Praise for *The Unthinkable Truth*

"MUST READ. INCREDIBLE... PREPARE TO HAVE
THOUGHT PROVOKED."

- David Powers, author and professor of computer and
cognitive science

"PACY AND EXCITING... WHILE MAKING YOU
THINK."

- Matt Graydon, author and journalist

"A SOLID WRITER WITH A SOLID HOOK."

- Douglas E. Richards, *New York Times* bestselling author of
Mind's Eye

THE
UNTHINKABLE
TRUTH

YONA BOUSKILA

CRANTHORPE
—MILLNER—
PUBLISHERS

First published by Cranthorpe Millner Publishers (2024)

ISBN 978-1-80378-201-0 (Paperback)

www.cranthorpemillner.com

Cranthorpe Millner Publishers

Printed and bound by CPI Group (UK) Ltd
Croydon, CR0 4YY

For my mother whose zest for life and love of books were infectious

Author's Note

All research studies mentioned are real and published in peer-reviewed scientific journals. Most of the rest is a pure figment of the imagination.

"All truth passes through three stages. First, it is ridiculed. Second, it is violently opposed. Third, it is accepted as being self-evident."

Arthur Schopenhauer

1

George Bennet gazed at the picture of Ella on the mantelpiece. He wanted to ask for her forgiveness, but it was too much. His courage fled him, and he shifted his eyes to the other end of the sofa he was sprawled on, where his bare toes rubbed against the cold leather armrest. A plate on the nearby coffee table snubbed him with its dry strip of bacon, congealed yolk and slice of half-eaten burnt toast. He groaned. Just outside the window of his Boston condo, the green summer leaves of the yellowwood tree offered a more palatable view.

Then the landline rang.

Damn! Should've unplugged it.

It chirruped seven times before the answerphone kicked in.

'Hi, Professor Bennet. It's Ben from UNESCO. Just checking that you received the upgrade to business class we arranged. Your mobile went straight to voicemail, so not sure you'll get this message. You're probably on your way to the airport already. Have a nice flight and I look forward to seeing you in Paris.'

There was a click and the call ended.

George cringed. The voice had invaded his solitude, exposed the state of him and his condo to its prying ... eyes? Ears? Whatever. It made him uncomfortable; that's what mattered. He rose, smoothed his rumpled pyjamas and took the dirty plate to the kitchen, where it balanced on top of a foot-high pile of crusty dishes in the stainless-steel sink. Then he lumbered upstairs to his study, slumped in his swivel chair and fired up the laptop.

A barrage of unread emails assaulted him, most acknowledging his out-of-office message, some enquiring about his health or passing on good wishes.

He couldn't manage a single reply, although knew he ought to, at least to the few friends he hadn't cut off completely. Of course, as director, he was automatically included in most committee messages and those distributed more generally to the MIT Center for Theoretical Physics, but he didn't need to read those. They were usually boring anyway – announcements about lectures, the occasional invite to dinners and conflicts between colleagues that amounted to playground squabbles waged at the institutional level. He'd thought he'd miss the intellectual engagement, miss being the first to peer-review manuscripts with exciting new ideas and discoveries, but that's not what had transpired. He didn't care about any of the hundreds of messages that had accumulated over the past four months. Not a single one.

He searched for "Paris" and opened the latest message.

An electronic ticket with his name and flight details

appeared on-screen. He checked the time; the gate was closing in four hours. He could still make it.

He leaned back and shut his eyes. The meeting with Ben at a Boston café a couple of weeks ago surfaced, and he ran through their conversation, trying to work out why he'd said yes.

'You must be Professor Bennet.' That's how it had started.

He had looked up from the depths of his latte and into the face of a youngish man in a black suit with the bearing of either a diplomat or a Wall Street shark.

'Ben McFarland. We spoke last week.'

He'd sat down at George's table, uninvited, folded up a pair of sunglasses and slid them into his breast pocket while extending his free hand across the table. George had flinched at the firm handshake.

Grinning from ear to ear, Ben waved over the waitress and ordered a large pot of tea and a slice of cheesecake. George expected some small talk – *Great weather for this time of year, huh?* – but Ben's opening was far more direct.

'What do you know about DABI?'

George blinked at the question. DABI was The Definite Answers to Big Issues project. 'I know it aims to analyse and solve some of the most complex and intriguing questions facing humanity,' he replied, 'and that those involved are given the best tools and conditions available.'

Ben sat up straight and rubbed his hands together. 'Good, good. You're up to date. Well, we established a DABI team to explore certain aspects of the human mind a while ago, and there have been some ... unexpected and disturbing developments. So, we've decided to assemble a new, larger team of prominent experts from every relevant field to get to the bottom of it.'

George had been flattered that a UN representative had come all the way from Europe to recruit him. Shame this wasn't his speciality. 'The human mind? You do know that my expertise is in theoretical physics and cosmology.'

Ben had nodded and launched into his spiel. That's what it had felt like, too – a spiel, a patter, the kind that car salesmen use with new buyers and army recruiters employ on gullible young men. George was being recruited, but by the end of an hour-long conversation, he'd still not understood for *what*.

Ben had been quite persuasive, insisting that George's contribution would be absolutely critical to unravelling a great, age-old mystery. But he'd been cagey about the details. All would be revealed – that was how Ben had put it – at a kick-off meeting with the entire team at UNESCO headquarters in Paris.

George sighed at the memory. Ben was a good salesman. So good, in fact, that George had somehow agreed to participate, though he was damned if he recalled ever saying those words. He now concluded that it'd been nothing more than a desperate attempt to distract himself from the memory of Ella.

But it had been a mistake. He wasn't ready to leave the safety of home, much less go abroad and face new people. Not yet.

He reached out to shut the laptop but withdrew his hand

and stared at the ticket on the glowing screen.

Paris.

He pressed his eyes with his thumbs. What was this big puzzle he was supposed to help solve? Why did they choose him?

When he opened his eyes again, the ticket had gone and Ella beamed straight at him with her lovely smile, the grey skeleton of the Eiffel Tower behind her.

'Ella, darling,' he whispered.

If only they could go to Paris again. Since her departure a year earlier, he hadn't been able to focus on work ... hadn't been able to focus on anything, for that matter. The world felt tasteless, meaningless, and more so these past four months. Occasionally, he'd find comfort by talking to her in his mind, but it was a poor substitute for conversations that were no longer possible. That open smile – God, he missed it so much – soothed him in the worst of times.

He could imagine what she'd say. 'Get off your arse and go. You might even enjoy it. You love mysteries.' He could almost swear she was mouthing the words from the screen. George touched the desk. Her image was replaced by the boarding pass. He clicked the print icon and headed to the bathroom.

Pyjama top removed, he stared at himself in the mirror. Still in good shape, though the week-long ginger beard on his haggard face needed attention. *Must pack a shaver.*

He ordered a taxi, threw on his usual conference attire – striped shirt and brown suede jacket – and crammed spare clothes, passport and boarding pass into a duffle bag before

5

rushing downstairs. If he moved fast enough, he might outrun his second thoughts.

As he slammed the front door, he heard the plates in the sink crashing to the floor.

* * *

Logan's Terminal E was surprisingly empty; it seemed his Paris flight was the only one leaving that afternoon. He headed for the nearest toilets and shaved thoroughly, then collapsed on a free couch in the Air France lounge. The other passengers were in expensive suits and tapping furiously on their laptops. Probably business travellers. George glanced at the generous buffet table and dismissed any thought of getting up.

Was he supposed to give a talk? He'd prepared nothing. He skimmed the emails from Ben – a non-disclosure agreement he couldn't even remember signing and matters of logistics. Two details attracted his attention – Ben's reassurance that the project had an entirely peaceful nature and the word "Skudder". The name was vaguely familiar.

A smiley waitress offered him fresh coffee. He took a long sip and ran the name through Google.

The top hit was the official UNESCO website – Skudder was head of the DABI programme. George studied the image of a short balding man with thin lips, round glasses and a bright orange tie. Odd-looking chap. He clicked back and scrolled through several pages of mundane links. A newspaper article that Skudder had authored caught his eye: *Ethical Eugenics for a Better World*.

He slumped and stared up at the white ceiling tiles. Eugenics? *Damn it.*

Opening the link, he scanned the lengthy article, noting several recurrent phrases – "modern genetic technologies", "eradication of undesired diseases", "proliferation of positive qualities". The article ended with a rhetorical question that George had to read several times: "Isn't it high time that humanity freed itself from its old inhibitions and harnessed the miracles of science to build a brighter future?"

The words made him feel slightly dizzy. This was starting to feel like the Psi project all over again. Shrouded in secrecy, the apparently legitimate academic exercise in quantum theory had dealt with what's often referred to as "spooky action at a distance". The project had been interesting, though not at all spooky. And it had soon become clear that its true purpose was to activate some new weapon, not improve humanity. George's pacifist ideology was well known, and the deception had been deliberate, which had both infuriated and saddened him in equal measure. He'd quit in protest.

And now this. A project with someone who advocated "ethical eugenics". He glanced at the clock on the departure screen. There was still time to leave, go home and pretend he'd never even considered getting on the plane. He could do those dishes, the ones that hadn't broken, at least, and then ... and then what? *Sit and stare at her picture until I melt?*

'Air France Flight 333 to Paris, now boarding business class. Business passengers for Air France Flight 333, please report to ...'

George walked towards the gate.

2

George wandered in a fugue state through the mostly empty airport and out to the taxi rank. He'd asked the stewards not to disturb him on the night flight until landing, and he'd slept surprisingly deeply. Only as the early-morning sun dripped through the ornate windows of the hotel on the Right Bank did his brain fog begin to clear.

He dropped off his luggage and walked to a café around the corner for a quick breakfast of croissants and coffee, then joined the hoards in the Métro station; it was something he hadn't done in a while. As he emerged at street level in the 16th arrondissement, the stench of urine assaulted his nostrils. Some things never changed.

At least the sun was shining as he walked over Pont d'léna to the other side of the Seine. After the seven-hour flight, he needed the exercise and quickened his pace; watching the Eiffel Tower looming larger and larger, he proceeded until he was right beneath it. A young-looking woman in a flowery dress, holding two ice cream cones, crossed his path. For a moment he thought it was Ella. He stopped. Followed her for a while with his eyes then looked up towards the belly of the tower and closed them.

A homeless man in greasy clothing sat on the ground, leaning against the railings surrounding one of the tower's massive girders. Most tourists passed by without even a glance, much less a donation. One of the security guards would shoo him away before long. He approached the elderly man and rifled through a thin wad of freshly minted cash he'd exchanged at the airport. Peeling off what he thought was a small note, he placed it onto a frayed rug lying across the man's lap. The man's rheumy eyes widened, and old, blackened fingers gripped the hundred euro note.

George smiled – *That'll make his day* – and walked towards Place de Fontenoy, his destination for the next few days, a slight spring in his step, a renewed sense of ... what was it? Purpose? It had been two years since his last visit to Paris. He'd come with Ella and they'd done all the usual touristy things. It had been fun, romantic.

Nothing was romantic now, probably never would be, but Paris was still Paris, and he was here to do important work. He hoped. At the very least, it felt good to be needed again.

The tourists dwindled as he passed between two long rows of perfectly manicured trees – cubes on one side, pyramids on the other – in the Champ de Mars. The pleasant smell of freshly cut grass filled his senses. Just beyond the edge of the park stood an impressive 18th century military school building. He paused, taking in the striking French baroque facade with its massive columns and fine statues. A white clock face adorned a dark dome topped by the national flag. He consulted the map on his phone; the UNESCO building was just behind this large complex. So he took a right turn in front of a bronze statue of a French general on horseback and came to a junction surrounded by classical and elegant buildings with yellowish stone and ornate balconies. Were they even used by the residents or simply for the benefit of the pedestrians below?

The modern edifice of 7 Place de Fontenoy looked different from the Google image. The structure rested on seventy-two columns of concrete piling and featured row upon row of symmetrical and impersonal glass panes. It might have been confused with an imposing apartment building, but the collection of plush black cars parked outside was a giveaway – this was no ordinary residential complex. He followed the perimeter fence and the forest of poles with their colourful flags flapping gently in the morning breeze.

UNESCO's headquarters had been nicknamed the three-pointed star because of its Y-shaped design crafted by three architects of different nationalities under the direction of an international committee. Unfortunately, this outstanding architectural marvel could only be appreciated from the air – not from where George stood.

'What on earth am I doing here?' he murmured.

Unanswered questions didn't faze him. His entire field of study dealt with those, and he easily accepted that Mother Nature rarely parted willingly with her secrets. But this project was different. Ben had obviously known exactly what it was about but had kept him in the dark.

The slight elation he'd felt beneath the Eiffel Tower dissipated. He could still change his mind, go back to the hotel, send an apologetic message to Ben, pull out. But then ... then he'd *never* know. And if he was honest with himself, which he rarely was, he was desperately curious. He could always bail out if it truly didn't feel right. Besides, maybe it would help stop the nagging thoughts about Ella – at least for a few days.

He ambled towards the ambitiously concaved main entrance, where elegantly dressed people came and went. In the foyer, a large group of visitors on a guided tour blocked his way.

'This building wasn't always the home of UNESCO,' the tour guide informed the visitors. 'When the headquarters moved from London to Paris in 1946, it was based in the Hotel Majestic on the Avenue Kléber, just across the river.' He pointed towards the entrance. 'The hotel was quickly refitted after the liberation from German occupation. In those days, working conditions were hardly ideal. The largest bedrooms were allocated to secretaries, and several had to share the space and store their files in wardrobes. Middle-grade professionals were placed in disused bathrooms and kept their papers in the tub. Before we move on, please look to your right ...'

George considered joining the group. Perhaps he could learn more about the organisation. Surely there was more to UNESCO than declaring heritage sites for the benefit of travel brochures. He glanced at his wristwatch. No, he needed to hurry; he was already in danger of being late.

At the far end of the foyer, a smiling receptionist greeted him, but was then distracted by a raised voice next to the security X-ray machine.

'I'm not leaving anything at reception!' a man said with a strong German accent.

'Sir, I'm afraid mobile phones and other communication devices are not allowed in the building,' the uniformed guard replied.

'But it doesn't make sense. You can board any flight with an electronic device. Why is it a problem here?'

'I'm sorry, but that's our policy.'

'My whole life is in this mobile. Just tell me, what are you afraid of?'

'Sir, I'm not making the policy here. If you want to enter, you'll have to hand over your phone and put it in this envelope. You'll get it back when you exit.'

The man shoved his phone angrily into the envelope and strode away.

'Sorry about that,' the receptionist said with an apologetic smile. 'There's always someone.' She checked her monitor and handed George a visitor's pass on a lanyard. 'Please wear this at all times while in the building. And please hand over your phone here, if you would. We take security very seriously.'

'Yeah, I noticed,' George said, passing her his phone. 'Has anything happened here recently?'

'Oh no, not at all, Professor' – she consulted the monitor again – 'Bennet. But we'd like to keep it that way. One of my colleagues will escort you to your meeting place. Security check is over there.'

Without a hint of a smile, the security guard asked him to empty his pockets and place the contents into a small tray next to his bag on the conveyer belt.

George passed through the metal detector and waited patiently while another severe-looking guard pored over the image of his bag and its contents.

The guard glared at him. 'You can't enter with a laptop. Could you hand it over, please?'

'Really?'

'Yes, really. It can be used as a communication device, so you'll have to leave it at reception.'

George fished it out, and the receptionist led him through the main corridor, all white linoleum and gold fringe, to the elevator lobby. A strange mixture of excitement and apprehension filled his chest. This was uncharted territory. Meeting a new group of people on a project he knew nothing about. God only knew what he was walking into.

When the elevator pinged, they got out at the fourth floor, walked down a series of long corridors lined with offices and conference rooms and stopped by a set of double wooden doors with a security swipe to the right. The receptionist slid her badge through and ushered George into a large lounge area.

'Mr McFarland will arrive shortly,' she said. 'I'm to ask you to get acquainted with your colleagues. Coffee is on the buffet trolley.'

She swept out of the room and the doors locked with a click. He hadn't even had time to thank her.

The room reminded him of a hotel lobby – orange and brown leather armchairs and settees surrounding coffee tables, floor-to-ceiling glass windows, a coffee machine, and china cups and saucers on a buffet trolley dressed with white linen. A few people gathered near the window wall overlooking the boulevard, but George didn't recognise anyone, except …

'Takahashi!'

A Japanese man with a shaggy goatee and white Panama hat glanced up, gazed at him for a moment then raised a hand – *hello* and *not now* – and returned to his book. George approached his friend and craned his neck to peer over the shoulder of one of the world's finest professors of philosophy. Takahashi was scribbling intently in a logic puzzle book resting on his lap.

'Are you—?'

Another wave of Takahashi's hand silenced him.

Quite typical. The man hadn't changed.

George slid into the closest armchair, resigned to awaiting the conclusion of Takahashi's direly important problem. He was about to get up again and pour himself a coffee from the buffet trolley when a petite woman took the seat next to him, crossed one leg over the other and arranged her elegant blue dress across her knee.

14

George smiled and introduced himself.

The woman blinked, as if she'd just noticed him, glanced at his name tag and returned the smile. 'Meghan Mercer. I've heard of you, Professor Bennet.'

'That's flattering.'

'Not at all. One of your books did the rounds in The Hague. Well, at least among my colleagues. I'm with the ICC.'

It was George's turn to blink. 'Is the International Criminal Court relevant to what we're doing here?'

'To be honest, I'm not entirely sure,' she replied. 'Ben said my leading role in setting the policy on accountability in diminished-responsibility cases would be very useful, but he gave me no details – except that all would be revealed at today's kick-off meeting.'

'Yes, sounds familiar. It's a puzzle with pieces that don't make much sense. Takahashi' – he nodded at his friend – 'is a professor of philosophy. I'm a physicist. Who knows? Maybe we'll have an oceanographer and a dietitian too.'

Meghan laughed. 'The two over there,' she said, motioning discreetly towards a couple talking animatedly on a settee, 'are psychologists of some sort, from what I gathered ... Helen and Max.'

George glanced at them. 'I saw that man earlier in reception. He made a big fuss about having to leave his mobile there. Seems like they know each other.'

'Not necessarily. Perhaps they're both extroverts who've just met.'

'I must agree with the lady,' Takahashi said, raising his head from the puzzle book. 'One should never jump to conclusions.' He got up, which didn't add much to his height, and approached George with a warm smile, both hands extended. 'How are you, George?'

'I'm all right,' he lied, hoping Takahashi wouldn't ask about Ella. 'Took some time off from all the usual pressures.'

'Rest, eh? That's good. But hopefully you're still active. I think you and I have a few more papers we could write together.'

'Absolutely,' George said weakly. 'Maybe we can find some time to chat at breaks between sessions.' He glanced at Meghan, who was staring at the carpet. 'This is Meghan Mercer.'

'Kazuki Takahashi,' the philosopher said, sweeping off his Panama and bowing.

Meghan smiled and shook his hand.

'Meghan and I were trying to figure out what brings us all together,' George said. 'Any ideas?'

'Unlike my book of puzzles, where all the information is provided, I don't think we're the full group yet. We're still waiting for three more visitors.'

'Three? How did you figure that out?'

'Quite simple. When I arrived at reception, there were eight visitor badges in the basket. I received one, and four people have come after me. Ben McFarland works here, so he doesn't need one.'

'Ah, you never cease to amaze me,' George said. 'I should probably start practising logic puzzles too.'

Meghan smirked. 'Or perhaps just wait for Ben to explain it all.'

'Where's the fun in that?' Takahashi said.

The double doors opened and the receptionist entered, flanked by a woman and a young man. She pointed towards the group and walked away.

'I'll be damned,' Takahashi said, and rose to his feet. 'My esteemed colleague Professor Gertrude Kirkpatrick. Well, well, this conference, or whatever it's going to be, will certainly be very interesting.'

A grimace spread across Gertrude's deeply lined face. 'Long time no see,' she said as she crossed the room.

She wore a formal black skirt and white blouse. In contrast, her much younger companion's hands were stuffed into the pockets of a leather bomber jacket.

'Yes,' Takahashi said. He grinned and grasped her outstretched hand. 'But it seems we still manage to keep in touch regularly via very public correspondence after each article I publish.'

Gertrude pulled back, glaring down her nose at the little man. 'Believe me, I'd rather do other things, but you leave me no choice.'

'I'm glad I keep you busy,' he said, and turned abruptly to the man. 'Where are my manners? I'm Kazuki Takahashi, specialising in philosophy. And you are ...?'

'Jerry Stokes. Neuroscientist. Nice to meet you!' he replied, combing his fingers through an untidy mane of dark hair.

'Oh! Then you must've heard of the last person we're waiting for,' Meghan said. 'Professor Grinberg.'

Jerry gawped at her. 'Grinberg? As in Malcolm Grinberg?'

'Yes. That's how he introduced himself. We met at the airport and started chatting when we realised we were heading to the same event. Why? Should I have heard of him?'

Jerry bounced on the balls of his feet, more an eager puppy than an esteemed neuroscientist. 'Well, he's one of those living legends. Authored many classical textbooks and hundreds of scientific papers in brain research. *And* a Nobel laureate. So yes, you may have heard his name before,' he said with a chuckle. 'Who else is on the guest list?'

'I think the puzzle is nearly complete,' Takahashi said. 'We've two neuroscientists, two psychologists, two philosophers, one physicist-slash-cosmologist and a legal expert. But we still don't know why we're here. It's either Noah's Ark or' – he chuckled – 'a murder-mystery dinner party.'

3

Two men crossed the lounge, approaching their group. Ben, in a black suit, had the practical, urgent gait George often noticed in people with little doubt about themselves or their place in the world. An attitude he was envious of, even though it often came with a bravado he found somewhat repulsive. The other man's bearing was more measured – calm, assured. He wore an open waistcoat over a chequered shirt with a woven tie. Grinberg, surely. The last participant. An archetypal academic.

Without a word, Ben motioned to the group to follow him. They fell into step, passing through the double doors at the far end of the lounge two at a time, like they were heading into an important business meeting. *Or an interrogation*, George thought. He glanced down at Takahashi, who barely came to his elbow. The professor gave him a quick smile and a wink. He was clearly enjoying himself.

They entered a room that seemed an extension of the lounge along the glass facade, partitioned by a wood-clad interior wall to create some sort of a boardroom. A large mahogany table dominated most of the space and was surrounded by ten comfortably padded swivel chairs. Unlike the beige carpet in the lounge, this room had parquet flooring. George found the space somewhat characterless but not unpleasant. He sat down facing the most attractive feature, which ironically wasn't in the room at all: the impressive Paris skyline through the window wall. The Eiffel Tower in the near distance caught his attention. Not realising what a challenge it was, he had tried to climb the tower with Ella, but they'd given up at the first floor. Now it seemed to silently mock him.

'Welcome, everyone,' he heard Ben say. But the voice receded as George recalled the look in her eyes when they'd stood gazing out from the terrace, her breath coming in gentle gasps. He should have known, even then …

He snapped back into the moment when Ben mentioned his name.

'Professor Bennet has kindly agreed to join the project, and brings his authoritative knowledge of physics as well as his contributions to our understanding of the nature of reality. He's authored countless original scientific articles, as well as a number of bestselling books on science and the philosophy of science that demonstrate his interest in the bigger picture – beyond his expertise in theoretical physics and cosmology. But there's another reason we asked such a prominent scientist to attend the discussions.' Ben paused, and their eyes met for several seconds.

He frowned. *What in the hell are you after, Ben?*

'Thanks to his analytical mind and scientific rigour,' Ben continued, 'he ticks all the boxes required for an impartial observer who can assess the quality of the evidence and the final conclusion. If we arrive at one, that is.'

George had never felt comfortable with praise, and even less so now, what with Ben looking at him so ... oddly. He'd heard this before, almost word for word, in the café when Ben tried to recruit him. It wasn't even praise. Not really. More like a ploy. And once more, it left him with a sense of disconnection, disconcertion. Just what was Ben really playing at?

Ben nodded to his left. 'We borrowed Meghan Mercer from The Hague. She's a high court judge and brings a vast legal knowledge to the table, especially in the area of personal responsibility.'

He glanced at Meghan. Sitting a few seats down from him, she was an attractive young woman, olive skin, slender, long dark hair, sparkly eyes. A high court judge? She hadn't mentioned that. She didn't look like one either – too thin, too young, too pretty, not at all like the elderly gentleman in a black robe wearing a severe expression that he would have pictured.

Ben gestured towards Takahashi and Gertrude, who sat on opposite sides of the table. 'And we're lucky to have two such prominent professors of philosophy.'

George couldn't help but notice Gertrude's clenched jaw as Ben described Takahashi's reputation as a leading figure in logic and ethics. She reminded him of the first PA he'd inherited from the retiring head of the Centre at MIT. *Scary woman.*

Her expression relaxed when Ben introduced her as a prolific author of articles and books in the emerging field of evidence-based philosophy.

'Next,' Ben continued, taking a few steps, 'I'd like to introduce our two cognitive psychologists, Helen Casey and Max Schreiber. Conveniently, they're sitting next to each other. You may have come across Helen if you follow TED talks. Ten years ago she gave one on child development that went viral.'

Helen offered an infectious smile, her gentle, long-lashed eyes lighting up as she acknowledged Ben's compliments. With her cheerful abstract floral shirt and loose, flowing trousers, she stood out from most of the women he'd met in academia. The men too, come to think of it.

Max, the German who'd made such a stink at security, couldn't have been more different if he'd tried – short hair, which accentuated his large ears, penetrating eyes and drab academic garb.

He glanced at Helen again. With her glossy chestnut bob, she was certainly pretty, but there was something more, perhaps the kindness in her eyes. He was puzzling over what it was as Ben wrapped up Max's introduction. Something to do with experimental psychology.

A side door opened and a short bald man wearing a ridiculously bright yellow tie entered the room. He greeted Ben with a quick nod.

'Skudder,' Ben said. 'I'm almost done introducing the group.'

Skudder raised his hand and shook his head. 'I've been following it from my office. Just ignore me.'

Ignore him? In that tie? George mused. And how had he been able to follow the introductions from his office?

Ben turned back to the group. 'Skudder heads up the DABI programme. I'm sure we'll hear from him soon. Now to the last pair of experts in this think tank. Jerry Stokes and Malcolm Grinberg. Two neuroscientists who've probably met each other before, right?'

The two looked at each other. Jerry nodded and started chewing on a strand of his hair.

George studied the two men. Jerry was somewhere in his early forties, had shoulder-length dark hair and wore a black bomber jacket over a colourful shirt. Not your usual scientist. In contrast, Grinberg looked like someone's good-natured grandpa, short moustache, bald crown, a warm smile.

'Malcolm Grinberg,' Ben announced, 'won the Nobel Prize for his work on neuronal networks and their function in the brain. We're very fortunate to have the benefit of his unparalleled understanding of the field and its history. Last but not least, Jerry Stokes is both a neuroscientist and a clinician, a rare combination that may prove vital for our goal.'

Jerry flashed an embarrassed smile then proceeded to tie his hair in a ponytail.

Ben seemed about to say something else when Skudder approached and buttonholed him. They stepped to the side and had a brief, inaudible conversation.

'The plot thickens,' Takahashi whispered.

Skudder then sat down in a chair away from the others, and Ben returned to the table, rapping on its polished surface for attention.

'Ladies and gentlemen, before we move on, I'd like to introduce to you one more member of our group. Please meet Sherlock.' He pointed to a small sphere on the far end of the table.

George had thought it was some kind of speaker phone for conference calls.

A sequence of blue lights flashed around the equator of the tennis ball-sized device, then stopped, revealing a series of equidistant holes that separated the opaque white bottom and the dark glass top.

Takahashi, who sat next to it, nudged the orb with his index finger.

It didn't budge.

'It's held in place by a powerful magnet that can be switched off,' Ben said. 'I'm sure you've all heard of IBM's Watson, which answered questions posed in natural language. It won *Jeopardy* against the best human players. Well, Sherlock is superior by several orders of magnitude, hence his name.' He paused at the trickle of laughter.

Takahashi raised a hand. 'Except that Watson was named after the company's first CEO, Thomas Watson, not Arthur Conan Doyle's hero,' he said with a wry smile.

Good old Takahashi, George thought. *Couldn't let such an inaccuracy pass unchallenged.*

But Ben was unfazed. 'Sherlock is a supercomputer, equipped with third-generation artificial intelligence capabilities, more commonly known as AI. He can assimilate vast amounts of information, learn from mistakes and use sophisticated analysis to identify patterns.'

George took a breath and shifted in his seat. He'd never liked people talking about computers as though they were human. AI was a wonderful tool and terrifyingly accurate, but he preferred the human mind.

'Sherlock has access to all published human knowledge,' Ben continued, 'and can critically analyse it almost instantaneously. He also assesses his own performance and improves on it.'

'Really?' Gertrude said. 'Wouldn't that require a large supercomputer?' She appeared both bemused and bewildered. 'Are you saying that all this is now crammed inside this little ball?'

Ben gave a feigned smile. 'No, not really. What you see here is just the communication interface. Most of the hardware's located in a highly secure part of this building.'

The blue lights on the orb's surface flickered. 'Hello, nice to meet you all,' it said in a friendly and disturbingly normal voice.

George raised his eyebrows. The voice was soft, natural, human. Ben grinned, but no one else responded for a long while; they just stared at the queer little orb that had addressed them like colleagues.

It was Meghan who broke the awkward silence. 'Does Sherlock have a wake word, like, "Hey, Siri"?'

'I'll let Sherlock answer that,' Ben said.

The orb's blue points of light flashed in all directions. 'There's no need, Meghan. I can tell the difference between your talking about me and talking to me.'

Ben's grin widened.

'Are we being recorded by this thing?' Helen asked.

It was an excellent question.

'Yes, voice-recorded at all times,' Ben said. 'I was just getting to that. Sherlock is our official minute-taker, which leaves us free to focus on the presentations and discussions.'

'But can we trust him? Her? It?' Helen rolled a pen between her fingers and regarded the orb with evident distrust.

'I'd trust him with my own life,' Ben said. 'Not only is he more capable at most things than a human being, he's also *incapable* of lying. Why? Are you worried about an AI takeover, like in *Terminator*?'

'Well, maybe not that extreme, but—'

'No such risk,' he said with a confident smile. 'This is not Skynet. You can rest assured that Sherlock's been programmed to be entirely loyal to the UN and to adhere strictly to our code of conduct. That includes, of course, the revised moral laws of robotics. On top of that, he's equipped with an ethical black box.'

'Sorry,' Helen said, running a hand through her hair, 'you're going to have to explain what the hell an ethical black box is.'

'It's equivalent to the flight data recorder in an aircraft. It basically means that the internal process of making ethical decisions is completely transparent, so if something goes wrong, we can replay what Sherlock was thinking and analyse it.'

She gave an amused grimace. 'What ethical decisions are we talking about here?'

'Well, this safety mechanism is probably not all that relevant to this project,' Ben replied with an apologetic smile, 'because Sherlock will be acting mainly as a helper, but ethical black boxes come as standard with such high-level AI ... as a general precaution.'

He's deflecting, George thought, and glanced at Takahashi, whose brows were drawn together as he gazed at the orb that could, apparently, reason ethically.

'Is there anything else we should know about Sherlock?' Takahashi asked. 'Such as, perhaps, why he's not just doing the work for us, given that he's so capable?'

Before Ben could answer, the double doors opened and a caterer wheeled in a trolley laden with metal jugs and an assortment of biscuits. For a while there was silence as Ben poured himself a cup of coffee and stirred it gently, as though buying time.

'Mr McFarland?' Takahashi pressed.

Ben tapped his spoon against the cup and took a slow sip. 'Because this is a very human debate and he is not human. Sherlock has a unique personality, and some corresponding quirks. That's entirely normal at this level of intelligence and complexity.' He took another sip of coffee and returned to the table. 'In fact, we selected him for this project because of

27

his temperament, more so than his intelligence. His creators described him as calm and stubborn, someone who searches for creative new ways to tackle a difficult problem and who rarely gives up. You could say he leaves no chip unturned to reach his assigned goal. We couldn't predict this trait in advance, but once we noticed it, Sherlock became very desirable. We're incredibly lucky to have him here. Please feel free to ask him for any piece of information or research you might need to move this project forward.'

Ben wheeled a chair away from the table and dropped into it, his performance over. And yet he had barely answered the second part of Takahashi's question. With less enthusiasm, he got down to the mundanities. The security badges allowed free movement within the conference room, lounge and surrounding area, including the front door to the perimeter corridor. The toilets at the far end of the lounge could be accessed without the security badge. The rest of the building was out of bounds; the badges wouldn't open any other door. The security was so high mainly because the building also housed UNESCO's entire archive, though he didn't specify the additional measures in place.

'What about getting out of here?' Max asked, a concerned look on his face.

'Well, for lunch, I'll take you out through this maze to a nearby restaurant. Or we'll order food in. We have an excellent provider.'

'But what about fire or other emergencies?' Max asked, his fingers drumming the table, sweat beading on his upper lip.

'I'll feel much more ... *entspannt* ... How do you say that in English? Relaxed, much more relaxed if I know I can get out of here at any moment. I am *klaustrophobisch*. It's important to me that the doors to this room stay open at all times, *ja*?'

'Sure,' Ben said calmly, 'we can keep the back door to the lounge open. In case of fire, the doors automatically unlock, and you can get out through the stairwell in the main corridor. Just follow the green emergency signs.'

Max slumped back in his chair and his fingers quieted.

'If I may interrupt,' Helen said, 'I think we were kept somewhat in the dark about the exact purpose of this project. Ben, maybe this would be a good time to tell us what exactly we're all doing here.'

4

For what seemed an inordinate amount of time, Ben was silent, and George became aware of emergency blue lights in the distance, perhaps a police car or ambulance. The siren wailings were not audible through the thick glass. It was strange that Ben seemed so reticent to declare the mission statement. He had gathered a group of very eminent experts together, yet no one was sure why they were here.

Eventually Ben rose and feigned a smile, one that didn't reach his eyes. 'I was just getting to our mission statement.' He gestured wide with his arms. 'From the dawn of civilisation, men took the existence of free will pretty much for granted – holding others and themselves responsible for their actions – with occasional fierce debates about the extent of that freedom. There are, of course, objective constraints all around us. Gravity, for example, fixed public transport schedules, laws, other people's actions, etcetera, etcetera. These will *not* be the focus of our inquiry. The main question this think tank has been assigned to tackle concerns personal freedom. To what extent does a person actually have any control over their decisions and actions? I'm talking about free will – whether we have it and how much.'

'But free will is one of the oldest questions in philosophy,' Gertrude said, stroking her chin. 'What's new here?'

Ben poured a fresh cup of coffee. 'Don't be shy – the drinks are for everyone.' He returned to his seat and paused. George couldn't be sure if he was playing for time again or earnestly formulating an answer.

'Sure,' he said. 'There are thousands of books, tens of thousands of articles and millions of internet pages on the subject, not to mention the unwritten debates that have taken place anywhere from the pub to the living room to the conference venue, pretty much since abstract language evolved. But bottom line, after all those efforts, there's no definite conclusion. It's still considered an open question. Of course, you could dismiss the whole thing as a purely intellectual quest for people who have nothing better to do, or even as a complete waste of time. Fair enough.' He slurped his coffee. 'But the notion of personal freedom or agency, the ability to act independently and to make free choices, is one of the most fundamental assumptions behind human civilisation.'

Takahashi was constructing a complex doodle on his writing pad, but George knew from experience that he was also listening intently and no doubt wondering where Ben was taking this.

Ben began pacing back and forth at the head of the table. 'The implications are huge, and far from theoretical.

They affect moral responsibility, praise and blame, law and punishment, even emotions like pride, shame and guilt. If you think about it, the rule of law and all religions are based on personal responsibility. The definite answer to this key question would affect almost every aspect of life.'

Ben drained his cup, put it on the table and continued pacing. 'With the rare exceptions of mental disturbance and other unique conditions, the most common assumption is that we all have a true personal freedom. Since ancient times, philosophers, theologians and thinkers have debated this subject with meticulous arguments and counter-arguments but used little concrete evidence.'

'I think we all know this,' Takahashi said without lifting his gaze from the doodle, which looked increasingly like an elephant with its trunk in the air. 'Are you suggesting that modern science can now find the answer?'

Ben stopped pacing and glared at him. 'Modern science combined with modern thinking might. We're now fortunate enough to live in an era – one that's only a few decades old – in which science can provide the necessary tools and knowledge to examine this fundamental question thoroughly. Rather than just arguing about it, for the first time in the history of humankind, we can tackle this mystery right here in this room and discover the true level of freedom we actually have. For this purpose, we've assembled an interdisciplinary team of distinguished world experts from all the relevant fields – neuroscience, cognitive psychology, philosophy, physics and law – as well as the most powerful AI available to date.'

'Thank you,' Sherlock said.

Ben chuckled. 'And probably the politest one too.'

There was nervous laughter around the room, which George didn't join in. Something was odd about all this, but he couldn't quite put his finger on it. Even if they finally concluded that people did or didn't have free will – what difference would it make?

'There's one more thing I want to emphasise before we start,' Ben continued. 'The whole idea here is that we consider only solid, verifiable facts.' He scanned the faces around the table. 'And the emphasis is on *solid*. There are already enough books and articles filled with theoretical and unsubstantiated ideas. Some would call it philosophical mumbo-jumbo.'

Gertrude rolled her eyes then shook her head. That did the trick – Ben noticed her.

'Look, all I'm saying is that we're here to get to the truth and reach a conclusive answer, if that's at all possible.'

At that moment, Skudder stood up and walked over to the head of the table, brought his hands up to his mouth in the prayer position and exhaled through his nose. 'Thank you, Ben. Before you all start on this monumental project, I'd like to say a few words. I've always been fascinated by the human mind, and one thing is quite clear: our understanding of the world around us is filtered by our senses, our past experiences and our internal logic. There is simply no escape from the perception of our minds, even in the most objective of sciences – physics.'

He shot a glance at George, who remained deliberately impassive.

'So, attempting to solve one of the deepest and oldest mysteries of the human mind is incredibly exciting for me. But let me be crystal clear. I absolutely don't want you to continue the philosophical discussions that have been going on for at least two millennia, or even to consider the opinion of leading figures on the subject. None of these have brought us any closer to a definite conclusion. More than that, you also have to forget your personal view on this matter. It won't be easy, but that's the *only* way to start from scratch. What I do want from you is an unflinching multidisciplinary investigation that uses science-based evidence and gives me' – he stabbed the table with a pen after each word – 'a clear ... answer ... either ... way. That's not some ludicrous goal; it should be possible. I've carefully selected you as the brightest minds in your fields, and thanks to Sherlock, the entire knowledge of humanity is at the tips of your fingers. All the necessary ingredients are right here. This may very well mean a breakthrough of historical proportions, one that means we understand our true nature. And that, my friends, could lead to the most monumental change in the direction of human civilisation.'

Direction? George thought. Human civilisation seemed to progress very randomly and often backwards. So what was he talking about? He was about to ask for clarification when Skudder clapped his hands together, wished them good luck and left.

5

George scanned the catered lunch with little enthusiasm. His stomach was doing flips, though whether from the continued uncertainty about this "conference" or because he was still jet-lagged, he didn't know. Max seemed to have no such problems – for a man who had just been sweating out his claustrophobia, he was eating well, loading up on the baguettes, cheese, poached salmon fillet swirled with dill and a massive glass of pineapple juice. George decided he could probably stomach half a baguette. He spread it meticulously with butter, poured himself some freshly squeezed orange juice and returned to his seat, aware of the clank of cutlery against china plates as the group ate.

'I was just thinking,' Meghan said between bites of carrot batons, 'would it be possible to come up with one neat and definite experiment to resolve this question, a kind of a litmus test? Then we could all go home early.'

'If only that was possible,' Gertrude said, waving her fork around. 'According to the ancient Principle of Alternative

Possibilities, the typical test to exemplify your free will to carry out a certain action would involve demonstrating that you *could* have done another action instead at that *specific moment.*'

Takahashi's head bobbed.

'Sounds straight-forward enough,' Meghan said. 'Just repeat the same situation several times and give a person a few options to choose from.'

'It can only be a thought experiment, though,' George said. 'It's just too complicated.'

'How? Don't you replicate physics experiments, sometimes even in different labs?'

'There's no comparison. In physics you can control all the important conditions – and normally there aren't many – but the human brain, that's something else. It's *the* most complex object in the universe.'

'That we know of, you mean,' Takahashi said, grinning with all his teeth.

'Yes, of course,' George said, and bit into his baguette.

Grinberg pushed his reading glasses to the top of his head. 'I think it's fair to say that while external conditions could roughly be replicated, internal ones couldn't. Take, for example, brain chemistry and connectivity – they change all the time, so we could never be sure if any of them were responsible for the choice. In other words, you'd be a slightly different person with each choice.'

'You can't cross the same river twice,' Takahashi said cheerfully. He paused at George's blank stare. 'Heraclitus.'

'You can't cross the same river even once,' Gertrude said, and stabbed her fish viciously, 'since both you and the river are constantly changing.'

Meghan waved her hand. 'Okay, fine. So if there's no decisive experiment, how are we going to tackle this?'

A few eyes turned to Ben, who swallowed the cracker he'd been chewing on silently for most of the conversation.

'Don't look at me. You're the experts. I expect *you* to come up with the best way to solve it. Once and for all.'

There was a long silence, broken only by the faint sound of car horns blaring in the street below. George stared at his half-eaten baguette. He understood Meghan's urgency and wanted suddenly to be at home. Was it really only a few hours ago he'd been gazing at Ella's photograph and refusing to answer the phone? 'It'll have to be the hard way,' he said. 'Going through the best scientific evidence available. Seeing if we can get to the truth. But there's a whole different type of challenge here.' He paused. It was difficult, reasoning things out in front of other people. 'Pardon my French, but most philosophers know shit about science. With a few exceptions, of course.'

He winked at Takahashi. Gertrude, just beyond, scowled at him. 'On the other hand,' he continued, 'most scientists wouldn't touch philosophy with a barge pole. It's considered career suicide. It didn't use to be like that – Isaac Newton was a philosopher *and* a scientist. So was Einstein. Even Oppenheimer. But right now, the two camps just hurl insults at each other without any progress. So, for the sake of this project, I think we have to set these things aside. Consider ourselves … scientist-philosophers! To have any chance of cracking this ancient riddle, we're going to need the best of both of us. There's no room for the old animosities and suspicions.' He glanced at Gertrude, whose scowl hadn't changed, but she didn't meet his eyes.

'Agreed,' Takahashi said.

'Agreed,' Grinberg said.

'Agreed,' Gertrude finally mumbled.

'I do have a question for Ben,' Helen said, her lips pursed. 'I'd like to know what you intend to *do* with this truth – assuming we manage to agree on such a thing.' She arched an eyebrow. 'And by *you*, do I mean DABI, the UN, or—'

'Something more sinister?' George suggested, tapping a pencil on the provided yellow notepad, glad that he had finally had the guts to bring this up.

Ben shifted in his chair and cleared his throat. 'Of course. That's fair. Well … the possibilities are exciting, of course. If we're able to arrive at this truth, the knowledge itself may affect society. So … we may need to tread carefully. But I can assure you, there's no specific plan at the moment, other than finding the truth, whatever it is … Right' – he stood abruptly – 'when we finish our lunch break in fifteen minutes, I suggest Helen opens the discussion. That way you can choose how we begin. How about that?'

Helen nodded weakly.

George's stomach flipped again, and he abandoned the baguette. Once more, Ben hadn't come close to giving a straight answer.

6

When lunch ended, the group broke into pods of twos and threes. Only Helen remained separate, most of her plate untouched. She moved to the window wall that overlooked the street below and wrapped her arms around herself.

George debated with himself whether to go over, ask if she was okay – after all, she was just a few steps away – but maybe it was something personal that she'd rather not share. Then Max walked over and stood beside her.

It was too late. He'd missed his chance.

'What did you think of the mission statement?' Max asked.

Helen jolted and looked at him, eyes wide. 'Sorry, I was miles away. What?'

'The mission statement. What did you think?'

'Honestly? I can hardly remember it now.'

'You're not excited to be a part of this anymore?'

'Yes, sure. It's just that Ben put me in the spotlight and I wasn't expecting it. I agreed to go first and I don't know what to do.' She breathed a soft laugh. 'Now I feel like a silly schoolgirl who forgot to do her homework.'

'But you were brilliant in that TED talk,' Max reassured her. 'Actually, one of my colleagues at the University of Hamburg shows it regularly to his new students as part of his ... how do you say in English ... pep, pep something.'

'Pep talk. Well, that was very different. I was prepared. In fact, for those fifteen minutes on stage, I'd prepared for a whole week.'

Max folded his arms, staring at his feet. 'I see. That was really unfair of Ben. I don't think he liked it that you challenged him, but I thought you were great. A challenge always makes people think harder.'

Helen shrugged. 'Yes, maybe, but right now I've only a few minutes to prepare and my mind is blank.'

Max cleared his throat. 'Well, how about something you know back to front? Maybe some kind of demonstration of a relevant cognitive principle? Something you could do with your eyes closed.'

Helen's face, which had been creased with a frown, relaxed, and her eyes seemed to brighten. 'That's it! You're a genius, Max.'

'Happy to help,' he said, turning away. He looked confused. 'I'll see you in a few minutes.' But after a few steps he looked back at her. 'I'm sure you'll do just fine, Helen.'

As she beamed at Max, George felt a surprising twinge of jealousy, which was odd.

Five minutes later, they reconvened around the mahogany table and the room quieted. Ben gestured towards Helen.

She straightened in her seat and cleared her throat. 'I'd like to start with a little demonstration ... but it requires your participation.'

There was a low murmur and a few eyerolls.

She bit her lip. 'You'll all know about mindfulness and meditation, and no doubt you've all had a go. Apologies to anyone who's a regular practitioner.'

Meghan straightened her spine and lowered her gaze. *Must be a regular*, George thought. And the notion surprised him.

'What are we supposed to do?' Jerry asked, popping a strand of hair into his mouth.

'Just stay in your seats and follow the instructions I'll give you in a minute.'

Takahashi waved both hands. 'Count me out. I'm done with school, and I don't miss it.'

'Grow up,' George muttered, and beamed at Helen. 'I'm in.'

She smiled back. 'Please bear with me. It'll take just five minutes and it's very relevant to our goal here.'

The grumbles subsided.

'Okay,' she said. 'Put your feet flat on the ground, straighten your back, rest your hands on your knees, then gently close your eyes.' She paused, waiting for everyone to comply. 'Now, focus all your attention on your breathing.'

The room calmed, and after a moment George closed his eyes, but not for long. Unable to resist, he took a peek. Everyone but Takahashi had followed her instructions. He gave the stubborn philosopher a nudge, but the man was immovable. Helen continued, her voice gentle, almost floating in his ears. He decided to go with the flow.

'For the next few minutes, focus on the sensation of air flowing in and out through your nostrils. Or focus on the rhythmic movements of your belly and chest as you breathe. That's all you have to do. You may find that your mind's wandering, perhaps reminiscing on the past, making some plans for the future, rehearsing a conversation ... That's normal. When that happens, just notice it and gently bring your attention back to your breathing.'

He pulled in a deep breath. *Focus. Breathe out. Ella wanted to have a child. Breathe in. Remember what you said? Out. Remember ... In. Ella. Out. Ella. In ...*

'Okay, open your eyes.'

He blinked, and the room gradually filled with chatter.

'That can't have been five minutes.'

'It was actually very relaxing.'

'I didn't manage to do it right.'

'It was annoying just sitting here doing absolutely nothing,' Gertrude said, flicking imaginary lint off the table.

'All right,' Helen said. 'I'd be interested to know how many of you managed to fully focus on your breathing with no distractions.' She looked around. No one responded. 'Okay, how many had up to three distractions?'

Gertrude nodded and looked around the room.

'Four to six?'

Jerry, Meghan and Helen raised their hands.

'More than you could count?'

George lifted his arm. *Ella. Nothing but Ella.* He smiled at the others with their hands up.

'Think about it for a minute,' Helen said. 'Here we are, a group of intelligent, self-disciplined people who must also be reasonably persistent. Yet not one of us could follow these simple instructions and focus on a single thought for just a few minutes despite our best attempts. I'm no different, by the way, even though I've been practising daily meditation for many years now. The mind has its own agenda, churning all kinds of thoughts around almost constantly whether we like it or not. And we're often powerless to stop it.'

'Sherlock, did you manage to stay focused?' Takahashi asked with a mischievous smile.

'It's like asking a fish if it can swim,' the orb replied. 'All my activities are hundred percent goal-oriented. I never get distracted.'

'Interesting,' Takahashi said, and paused for a moment. 'But you don't breathe, so what did you focus on?'

'On *your* breathing. All of you.'

Takahashi and George laughed almost simultaneously.

Max scratched his head. 'Hmm, this reminds me of a Harvard study that showed how mind-wandering is actually the brain's default mode of operation. They used an iPhone app to contact participants at random times during their waking hours and ask them questions about what they were doing at that moment, whether they were thinking about something other than what they were currently doing and how happy they were on a sliding scale from zero to a hundred. Apparently, mind-wandering happened nearly *half* the time.'

Helen smiled. 'That's an excellent confirmation of my point, Max. Thanks—'

'Let's get Sherlock to show us,' Max said.

The orb emitted a short burst of blue flashes followed by a low mechanical whirr. Two wooden panels in the front wall slid sideways, revealing a flickering widescreen. An image of twenty-two grey bubbles formed, each one's size proportionate to how often that activity had been reported. George leaned forward and studied the screen. The working, talking and watching TV activity bubbles were the largest. How mundane life looked when presented in this way.

'You can see how each activity was rated on the happiness scale,' Max said, pointing to the bottom of the image. 'Mind-wandering happened at least a third of the time in every type of activity ... except lovemaking. People are happier when their minds are focused on their current activity, but that's another story. In fact ...'

Something jostled George's arm; Meghan was fishing around in her bag under the table. Pulling out her phone, she clicked on the Messages app and began to type hurriedly with two thumbs.

What the hell was so important? He wondered.

At the top of Meghan's screen was a profile picture of a young man with a chiselled jawline and dark hair. Olivier. He could have been a movie star or a model. George read the text:

All brains and no fun at this meeting. Wish you could rescue me! xxx

Ah, so the judge was in love.

'Mobile phones aren't allowed.' Ben's stern voice startled him. His heart pounded as if he'd been caught by the headmaster, and his head jerked up.

'Meghan?' Ben said. 'Mobile phones aren't allowed in the building. Nothing personal – it applies to us employees as much as to visitors. All devices were supposed to be deposited in a safe at reception. I'm afraid I'll have to take it from you.' He reached across the table.

Meghan flushed, clenched her jaw and slid the phone to him.

'Don't you think this is a bit heavy-handed?' George muttered into Takahashi's ear. 'What do they think we're going to do – sell Sherlock's story to the tabloids?'

'You're too suspicious,' Takahashi replied. 'It's probably just corporate policy. You know how these bureaucrats think.'

'So how come Ben's kept his phone?' He nodded at the rectangular bulge in Ben's front pocket. 'He's hiding something. One may smile, and smile, and be a villain.'

Takahashi chuckled. 'I'm glad you know your Hamlet, but you should chill out, my friend. As Helen said, our minds are easily distracted, and right now we need to focus on our goal.'

7

Shunting his chair closer to the table, George glanced across at Helen, but she seemed to be deep in thought. She was sitting directly opposite him, staring into space, her interlaced fingers resting on the table. There was something about Helen, something about the way she moved, the way she tilted her head when listening and her directness when she spoke. It was her directness in particular that reminded him of Ella.

Looking down at his hands, at the Mont Blanc pen he had bought for Ella only months before her departure, he could still feel the warmth of her hands, see her sitting at her desk, hunched over a long letter she was writing. He still missed her, still woke in the middle of the night aching for her presence. It was always worse at night.

'Well,' Helen said suddenly, shifting in her seat, 'here's the strange thing.' She bit her lip and remained silent for a moment. 'A lifetime of experience shows us that we're responsible for our actions. We want to know the time, so we look at our watch; we feel hungry, so we make a sandwich; we think of a stroll in the park and go out to do it.' She paused and scanned the faces around the table. 'The obvious conclusion is that our conscious mind is an active force, or the engine for will, right? What else could it be?'

'Ah, but how do we form this unshaken conviction?' Max asked.

Helen seemed to think about this for a moment. 'You're probably thinking about the Theory of Apparent Mental Causation.' When Max nodded, she said, 'I wasn't going to go there quite yet, but ... Okay, would you like to elaborate on this theory? After all, it's your area.'

'If you insist.' Max moved forward in his chair, straightening his posture. 'First, it's not exactly a theory anymore. There's ample experimental evidence for causal perception, starting with the seminal life-long work of the Belgian psychologist Michotte, and many others after him. It all seems to point to three principles that lead to our strong sense of responsibility for our own actions: priority, consistency and exclusivity. I'll give you an example.'

Again, Max had hijacked Helen's presentation, George noticed. Was he an attention-seeker or did he just fancy her? He glanced at Helen, expecting her to respond, but she remained silent, so he looked away, trying not to make the vague feeling of attraction too obvious. He certainly wasn't interested in a new relationship, but Helen felt like a potential ally, and the way things were going, he might need one.

'Sounds a lot like David Hume,' Takahashi mumbled.

Max pursed his lips and glared at him. 'Maybe, but we're talking here about a thesis based on scientific observations, not the theories of some Scottish philosopher from the 18th century, *ja?*'

'Go ahead with your example,' Takahashi said with a dismissive wave.

Max shut his eyes and the room grew even more silent.

Jeez, they're like children in kindergarten, George thought. Max reminded him of an old colleague back home who used pregnant pauses in the middle of sentences to force people to pay attention. But Max looked almost asleep.

'George, let's say you're driving your Ferrari,' Max said suddenly.

He raised his eyebrows at Max's odd sense of humour, although it wasn't unwelcome. He suspected they were going to need a sense of humour before long.

'You're cruising along a quiet country lane, enjoying the sunny weather and open fields all around—'

'Should've mentioned I was in the country first. I would've driven the Citroën.'

Helen laughed.

'Stick with me. You notice that you're over the speed limit.'

George laughed. 'If I'm on a country lane, surrounded by fields, there wouldn't be a speed limit. Are you sure you want to use this example?'

Max looked annoyed. 'It's just an example, George. Besides, there *is* a speed limit on country lanes.'

'How fast am I going?'

'It doesn't matter. You're over the national speed limit, and as you're a good old chap, you adhere to the limit. What do you do?'

'Well, if I was over the national speed limit on a country lane, I'd be going one hell of a lick. I guess I'd slow down.'

'And you'd probably think you were responsible for that slowing down, wouldn't you, George? Because prior to slowing down you would've followed a sequence of steps – first thought then action. It's known as the Priority Principle. But if, say, you thought of pressing the brake only *after* slowing down, this unusual sequence would make you feel that you weren't responsible for the action.'

When no one responded, Max glanced around, but even Takahashi was scratching his beard and said nothing. 'Now let's say you didn't think about slowing down,' he continued, 'and found your foot pressing on the brake; the inconsistency between thought and action, again, may make you feel like you didn't do it – especially if you were a new driver. That's the Consistency Principle.' George nodded. The whole explanation seemed a bit obvious. 'Now imagine that you noticed your passenger's hand was on the handbrake.'

'What, someone's been in my car with me the whole time?'

Max rolled his eyes. 'Concentrate, George. You'd be furious, right?'

'Yes, I guess so.'

'But you'd also be inclined to feel less responsible for the car slowing down, even if you'd just thought of doing so. And that, ladies and gentlemen, is the Exclusivity Principle,' said Max with a triumphant smile, and relaxed into his seat.

'In other words,' Helen said, finally looking at George, 'only when all three principles are fulfilled do you have the feeling that you acted out of your own initiative.'

'Exactly!' Max said.

Gertrude sat up straighter, the pen she was playing with balanced between her fingers. 'Well, these principles are very neat, but they only explain a *feeling* of ownership, so it doesn't necessarily reflect reality, does it?'

Max opened his mouth to reply, but Gertrude was still going. 'Even the Priority Principle is a myth. No matter how regular a sequence of events is, it doesn't necessarily mean causality. Night always follows day, right? But it'd be an obvious mistake to conclude that the day causes the night, as we all know that the rotation of the earth near the sun is the cause of both.'

'I agree with you for a change.' Takahashi stood up abruptly. 'As one of my teachers liked to remind us in every lecture, "Falling barometers are regularly followed by storms but do not cause them."' He leaned with both hands on the table, facing Max in a more combative manner than George had ever seen in him before. 'Imagine for a moment that a certain thought always occurs before a certain action, but the thought isn't causing the action in any way. You'd probably still perceive it as the cause, wouldn't you?'

'Yes, but that's just a theoretical possibility, isn't it?' Max said, scowling. 'Definitely not the most intuitive one.'

Takahashi started. 'It is *not* theoretical—'

Helen raised her hand like a teacher calming a noisy classroom. 'Please, please, with all due respect to philosophical discussions, I'd like to go through some hard evidence on how this sense of responsibility of one's actions develops from a young age.'

For a moment, the three remained poised like a tableau, Takahashi leaning over, poking his finger in Max's face, Gertrude leaning back, a smirk on her lips, and poor Max just sitting there, paralysed by the intensity of the debate. Just like George was. After a moment, Takahashi slowly lowered himself back into his seat, giving a brief nod of apology to Helen.

As soon as the tension relaxed, Helen exhaled a loud sigh. 'Newborn babies. They appear to have little or no control over their actions.'

Meghan's eyes widened. 'What about smiling?'

'Ah!' Helen said. 'Smiling. Classical theories of psychological development suggest that voluntary control of actions, such as smiling, develops in the first months as a result of parental reinforcement. So humans learn to become agents not only over their own bodies but also their environment, and that includes their caregivers too.'

George laughed. 'I thought it was caused by wind.'

Helen gave him an amused smile.

'Um ... how are we defining agent here?' Meghan asked.

'Spiders and thermostats,' Takahashi blurted out. 'An agent is anything that perceives its environment and acts on that environment. That includes animals, plants and even robots –

especially those with artificial intelligence,' he added, looking directly at the orb. 'Isn't that right, Sherlock?'

The blue lights flashed. 'That is correct,' the device said in its precise diction. 'All you need to build an agent is three basic components: a sensor, a processor and an effector. A thermostat controlling central heating is a classic example of—'

'Okay, I think we get the picture,' Takahashi said.

'Talking of thermostats,' Meghan said, wrapping slender arms around her ribcage, 'I know it's summer now, but I'm absolutely freezing in here. Would any of you mind if we increased the temperature a bit?'

When nobody objected, Ben got up to change the setting on the control box by the door. Takahashi watched him and said, 'Maybe I should just mention that an *ideal* agent is one that has intention and conscious will, unlike a thermostat. Most people believe they are ideal agents and could tell you not only *what* they are doing but also *why*; if they can't, they are normally unconscious, drugged or crazy. Now, Ben, could you tell us why you got up?'

'Yes, I can,' Ben said, returning to his seat. 'Which proves that I'm not crazy.'

'I'm relieved,' Helen said with a genuine smile. 'As I was saying, initial learning in humans starts at a very early age, even before first autobiographical memories, but the learning process continues well into adulthood. That's why many legal systems recognise that a person only reaches a fully developed sense of agency and responsibility at the age of eighteen.'

'Depends on the country,' Meghan blurted.

'Yes, of course. It was just an example.' Helen took a long sip from her glass of mineral water. 'But this lengthy learning process starts very differently. Young children don't seem to understand that intention is supposed to precede action. Sherlock, would you show the University of Michigan bucket video?'

On-screen, a three-year-old boy with blond hair stood in front of three colourful buckets, holding a beanbag. Straining his face, he aimed the beanbag and tossed it towards the buckets. 'In this elegant study,' Helen said, 'children were asked to name in advance the colour of the bucket they intended to hit and were given a coloured chip to remind them. Some buckets had a picture hidden at the bottom; if they hit them, they were awarded a mark on a score sheet. So far, so good. But when the children won by hitting a bucket they didn't intend to, the youngest children claimed more often that they had been trying to hit the winner all along, compared to the four and five-year-olds.' Finishing up, she brushed an invisible speck of something off her blouse.

George took in every word, like a thirsty fox in the desert would gulp cool water. *The delivery's impressive, all right, but there's something else about her ...* He racked his brain for some question or comment, something that would impress her. Or at least make her glance his way again. The best he could come up with was: 'I can accept that kids will invent false intentions after the fact, but surely with age we grow out of it, right?'

'And I don't blame you for thinking that,' Helen replied, and rewarded his paltry effort with a smile. 'After all, grown-ups know very well that an intention cannot come after the action is over. But we often slip back into old habits. In the fifties, Leon Festinger proposed that inconsistencies between a person's attitudes and behaviours produce uncomfortable psychological effects. So, in an attempt to eliminate this feeling of dissonance, people will revise their attitudes to justify their action. A classic example is the keen smoker who claims to be against smoking – to reduce this inconsistency, they may minimise the health consequences or claim they have little choice in the matter.'

A loud thud resounded as Max put his glass of water down heavily on the table and raised a hand. Definitely an attention-seeker, concluded George even before Max started talking. 'Talking of cognitive dissonance, a more relevant example is the paradoxical change in opinion. It happens when people are led to believe they are free to choose their behaviour rather than being forced to comply.'

'Are you talking about mind manipulation or normal behaviour?' George asked, glancing at Helen, who was now frowning at Max.

'Well, both. The principles can be used to coerce people into doing tasks they may not want to do, but it's also common in everyday life, from politics to the workplace. There's a nice example from a study by the University of Wisconsin to demonstrate this, if I may.' Max continued without waiting for a response, 'In one trial, a group of students were told that their university was debating a ten-percent increase in tuition fees and wanted to thoroughly review both sides of the argument.

Half the students were given no choice and were asked to write an essay justifying a fee rise. The other half were given a choice of which opinion to justify but were still asked politely to help with the fee-rise arguments since the university had sufficient arguments against it. I should mention that initially, all students strongly opposed a tuition fee increase, but after this exercise, those who had choice changed their private opinion.'

'I read that study,' Helen said. 'These results were replicated many times by different groups and settings, but what I find most astonishing is that when those who had choice were asked to describe their previous attitude, they reported that they agreed with the essay all along, just like the three-year-old kids with the buckets. They erased their original opinion entirely to avoid the conflict.'

George rubbed his fingertips on the surface of the table, tracing the flow of the wood grain. Even in disagreement there was something warm about Helen, something he trusted. But he also liked how elegantly she handled Max's constant interruptions. *Quite a pest, this man.*

'I must interrupt here,' Takahashi said. 'We've seen the conditions that create the feeling of responsibility for our everyday actions, and that it develops with age, but these are just feelings.' He smiled. 'The psychologists in the room must forgive me for saying that – I really have nothing against feelings – but the mind is known to play tricks on us.' He scanned the faces. 'The *sense* of authorship may have nothing to do with what actually happens here.'

Max glared at him. 'So what's your alternative explanation?' His voice dripped with contempt.

'Well, I can think of at least one alternative. Maybe the sense of responsibility is just that, a sense that happens to be misguided, and the decision itself is somehow predetermined.'

George felt annoyance rising in his chest. Although he was very fond of his old friend, he knew that once he got on his high philosophical horse, it'd be hard to get him off it. 'Hold on. It looks like we're veering into the theoretical zone again. Is there some hard science on volition, or desire to act, in the brain? I don't know, maybe something like a location or a mechanism?'

'I resent this attitude,' Max said. He picked up his pen and began clicking it repeatedly. 'Why does hard science have to be physical for you? What about psychology? Is it any less real?'

George laughed and was pleased to see Helen smiling at him again. 'Your frustration looks pretty real to me,' he said, 'but as a physicist, I'm biased towards things I can see, measure and understand. It's not that you can't measure things in cognitive psychology – I'm sure you can – but once you do, the interpretations can be quite theoretical and ... ambiguous.'

'Okay, I give up. Is there any physical evidence related to volition?' Max asked the room.

Helen was about to speak again when Ben interrupted her by standing up. 'Sorry, we need to wrap up for today – they're closing the building for the evening soon – but I can assure you that tomorrow morning we'll be able to continue from this point. Isn't that right, Sherlock?'

'Absolutely,' came the answer. 'From this exact point.'

'Excellent,' Ben said as he gathered his belongings. 'Now, just to remind you all, this evening we've a Seine River gourmet dinner cruise.' Max's eyes widened, as if he hadn't known. 'We'll meet by the rhino outside Musée d'Orsay at 7.30 p.m. and walk to the boat together. Dress code, smart casual.' Without waiting for confirmation, he strode out from the room, leaving behind a perplexed group of academics.

George watched him go. He hadn't forgotten about the river cruise. In fact, it had been worrying him. Coming to Paris had certainly cheered him up a bit, but not completely, and he wondered how he would deal with the socialising. He'd taken a river cruise with Ella when they were last in Paris. She'd been happy then; they'd both been happy – despite the circumstances. On the way from the airport earlier that morning his taxi had passed the hotel they stayed at. Just seeing it made his chest ache with physical pain. Would the river cruise hurt even more?

8

By a twist of good fortune, for which George wondered whether he should thank coincidence, the stars or quantum physics, it turned out that he and Helen were staying in the same hotel, so they agreed to make the journey that evening together. After a short ride on the Métro to a station near the river, they walked along the Left Bank, admiring the illuminated bridges and the reflections of the nearby buildings, the calm water occasionally disturbed by a cruise boat filled with tourists, some of them shouting and snapping pictures with upheld phones.

It was a pleasant walk, but after a while he realised that they hadn't said a word to one another, not one. The last time he'd walked along the Seine, he'd been with Ella, a very different woman, but the silence between him and Helen was just as companionable. It was a strange revelation; usually he was uncomfortable with silences.

At that moment, a cyclist whizzed by, causing Helen to suddenly step closer to him, her elbow brushing his. 'Sorry, I was daydreaming,' she said, smiling at him. She chuckled. 'Or maybe that's eveningdreaming. Is this your first time in Paris?'

'No. I've been here quite a few times – for conferences, mainly. You?'

She shook her head. 'It's my first time. Not for want of trying, of course.'

'That's hard to believe.'

'Why?'

'You just seem so natural here.' *Smooth, boy, real smooth.*

She laughed. 'I'm just following your lead.'

A few yards further on, they came across a portrait artist sitting at the edge of the embankment. He was putting the final touches to a charcoal picture of a little girl with pigtails. Helen slowed, then stopped to study the portrait, which was almost finished.

She turned to him. 'Wow, he's really good. I've always wanted a portrait done. You don't have to wait for me. I'll meet you at the boat.'

George looked ahead to where the restaurant boat was moored. They weren't far away now. He shrugged. 'Sure. I'll see you by the rhino statue. Don't be late. The boat may leave without you.'

As soon as he started walking away, he regretted not staying with her, so he slowed his walk and looked back. The artist was handing the drawing to the little girl, who immediately skipped towards her parents, joyfully holding the portrait above her head. The artist must have been good at spotting potential customers; he was already speaking to Helen.

He continued along the riverbank, trying to rebuff the thoughts of his faux pas. After all, Helen was just a colleague. She was kind and spontaneous, but so were plenty of other women. By the time he arrived at the brightly illuminated open space near the entrance to the museum, he'd concluded that continuing down any path that included Helen was a bad idea.

Ben was already there, slapping the cast-iron rhino statue, making a hollow sound.

'Now why the hell did they decide that a rhino was a good idea ...' he was saying to Max, but trailed off when he saw George approaching. 'Hi, George. Glad you could make it. Have you seen Helen?'

'She'll be along in a minute. Having her portrait done.' He leaned against the cold base of the statue, watching the slow stream of visitors pouring out of Musée d'Orsay and heading for the riverbank. Then Ben went off on his rhino rant again.

Fifteen minutes later, Grinberg and Helen arrived together, with Takahashi bringing up the rear. Jerry and Meghan joined the group from the opposite direction.

'Okay, we're all here,' Ben said. 'Gertrude isn't well and decided to have an early night. Maybe something she ate.'

'A small child?' George whispered into Helen's ear, causing her to giggle. 'How was the portrait?'

'It's really good,' she said, waving the rolled-up drawing. 'I'll show you later.'

Crossing the road, they made their way down a wide set of steps towards the boat. A smiling stewardess in a grey silk waistcoat with a red tie welcomed them as she unhooked the velvet rope across the gangplank, and just beyond, another steward in an identical uniform was holding a tray with champagne flutes. George watched from the very back of the queue as they climbed on board and collected a drink – all except Takahashi and Meghan. When he reached the steward, he took a glass and stepped into the dining area, lowering his head to avoid the door frame. The carpet was soft under his feet. All the tables had white linen, but only two were fully made up with plates, cutlery and napkins, one on each side of the boat. Soft orange lights flickered through elegant candle holders, which reflected in the windows and roof in all directions. It looked like this luxury boat was meant for a bigger party than eight, and he wondered if Ben had booked out all the other tables. He made his way to where Helen, Max and Takahashi were already seated.

'You said that it's your first visit to Paris,' George said, sliding into his seat beside Helen. 'Is Mr Casey not the type to whisk you away on a romantic holiday?'

She laughed. 'There is no Mr Casey … or any other partner.'

Ignoring the lightening of his heart, he tried to make a joke of it. 'That's even harder to believe. An intelligent and attractive woman …'

'I'm glad you said intelligent before attractive. I guess I never found the right partner.' She paused. 'Well, that's not entirely true.'

'Why, what happened with Mr Perfect?'

61

'Oh no, I meant Charlie. I had the artist draw him from a picture.' She pulled out the portrait from her bag and showed it to him.

He glanced at the chocolate-coloured labradoodle with its tongue out. 'What, he's never offered to take you to Paris?'

'Never,' she said, chuckling. 'But he's loyal and affectionate. What else do I need?'

'A good conversation?'

She laughed. 'That probably *is* the only weakness in the relationship. He's an excellent listener though. Have you been to Paris with Mrs Bennet?'

He hesitated, remembering. 'Yes. I had the most amazing week here with Ella. Two years ago.'

'But she's not here this time?'

A waiter arrived and handed out menus. George scanned his as the waiter reeled off the specials, but didn't hear a word; he was too consumed by Ella. It was now or never, because there'd be no way to explain it away if he lied. And why should he lie? There was nothing shameful in being a ... a widower.

So as soon as the waiter finished, George turned to Helen, certain she could hear his heartbeat from where she sat. 'I lost my wife to Huntington's disease last year.'

Her face went blank, then sad. 'Oh no, I'm so sorry, George. I had no idea.'

'That's all right. I think Paris will always be very special for me. It was our last trip together. Regardless, it's a beautiful city.'

'So Ella's ... condition deteriorated quickly after your trip?'

62

'No ... not really.' He went silent. He'd done this to himself, blurting things out, telling this woman, a near stranger, things that she didn't need to know. Then he heard himself speaking. 'She'd started dropping things, stumbling, forgetting names. It was distressing, but not too terrible.' He realigned the cutlery before him, knives straight, forks straight, spoon horizontal. 'Well, there were the changes in personality. She'd rarely been irritable before.'

'So what happened?' Helen asked, her voice concerned.

'We read everything we could find on the disease.' He hesitated and swallowed hard. 'We learned that there was no prospect of a cure. At the later stages, she wouldn't be able to walk or talk, meaning full-time care.'

'And then?'

'Then it was all over. Twenty-three years together, gone, just like that.'

'I'm so sorry, my friend,' whispered Takahashi. He started and glanced at the little man's kind face. Of course. He hadn't even told Takahashi.

Max paused briefly from his detailed analysis of the menu and the food quality he was expecting, realising that Takahashi wasn't listening.

George drained his champagne glass. 'It's still early days. Someday, I'll get over it. Actually, as a psychologist, *you* can probably tell *me* when that's likely to be.'

Helen sighed. 'I really don't know, I'm just a cognitive psychologist. And I've never experienced such a loss.'

He glanced through the window at an impressive illuminated building passing by and recognised the Conciergerie, a former prison during the French Revolution, thanks to its distinctive dark roof cones. 'She was my soulmate for twenty-three years,' he said pensively. 'There's no replacing her.'

The waiter came back, but George hadn't understood any of the menu. He quickly scanned it and was relieved to see that each course had only four options. From the other table, he could hear Meghan protesting about the very limited vegetarian selection.

'I'll ... I'll start with the onion soup,' he managed. The waiter nodded and finally left, leaving the table in an uncomfortable silence once more. George searched around for something to talk about that wasn't his wife. 'So, um, Max, I'm just wondering, what attracted you to psychology? I mean, it's a fascinating area, but was it a life-long interest of yours?'

'Ha, funny you should ask,' Max said, and dabbed his mouth with a napkin. 'It was actually one event in my childhood that triggered my interest.'

'Oh! Can you tell us?' Helen asked, leaning forward and resting her elbows on the table.

Max gave her a grin that showed too many of his teeth. '*Ja*, of course. Do you want the long version or the short version?'

'Let's start with the short version, shall we?' George muttered.

'Well, it was just after school. Me and my best friends, Ryker and Sabine, went to play hide-and-seek in the field behind the old school building, as we often did. It was Sabine's turn to find us that day, but I had a secret plan, you see.'

'How old were you?' Helen asked with a dreamy smile.

'Oh, probably eight or nine. Anyway, each classroom had a cupboard with teaching supplies, but those were normally locked so no pupil would help themselves to the tempting new stationery. That day during class, I'd noticed that the cupboard was slightly ajar, so I'd shut it just before leaving the classroom and conjured up a cunning plan. I insisted that Sabine would count till fifty and used the time to run across the field back into the school. That was quite scary as we weren't supposed to be there after hours, but I managed to sneak back into my classroom without being caught by the caretaker.'

The waiter came back with the starters. George inspected the French onion soup in front of him – steaming, delicious but somehow off-putting with the floating slice of bread covered in melted cheese. He poked the bread with his spoon. The slice kept surfacing.

Max paused to look wide-eyed at his foie gras with truffle shavings. 'To cut a long story short, I hid inside the cupboard and my friends couldn't find me. The problem was that I fell asleep inside it. When I woke up a few hours later, it was already dark and the caretaker had locked the classroom door. I spent the whole night in there, shaking and sobbing.'

'That's terrible,' Helen said.

'Well, they found me in the morning, but since then I don't like to be in locked spaces unless it's my own home, where I keep the keys in my pocket at all times. But that's the incident that piqued my interest in psychology. I was particularly fascinated by how a single event can shape a person's reactions for life. Now, let's eat. I'm starving.'

'Have you ever studied this condition as a result?' George asked, but Max was already deep into his starter and deaf to the world.

He ate quickly, suddenly feeling a bit oppressed by the company, the noise, the chatter. It was too much for one day – and also probably the most people he'd been around since Ella's death. When he finished his soup, he excused himself and made his way out to the open deck in the bow. A warm breeze caressed his face, and after a while his spirits lifted. He hated to admit it, but despite enjoying Helen's company, he preferred to be alone with his thoughts. There was an odd contradiction about being in Paris, because in a strange way, Ella was still alive here. Paris even smelled like her. Leaning over the handrail, he watched the ripples of the water as the boat cut through its glassy surface.

The illuminated Eiffel Tower passing by reminded him of that last conference, where he'd delivered the keynote speech on physics and the nature of reality. He'd certainly enjoyed all the attention after the talk and the intellectual discussions over meals and in the corridors of the conference centre, but the most memorable part of that visit was the time he'd spent alone with Ella. She normally didn't accompany him on such conferences but had made an exception on that occasion.

'Wouldn't it be nice if we spent a few days exploring Paris?' she'd said when he told her about the conference invitation.

He'd agreed immediately and later wondered why they'd never done that before. The idea that you shouldn't mix business and pleasure had been embedded in his mind without his ever questioning its validity. Holidays were purely holidays and work trips were purely work. That Paris trip was different because they'd already received the bad news, and both had an urge to enjoy life and each other's company to the full before it was too late. On their last day in Paris, they scaled the stairs up the famous tower, stopping every few minutes for a hug when Ella was too tired. They finally reached the first-level gallery, huffing and puffing, but were restored as they strolled around the balcony's outer perimeter, taking in the view below while trying to dodge visitors taking photos with long selfie sticks. He'd been eager to see the names of the country's scientists that Alexandre-Gustave Eiffel had engraved somewhere on the first level. After an unsuccessful search he'd asked a friendly guard, who explained that the engravings of the letters, each sixty centimetres in height, were located below the balcony, so they could only be viewed from the ground. 'Apparently,' the guard explained in a heavy French accent, 'Monsieur Eiffel did not include a single woman in this list of seventy-two scientists and engineers. This is outrageous, do you not think?'

George had sensed the genuine indignation in her voice and offered a sympathetic smile. 'Well, it was a long time ago,' he'd said. 'I doubt it would happen these days.'

The guard had laughed. 'I would not be so sure, monsieur.'

Finally, they'd used the lift to get to the top floor and climbed up the last few stairs to the observation balcony. The constant swaying of the tower took them both by surprise. Ella had grown dizzy and held on to him tightly as they peered into Eiffel's laboratory, where French scientists had studied astronomy, meteorology, aerodynamics and physiology and conducted experiments with various devices, including the famous Foucault's Pendulum.

'That was a time when one person could quite easily master a variety of fields, just like Leonardo da Vinci,' he'd told Ella with a hint of jealousy. She had smiled lovingly and placed a gentle kiss on his lips.

'Hey, here you are,' came a voice to his left. Takahashi was leaning on the handrail next to him, gazing at the slowly moving riverbank. 'How *are* you?'

'I'm ... I'm fine,' he replied with relief, still staring ahead.

'They will call us when the main dish is served.'

'Good.'

'Maybe we could find a free evening away from this crowd and have a good old catch-up. What do you say?'

'Sounds good,' he replied, offering Takahashi a reticent smile.

And then Max and Helen burst onto the deck, wine glasses in hand. Max was recounting an amusing incident, gesticulating enthusiastically with his free hand, causing them both to laugh loudly. He put an arm around Helen and led her to the opposite side of the deck. Takahashi winked discreetly at George, who remained sombre.

What a jerk.

Before long, the rest of the group filled in the deck, talking, laughing, acting like people on a holiday. The boat was approaching the Pont de Bir-Hakeim. From a distance, George could see flashing blue lights on both ends of the bridge with more police cars heading there along the riverbanks. As they came closer, the shouts of the crowd and banners on the bridge attracted everyone's attention and they looked up. Suddenly, someone released a long and narrow banner, which quickly unfurled straight down over the side of the bridge, nearly reaching the water level. George just managed to read the vertical letters "*arrêter la mondialisation*" when the boat made a sharp maneuverer to the left in an attempt to avoid it. The bottom of the banner brushed the handrail, crossed the deck from the side, then slapped the glass roof covering the dining area hard. He ducked and turned to see Max lose his balance and nearly fall backwards on the deck. At the last moment he clutched the handrail, saving his glass but spilling the red wine on Helen's cream blouse. Takahashi remained standing, holding his hat tightly with both hands. It was all over in seconds. The captain steered the boat back to its original course towards the arch, and after a brief apology over the Tannoy, they emerged safely on the other side of the bridge.

George exchanged looks with Helen, who was wiping her blouse with a tissue. Her look said, *That certainly spiced things up a bit.*

'Good Lord,' Meghan said as they recovered. 'What do they want?'

'Oh, the usual,' Ben said, still looking back at the unfurled banner. 'Just another anti-globalisation demo. Skudder's got some ideas on how to handle these disruptions.'

'Oh? How?'

Ben cleared his throat. 'I mean ... I think he has. Skudder doesn't share his thinking with me.'

George tried to read his expression in the dim light, the brief but discernible furrowing of his brow. 'Ben ...' he began.

'Sorry, I need to make a phone call,' Ben said, and left the deck.

9

The following day, when the playback of the final few minutes from last evening's discussion was projected on-screen raised some chuckles of embarrassment, it seemed to George that the river adventure was far from everyone's mind. He was mulling over Ben's strange comment and evasiveness during the cruise when he noticed something else. Leaning over towards Takahashi, he whispered, 'Strange that we weren't told we were being filmed, or asked to give our consent, don't you think?' Takahashi nodded but said nothing. George straightened. Perhaps he *was* the only one suspicious of this whole enterprise.

When the playback finished, Grinberg wheeled his chair backwards, got to his feet and started pacing around the room, hands behind his back. All eyes followed him. 'Before replying to George and Max on the physical evidence for volition in the brain,' he said, 'I'd better mention briefly the left-brain interpreter concept, which I'm sure some of you know already.' He looked at the blank faces. 'No? Okay, it was developed by the psychologist Michael Gazzaniga and the neuroscientist Joseph LeDoux.' He stopped his pacing for a moment. 'Actually, it all started in the 1950s with the work by Roger Sperry on split-brain patients. He discovered that the two brain hemispheres have functional specialisation, and for that he got the Nobel Prize in Physiology or Medicine in 1981.'

'Sorry,' interrupted Gertrude, 'so which one was it? Physiology or medicine?'

Takahashi burst out laughing.

'What's so funny?' She glowered at him and stood up. A loud ripping sound came from her skirt as it got caught in the chair. She quickly sat down again, her cheeks flushed.

George stifled a laugh. *Not so arrogant now.*

'Physiology or Medicine is the name of this prize,' Grinberg said. 'So, as I was saying ... in the 1960s, Sperry was joined by Gazzaniga, a psychobiology student at Caltech, whose clear summaries of their collaborative work are widely cited in textbooks.'

George watched Max drumming his fingers silently on the table and wondered if Grinberg had noticed it too. He was starting to get impatient himself.

'To cut a long story short,' continued Grinberg, 'the brain-splitting surgeries aimed to treat severe epilepsy and involved severing the corpus callosum, the bundle of fibres that carry signals between the two hemispheres. The left one is often responsible for speech and analytical capacity and the right one helps the recognition of visual patterns. That's obviously an oversimplification, and I hope you'll forgive me for that.

Interestingly, the surgery didn't seem to affect these patients' personality, intelligence or emotions. But when the right brain was presented with pictures or words, there was no response for the simple reason that the information couldn't pass to the speech centre in the left brain.'

'So what happened?' said George, trying to move things a bit faster.

'You'll see soon,' replied Grinberg, not unkindly. 'Once the instruction "walk" was presented to the right brain, the patient known as JW got up to leave the testing van. When asked where he was going, the patient's left brain quickly improvised, "I'm going into the house to get a Coke." When the word "laugh" was flashed to the right brain, the patient would often laugh and his explanation was an obvious confabulation. "You guys come up and test us every month. What a way to make a living."'

Meghan raised a tentative hand. 'Sorry for the naive question, but how do you present images to only one side of the brain?'

George nodded. It was a good question.

'Ah,' said Grinberg, and stroked his moustache. 'Well, you flash an image on the opposite side of the screen. Because of the way the brain is wired to the eyes, the right visual field activates the left brain and vice versa. So, based on decades of research, Gazzaniga constructed this theory that the left brain is functioning as an interpreter. It observes everything and immediately constructs a hypothesis as to why particular actions occurred. In fact, the interpreter need not be privy to the reason for a response. It will take the behaviour at face value and fit the event into the ongoing belief system that it's already constructed.'

Jerry, the other neuroscientist on the team, was nodding away, his black mane of hair bobbing up and down. 'In other words, your left brain invents intentions on a regular basis *after* observing your behaviour.'

Grinberg took his seat at the table, smiling smugly. He folded his reading glasses and dropped them straight into his coffee cup. Realising what he'd done, he quickly fished them out and wiped them with a napkin.

George smiled – a scatterbrain neuroscientist with a Nobel Prize was ironic and endearing in equal measures.

Takahashi took off his white Panama hat. 'Very impressive,' he said, twirling the hat around his finger. 'But are there more natural examples? A surgery tinkering with the normal function and connectivity of the brain is useful, but it's also quite artificial, don't you think?' His glance alternated between Grinberg and Jerry on the opposite sides of the table.

The two exchanged looks that George couldn't read, then Grinberg gestured to Jerry to take the question.

'In fact, localised brain lesions are still considered the gold standard for identifying the function of specific brain areas,' Jerry said. 'And this is the case to this day, even though we have modern tools such as brain stimulation and imaging to decipher function. But you know, there is a host of naturally occurring neurological syndromes that give rise to abnormal volition. Maybe we should look at those next.'

'That would be interesting,' George said, 'but are we still focusing on the physical evidence for free will?'

Ben nodded. 'Yes, we must have a definitive answer. Skudder will accept nothing less.'

Skudder? He's not even here. Besides, we're the experts.

'Of course, of course,' Jerry replied. 'The generation of volition is central to our goal. I'll get to that in a minute, but first a bit on these fascinating syndromes.' There was a glint in his eyes that betrayed his excitement. 'On one extreme, there are those with decreased volition. We call them hypovolition. A typical example is the known passivity in schizophrenia. Patients experiencing delusions of control make normal movements but claim that someone or something else is controlling them rather than their own will. On the other extreme, we have those syndromes that exhibit hypervolition, like Huntington's disease.'

George flinched. It was unfortunate that Jerry had mentioned that, bringing up unintentionally the pain he still felt, the frustration and sense of loss. He glanced at Helen. Their eyes met only briefly, but long enough for him to notice her concerned look.

'These patients,' continued Jerry, 'have jerky, involuntary movements of mainly the shoulders, hips and face. Anyway, many neurologists noticed that in the early course of the disease, patients claim that these uncontrolled movements are voluntary, especially when they are relatively infrequent. When asked if they made the movement on purpose or if it just happened to them, they often replied with things like "I was scratching my head" or "I was just stretching".'

George's mind drifted to Ella again. In the early days of her disease, he'd noticed occasional shoulder jerks. At first, he hadn't said anything, dismissing it as just stress at work that had finally got to her. She'd often complained that customers were really rude to her at the pharmacy. But then she also started dropping things ... 'Stop watching me like a hawk,' she'd snap. 'It was just an accident. Could happen to anyone.' She'd never snapped at him like that before ...

'Okay, back to the physical evidence you wanted to hear about, George.'

He looked up from his yellow notepad. Jerry was talking directly to him. 'There is this very elegant study from Harvard Medical School,' he began, 'that looked closely at two syndromes that disrupt the perception of free will. Just to remind you all, this perception has two components, agency and volition. The first is the sense of responsibility for our actions and the second is the desire to act. We'll start with agency. One rare condition that disrupts it is called the alien hand syndrome.' He smiled as a few heads nodded. 'I guess some of you are familiar with Peter Sellers in *Dr Strangelove*? Sherlock, please show us a relevant clip.'

A black-and-white image of Peter Sellers appeared on-screen. He was sitting in a wheelchair, answering questions from the US president in a heavy German accent, when suddenly his prosthetic right hand in a black leather glove shot up in a Nazi salute. His left hand quickly restrained it. The clip stopped as Dr Strangelove's left hand was desperately trying to prise away his gloved hand from a choking grip on his throat.

'It's comic in the film,' Jerry said, after instructing Sherlock to stop the clip, 'but in reality, I can assure you, it's quite distressing to the patient.' He undid the elastic band holding his ponytail and looped it around his hand. 'Patients typically experience one hand as acting autonomously and may find it moving at cross purposes with their conscious intention. In one case, a patient was playing draughts when his left hand made a move he did not wish to make, but when he corrected the move with the right hand, the left hand repeated the false move. The left hand might undo buttons as the right hand tries to button the shirt. You get the picture.'

George thought about this strange condition and wondered if the person suffering from it could see the absurdity of it. Probably not.

'What causes this syndrome?' Ben asked.

'It could develop after a stroke, trauma, tumour or other conditions that damage the frontal lobe on the side of the brain opposite the affected hand.' Jerry tucked a strand of hair into his mouth and chewed it. 'Next they looked at another condition that affects volition and causes diminished motivation. That's a classic example of hypovolition.'

All this talk about syndromes was making George slightly dizzy. He got up and approached the window wall, smiling apologetically to Jerry for the interruption. The view of the street below with healthy people walking about had a calming effect and he continued listening from there.

'Here, brain damage from stroke, for example, results in the lack of spontaneous behaviour, or apathy. In its most extreme form, called akinetic mutism, patients exhibit greatly reduced movements, gestures and speech but without any weakness or other causes. Now, the Harvard group analysed in detail the locations of the brain damage that caused these two disorders of the free will, and that's where things get really interesting.' Jerry stopped speaking and George turned away from the window to see Jerry rolling up his sleeves. 'They found that damage that disrupts agency, where patients felt they were not responsible for their hand movement, occurred in many different brain areas *but* always within a single network of nerve fibres.' He turned to the orb. 'Sherlock, load the image.'

A large map of the human brain appeared on-screen. An area located in the inner side of each cerebral hemisphere towards the rear was painted red and labelled "precuneus", with a network of fluorescent orange lines leading to it.

'It's a case of all roads lead to Rome. This network is defined by its connection to the red area. If we now look at damage that disrupts volition, where patients had very little motivation, it was confined, again, to a single but different network.'

On-screen, Sherlock highlighted a collar-shaped area in blue. It was tucked deep between the two cerebral hemispheres in the front and labelled "anterior cingulate", with a network of fluorescent green lines leading to it.

That's very neat, George thought. *Orange network is agency, green network is volition. If only the rest of science was so clear-cut and simple.*

'Sorry, I can't see the difference between the colours,' Max said. 'I'm colour blind.'

'Good job you're not an electrician then,' Gertrude said.

'Maybe Sherlock can make the volition network flash,' Jerry suggested, then immediately added, 'That's great, thank you, Sherlock. Okay, now we'll map the locations where brain stimulation alters the perception of free will compared to control stimulations that did not, just as these researchers did.' He turned to the orb. 'Sherlock, please load the video.'

A series of black stars and dots popped up at random locations across the image of the brain. Most of the stars overlaid on the orange and green networks. The dots did not.

'Bingo,' Jerry cried. 'With a 94 percent match and a significant difference, this brilliant work provides the anatomical location for our perception of free will.'

Soon after George returned to his seat, he felt a tap on his shoulder and looked to his right. Helen retracted her hand from behind Takahashi and whispered, 'Sharp mind in scruffy clothes. Looks can be so misleading.'

George gave a vague nod. He was rarely lost for words, but at this moment he was. This study provided just the evidence he'd asked for but hadn't thought existed. A concrete physical confirmation for a location was the strongest evidence so far. Perhaps they would find a firm resolution for this old puzzle after all. He felt the hairs on the nape of his neck rising. Then doubts started creeping in. *Location is nice, but ...*

'Wait a minute, Jerry,' Takahashi said. 'Sorry to be a pain, but did you just say *perception*?'

'Yes, why?'

'Well, just because there is an area in the brain that's responsible for our *perception* of free will, doesn't mean we actually *have* a free will, does it?'

Exactly. Takahashi read my mind.

10

As soon as Ben left the room for an impromptu comfort break, the conversation focused on phones, or rather the lack of them.

'What I find the most upsetting about it,' said Gertrude, 'is that I can't read my news feed. It's almost an addiction, I know, but a healthy one. Must keep up with world events.'

George pictured Gertrude watching the evening news from her armchair, sipping gin and tonic and swearing at anyone she found disagreeable on-screen. Was she talking to herself or to a meek husband? He couldn't quite decide.

'I actually miss my social media,' said Jerry. 'Now I have to wait until the evening to find out what my friends are up to.'

Gertrude rolled her eyes.

'I don't miss social media,' said Grinberg with a smile. 'In fact, it's only recently that I stopped carrying the photos of my grandchildren in my wallet. Went digital. But of course, they're on my phone, so I can't show them to you.'

'How many do you have?' asked George.

'Photos or grandchildren?' He chuckled. 'Five gorgeous grandkids from three children.'

A few minutes later, when Ben entered the room, the conversation died out abruptly. A light snoring caught George's attention and he saw that Grinberg's head had slumped on his chest. Feeling embarrassed on Grinberg's behalf, he tried a discrete cough. When that failed, he nudged him gently with his elbow. Grinberg opened his eyes and fumbled for his reading glasses. He put them on and casually looked at his notes.

Ben nodded towards Jerry, prompting him to continue the discussion.

'You're absolutely right,' Jerry said, facing Takahashi. 'Perception of free will doesn't prove that it exists. In fact, in some circumstances the perception is clearly false. Take, for example, hypnosis, a subject that's fascinated me since I witnessed a demonstration at medical school. Let's listen to Albert Moll, an early hypnosis researcher, recounting a typical example of posthypnotic suggestion. Sherlock, could you please read for us the incident with the flowerpot from Moll's book *Hypnotism*?'

Sherlock's lights flickered briefly, then it found its voice. 'Absolutely. It's on page 153,' stated the orb. 'I tell a hypnotised subject that when he wakes he is to take a flowerpot from the window, wrap it in a cloth, put it on the sofa and bow to it three times. All of which he does. When he is asked for his reasons, he answers, "You know, when I woke and saw the flowerpot there, I thought that as it was rather cold, the flowerpot had better be warmed a little, or else the plant would die. So I wrapped it in the cloth, and then I thought that as the sofa was near the fire, I would put the flowerpot on it; and I bowed because I was pleased with myself for having such a bright idea." He added that he did not consider the proceeding foolish because he had told me his reasons for so acting.'

'Ah, yes,' Max said with an amused smile, waving a silent thank you at Sherlock. 'It was the posthypnotic suggestion that led Sigmund Freud to develop the concept of Defensive Rationalisation. He basically said that each of us can sometimes be like the person who carries out a posthypnotic suggestion. So if you ask almost anyone why they are acting this way, instead of saying that they have no idea, they're compelled to invent some obviously unsatisfactory reason. According to Freud, such confabulation of impossible intentions happens in everyday life when the true intentions are troubling. The motive for people to invent or distort the reason for their behaviour after the fact, the theory goes, is to cover up the true causes because these are unconscious, unbearable or just unseemly.'

'I hope we're not getting into psychoanalytical theory now,' Gertrude said, twiddling her pen.

'Any problem with that?' snapped Max.

She leaned back in her seat and bounced the pen on the table. 'Personally, I have no problem with psychoanalysis. On the contrary, I find it full of fascinating fairy tales about the mind. But if we want firm answers, we'd better stick with solid evidence.' She smiled at him, displaying a row of yellow teeth.

George watched Max rolling up his right sleeve as if getting ready to punch her. Instead, he shook his head. 'If you paid any attention—'

'Okay,' Jerry interrupted. 'If I may continue ... the reason I brought up posthypnotic suggestion is that susceptible people have a strong impression that they freely willed their actions. Studies show that between 15 and 55 percent of them feel their actions were voluntary. You see? People can easily confuse a request from a stranger with their own will and feel compelled to invent intentions because they expect to have them.'

'Wait a minute,' Gertrude said. 'I don't know much about hypnosis, but it's clearly a unique state of mind and hardly a typical everyday behaviour. Besides, not everyone is suggestible.'

'Well, estimates show that between 10 and 20 percent of people are susceptible to hypnosis, so quite a significant chunk of the population. But it's really the concept that matters here.'

George drew a spiral on his notepad, in which he hadn't taken many notes. He could see the point Gertrude had made. Not only was hypnosis far from an everyday activity, but the fact that most people can't even be hypnotised made it difficult to reach a general conclusion. Besides, stage hypnotists must have a clever way to select susceptible volunteers for the show to succeed.

'Okay, you want a different example from everyday behaviour? Fine!' Jerry straightened his back and stroked his ponytail, ready to pounce. 'There's a whole host of strange situations, often called automatisms, where people's actions are detached from their intention. Take, for example, the practices in the late 19th century – spiritualist trends like automatic writing, Ouija board spelling, channelling and what not.'

'I think these practices are still common in certain circles these days,' Max said with a wry smile.

'I'm not surprised,' Jerry said, relaxing his shoulders. 'I guess the attraction of the supernatural can be powerful even in the era of modern science. Anyway, back to my point. Let's look for a moment at the practice of table-turning. A group of people sat around a light table with hands resting on its surface, waiting. Many participants were sceptics, yet often after a long and tense wait, the table started rotating, rocking from side to side or performing other movements. Most spiritualists ascribed the table movements to the agency of spirits or ghosts, but Michael Faraday proved conclusively that it had nothing to do with the supernatural.'

George brightened at this. The conversation was becoming a bit more interesting. He'd had no idea that Faraday was a debunker. 'Was this *the* Faraday?' he asked. 'The English physicist who's considered the father of electromagnetism?'

'The very man,' Jerry said excitedly. 'He actually used a simple apparatus made of two sliding boards fastened with elastic bands between the hands and the table to investigate the movement. Not surprisingly, he demonstrated that the movement originated from the participants themselves, who reported no experience of willing the action. Instead, they were amazed at the table's animation. Again, in these cases, people's experience of will was entirely misleading about the true cause of their actions.'

'Here we go again,' Gertrude said, rolling her eyes. 'That's just another exotic story of a bunch of gullible imbeciles in highly unusual circumstances. Is that the best example you can give us? Because I'm not impressed.'

George closed his eyes and the arguing voices faded away. Soon after the group placed their hands on the large table, it started rocking gently from side to side, then levitating slowly together with the people around it as one, all the way to the ceiling.

All except Gertrude. She was sitting firmly in her chair, looking up and sulking.

He smiled and opened his eyes.

'Well, I've already realised that it's hard to impress you,' retorted Jerry.

'Someone has to be critical here.' Gertrude looked around the table disapprovingly. 'And it just happened to be me this time.'

'As much as I hate to admit it, I think she has a point,' George said. 'Are there more normal, everyday situations that we could look at?'

'I don't know about normal,' Helen said, 'but there are certainly psychological experiments that looked at attribution of choice and will, with startling results.'

'Okay,' Gertrude said with a smile of satisfaction. 'I'm all ears. Startle me.'

George grimaced. Gertrude's challenge felt almost personal. He turned towards Helen, hoping she'd handle this gracefully.

'Let me start with something called choice blindness,' Helen began, apparently oblivious to Gertrude's contempt. 'Researchers from Lund and New York Universities showed pairs of pictures of female faces to both male and female participants and asked them to choose which face they found most attractive. Immediately after the selection they were asked to describe the reasons for their choice. Sneakily, in some trials, they used sleight of hand to exchange one face with the other that the participants did not choose.'

'And no one noticed the exchange?' asked George.

'Actually, some did,' she replied with a smile, 'but only about 13 percent. Even in the best cases, when faces were particularly different and participants had unlimited time for deliberation, no more than 26 percent detected the exchange. That's not all. When participants went on to explain in detail the reasons for their choices, they were actually justifying the face they had not picked.'

Amazing, thought George. *Just like the three-year-old children with the bucket.*

'In other words,' Helen concluded, 'they were mistaken about their own intentions and confabulated an explanation to match the final outcome.'

George glanced at Gertrude. Maybe that would shut the snappy alligator up.

'Ah, sounds like the ideal agent was caught with his pants down,' Takahashi said with a chuckle.

Gertrude held her head with both hands like she was trying to keep it from exploding. 'What does an ideal agent have to do with this?'

'As the ideal agents we all believe we are, we expect to have conscious goals and to know what they are before we pursue them,' Helen replied. 'But as this experiment shows, the sense of agency seems to be nothing but a retroactive confabulation. A strategy to fill in the gaps and explain our own actions or choices *after* the fact.'

'That's quite a big claim,' Gertrude said, glaring at Helen. 'I hope you have more evidence than just selecting attractive faces from cards.'

George alternated his gaze between Gertrude and Helen as if watching a tense table tennis match.

'I certainly do. One experiment, often called I-spy, showed how easily people can be fooled into believing they caused an action freely that in reality they were forced to do.' Gertrude raised her left eyebrow in response and Helen continued, 'Researchers from the University of Virginia asked volunteers to move a cursor on a screen covered with photos of different toys from a children's book. They shared the computer mouse with an experimental confederate, or an actor if you like, who gently forced the movement without their knowledge. They each heard very different things over a set of headphones. The confederate heard clear instructions on what item to stop on and when. But the volunteer heard music and a single word, such as "monkey", which was one of the items on the screen. Now, amazingly, the volunteers reported feeling that their movement was intentional when the word "monkey" was played one or five seconds before the forced stop on that item, as if it were their own intention. On the other hand, they did not feel it was their own intention if they heard the item much earlier or just one second after the forced stop. In other words, people think they cause an action when the relevant thought is primed just before the action, whether they actually performed it or not.'

'Sounds like the word over the headphone implanted a thought in their mind that was perceived as an internal intention,' Gertrude said, then paused as if to consider what she'd just said. 'Very impressive,' she mumbled. 'But this effect was on moving a computer mouse. Are there any examples out there with substantial effect? Maybe with more complex behaviour or something with more consequences?'

'A computer mouse can have far-reaching consequences, my friend,' Takahashi said with a grin. Gertrude winced. 'From controlling a remote surgical operation to launching a ballistic missile.'

'Well,' Helen said, 'there are plenty of examples of what psychologists call priming, and they don't even have to be activated by words. Let's take the Yale study that looked at the effects of touching cold and warm objects, okay?'

'Sure, why not.' Gertrude leaned back in her chair with her hands clasped behind her head and that same smug scepticism on her face.

'So, in this study, participants were greeted by a confederate in the lobby who accompanied them to the laboratory. Now, during the elevator ride, the participants were asked to hold a cup of coffee while the confederate wrote down their details. Some held a hot drink and others an ice-cold drink. When they arrived in the lab, they had to fill in a questionnaire on the personality traits of the person that brought them there from the lobby. Apparently, this brief coffee cup manipulation significantly affected their responses. Those who held the hot coffee tended to describe the target person's personality as warm, generous and caring, but those who held the iced coffee described the person as cold, uncaring, etcetera. There was no difference on traits unrelated to the warm-cold type.'

Takahashi chuckled. 'I better tell that to my daughters before they go on a date.'

'You'd better,' Helen said, laughing too. 'But that's not all. In another study from the same series, they looked at generosity. I guess that would constitute a substantial behaviour in your dictionary,' she said, looking to Gertrude. Gertrude's face remained impassive. 'They asked participants to inspect a hot or cold therapeutic pad in their hands under the pretext of an assessment and rate it for effectiveness. The real test came only later.'

'We are such a bunch of manipulating liars, aren't we?' Max said.

'Certainly sounds like you are,' Gertrude agreed.

'As a reward for taking part in the study,' Helen continued, 'participants were offered a gift either for a friend or for themselves—'

'Let me guess,' interrupted Gertrude. 'Holding the warm pad caused them to choose a gift for a friend and the cold pad a gift for themselves.'

Helen's face lit up. 'Yup, you got it. Most of them followed this rule – unknowingly, of course. So you see, something as highly regarded as altruistic or generous behaviour can be triggered by a simple and brief contact with a warm object, and vice versa.'

'Shocking!' Takahashi said.

Grinberg cleared his throat. 'I must say, I'm not entirely surprised. And not just because at my age I've seen it all before.'

The focus shifted to Grinberg. Even George shuffled forward to the edge of his seat.

'The area in the brain that responds to temperature acts on two very different levels. Sherlock, can you show us the location of the insula?'

On-screen, a side-view picture of the human brain appeared. Two metal saddle hooks separated the temporal lobe from the frontal lobe along the large fissure to reveal a smooth area deep inside.

'Thank you, that's great, Sherlock.'

'You're welcome. At your service anytime.'

Grinberg ignored the response. 'This smooth area, among others, becomes active during temperature and touch sensation; that's the physical aspect. But at another level, it's also involved with feelings of trust, empathy and social emotions like guilt and embarrassment. So that could explain nicely the effect of temperature sensation with the impressions of personality and prosocial behaviour toward other people.'

'Not only that,' Max said with excitement, 'it could also explain why early-childhood experiences of physical warmth from caregivers are so important for the normal development of interpersonal trust in adulthood.'

Helen frowned. 'Well, yes, that's a possibility. But let's stay on course with our main goal here to determine if we have free will. I'd like to share with you one or two more surprising examples, if I may.'

Her eyes met George's and he gave her a reassuring smile.

'Social behaviour is also affected by subtle implanted thoughts. In a study by New York University, participants completed a scrambled-sentence test in what they thought was the main experiment. As part of this test, some of them were exposed to words related to rudeness, like "annoyingly" and "obnoxious", others to politeness, like "considerate" and "appreciate", and yet others to neutral words like "occasionally" and "watches". They were all instructed to look for the experimenter once they'd finished the test so they could receive a second test, but the experimenter was engaged in a staged conversation for a whole ten minutes. Now the real test was their responses. A full 63 percent of those primed with rudeness interrupted the conversation. Only 37 percent of the control group and 17 percent of those primed with politeness did the same.'

George rested his chin on his hands, staring at Helen. He'd never thought people's behaviour could be so easily manipulated, and so quickly.

'A similar picture emerged from another study by the Universities of Miami and Florida, where priming with words related to hostility led to participants giving longer electric shocks to a confederate.'

'Ouch,' Meghan said. 'You guys are cruel.'

'Don't worry, nobody was harmed in this experiment. The confederates faked their responses.'

'Phew, that's reassuring. It actually reminds me of my nephews. They're four and eight, and after watching a mildly violent cartoon they often act out the actions.'

'Hold on,' Gertrude cried. 'Family examples aside, are you saying, Helen, that the behaviour of adults in your experiment was determined by a few words they were exposed to, rather than their life experiences, character and choice?'

'That's exactly what I'm saying. They had, in effect, no freedom of choice, even though they probably thought they did.'

The chair creaked as Ben, silent throughout the whole exchange, shifted forward.

11

George got up and wandered over to the window wall. They were still debating the examples of word suggestion and he needed a break. In many ways he appreciated Gertrude's challenges, since counter-arguments must be aired for a balanced discussion, but she was just so annoying – and he had to admit that it prickled when she was nasty to Helen. He gazed down at the traffic. A large truck was offloading supplies into a nearby building, causing a traffic jam; drivers were getting out of cars and gesticulating aggressively.

When he wandered back to the table, Gertrude still had Helen fixed with a steely gaze. 'I have a problem with that. If this claim is correct, and exposure to words can affect behaviour to such an extent, I'd expect it to work every single time. I mean 100 percent, not 63 percent.'

'Ah, yes, that's a common criticism,' Helen replied, shifting in her seat. 'The thing is that in psychology, unlike in physics, the experimental design can never control hundred percent of the conditions. So although the effect of the words was pretty powerful, as we saw, it's impossible to control other potential inputs that could affect the participants.'

'What about reproducibility?' Gertrude said, her face growing red. 'Has this priming business been replicated or are these just anecdotal examples?'

'Priming effects are widely accepted among social psychologists,' said Helen heatedly. 'Some studies have been replicated over two hundred times. In fact, there are many hundreds ... *thousands* of peer-reviewed studies in this field.'

'Absolutely,' intervened Max. 'I'm with Helen on this, hundred and ten percent.'

Sherlock's blue lights suddenly flashed. 'A hundred and ten percent in this case is factually incorrect,' the orb said in a kindly voice. 'As of this moment, there are precisely 5,614 scientific articles on the subject.'

That's impressive, thought George. *Not many areas in science get so much attention.*

'Thank you for the precision,' Helen said. 'So that's a highly established phenomenon that affects an individual's behaviour and social behaviour and is automatic – entirely outside conscious control.'

'Do you mind if I comment?' George asked, giving Helen a friendly smile.

'Not at all. Fire away.'

'I was just wondering, is it possible that priming affects mainly *how* we achieve our goals, but we still choose what goals to pursue?'

Helen brushed a stray strand of hair from her forehead, and he caught a whiff of her apple shampoo, giving him a fleeting image of her standing in front of the large mirror in her hotel room, head tilted, drying her hair with a white towel.

Helen straightened her back, as if it was painful, which wouldn't surprise him with all the sitting about. 'I'm glad you asked that, because it brings me nicely to the last example of priming I want to share. I promise. It's probably one of the most profound and shocking in terms of free will. Another New York University study used the familiar language test to prime participants with words related to achievement. In a seemingly unrelated experiment, they were given a set of Scrabble letter tiles and asked to find as many words as they could in three minutes.'

Gertrude drummed on her chin, still staring at Helen with the same steely, annoyed expression. The woman was goddamned exasperating.

Helen took a quick sip of water. 'The experimenter left the room. After the three minutes were up, she instructed the participants through an intercom to stop, but continued to watch them via a hidden video camera. A full 55 percent of those primed for achievement continued to look for more words after they were told to stop, often looking nervously at the door, compared to just 21 percent in the control condition.'

The drumming stopped. At last Gertrude was taking notice.

'There are other studies with variations on the goal-inducing theme, but the overall results are quite consistent.

Behavioural goals can be implanted in people's minds, and they will adopt them as their own while remaining completely oblivious to the source of their goals.'

'A perfect solution for totalitarian regimes,' Takahashi said with a bemused smile. 'Achieving behavioural control without the use of force or intimidation.'

As Takahashi spoke, George caught Ben out of the corner of his eye. The blood had completely drained from his face. He looked around. No one else seemed to have noticed. *Am I getting paranoid?*

'Jokes aside,' Meghan said, 'surely priming would not affect a deliberate and careful decision in court, for example, right?'

Helen burst out laughing. 'I can see why you'd say that, Meghan. Law comes with the expectation that judges are the last bastion of pure rational thinking, unaffected by irrelevant influences. Well, bad news! Studies have shown that defendants have an advantage just by being physically attractive or possessing an innocent baby face.'

'Yes, but as that's quite well known, it could be controlled.'

'How about unexpected effects, such as the type of chair the judge is sitting on?'

'You're joking, right?'

'Not at all.' Helen seemed to be enjoying making her legal colleague uncomfortable. 'This remarkable study was performed by scientists from Yale, Stanford, Arizona and two institutions in Berlin. They presented students with four hypothetical crime scenarios, anywhere from a youth stealing a television set to a repeat offender who robbed a bank with accomplices and killed a guard. For each scenario, participants were asked to give their judgement on how long the offender should spend in jail and what fine they should pay for their crime. While completing these questionnaires, the participants were seated on either a hard wooden chair or a soft cushioned chair. Now, the results showed that the concept of "hard on crime" has a very literal meaning. Those seated on the hard chairs assigned harsher punishments than those seated on soft chairs in all four scenarios.'

'Maybe they handed out harsher punishments because they were simply annoyed by the uncomfortable chair,' Takahashi said with a grin.

'It doesn't look that way,' Helen said. 'The results were similar when they simply touched a hard wooden object, compared to an identical but soft foam object, just before assessing various crime scenarios.'

'That's incredible,' Meghan said. 'In my early career, when I was a district judge, I had a colleague ... Actually, better not to name names. He was known to pass particularly harsh sentences. In the legal profession it's not acceptable to criticise colleagues openly, but of course we are humans too.'

'Are you?' muttered Gertrude.

George gawped in horror and then glanced at Meghan, but she didn't seem to have heard the insult, or pretended not to.

'After the refurbishment of the courts,' Meghan continued, 'the harsh judge softened considerably. Now that I think about it, they also replaced the hard chairs with much softer ones. Of course, this wasn't tested scientifically, but it certainly makes sense now.'

'How about you?' Gertrude said. 'Have you softened your judgements after the refurbishment?'

Meghan smiled. 'I can't really tell. You should ask my colleagues.'

'Very interesting,' Helen said. 'But there is even more to it. The researchers then performed these same assessments while the participants were lying inside a functional MRI scanner that measured their brain activity. Apparently, the stronger the tactile effect of hard on crime, the more active their somatosensory cortex became during the judgement phase.'

'Fascinating!' Grinberg said, beaming. 'The fact that the somatosensory cortex is activated when touching objects is a basic physiology fact that every second-year biology and psychology student knows, but this study extends the role of that region to a much more complex behaviour: tactile priming effect on judgement.'

'I find it really depressing,' Meghan said. 'Just makes you wonder what other random things control our behaviour.' After a short pause, her eyes lit up. 'But this study tested lay people, right? Not experienced judges who are trained to follow certain guidelines. So perhaps my colleague's case was just an anomaly.'

'It's a possibility, but an unlikely one,' Helen said. 'Field studies in California courtrooms, for example, showed that even very experienced judges are not immune to extra-legal factors. So I wouldn't be surprised if they're also prone to this hard-on-crime effect. But that's a minor point, really. The main conclusion from thousands of studies is that nobody is immune to priming, automaticity and other unconscious effects.'

Max rose to his feet and picked his way carefully across the room to the flip chart. 'It's all about decision-making. You see, there's strong evidence that two separate systems help us make decisions.' He drew two large ovals in green marker pen and wrote "SYSTEM 1 – FAST" in one and "SYSTEM 2 – SLOW" in the other. 'This idea was expounded by Daniel Kahneman, the Nobel Laureate in Economics of 2002. Now the main characteristic of System 1 is speed.' He drew multiple arrows leading to the left oval, each connecting to a single word, "automatic", "emotional", "stereotypic", "unconscious".

'Wait,' Ben said. 'Is there any hard evidence for this? I think we all know how sexy theoretical ideas seem initially.'

Max wiped sweat from his forehead. 'I'm not sure what kind of evidence you're after.'

'As I said at the outset, we are looking for hard evidence, something that can be measured and either proved or disproved.'

'Actually,' Grinberg said, patting a hand against his chest, 'there is direct evidence from brain studies on the DMN. That's, uh, the Default Mode Network. Basically, it's a network of brain regions that are active when the brain is resting or mind-wandering. And by active, I mean a slow, synchronised electrical activity of less than once every ten seconds. You're probably wondering what else it does, right? Well, a variety of different things like thinking about others, thinking about one's self, remembering the past and envisioning the future. But it falls silent when we engage in goal-oriented tasks.'

'Sounds to me like a pretty useless daydreaming area,' Gertrude said. 'Is it related somehow to decision-making or are you just getting carried away telling us everything you know?'

George was getting annoyed now. Gertrude wasn't just keeping a balance in the debate; she was being purposely rude, and he wondered why. It was certainly true that the purpose of this debate had never truly been explained, and he was beginning to feel uneasy about the whole scenario, but that didn't excuse Gertrude.

Grinberg looked crestfallen. 'Sorry, yes, I do get carried away sometimes, but in this case it's very relevant. This network allows us to switch to autopilot once we're familiar with a task.'

'Nice,' Max said. 'That would provide an actual location for the fast automatic decision-making system.' He pointed to the flip chart. 'Please, tell us more about it.'

'It was shown during card games,' Grinberg said, grinning. 'Well, not exactly games. Researchers at the University of Cambridge showed volunteers four cards and asked them to match a target card to one of them while lying in an fMRI scanner. There were three possible matching rules, by colour, shape or number, but they had to figure out for themselves which rule to use by trial and error. Apparently, during the acquisition period when they learned the rules, the dorsal attention network was active, but when they applied the rules they'd already learned, the DMN was active. So ... I present to you the brain's autopilot! The very system that allows us to drive effortlessly along a familiar route while daydreaming and to make countless daily routine decisions.'

'Okay, okay,' Gertrude said, raising both hands in surrender. 'You've convinced me that many automatic decisions are not under our conscious control, so we obviously can't claim free will for those, but what about System 2, or just big, life-changing decisions?'

George shifted in his seat. He felt at last that they were getting somewhere. The argument that little decisions are often entirely automatic was persuasive. But if Grinberg could prove the same for major decisions, that'd be a home run. And also quite disturbing. He looked back at Ben, whose colour seemed to have returned.

'Yes, you'd think we have control over these types of decisions, wouldn't you?' Max said. 'After all, according to Kahneman, System 2 of thought and decision-making is slow, deliberative, infrequent, logical, calculating and, above all ... conscious.' He added these words on the flip chart with arrows leading to the right oval, then turned back to face the group with an expression of triumph.

Gertrude looked Grinberg straight in the eyes. 'Do we know what happens in the brain when deliberate decisions are taken? I mean like in major life decisions.'

Grinberg shook his head, lips pursed. 'Unfortunately, we're not there yet. These processes are just too complicated. They happen over a long period of time and are influenced by many life experiences.'

'Not necessarily,' Max said.

'What, are you a brain expert now?' Grinberg retorted.

'No, but studying the brain is not the answer for everything, you know? Sometimes all you need is a creative way to tackle a difficult problem.'

'What *are* you talking about?' Grinberg asked, his voice rising to a squeak.

'A careful analysis of public records – that's all you need,' Max said, and paused unnecessarily as the intriguing claim had already focused everyone's attention on him. 'Let me start from the start,' he finally continued. 'Most people have generally favourable opinions about themselves, and the motivation to feel good about yourself explains a lot of social behaviours. Take, for example, students' evaluations of professors' teaching skills. They're more favourable towards professors who gave them more lenient grades, probably because it satisfies their desire for good feedback.'

'That's not related to major life decisions.'

'Ah, but it is. You see, people's positive automatic associations about themselves can influence their feelings about almost anything in life, including major decisions like their choice of a place to live, their career and even their life partner. This principle is called ...' He wrote "IMPLICIT EGOTISM" on the flip chart and circled it, pressing the marker pen so hard that it screeched. Gertrude jammed her hands over her ears in a mockery of annoyance.

George stifled a smile as Max plunged ahead through the silence. 'Studies from the eighties and nineties found that people prefer the letters that appear in their own name and numbers that appear in their birthday over other letters and numbers. Now, these findings gave rise to a radical idea tested by researchers from the State University of New York at Buffalo. They asked themselves whether these seemingly meaningless preferences can affect major decisions like contributions to political campaigns. What they found was pretty shocking. During the 2000 US presidential campaign, people with a last name that began with B or G were more likely to be donating money to the election funds of Bush and Gore, respectively.'

'So?' said Gertrude.

Max rolled his shoulders. 'Okay, how about a choice of partner? Is that major enough?' He continued without waiting for a response. 'In another study, they looked at the public records in Texas and analysed every woman who gave birth in the state during one full year. Guess what? Women tended to marry men who shared their maiden name initial at a rate of more than 40 percent above pure chance.'

Max was sweating profusely. Perspiration dripped down his neck and onto his collar. 'And if you think this is just a fluke, think again. This choice of partner was found in a wide range of cultural and ethnic groups from the 19th to the 21st centuries.'

'This could have been a truly fascinating discovery,' George said. 'But, as a physicist, I'm always sceptical when there is a risk of cherry-picking results. I'm not sure I believe it. You see, even the best-intentioned researcher could've conducted lots of archival studies and then cherry-picked only those that supported their pet hypothesis. Few scientific journals are interested in publishing negative results, so you end up with a biased selection. I really don't blame you, Max, but publication bias is the bane of modern science. And this is just one potential weakness; I'm sure there are others.'

'That's fine, George, I don't take it personally.' Max adjusted his sweat-drenched collar.

George waved a dismissive hand.

'Luckily, you are not the first to raise objections to these findings,' Max continued. 'How about we both stay here in the break and I'll take you through their rebuttal?'

'Sounds good, but I'd suggest that Helen joins us too. And not because of her matching maiden name but because of her expertise in the field.'

Helen laughed out loud. 'I don't have a maiden name, but I hope it doesn't disqualify me from anything.'

Max looked confused.

George had concluded a while ago that the man lacked all sense of humour, and hoped Helen had noticed that too. And then, quite out of the blue, he wondered why he was thinking that. Why would he care whether Helen found Max humourless? He certainly liked her. There was something about her that reminded him of Ella, although he couldn't quite put his finger on what it was.

In the break, people left the conference room to stretch their legs in the lounge. Max, Helen, George and Takahashi, who was busy drawing doodles, remained behind. Helen and George moved closer to the screen as Max guzzled down water.

'As you'll see,' Max said, wiping his mouth, 'the researchers have responded to all the criticism thrown at them, but I'll let you be the judge of their success. Sherlock, please bring up the rebuttal paper.'

An article flashed onto the screen. George and Helen leaned forward and read it intently. Takahashi, quiet at the back of the room, didn't seem to be paying attention.

After a while, George leaned back in his chair. 'I see what you mean. They'd taken all the standard methodological precautions, and not only replicated their results several times but had never seen a meaningful reversal of them. I'm happy with that.' He turned to Helen. 'What do *you* think?'

'I agree. It looks to me like they addressed all the criticism. I just wonder what other life decisions they investigated.'

Max gave an audible sigh. 'Ah, the list is quite long. But maybe I should mention place of residence. They used a sample of more than seventy-five thousand women and found that a high proportion resided in states that resemble their first name. For example, there are more women named Florence in Florida, Georgia in Georgia, Louise in Louisiana and Virginia in Virginia.'

'Obviously, that could not apply to every name or everyone,' Takahashi said, lifting his eyes from his doodle. He had drawn a very big, long-eared rabbit.

'Of course not. The name effect was significant, with an average of 44 percent above chance alone, but it doesn't end with place of residence. First name also affects choice of career. So people with the name Dennis or Denise are overrepresented among dentists, for example.'

'That reminds me of Happy Families,' said Gertrude, who had come to stand in the doorway.

George turned to her. *Gertrude. Granny. Gastroenterologist. Garbage man ... woman.*

'What?' Max said.

'It's a British card game I used to play as a child. Each card had a tradesman with his title and family name: Mr Bun the Baker, Mr Soot the Sweeper and Mr Pots the Painter.'

Helen and George exchanged a glance.

Takahashi's smile broadened. 'Well, I don't think this exciting card game has arrived in the US yet. Now, back to the fascinating implicit egotism principle. It can't explain everything, that is clear, but if decisions such as where we live, what career we choose and who we fall in love with can be controlled by such a random thing as the name our parents gave us, then our rational choices when we make major life decisions seem to be, at least partly, an illusion.'

'Or maybe entirely an illusion,' murmured George.

12

During the break, Helen and Meghan went together to the toilets. When they got there, they found Gertrude standing in front of a full-length mirror. She was inspecting the rip in her skirt and muttering something unintelligible. Helen gazed at her. She seemed suddenly more human in these circumstances.

'You're in luck,' Helen said. 'I've got a travel sewing kit with black thread.'

'Oh, that would be great,' Gertrude said with a rare smile.

Helen was surprised. She hadn't thought the woman capable of smiling. Rummaging through her handbag, she found the sewing kit and handed it to Gertrude.

'I always carry it with me just for this kind of accident.'

'I can't thank you enough. This is so embarrassing. I often have to mend my clothes at home as my cats have little respect for designer brands, but here I thought I'd be safe.'

'Oh, you have a cat?' Meghan said. 'Me too! How many?'

'Nine.'

'Wow! How do you manage taking care of them *and* lecturing at the university?'

'Oh, that's easy. They pretty much take care of themselves. Much better than men, I can assure you. Could you imagine having someone like Jerry at home?'

Jerry? wondered Helen. *He seems such a lovely chap.*

Gertrude lifted her head from her stitching. 'Chewing his long hair all the time – it's disgusting. He reminds me my Persian cat. Do you think he throws up furballs?'

Meghan and Helen burst out laughing. They were still laughing when they entered their cubicles.

* * *

George sat in an armchair facing the window wall. For the first time in months, he felt relaxed. The people seemed pleasant enough and the discussions were more interesting than he'd expected. Being engaged in academic subjects again seemed to be all he needed right now. The only niggling issue that spoiled it a bit was Ben's strange behaviour. First, smuggling in a phone when not even employees were allowed to bring them into the building, then his evasive responses, like when Helen asked him what they'd do with the conclusion, and the latest – his alarmed response to Takahashi's flippant comment on totalitarian regimes. Then again, maybe distancing himself from people for several months was making him imagine things. He couldn't be sure.

He exhaled deeply and clasped his hands behind his head, gazing at the city below. In the reflection he saw Meghan and Helen approaching and sitting down on an orange sofa just behind him.

'So tell me about this guy,' Helen said.

'Well ... he's the most attractive man in the Office of the Prosecutor by far,' Meghan replied. 'Even my cynical twenty-three-year-old assistant conceded that. There are persistent rumours that he used to be a spook before he made a career change to law, but I haven't had time to look into it. He's such lovely company that I don't really care what he did.'

'Wow, sounds like you're smitten.'

'Yes, I probably am, and this is the first time we've spent a night in separate cities.'

'So? Are you worried?'

'The Hague is hardly a million miles from Paris, but that's not the point. We've only been dating for three months now, and he's agreed we're exclusive, but I'm not sure I trust him. Dating someone that desirable comes at a price; I know that from bitter experience. We've been texting each other first thing in the morning and last thing at night, but almost never during the working day.'

'Sounds reasonable.'

'Yeah, the only thing is that yesterday, after my first night away, there was no message from Olivier, and I'd already texted him twice that morning. Do you think I blew it by messaging him again before Ben confiscated my phone?'

'Did you try calling him after the river cruise?'

'No, it was too late. And now after yesterday's disgrace, I can't afford to get caught again.'

'Don't worry ...'

George couldn't hear all the words, but the laughter that followed reassured him that all was well. *How nice it is to have someone to confide with, to share the deepest thoughts and concerns. Like Ella.*

He waited a while on the armchair for the two to make their way back to the conference room. It would be embarrassing to be caught eavesdropping on their private conversation. When he finally joined the rest of the group, he was met with an unusually satisfied expression on Gertrude's face and couldn't help wondering what had caused such a thing.

'I'd like to start this discussion with mice,' Grinberg began once everyone had settled into their seats. 'Please bear with me. I, uh, I seem to have lost my glasses ...' He fumbled about in his pockets. 'I'm sure I had them a minute ago ...'

'They're on your head,' Helen said.

'Ah! Thank you!' Grinberg slid the glasses over his nose, consulted his yellow writing pad and turned to the orb. 'Sherlock, would you please play the mouse video from Columbia University?'

On-screen, a cute grey mouse appeared. From the blue cap on its head, a thin transparent tube projected upwards. The mouse explored its cage intently, ignoring a pile of food pellets and a dish of water.

'Watch what happens when the blue light is turned on,' Grinberg said.

As soon as the tube turned blue, the mouse rushed to the dish and started drinking eagerly. The blue light went off, and it stopped. This sequence of events was repeated a few times with the same results.

'What you're witnessing here is a demonstration of the on-switch of thirst. This brilliant study identified a specific group of neurones in the hypothalamus that are responsible for thirst. As you've just seen, each time they were activated, the mouse immediately searched for water and started drinking. And that is—'

'Wait,' Helen said, 'since when is the brain activated by light? I thought it was only the eyes ...'

'You're correct, Helen. The brain is not normally sensitive to direct light. But here, the researchers used optogenetic activation.'

'Which is ...?'

'Yes, of course, I shouldn't assume ... Well, it's a biological technique that uses light to control cells by genetically modifying them so they become electrically active when exposed to light. It's a bit like what happens naturally in photoreceptor cells of the retina. Now the interesting thing is ...' He beamed. 'That this drinking behaviour was triggered reliably even in mice that had unlimited water.'

'Nice,' Helen said. 'So there is a thirst-ON button. How about a thirst-OFF button?'

'People might think I paid you to ask that question,' Grinberg said with a chuckle. 'In fact, there is one. The same study identified another group of neurones that when activated stopped the drinking behaviour even in thirsty mice.'

'Yes, that's interesting,' Gertrude said, 'as far as mice are concerned, but I fail to see how this is relevant to our main question. You know ... free will in humans?'

Grinberg placed his reading glasses on the table and leaned back in his chair. 'Well, you see, these on-off switches are consistent, immediate and reliable, just like a man-made machine. You press a button and hey presto, the same thing happens nearly *every single time*. The ethnologist Konrad Lorenz described automatic behaviours in response to external triggers a long time ago. He called them fixed-action patterns. But he had no idea how they worked. For example, a goose would roll a displaced egg back to the nest with its beak, but if you removed the egg partway through, it would complete the action with an imaginary egg. Obviously, adult humans don't have this type of simple automatic behaviour, except perhaps for ...' He yawned and looked around the room. Takahashi and Gertrude yawned almost in unison. George stifled a yawn. 'Yes, I was hoping for that,' he said with a satisfied smile. 'Yawning is contagious. They are triggered in other people just by watching a yawn and are difficult to stop once started. But I think the general principle may very well apply to a variety of completely different situations. Take, for example, all those irresistible responses we see in addiction, compulsion or just normal likes and dislikes. So ... it raises the possibility that a set of automatic switches with wide levels of complexity operate in our brain to control many, if not all, human behaviours.'

'And that would leave no room for free will,' interjected Takahashi.

'*Exactly!*' he exclaimed, and stuck the end of one arm of his glasses in his mouth.

'Wow,' Gertrude said, glaring at Takahashi. 'That's a huge leap. What about deliberations, accumulation of experience and endless other complexities? To be frank, I'm surprised to hear such a sweeping conclusion from someone who specialises in logic.'

Takahashi spread his hands. 'You asked what the relevance of this study is, so I responded. At this stage I guess it's just a hypothesis, right?' He looked at Grinberg. 'But certainly one we must consider very seriously and thoroughly.'

'Please bear with me,' Grinberg said. 'I'm just getting started. Let's imagine that on a sunny Sunday morning you're sitting comfortably in a deckchair on your porch, reading a good novel. Although you are engrossed in the plot, something is missing. It'd be nice to have a cool drink now, you think. You insert a bookmark, put down your book and get up to make a refreshing lemonade. Soon you're sipping from the drink and immersing yourself back into the plot.'

George's mind drifted to Nantasket Beach, the sun still high in the sky. Ella is reading a thick novel on the deckchair next to him, he's eyeing the picnic basket full of cool drinks and ...

Grinberg's voice cut into his thoughts. 'Now, on the surface, this seems like a perfect example of exercising your free will. You chose consciously if and when to get up, right?'

Grinberg didn't wait for an answer. 'Not necessarily. There is an alternative explanation.' He paused, glancing around like an actor on the stage. 'There are structures near the hypothalamus, called the circumventricular organs, that are rich in blood capillaries and neurones that respond to a drop in water content. As you were sitting in the sun you got slightly dehydrated and your thirst neurones sensed that, responding just like in the mice and making you get up and prepare a drink. The rest could've been a confabulation on how nice it would be to have cool lemonade while reading. The other difference is that the mice were not offered lemonade,' he said with a chuckle.

Gertrude did not find this amusing. 'This is sheer speculation.'

'Well, the brain is known to play tricks on us. Blindsight is just one example of many proven cases where the brain affects our behaviour without our conscious awareness. Jerry, that's your area. Will you enlighten us on this?'

'Oh, yeah, sure,' Jerry said with a wide grin. 'It's a fascinating phenomenon. People who have suffered from damage to their primary visual cortex' – he placed his palm on the back of his head to indicate its location – 'insist they're blind, but can still make correct decisions based on sight.'

That's weird.

'But how is that possible?' exclaimed Gertrude. 'Aren't they just lying?'

'Blind people with such damage confess that they cannot see, but when asked to guess answers about the shape, orientation and movement of objects in front of them, they do amazingly well. One patient, known as TN, had two strokes that destroyed both sides of his visual cortex, causing clinical blindness over his entire visual field. This was confirmed by imaging and clinical tests. He behaved like a blind person, using a cane for walking and all the rest of it, but when asked to walk along a corridor arranged with many obstacles without his cane, he managed to navigate around them skilfully without colliding even once.'

'You still didn't answer my question. How is it possible?'

'I don't think there's a full explanation yet, except that they aren't aware that they've some rudimentary vision. The important take-home message here is that blindsight and many other phenomena are consistent with the idea that consciousness plays only a peripheral role in our behaviour.'

'So it is just an *idea*,' Gertrude said, pouncing on the choice of word. 'And this is, again, a case of a brain damage. We should really focus on normal ...' She stared at Jerry's hair, now tied in a ponytail. 'I mean, healthy people.'

'Thanks, Jerry,' Grinberg said, before turning to Gertrude. 'At this stage of the discussion, yes, it's just a hypothesis, but let's examine it with the solid evidence that is available to us in ... *healthy* people, okay?'

Gertrude folded her arms across her chest. 'I'm listening.'

'Right. From a practical, scientific point of view, you could say that there are two basic possibilities regarding the free-will question in the brain. Phrasing it very crudely, it's all about the order of events.' Picking up his glasses, he used them to stab the air as he spoke. 'If there is free will, our *will* somehow initiates a signal in the brain, leading eventually to a purposeful behaviour. On the other hand, if there isn't, then our *brain* initiates the signal for behaviour and we simply justify our action as an afterthought.'

'Wait a minute!' Max cried, half rising from his seat. 'If we're talking about the reasons for behaviour, shouldn't we first consider the nature versus nurture debate?'

George looked at Max's red face. *Sure, good point, but why get so excited over it?*

'Yes, we are obviously the product of the two,' Grinberg said calmly, 'but regardless of the relative contribution of nature and nurture, both converge eventually to affect brain function, leading to the initiation of any conscious behaviour. And *that's* what we're interested in here.'

Max relaxed back into his seat and Grinberg continued, 'So ... as I said before, the key to finding the correct option is teasing out the order of events leading up to a conscious behaviour. Say you pick up a pencil to write a note to your partner. According to the first option, you first decide consciously to pick it up. That somehow generates the decision signal in your brain, which then leads to another signal to your hand.' He slowly lifted a pencil off the table. After a look around the table, he put the pencil back down. 'According to the second option, where there is no free will, it's your *brain* that generates the initial decision signal to pick up the pencil. Only then do you feel that you made a decision, and finally your brain sends another signal to move your hand.' Again he

117

lifted up the pencil, and froze. 'Distinguishing between these two options, and finding the true order of events, could resolve this old question. Can we agree on this general concept?'

'Not really,' Max said. 'It's just too simplistic. The decision to pick up a pencil is very different from purchasing a house or ... asking someone on a date, don't you think?' Max looked at Helen, who immediately shifted her gaze away.

George tried to suppress a smile, but he doubted he was successful.

'For the moment I'm using *behaviour* in the widest sense, as long as it's conscious and voluntary,' Grinberg said. 'I'd even include deliberate thoughts in it.'

Max sat back, his lower lip protruding slightly, but he said nothing more.

'Okay, back to facts now,' Grinberg continued. 'In the early 1980s a study by the University of California, San Francisco set out to test just that. It later became known as the Libet Experiment after the lead scientist.'

'It's probably the most quoted scientific study in the philosophy of free will,' Takahashi said.

'I'm glad to hear that some philosophers base their opinions on evidence,' Grinberg said with a wry smile. 'I just hope you're not stuck in the 1980s.'

'I have the feeling you'll bring us all up to speed.'

'That's exactly my intention.'

'Hasn't the Libet Experiment been discredited?' Max asked with a smug smile.

'I wouldn't say discredited, but it certainly had a few flaws in its interpretation. Anyway, for the benefit of those who aren't familiar with it, Libet instructed subjects to move a finger whenever they felt like it and to note the time they first became aware of the urge or intention to do it by looking at a precise clock. Meanwhile, the electrical activity in their brain was recorded using electroencephalogram, as well as the muscle activity of their finger. As expected, the urge to move the finger occurred before the actual movement, preceding it by about 150 milliseconds. What's more, Libet found that an electrical activity, called the readiness potential, started in the brain about 350 milliseconds before that urge to move. Apparently the signal originated from a specific brain region called the supplementary motor area – the SMA. Neuroscientists don't like long names.' He took a sip of water. 'As you can appreciate, the result agrees with the second option I described earlier, leading to the suspicion that our conscious will is *not* the original cause of our action since the brain had already made an unconscious decision to move the finger beforehand, and not the other way around.'

'So, there is no free will and we can all go home now, right?' Meghan asked with a grin.

'Not so fast,' Ben said. 'We've a lot more work to do before ... before we are absolutely sure of the answer.'

'Oh, I wasn't serious,' she shot back. 'Grinberg, do we know what the exact function of this brain area is? What's its name again?'

'Let's start with its location,' Grinberg said. 'Sherlock, could you show us a brain map, please?'

On-screen, a three-dimensional rotating map of a human brain appeared. The surface was covered with the typical ridges and furrows on the outer layer of the cortex. Roughly at the centre, a blue ridge resembling a hairband was situated just behind a squarish area of ridges flashing in bright green.

'The blue ridge, the precentral gyrus, is the location of the primary motor cortex, which activates our muscles. The flashing green area is the SMA, where a signal originated before the urge to move. Thanks for the cool effect, Sherlock.'

'You're welcome,' came the answer from the orb.

'So what's the function of the SMA?' insisted Meghan.

Grinberg placed his glasses on the table deliberately. 'To be honest, it's not entirely clear, but we do know that it's implicated in different aspects of movement, such as the control of postural stability, coordination of action sequences, coordination of both hands' movement and, as in Libet's experiment, the initiation of internally generated movement.'

'So it's not really involved in decision-making, is it?' Meghan asked.

'Correct. At least not that we know of.' He laughed. 'You're sharp! Would you consider working in my lab?'

'You'd need to take extra insurance. I've two left hands.'

'Am I missing something?' Helen asked. 'For our purposes, isn't it enough just to know that there is a specific brain signal before we make a decision rather than after it?'

'Ah, if only it were that simple,' Grinberg said. 'I didn't really want to enter into the weaknesses of this study, but you've really talked me into it,' he said with a mischievous smile. 'The whole premise relies on precise time measurement. So although electrical activity in both the brain and the finger can be measured very accurately, determining the time of a reported urge is much trickier. After all, the events were separated by just a third of a second, so if somehow the time of the mental event was unreliable, as some critics claim, the whole argument would collapse like a sandcastle at high tide. Mind you, these results were replicated in several other labs, but none has fully addressed the critics' concerns.'

'As you mentioned weaknesses,' Max said with a smirk, 'I've a bigger bone to pick here. This experiment looked at one very simple decision, and I think you'd agree that most human behaviour is a bit more complex than moving a finger. We often take our time, we deliberate. Unless we spent most of our life twiddling our thumbs, I don't really see how we could generalise to answer one of the biggest and most fundamental questions in philosophy ...' His voice trailed off as the double doors opened. A high stack of pizzas entered the room with just the head of the delivery man visible at the top. 'Well, this trumps any philosophical question. I'm starving.'

13

To George's surprise, Ben got up and helped the delivery man place the stack of pizzas on the table, smiling broadly to the receptionist who was holding the doors open. Not that he thought Ben was averse to such physical involvement, but for a reason he couldn't quite fathom, it looked like an act.

'I wasn't sure what pizza you all like,' Ben said, addressing everyone, 'so I ordered a variety.'

Max heaved himself out of his chair and started inspecting the boxes with a glint in his eyes.

'Anything vegetarian?' Meghan asked from the far end of the table.

Ben slid one towards her. 'Margherita okay?'

As he passed out the rest of the pizzas, George's nostrils were assaulted by a strong cocktail of melted cheese, roasted peppers, chicken and caramelised onion. He had to admit, he loved pizzas made in Europe. Pizzas in Boston were usually abysmal. Soon after grabbing a brie and bacon for himself, the only sound in the room was that of munching.

'There's nothing like food to silence a bunch of intellectuals,' Helen said between bites.

'Then I'm afraid I'm going to ruin your theory,' Grinberg said through a mouth of pepperoni. 'I was just going to answer Max before I forget. To be honest, I don't think we'd be here today discussing this if we only had the Libet Experiment to rely on. At the time it was a discovery that caused a lot of excitement, but in retrospect, it's just not conclusive enough to draw the far-reaching conclusions we need here. So let's move on to more modern evidence.'

'What, now?' Jerry complained.

'Well, not immediately, but I've arranged a live demonstration for us not far from here at the Paris Brain Institute, soon after lunch. It has to do with a monumental experiment that was first conducted by German researchers, mostly from the Max Planck Institute. Luckily, a good friend and colleague of mine, Professor Rousseau, has agreed to replicate it for us.'

Jerry raised his eyebrows and took a large bite from his wedge of mushroom pizza.

'Is he a good painter of frightened tigers, by any chance?' asked Takahashi.

Grinberg chuckled. He wiped his mouth with a paper napkin and folded it carefully. 'Professor Rousseau is a she, and actually, Juliette is a great lover of art exhibitions and has done some impressive oil paintings herself, but so far they only hang in her living room; I don't think there is any relation to Henri Rousseau.'

George wondered if the personal knowledge suggested some romantic liaison between them and smiled at this possibility, suddenly seeing a young Grinberg as a ladies' man with a full head of hair but still wearing his chequered shirt.

After they finished lunch, Helen gathered the empty pizza boxes and piled them up on the corner of the table. Then everyone followed Ben as he led the way through the maze of corridors on the fourth floor and down to the main entrance. As they approached the white minibus that waited for them in the baking sun, Max rushed ahead and climbed up just behind Helen. George watched with dismay as the two sat next to each other. The smell of Max's hair oil was strong in the confined space, and George was glad of the extra Calvin Klein aftershave he'd drenched himself with that morning from the long-lost bottle he'd found at the bottom of his travel bag. He consoled himself by taking a window seat.

Sitting on his own, he watched the quintessential Parisian-style buildings passing by along Boulevard de Port-Royal. On his right, a modern-looking skyscraper with its reflective glass facade stood in stark contrast. His gaze took him up to the top of the building. Ben remarked that it was Montparnasse Tower, and George nodded absent-mindedly. For once, he was enjoying doing nothing. Not a single thought crossed his mind. When the minibus stopped just outside the main entrance of the hospital, he glanced at his watch with a pang of disappointment. The twenty-minute journey had passed way too quickly for his liking.

Stepping out of the van, he noticed the large sign over the entrance: "HÔPITAL UNIVERSITAIRE LA PITIÉ-SALPÊTRIÈRE". It was vaguely familiar. Then he recalled seeing the name repeated over and over in the news years ago. Soon after Princess Diana's tragic car accident, she was rushed here in an attempt to save her life. Considering that it was the biggest hospital in France, he was quite impressed that Grinberg, who lived in the US, knew his way around.

Leading the group between an endless forest of buildings and alleys without hesitation, Grinberg took them all the way to a massive curved structure. The building had a smooth silvery wing jutting out on each side. Under the child-like line drawing of a face with a brain in orange, the title announced "INSTITUT DU CERVEAU".

There was plenty of space in the elevator for the nine of them and the uniformed porter who joined them at the last minute, pushing a nervously smiling patient on a hospital bed, who looked embarrassed with all the attention. Grinberg waited for the porter to press his destination, the third floor, then pushed the button for Level −1. When the doors finally opened following the journey up and down, they all spilled out into the CENIR, the Neuroimaging Research Centre. Within minutes of the receptionist making a phone call, a stunning redheaded woman wearing a lab coat emerged through the double doors. George estimated she was in her late fifties.

'Malcolm! So nice to see you again,' she said in a strong French accent, ignoring the rest of the group.

Grinberg only managed to say 'Juliette' before she took both his hands and gave him the mandatory double kiss, one on each cheek. She then noticed George and gave him a brief smile, one he was used to receiving when meeting a fellow ginger, as if they belonged to a separate species. Before he had time to respond, she'd already motioned to the group to follow her and continued to converse excitedly with Grinberg. They clearly had a lot to talk about. She led them to a room with a large white scanner close to the far wall. A patient table protruded from the cylinder's circular opening.

'Well,' she said when everyone had formed a semi-circle around the machine, 'I understand that you want a little demonstration of the Max Planck Institute experiment. That's all ready, but I also have a little surprise for you. I'm sure you'll love it,' she added with a knowing smile. 'But before we start, I probably should explain a little, since none of you are in this field except Malcolm.'

'Actually, Jerry Stokes is a neuroscientist too,' said Grinberg. Jerry waved in response.

'Oh, sorry, sorry. Okay, I'll just explain to the rest of you that we have here' – and she gestured proudly towards the machine – 'a 3T MRI Siemens PRISMA scanner with 64 channels. I should probably mention that with a magnetic strength of three tesla and so many channels, we get pretty decent images. Details aside, this scanner allows us to visualise brain activity using a technique called functional magnetic resonance imaging, or fMRI in short. It basically measures the blood flow in the brain, which is a good indication of electrical activity. The more blood flowing in a certain area, the more active it is. Right. Before we start, I'll need a volunteer.'

There was silence as everyone looked at each other.

'There is nothing to worry about,' Juliette said with a smile. 'It's not painful or damaging in any way. So?'

'I'm not entering this metal coffin,' announced Max.

After a long moment, Helen said, 'I'll do it. Always wanted to see my brain in action.'

'Good. Good. So, please, remove any metallic objects on you before you lie down on this bed. We don't want anything flying across the room.'

Helen removed the belt with its silver buckle from her trousers, a watch, a pearl neckless and a pair of green tear-drop earrings. She placed them in her handbag and handed it to George, who happened to be standing next to her. A technician helped Helen to climb onto the table and adjusted the pillow. He then gave her virtual reality goggles to wear and placed a set of headphones with a mouthpiece over her ears and adjusted the straps. With the complex apparatus, George could only recognise Helen by her chestnut hair.

The technician then placed a small remote with a single button in each of Helen's hands. A mechanical sound was heard as the table with Helen on it slid smoothly inside the scanner.

'Is everything all right?' asked Juliette.

Helen, who was now inside the cylinder, flashed a thumbs up.

'Good stuff, but you know you can talk, right?'

Infectious laughter came from deep inside the scanner.

'Okay, I'll explain everything via the headset from the control room.'

Juliette led the group to an adjacent room with a thick glass window, through which the MRI scanner was visible. She sat down in front of three monitors and quickly tapped on a keyboard. Leaning forward towards a microphone, she pressed a button. 'Can you hear me, Helen?'

'Loud and clear,' came the answer in a somewhat shaky voice.

George moved a bit closer to the window and watched the scanner on the other side, Helen's pink socks poking out from the cylinder.

'Good, good stuff. When the scan starts, Helen, you'll hear loud clicks. This is normal and indicates the machine is working. All you have to do then is decide, in your own time, which of the two buttons in your hands to press, either the left or the right, and press it immediately. At the same time, you should look at the stream of letters that will show in your goggles and tell us what letter appeared at the exact moment you made your conscious decision. Okay?

'Sounds easy enough,' said Helen.

Juliette turned towards the group crowding the room just behind her. 'Each letter represents, in effect, a point in time like a clock, so by memorising the letter, Helen can tell us accurately when she made her decision, dodging any delay of reaction time.'

'I'm sorry,' intervened Gertrude, 'but how does this method solve the issue of accuracy?'

'Let's wait and see,' said Grinberg. 'I think the answer will be obvious.'

Juliette thanked him with a nod and continued, 'Now, since just replicating the results from the German team isn't exciting enough – we've already done that many times – I have prepared for you a really cool twist.'

'A twist?' said Grinberg. 'What is it?'

'Patience, patience. All will be revealed in good time,' said Juliette with a mischievous smile. 'First we need a few runs to let the system adapt to Helen's unique brain activity. Helen, are you ready?'

'Ready as I'll ever be.'

Juliette selected a few tick boxes on the control screen then hit the enter key. Immediately, muffled clicks from the active MRI machine came over the microphone.

After a few moments, George heard Helen's voice. 'G.'

'Again,' shouted Juliette.

This time, after a long delay, "D" came through the microphone.

Everyone was glued to the upper screen, where several black-and-white images of brain sections appeared with red and orange hot spots in places. The puzzled looks on their faces suggested to George that no one knew exactly what was going on, with the exception of the neuroscientists.

After a few repetitions, Juliette leaned forward and pressed the button on the microphone base. 'Okay, Helen, let's take a short break.' She turned to the group. 'Mon Dieu. You're staring at the wrong screen. Look here, at the bottom one. I'll run the traces again.' She tapped the keyboard and a blue trace ran across the white screen in a straight line from left to right. Close to the right edge, it formed a sharp peak then immediately a second one, and the letter "L" appeared next to it. A similar pattern formed just below with each run, with either "L" or "R" at the end. 'As you can see,' Juliette said, pointing to the right peak, 'this is the point in time when Helen pressed the button. In this case the left one, hence the letter "L". The first peak is when Helen reported making her conscious decision, which button to press. We call this time zero. If you look at all these runs, you can see that she made her decision about a second before actually pressing the button. So far so good?'

Everyone nodded.

'Okay. Now to the exciting stuff. What we have here that the original researchers didn't is a computer with incredibly fast processing power that can do the analysis in real time rather than only later. So, we'll repeat the same procedure, but this time, the software will run some sophisticated analysis on Helen's brain activity in real time and see what happens. Okay?'

'So that's the twist,' said Grinberg, 'real-time analysis. Very impressive.'

'I knew you'd like that,' said Juliette, beaming. 'Luckily, thanks to the German study, we already know which two areas have the earliest predictive information, so we'll focus on them.'

'Predictive information? What's that?' asked Meghan.

'Good question. Well, basically these areas have the ability to predict which button will be pressed. In other words, they have that knowledge in advance, and if we do the right analysis, we too will know that in real time.

'Okay, let's do it,' said Juliette enthusiastically. She pressed the microphone button. 'Helen, we'll repeat it a few more times and then finish.'

'Oh good, I'm getting a bit bored here.'

'Yes, I know, darling. All the action is actually here, but I'll show you everything when we've finished the last batch.'

'I can't wait to see it.'

Juliette selected some additional settings on the control monitor and the machine's familiar muffled clicks started. The tension in the room was palpable. Everyone was glued to the bottom screen, where the first blue trace started moving across in a straight line. 'The first peak is new and will show us when the initial decision was identified by the brain activity and which is the predicted button.' As soon as she'd said that, the trace shot up and back down. 'Here it is, guys!' The letter "R" appeared next to it. 'Look, look,' Juliette called, pointing to the letter. A few seconds later, Helen's voice came through the microphone. 'Z.' Soon the second peak appeared, followed by the third peak, and the letter "R" appeared again next to it. 'Bingo!' shouted Juliette.

There were gasps in the room.

'You're doing great,' said Juliette into the microphone. 'Let's repeat this a few more times, just in case it was a fluke.'

George moved closer to the screen as the next few traces ran just below the first and repeated a similar pattern of peaks. 'Not only is the correct button predicted every time without fail,' he said with amazement, 'but Helen's intention became known to us about seven seconds before she made her decision!'

'If only clairvoyants had that ability,' said Takahashi with a chuckle.

'That's right,' said Juliette, ignoring the comment. She pointed to the number "−7" on the bottom axis. 'In fact, the fMRI is a bit sluggish in responding to brain activity, so we could safely add three seconds. Meaning that the decision was formed in Helen's brain up to a full ten seconds *before* she became aware of it.'

'Brilliant,' said Grinberg with a satisfied smile. 'Maybe I should just add that since these regions encoded the predicted choice so much earlier than the moment Helen reported making the choice, she couldn't *possibly* be responsible for making the decision. It was made for her.'

The room fell silent. George leaned back to absorb the implications. This may just be the critical result they needed to reach a conclusive outcome. Again, he felt the hair on the nape of his neck rising. And then he noticed the blank expression on Ben's face. *I don't think he got it.*

At that moment the technician opened the door and let Helen into the crowded room. She looked around at the stunned faces. 'What did I miss?'

'Everything,' said Grinberg, 'but Juliette will you show you in a minute. Now, I guess,' he continued, staring at Gertrude,

'I don't need to tell you that with such a long interval, any concern over the exact decision time simply evaporates.'

'This is incredible,' Takahashi said.

'Yes, very exciting stuff,' added George, glancing at Gertrude.

Ben looked around, paused, then shook his head. 'I'm so sorry, but it looks like I'm the only one who doesn't quite get this. Could you tell me in one-syllable words why it's so significant that two areas of, say, my brain would be able to ... predict – I think that was the verb, wasn't it, Professor Grinberg? – would be able to predict that I'm about to press the left rather than the right button? It's still my brain doing both the predicting and the choosing, isn't it? So how does this make me less in control over my own actions – it's still *my brain* and therefore *my decision*, right?'

'Ben,' Grinberg said in a fatherly tone, 'your brain, as important as it is, is just an organ, like your stomach; it's not exactly you. I'm sure you'd accept that *you* as a person have zero control over your natural digestive processes, right?'

'Sure, but we're talking about free will, not a chemical process.'

'Well, the fact that these brain areas could *predict* which button Helen would press means that they already *knew* the outcome *before* she made her conscious decision. In other words, they must have *dictated* her decision. So in effect, this experiment showed that you, as a person, have zero control over your brain and your decisions, just as you've no control over your digestion. Therefore, your actions are also out of your control. Is that clearer now?'

'Hmm, I think so ...' Ben said weakly.

Grinberg scratched his bald scalp. 'Think so? That's not good. I obviously didn't explain it very well.'

'May I?' asked Takahashi.

Grinberg nodded, but then looked at his watch. 'Sorry. Hold that thought till we're back in the conference room.'

Juliette looked up from her computer monitor, directly at Grinberg. 'Leaving already?' she said with utter disappointment in her voice.

'It was very kind of you to help us, but I don't want to take any more of your precious time.'

'Nonsense. You're always welcome here, *mon chér.*'

'That's very generous of you, but we still have a lot of work to do,' said Grinberg.

'Oh well. Maybe you and I could catch up one evening while you're in Paris? For old times' sake?

'Er ... maybe,' he replied, blushing like a freshly peeled beetroot – a response that led George to suspect that any romantic feelings they may have had were no longer mutual.

Ben thanked Professor Rousseau and the group left the lab.

Overcome by curiosity, George approached Grinberg discreetly on their way back to the minibus. 'Looks like Juliette was very keen on you back there. Were you an item?'

Grinberg let out a guffaw. 'Juliette is keen on a lot of things,' he said, 'but my ex was less keen about my frequent trips to Paris, if you see what I mean.'

George nodded, contemplating whether to ask what happened, but then concluded that if Grinberg wanted to tell him more, he would've done so already.

* * *

There was a lot of chatter when they entered the conference room. The group was upbeat and George felt it too. The unexpected outing to a super-modern lab was refreshing after the endless discussions in a closed room. But more importantly, the remarkable demonstration, which bordered on something out of a science fiction film, had given him a boost of energy and morale.

When they all took their seats, Takahashi raised his hand. 'Okay, Ben,' he said, 'the brain is not my area, but analogies are.' Clasping his hands tightly with a mischievous smile spreading on his face, he continued, 'Imagine you're a jury member trying to determine the responsibility of a security guard in a shopping mall who had attacked a young woman. In court, the prosecution presents a clip from CCTV footage, where you see a woman in orange trousers strolling casually, stopping intermittently to do window shopping. Then, the guard, who so far was standing still, suddenly breaks into a run, jumps on the woman and wrestles her to the ground. Having been presented with just this information, what do you make of it?'

Ben shook his head slowly, grimacing. 'Looks like an unprovoked attack by the guard. Why?'

'Exactly! But then the defence lawyer plays a recording of what the guard heard in his earpiece just a few seconds earlier. The head of security was yelling in his ear to stop that woman in orange trousers at any cost because she was a professional shoplifter who had just done a big job at the jewellery store.' An amused smile spread on Takahashi's face. 'So, I hope you see now that knowing the full chain of events is absolutely crucial to figuring out who gives the order for an action and who just executes it. Back to Professor Grinberg's experiment—'

'It's not my experiment,' said Grinberg.

'Yes, yes, I know,' shot Takahashi before turning back to Ben. 'This epic result revealed who is *actually* yelling the orders, so to speak, and it's not you, although you feel *as if* it is.'

Ben nodded vigorously. His right hand started shaking and he slid it under the table.

George pinched his chin. Ben clearly got it at last, but he seemed more frightened than ever before, which was strange. *Solid evidence is exactly what he kept saying he wanted.* And now they had just that, so what was the problem? Perhaps it was not the answer Ben wanted. But why was it so frightening? What could happen?

'Now, perhaps I should mention,' continued Grinberg, 'that the results of the original study sent shock waves through the scientific community. Even Stephen Hawking picked up on this experiment and mentioned it in one of his books. But more importantly, a few years later, the study was repeated by researchers from the Max Planck Institute using a much more powerful scanner. In fact, seven tesla is more than double the magnetic strength we saw today.'

'That's a lot,' said Jerry. 'Such a machine produces high-resolution imaging down to a single cubic millimetre, with high temporal resolution too.'

'That's correct,' said Grinberg. 'Indeed, the new study accurately revealed both the location and time of the early decision-making process, with the main findings of the original study confirmed. Again, an early activity pattern that became stable over time could predict which button would be pressed way before the subjects became aware of their own decision. In other words, these areas encoded the decision.'

'But ten seconds is a very long time,' Gertrude said. 'Can't we change our mind during this period?'

Grinberg chuckled. 'I thought you were paying attention when we witnessed that Helen, like all the subjects in these studies, only became aware of her own decision about a second before pressing the button.'

'So?'

'So, you can't change your mind before you know you have made a decision, can you?'

Gertrude frowned, but remained silent.

'Before I forget,' said Helen, 'could you tell us what areas initiated the decision process before it entered awareness?'

Grinberg smiled at her. 'Sure, how can I refuse a question from such a lovely lady?'

Helen blushed.

'Well, one area was the frontopolar cortex. It's also called Brodmann Area 10, after the German anatomist Korbinian Brodmann. In the early 1900s, he defined the areas of the cerebral cortex based on their cytoarchitecture under a microscope and numbered them from 1 to 52.'

'So where is it?' pressed Helen.

'Yes, of course, I forget that not everyone is fascinated by the history of anatomy like me. It's basically at the very front tip of the brain. The other area was the parietal cortex, which extends from the very top of the brain towards the back. So the motor decision process seemed to originate first in the frontopolar cortex as an unconscious step, then it influenced the build-up of decision-related information in the parietal cortex, and later in the SMA, our old friend, where it could remain unconscious for a few more seconds.'

George chuckled. 'It sounds like consciousness is one of the last to be informed of the decision, but then it takes all the credit for it.'

'I never thought about it that way,' Grinberg said with a grin. 'But that's exactly what seems to happen.'

Max held his hand up and waved it awkwardly. 'Sorry to spoil the party, but I still have a major concern.' He rubbed his hands as if preparing for a fight. 'It's true that the main criticisms about the Libet Experiment were adequately addressed in these fMRI studies, but my main concern remains. Can we really extrapolate from the simple decision of which button to press to the much more complex decisions people make throughout their lives? Well, anyway, at least some people make complex decisions.'

Grinberg turned to Max. 'I see you are not easily pleased or impressed.'

Max grinned. 'You wouldn't be the first to say that.'

'Okay, if you expect to have a similar study for each and every human behaviour, that's simply ludicrous. But there are two fascinating studies with abstract decisions just for sceptics like yourself.'

Max shook his head, but Grinberg seemed to ignore that and plunged ahead with vigour. 'In the first one, again by researchers from the famous Max Planck Institute' – he shot a glance at Max – 'the subjects had to decide freely which mental arithmetic task to perform on two numbers, an addition or a subtraction, and at what time. They then had to report when they made the decision and, of course, the result. Interestingly, although the nature of the decision was not motor – as you know, calculation does not require muscles – the same two brain areas we mentioned earlier were involved and the decision was detected there up to four seconds before the person became aware of it. Taking into account the delayed response we have already talked about, it means that the actual intention was formed a few seconds earlier, around seven seconds before the conscious decision. The analysis could also predict with a high degree of accuracy when the participants would make their conscious decision.'

Max was nodding, but remained silent.

'The second study, by Australian scientists from the University of New South Wales, looked at imagery. The subjects were asked to choose between two predefined images, one with horizontal green and vertical red gratings and the other with the opposite colour and orientation. They then had to imagine their chosen image as vividly as possible and finally report their choice and the level of vividness. Well, in this vastly different paradigm, they found pretty much the same results. Activity patterns in four brain areas could predict the mental imagery content as early as eleven seconds before the person made a conscious and voluntary decision of what to imagine. In case you are wondering which areas, they included cortical areas, specifically the visual and frontal, as well as the thalamus and pons, which are deep inside the brain. Surprisingly, even the future vividness of the imagery could be predicted by the activity pattern in the primary visual cortex.'

'Aha,' exclaimed Gertrude. 'How can you be so sure that the subjects reported the decision time accurately? Isn't it possible that they reported the onset of imagery after they actually started doing it?'

'That would be very unlikely,' Grinberg said. 'With a gap of eleven seconds, the mistake would just be too great, so we could pretty much rule that out. But the researchers didn't take any chances and confirmed the reliability of the decision time using a clever psychophysical test.'

'Psycho-what?' Meghan asked.

'Psychophysical,' Grinberg said patiently. 'They used an objective test that participants simply could not control or cheat on to confirm the accuracy of the reported decision time. This was done by comparing free decision and forced decision using a well-known phenomenon called binocular rivalry. Now, without getting into the technical details, the important finding was that the reported timing of the free decision was proven categorically to be accurate.'

Very nice, thought George. With the potential weakness ruled out, he was satisfied that this study was solid.

Grinberg rose to his feet. 'For our purposes, the bottom line of all these studies is that between the two options – *you* control your brain or *your brain* controls you – the latter is correct.' He paused for a while. 'So ... if anyone has any other concerns or criticisms, please raise them now.'

There was silence in the room for a long while. George surveyed the faces around the table. Most looked relaxed but speechless. Ben was also looking around, but his stiff, upright posture and clenched jaw betrayed his tension. The person who had brought them here and encouraged them to come to a conclusion seemed, for some reason that George still couldn't decipher, visibly upset.

'Not a criticism,' George said. 'Just wanted to say that these additional results are truly remarkable.'

Grinberg nodded in agreement. Max and Gertrude exchanged glances but said nothing.

Grinberg scanned the faces around the table for a long while before slumping down in his chair. 'Very well then! But don't feel bad about it – the sharpest scientists in the field failed to find holes in these studies, so you are in good company. I think that this last study more than the others gives us a clue as to how decisions are made, at least for imagery. Sensory-like neuronal activity emerges spontaneously before volition, and when it's strong enough, passing a certain threshold, we experience it as our own free will. This, of course, may vary with different modalities, but it's clear that in a variety of decisions – whether about making a move, doing mental arithmetic or imagining something – brain activity representing the decision itself emerges well before the conscious decision is formed.'

Gertrude held her head with both hands. 'Just to make sure I've got this right. You're saying that when I make what feels to me like a completely free decision, what *actually* happens is that my brain has already made the decision *for* me in a very discreet fashion, behind the scenes and well in advance, correct?'

'That's what the evidence shows. We're following instructions without knowing it, but still feel in control.'

'Professor Grinberg, it sounds to me that based on this, we are *actually* just automatons.'

Grinberg nodded slowly. 'I'm afraid so. It's like we are all puppets on strings in the theatre of life, only the strings are invisible, such that the illusion of self-control is just perfect.'

'So who is the puppeteer?' Ben asked, frowning.

'The puppeteer? Well, that's just the laws of physics and chemistry that govern the functioning of the brain. Obviously, brains are different from each other due to differences in genetics, environment and the experiences we all had, but we hold no power *whatsoever* over the brain that governs us, just like the string puppet has no power over the puppeteer.'

Ben chuckled and got to his feet. All the tension seemed to have left his body. 'Well, well, well. That's a dramatic way to finish the last session for today. It looks like we all have something to think about, at least those of us who haven't heard this before. Have a good trip to your hotel and I'll see you all here in the morning.' He turned away and left the conference room in a hurry.

George didn't move. It was still only early afternoon, but Ben obviously considered the meeting over. His mind was flooded with questions and thoughts. *Have we reached the Holy Grail?* Was he just a string puppet obeying rules he hardly understood? Maybe there really was nothing he could do to save Ella. He wished he could talk to her now – share all of this with her.

14

On the Métro from the hotel the next morning, George spotted a familiar head with long, glossy dark hair at the far end of the carriage. His full head height above most people in a densely packed train had its advantages. He told Helen, who immediately made her way through the crowd, with George trying to catch up.

'Hey, Meghan, you're positively beaming!' Helen said with a grin. 'Does this remind you of the trains at home?'

Meghan glanced at her in surprise. 'Not at all. The trains in The Hague are rarely this busy.'

'You're lucky. They are in New York. Can we join you?'

'Absolutely. I could do with the company. I had a lovely chat with Olivier this morning. He wants to come over here once I'm free.'

'Ah, that's sweet.'

'Yes. It'll be our first mini-holiday together. Very exciting!'

'Nice,' Helen said. A crackling announcement in French blared over the speakers, followed by a wave of exasperated responses from the passengers. Looking through the carriage window, Helen stood on her tiptoes to catch a glimpse of the station's name just before they entered the tunnel. 'Next stop is ours.'

'Not today,' George said. 'They've just announced that the train will not stop at the next two stations. We'll probably have to get a taxi if we still want to arrive on time.'

'Strange they didn't say it in English too,' Meghan said.

'Maybe something has just happened, so they haven't had a chance to prepare a translation.'

'Did they give any reason?'

'Only that the stations had to be closed for safety.'

Four minutes later, the train came to a stop at Edgar Quinet Station, and they all piled out. When they finally emerged at street level with the large crowd, the only two taxis in sight were already being mobbed, so Meghan pulled out her phone and brought up a map of Paris. 'We're only twenty-five minutes away on foot. Shall we walk?'

George looked around. A few streets away, the traffic seemed to be at a standstill. Sporadically beeping horns came from the junction ahead, and he wondered if that was the reason for the closed Métro stations. A small group of people stood on the pavement near the junction, all peering to their right. Something was going on, and he could now hear drumbeats and loud chanting. A large procession of mostly young people was flooding the road. In the increasing cacophony, he could hear a male voice shouting something in French through a megaphone, the crowd answering back in unison.

'What are they saying?' Meghan asked.

'I can't hear it very clearly!' George replied, raising his voice over the increasing din.

'Let's get closer – I want to read the placards.'

He glanced at Helen, but she just shrugged. 'We don't have much time.' Meanwhile, Meghan was already moving ahead towards the demonstrators, without looking back. They kept up with her. If she got swallowed by this crowd, they'd lose her for sure.

Meghan pointed to a placard written in English, held by a middle-aged woman with short grey hair.

WE APOLOGISE FOR ANY INCONVENIENCE
DURING
ESSENTIAL GLOBAL IMPROVEMENT WORKS

'This is great! George, look at that one over there – what does it say?'

It was written in French, so George obliged. 'Fear is the currency of control.'

'How about that one?'

He read the next placard. 'Put the world's people first.'

'I think we should leave,' Helen said.

'Wait, there's another one over there!' Meghan stepped off the pavement and into the crowd to read it better. 'Wow, that's brilliant.' The sign read:

MAKE ORWELL FICTION AGAIN

Before George could stop her, she approached a young man with shoulder-length hair. 'What's the protest about?' she shouted.

'We are sick and tired of corporate greed and control by big institutions,' he shouted in a heavy French accent. 'The government is not listening to the people and we've had enough.'

'Good luck!' she yelled, and turned around, but she'd only taken one step when he took the paper flower garland off his neck and put it around hers. She just smiled.

The crowd started moving faster, as if pushed by an invisible force, and George quickly lost sight of Meghan as the sea of people engulfed her.

He scanned the crowd. At the far end of the street, a line of horse-mounted police moved towards the mass of people. There were perhaps five or six of them and the horses looked skittish, but the crowd kept moving, pushed from behind. Then one of the horses reared, causing people to leap out of the way, some falling over each other in panic. The shouts turned angry. It was impossible to stop the momentum.

George wiped beads of anxious sweat from his forehead. *This doesn't look good. I really shouldn't be here.* 'I can't see Meghan!' he shouted to Helen.

'Shall we join the protest and look for her?'

'I guess we'll have to! Take my hand.' He stepped into the churning crowd, Helen just behind him.

George searched the weaving bodies for a stripy blue-and-white blouse, but there was no sign of Meghan. Three shots rang out behind them. As the vigorous pushing and shoving propelled them forward, a cloud of thin white smoke spread over the crowd, stinging his eyes. He let go of Helen's hand and rubbed them, but the pain got worse, pulsating now with increasing intensity. He peered through his tears, searching for Helen. She stood frozen just a few metres ahead. Moving quickly towards her, he grabbed her hand tightly.

'Let's move,' he shouted. 'They're using tear gas.'

Some of the protesters put on gas masks. Others covered their faces with scarves or pieces of cloth. George stooped low, hoping to hide from the gas among the moving bodies. He dragged Helen back to the relatively empty pavement. Her hand felt small and fragile in his. 'Are you okay?'

'Yes, I think so,' she said, looking up at him. 'You're properly crying.'

'I'm surprised you're not,' he said, wiping the tears with his shirtsleeve and looking around. 'Christ, there she is!'

Meghan was leaning with both hands against a wall, coughing hard. They ran towards her, lifted her by an arm on each side and walked away as one. 'Let's find a café and wash off this horrible stuff,' Helen said. 'But please, no more detours.'

15

When George, Helen and Meghan finally made it to the conference room, they found the others already seated, but there was no sign of Ben, which was surprising. Perhaps he too had been held up by the protest. Skudder, in a livid green tie and white shirt, was pacing back and forth by the window wall, and he looked furious. He stopped and faced them as they entered.

'Oh, here you are,' he growled. 'I bet you were held up by those damned demonstrators, right?'

'Yeah, you could say that,' George said as he took his seat between Helen and Meghan. 'The police were using tear gas. We had to clean up.'

But Skudder wasn't finished. 'Well, I apologise for the unacceptable chaos you've all experienced in recent days,' he said, 'on behalf of the mayor of Paris, not to mention the useless government now in power.'

'It's not your fault,' Meghan said, taking off the colourful flower garland and placing it carefully on the table. 'After all, it's quite commendable that free speech is not only legally protected here but actually practised.'

Skudder fixed her with a hard stare. 'Commendable? What's commendable? The chaos on the streets and the Métro? The widespread disruption to ordinary citizens going about their lives?'

George gazed at Skudder. The man had obviously avoided the protest. Why was he so angry? Protests were normal in Paris. Parisians were well known for voicing their opinions.

'Well, maybe that's a small price to pay,' Meghan said, 'when something is seriously rotten and needs fixing.'

'What do you mean?' Skudder demanded, placing his hands on his hips and stretching his turtleneck towards her.

'Perhaps it's history repeating itself. The French Revolution completely changed the social and political structure of this country, and those new ideas helped shape many of Europe's modern-day governments. So maybe something *positive* could come out of these peaceful demonstrations.' After a pause she added, 'And it'd help if the police weren't so heavy-handed.'

'Yes, yes,' Skudder said, nodding absent-mindedly. He glanced at the door as Ben entered, mug in hand. The smell of coffee was intense. 'There are much more peaceful and effective crowd control methods out there. Thankfully, science and technology have all the necessary tools to restore law and order and create the obedient society we all wish for.'

George glanced at Skudder in surprise. *What sort of crowd control has this man got in mind?* He looked around the table to see if he was the only one worried by this statement. Takahashi was squinting, as he often did when struggling to make sense of something, and Meghan had an eyebrow raised. *Okay, I'm not being paranoid.* Skudder did sound like a radical. Since when did an innocent demonstration mean a disobedient society? And in France of all places?

'Only baseless fears stop us from achieving this,' Skudder continued, his eyes gaining a disconcerting brightness. 'But not for long. Okay, enough of me jabbering away.'

George glanced at Helen. She was also staring at Skudder.

'Thank you,' Ben said, his gaze following Skudder as he left the room. He turned to the group and took a sip of coffee, looking embarrassed.

'You've not gathered us here so that we can hypnotise the commander-in-chief and put you in charge instead, have you, Ben?' Takahashi asked. George recognised Takahashi's dry sense of humour, but the provocation sounded serious.

Ben spluttered into his mug, but quickly regained his composure and dabbed at the spillage on his sleeve. 'If only life was that simple, Professor Takahashi,' he said with a weak smile.

George noticed the inscription on the mug: "WORLD'S BEST DAD".

'Where did he nick that mug from?' he whispered into Helen's ear.

'Oh, don't be so cynical,' she whispered back with a cheeky grin. 'Maybe he's a great dad.'

'Okay, as we saw yesterday,' Ben said, 'evidence from neuroscience is firmly against free will, and I wonder if there is any way around this from physics or philosophy, or anything else ...'

George studied Ben. He found it odd that there was no mention of the late start. Ben seemed eager to avoid anything controversial. Was it out of fear of Skudder, who was monitoring the proceedings from his office, or something else? He couldn't decide.

'After all,' Ben continued, 'we can't just give up on this most fundamental freedom we all feel we have without a proper fight.'

Takahashi chuckled. 'You wouldn't be the first to try and save our precious free will. At least since early Greek civilisation, people have grappled with the compatibility of the laws of nature and the apparent capacity of mankind to make conscious decisions. Maybe the Roman poet and philosopher Lucretius expressed it most nicely and poetically in his *De Rerum Natura*.'

'On the nature of things,' mumbled Gertrude.

'Yes, thank you,' Takahashi said with a warm smile. 'Sherlock, could you read the relevant verse for us?'

'Certainly,' responded the orb. 'If all movement is always interconnected, the new arising from the old in a determinate order – if the atoms never swerve so as to originate some new movement that will snap the bonds of fate, the everlasting sequence of cause and effect – what is the source of the free will possessed by living things throughout the earth?'

'Perfect. Thank you.'

'Sorry,' Helen said, 'did you just say "atoms" and "early Greek civilisation" in one sentence?'

'No,' said Sherlock, 'actually it was in two separate sentences.'

George chuckled. Takahashi gave a self-satisfied grin before replying, 'You did hear correctly. The creation of an atomic theory of the universe was initially a purely philosophical idea by a chap called Democritus, a pre-Socratic philosopher who lived in the fifth and fourth centuries BC. You see, us philosophers have often paved the way for science, and in this case, over two thousand years before any hard evidence.'

'Yes, I've always thought that's astonishing,' George said, getting up to pour himself coffee. 'We now know that several of the early atomic concepts are correct – for example, that atoms are constantly moving. They reached that conclusion without any observations or instruments. Truly remarkable.'

'Agreed. Now, back to the ancient Greeks. They had a perfect solution to the problem. In an attempt to reconcile the phenomenon of cause and effect – which the Epicureans had seen as typical of the physical world – with the conflict created by the apparent freedom of human behaviour, they came up with the idea that atoms occasionally exhibit random swerves.'

'Random swerves?' Jerry said. 'And what would cause them?'

'Well, one explanation could have been the Greek gods, of whom there were quite a few. Those gods had daily influence on people's lives. Problem solved.'

'Nice, nice,' Jerry said. 'Could we move on now from Greek mythology to more solid evidence?'

'Sure, we can move on,' Takahashi said. 'How about the 17th century? I'm sure you'll love this one.'

Jerry raised an eyebrow.

'When trying to address the mind–body problem, Descartes proposed that the body obeyed the laws of the physical world, but the soul, or the mind, acting through the pineal gland, is not restricted by these limitations. How about that?'

'Ridiculous!' Jerry said, crinkling his nose. 'After spending five years of my life studying the pineal, I can assure you and Mr Descartes that this gland obeys the physical laws as much as any other brain tissue.'

'And I trust you on this,' Takahashi said. 'I don't think anyone takes this idea seriously these days, but your colleague Eccles had a more recent proposal to save free will by employing modern physics – quantum mechanics.'

Ben, who had been staring at the table with a glazed, worried look on his face, jerked upright. 'Sorry, but who the hell is Eccles?'

'Eccles won the Nobel Prize in 1963 for his pioneering work on the synapse, and later turned philosopher,' Jerry explained. 'Looks like this transition later in life is relatively common among neuroscientists. Well, I, for one, hope to keep both feet on the ground till the end.'

'It was actually an interesting collaboration between Eccles and the physicist Beck,' Takahashi said. 'Joining forces, they claimed that at very short time scales, certain events in the synapse are governed by quantum principles. Now, I wouldn't dare explain these principles or their veracity when we have a quantum physics expert in the room.' He winked at George. 'But I'd just mention that according to Beck and Eccles, mental intention becomes effective by momentarily increasing the probability of neurotransmitter release at the synapse. George?'

George blinked. All the attention in the room had shifted to him. 'Well, yes,' he said, trying to find his footing. He hadn't expected to be put on the spot quite like this. 'I'm familiar with this particular theory, and I can say that the physics aspect is sound, but the problems lie elsewhere entirely. To start with, no explanation has ever been offered on how mental intention would interact with the physical world, at the quantum level or otherwise. It's like kicking the can down the road in the hope that someone will pick it up, but nobody does. The second problem is perhaps even bigger.' He took a sip of his coffee, contemplating his next move. 'As you all know, a quantum process is random by nature. So, the suggestion that a collection of random events would bring about a deliberate intention to achieve a specific goal simply doesn't make much sense.'

'Well then, maybe we now have an explanation of why so many human decisions seem entirely random and nonsensical,' said Takahashi, and burst out laughing.

'Seriously now,' Ben said, 'with all due respect to theories, I don't think they will take us very far. If we want to reach a solid conclusion, we must focus on solid scientific evidence. Evidence that can be proved or disproved. Please, no more of that ...' He seemed to be groping for the right word. Would he say "nonsense" and risk insulting respectable thinkers? wondered George. '... Those unprovable ideas, as attractive or convenient as they may be.'

There were nods of agreement around the table, and Takahashi continued, 'I'm with you on that, Ben. At this point, I'd like to introduce two of the fundamental principles behind what is often called The Causal Exclusion Problem.' Takahashi got to his feet and started pacing back and forth along the window wall with his hands behind his back, his chin drooping to his chest. He was engrossed in his own world in a way that George had never seen when he was in front of an audience before. He stopped by the white flip chart at the head of the table. 'There are actually four principles, but we only need to focus on the two most relevant ones for this discussion.' He uncapped a thick red marker and wrote in neat handwriting:

1. The Principle of Physical Causal Completeness: every physical event that has a cause has a sufficient physical cause.

'This is not my area of expertise,' Gertrude said, 'but I can already spot a problem with this principle. It does sound very reasonable, especially if one is not a science denier, *but* – would it still hold if it turns out that nature is not entirely deterministic? After all, we already know that at the subatomic level, where quantum mechanics operates, single events cannot be predicted with certainty. I wonder what our eminent physicist has to say about *that*.'

Takahashi gestured towards George again.

George hesitated. This was a tricky one. Explaining physics to non-physicists was never easy. He took a deep breath. 'Well, first, I should probably explain the difference between deterministic and probabilistic laws. Feel free to plug your ears if you know it already.'

'Enlighten us,' Ben said.

'Okay,' he began, taking another sip of coffee, 'so according to classical physics, nature is governed by deterministic laws, which mean that if we had an infinitely powerful computer and we knew all the laws of physics and current conditions, we could not only predict the future but also work out everything that had ever happened in the past with perfect precision. In quantum physics, on the other hand, even if we knew everything there is to know about a particle, we could only predict the probability, or chance, that a certain outcome would happen. For example, you could only predict that a particle has a 70 percent chance to be found in location A and 30 percent in location B, but never exactly where it is. Hence probabilistic laws. Einstein believed that the universe and its laws must be strictly deterministic, but we now know that certain aspects of the universe, especially in the small scale, are not.'

Ben squinted at him. 'That was very helpful. Thank you, George.'

George glanced at Ben. The thanks seemed genuine, but with Ben you could never tell. 'Back to Gertrude's question. The principle can easily be adapted for a probabilistic version without any problem. For example, some proposed rephrasing the principle as "every physical event has its probability fixed entirely by its physical past history". And that would work just as well. So, it wouldn't matter at all if the universe is deterministic or probabilistic or some combination of the two.'

'True,' Takahashi said. 'Philosophers often use the deterministic version just for the sake of simplicity. George, perhaps you could take us through the hard evidence for this principle from modern physics. After all, we're here to get to the truth rather than entertain philosophical ideas, as much as I like them.'

'I don't know about modern,' he replied, 'but it's certainly hard evidence. Without boring you with the details, I'd just say that the conservation laws provide a powerful proof of the first principle.'

'Any chance you could explain it to a non-physicist like myself?' Max asked.

'Well, actually it was one of your compatriots, Leibniz, who established the law of conservation of linear momentum.'

'*Ja, ja*, Leibniz, I know all about him,' Max said.

The little shit thinks he knows everything. Taken aback by his animosity towards Max, George moderated his tone and spoke to the room. 'He was a prominent German polymath in the 17th century.'

'Look,' snapped Max, 'I studied the Enlightenment period and Leibniz in school, but you lost me there with the word "momentum". I never liked math or physics.'

I can tell, George thought, smiling at Max. 'It's quite simple, really. All this law means is that the product of total mass times speed and direction of any set of bodies remains constant, regardless of how they interact. Think for a moment of a snooker ball rolling on a table and hitting two other, resting balls. If you add up the value of this product for each of the three balls together, the sum will remain constant at any point in time. I mean before, during and after the collision. And this law is universal. It'd be true in your local pub just as much as for a celestial collision between rigid planets in a faraway galaxy.'

'Nice. That was simple enough, but how does it prove anything?'

'Well, first I should also mention Hermann von Helmholtz ...' Looking at Max, George added with a smile, 'He's another German scientist that isn't so known outside the field. He lived a few centuries after Leibniz and added the law of conservation of energy. It's basically a similar idea but related to energy. You see, nature obeys strict laws of motion and energy, and together they govern pretty much every known object in the universe, including us. In fact, there isn't a single example of these laws having been broken.' He turned to the rest of the group. 'And believe me, there is nothing that brings more joy and fame to a scientist than finding an exception to an accepted law of nature. So ... these rigid universal laws of physics lead to the inevitable conclusion that every physical event must have a sufficient physical cause. The end.'

'Yes, I get that for pure physics,' Max said, furrowing his brow. 'But we are interested in human behaviour here – thoughts, emotions, desires and such.'

'Yes, but—'

'I'll stop you there, George.' Ben looked at Grinberg, who had his arms folded and his head slumped on his chest, snoring lightly. 'Maybe this is a good time to take a short break. Hopefully we'll be able to reach a common understanding when we reconvene.'

16

During the break, George found Takahashi sitting on a sofa. He was rifling through his bag and finally pulled out his puzzle book. Once that puzzle was started, there'd be no way of talking with him, so George slumped down on the sofa with a big sigh. 'I've been meaning to ask you something for a while now.'

'Shoot, my friend. What is it?'

'What do you think about Ben *now*?'

'Now? He's just the typical bureaucrat. Why?'

'No. Not that. I mean, did you notice his response when you mentioned that the implanted thoughts would be useful for a totalitarian regime?'

'Can't say I noticed. What did he do?'

'He went white as a sheet.'

Takahashi eyed him with an expression that said he'd finally gone around the bend. 'So what do you think is going on?'

George sighed again. He didn't know how to explain his feelings when they were just that – feelings. Nothing solid, nothing provable. No hard evidence, as Ben himself would say.

'It's not just that,' he said carefully. 'A lot of things he ... well, said, but also didn't say. Ben is very cagey. He won't really explain what our eventual conclusion will be used for. Then there's Skudder, making all kinds of insinuations and generalisations about obedience. I hate to say this, but I think we're involved in something we really shouldn't be involved in.'

And there it was. He'd gone back and forth with this; all the talking, all the debating, had given him a lift, made him feel warm, happy to be back in academia, to be talking with intelligent people about interesting topics. But Skudder's remarks about creating an obedient society had troubled him more than he realised, more than he knew until this moment.

But Takahashi still had that sceptical look on his face. 'Yes, both he and his superior said some strange things about crowd control, but a lot of people have odd views. Don't forget, we're in France, not under some totalitarian regime. The United Nations is a respectable organisation. Besides, we're free to leave and report anything now or later. All it takes is just one phone call. I don't think they'd dare do anything funny.'

'I know you were bothered by what Skudder said too. I saw it. And you forget that we don't have our phones with us. It's "against policy".' He made air quotes with his fingers.

'George, my friend, you are being paranoid. In many places mobile phones are against policy. We could get them back from reception at any moment.'

'I guess.'

'Listen, we will do this: I'll pay very close attention to how Ben reacts to things now, yes? And you … you try to relax.' Takahashi looked at his watch. 'We're due back in less than five minutes and I need a tinkle.'

* * *

It was an exhausted group who finally filed back into the conference room. George was getting quite sick of the sight of the table and the weird orb in the corner. The novelty had worn off.

'George,' said Jerry as they all got settled. 'Do you mind if I respond to Max?'

He glanced at Grinberg, Jerry's still snoozing colleague. 'By all means.' It was a relief. Maybe this would get things over and done with.

Jerry pulled a strand of wet hair out of his mouth and tucked it behind his ear. 'Max, I think it's more than just pure physics that proves the principle that every physical event has a sufficient physical cause. Let's consider neuroscience. True, our understanding of the brain isn't complete yet, but it has successfully demonstrated that neural processes are responsible for every behaviour tested so far and that specific brain regions are associated with movements, emotions, perceptions and cognition. So there is really compelling evidence that every behavioural event has a sufficient physical cause.'

'I couldn't put it in any better words,' Takahashi said. 'I just want to add that for these reasons, the Principle of

Physical Causal Completeness is considered by many as fully established.'

'Hold on, hold on,' Gertrude cried. Jumping up from her seat, she walked briskly towards the flip chart and underlined the word "sufficient". 'The principle, which by the way I fully accept, says every physical event has a *sufficient* physical cause. It doesn't rule out multiple causes, does it? So, for every behaviour, you could have both a physical cause in the form of brain activity and also a mental cause in the form of volition.' She jabbed the marker pen towards Takahashi like a sword.

'Theoretically yes, but practically no,' Takahashi said with a disarming smile. 'And I'll explain once you hand me your sword ... marker.'

She glared at him for several seconds, to the point that George was worried she was just going to throw the pen at him, but finally turned it over and returned to her seat without a fuss. Takahashi bowed and approached the flip chart.

'The second principle I wanted to bring here,' he said, writing on the chart, 'is the Principle of Causal Exclusion.'

2. No single event can have more than one sufficient cause occurring at any given time – unless it is a genuine case of causal overdetermination.

'Good,' Gertrude said with a triumphant smile. 'So you admit then that it could be overdetermination, with both physical and mental causes at play.'

'Definitely not,' he snapped, 'and you'll see why once we look at this a little deeper.' Takahashi closed his eyes for a long time. 'Okay, there are a few arguments that support this principle, but I think the main one, called the massive coincidence argument, will be more than enough. Unless, of course, my esteemed colleague Gertrude Kirkpatrick would like to hear them all.'

'It depends how strong it is.'

'Well, I'm sure we'll hear if you think it's not,' he said with a wink. He glanced around the group, lingering for a moment on Ben's face as he began to speak. 'I hope you'd all agree that in nature, cases of overdetermination, where multiple sufficient causes have the same effect, are a rare coincidence. For example, it'd be quite exceptional for a barn to burn down because of a simultaneous lightning strike *and* an arsonist dropping a match, right?'

'Well, it'd be the end of the arsonist,' George said with a chuckle.

'Yes, of course. But the two events happening together is very unlikely, if not impossible. Now, the act of behaviour from its very inception all the way to execution is a physical event. Thinking, decision-making, walking, talking, are all physical, either observable movement or electrical activity in the brain and muscle. As a physical event, each must have a sufficient physical cause. We saw that earlier. So ... for behaviour to have *another* sufficient cause, like a mental one, would be a case of causal overdetermination. But if you consider that there are billions of people in the world and each one initiates hundreds of behaviours a day, having more than that single sufficient physical cause would require *massive* amounts of coincidence. This is simply implausible.'

All eyes turned to Gertrude.

'Don't look at me,' she said. 'I'm a reasonable person really, and when I see a convincing argument, I keep my mouth shut.'

Takahashi chuckled. 'Some may disagree with you on that.'

But Max was not amused. He shook his head slowly. 'Are you seriously suggesting that a simplistic analogy of a burning barn is relevant to the causality in the human brain, which is considered to be the most complex object in the cosmos?'

Takahashi took off his Panama hat, turned it around slowly and inspected its rim. 'The short answer is yes,' he said, and placed his hat back where it belonged. 'It's not about barns or fires or even the brain. It's about multiple causes for anything at all. If you can find an example of something with more than a single and sufficient cause, just let me know. Oh, and it has to be common. I mean *very* common. Maybe something that happens every day to every person throughout their life, otherwise it doesn't qualify.'

Max didn't seem to have a response to that.

'You know what?' Takahashi said. 'I'll go through another argument. It's called the necessity argument. Suppose you and Helen are having red wine during a romantic dinner and simultaneously spill it on the pristinely white tablecloth.' There were several chuckles as Max blushed. George recalled the incident on the river cruise when Max spilled wine on Helen's blouse. He found himself smiling and was surprised at his glee that Takahashi would bring it up again. 'One stain is enough. Max's mishap without Helen's is individually sufficient to stain the tablecloth, right? So Helen's mishap is individually unnecessary. This is the case with overdetermining causes. They are each individually sufficient, therefore, not individually necessary. It's quite simple, really.'

Takahashi took a sip of water. 'Now, back to our subject. If behaviour is overdetermined, no single cause would be individually necessary, whether physical, mental or anything else, right? But, as I'm sure you all remember, we've already established that a physical cause is *always* necessary. So, any other non-physical cause is simply unnecessary, and that, my friends, covers our precious perceived choice too.'

'I think I understand now where all this is leading to,' Ben said. 'And frankly, this is quite a frightening thought.'

George tried to catch Takahashi's eyes, but his friend was just looking at the table.

Max pulled a sceptical face. 'Frightening? Why? I actually have another problem with all this. You've just concluded that physical events are sufficient to explain every physical event, and I accept that. Then you said that it also includes behaviour. So now, how do you explain that mental events like feelings, which are not physical, are also able to affect behaviour?'

Takahashi took a deep breath. 'Well, congratulations. You've just touched on one of the most challenging conundrums in philosophy, known as the mind–body dualism or the Hard Problem, or just "What the hell is consciousness?" The thing is that it's really irrelevant for our discussion.'

'Irrelevant? How come? I thought that free will and consciousness are part of the same issue, no?'

'Well, maybe one day these two subjects will be reconciled or united in some grand theory, but at the moment they are separate problems. You see, the fact is that science has contributed nothing so far to our understanding of the Hard Problem of consciousness. So it remains in the realm of philosophy. On the other hand, the free will issue can be addressed using scientific tools, as we're doing here.'

'But surely you must have some thoughts about consciousness and dualism.'

'More than just thoughts. In fact, I have spent most of my professional life wrestling with this fiendish question, and I believe I've found a possible satisfactory solution to it, but as I said, it's out of our scope right now.'

'That sounds intriguing,' Max said. 'Maybe I could invite you for a coffee one day and you'll tell me all about it?'

'I actually prefer tea. It'd take many pots of tea to cover this one, but if you're paying, I'm in. You'll have to sign a non-disclosure agreement though. It's still unpublished.'

George smiled again. He'd love to have another long conversation over a pot of tea with his friend and talk about consciousness. If Max wasn't there.

'Very well,' said Ben, and rose to his feet. He had a nervous tic in his left eye. 'Talking about NDAs, there seems to have been a problem with two of them. Meghan, you haven't signed yours, and Professor Takahashi, you signed as Mickey Mouse. I'll pop them over for you to sign before we continue. We need these fixed as soon as possible. Then, George, could you take the lead and give us your much anticipated summary? I want to know your thoughts on everything we've heard.'

This was not what George wanted to hear. He wasn't in the mood to take centre stage. Then he met Takahashi's gaze at last and saw a look of doubt on the little man's face. Takahashi had been watching Ben.

17

Ben left the room to get the non-disclosure agreements. As the door closed behind him, Meghan turned to look at Takahashi. 'I don't understand why all the secrecy. As I see it, we're involved in an intellectual investigation with no commercial value or security implications.'

'Agreed,' Takahashi said. 'Beforehand, I didn't know what the project was about, but now that I do, the secrecy is perplexing.'

'I'd say it's more worrying than perplexing,' George said. 'To me, the project is fascinating from every aspect, but largely innocuous. Yet, all this secrecy suggests there must be something we don't know yet. Maybe some unusual application?'

'Oh, c'mon,' Gertrude said. 'What is this supposed to be? A conspiracy?'

'Good question,' he replied. '*Is* there a conspiracy? I've a bad feeling about this. I'd just urge everyone to be cautious and—'

At that moment Ben returned, carrying a few forms in one hand and a briefcase in the other. Walking around the table, he handed Meghan and Takahashi a form each. 'Would be great if you could sign the two copies and return one to me before we proceed.'

'May I ask,' Takahashi said, 'what's the purpose of this NDA, and why the urgency?'

'Sure. Sure. You can always ask. Well, it's nothing much, really. The programme secretary likes to have all the paperwork by the books. She heard that we're approaching the end, so she panicked a bit that you might go home without signing. That's all.' He gave a Cheshire Cat smile.

George tried not to grimace. There was something wrong, very wrong. He tried to catch Takahashi's attention again, to find some way of telling him not to sign until they figured out what this was all about, but his friend was focused on Ben.

'And this is very important right now?' Takahashi asked.

'Yes. I mean, I'd like to get them done and given to the secretary.'

Takahashi looked at Meghan, shrugged, and then signed the papers. Meghan did the same after a short hesitation, and they both slid their copies across the table. Ben stowed them in his briefcase and locked it. 'Thank you, Professor Takahashi, for being our final expert witness in what has been a fascinating few days.' He turned to George. 'I'm sure I speak on behalf of everyone here when I say that we're all eager to hear your summary of the key points as well as the strength of the evidence as our impartial observer. So, George, over to you.'

Ben sat back down, kicked off his shoes and folded his arms on his chest. As he put his feet up on an adjacent chair, a pink crayon fell from his pocket to the floor.

Meghan picked up the crayon. 'You dropped something.'

'Ah, thanks,' he said with a crooked smile. 'My daughter often hides her things in my pockets.'

George raised his eyes from the densely written notepad in front of him and watched as Ben fiddled with the crayon. And he realised how little they knew about this man who had brought them here. He'd expressed no personal views during this entire discussion, except that comment he'd made in the Boston café about his passion for the truth. There had been no real insight into Ben's motivations, his background, his ... well, anything about him. All the other people around the table had long résumés and clear perspectives. Hell, even Gertrude had an online presence. Ben remained, even now, an enigma. Except that he had a daughter who liked pink crayons.

'George, the stage is yours,' Ben said.

'Yes, yes, thank you,' he said, realising that all eyes had been fixed on him for a while now. He put down the pen he was rolling back and forth between his fingers and took another long look at his notepad, then slowly scanned the faces around the table.

'Okay, I'll go in chronological order. First, we've seen that mind-wandering is our default mode in about half of our waking hours, and as we saw in a live demonstration' – he glanced at Helen, who returned a shy smile – 'trying to control our thoughts is often very difficult; thoughts have a mind of their own. We then looked at the concept of the ideal agent. Most people believe they are ideal agents who could tell you not only what they're doing but also why. In reality, things are much more complicated. The sense of responsibility for our own actions, or, if you like, the feeling of authorship, depends on three principles: priority, consistency and exclusivity. If any is missing, the sense of authorship can easily evaporate. Apparently, this sense of responsibility develops gradually from a young age, when children often assign their intentions after they complete an action and not before, as we've seen in the bucket experiment. As adults, we mostly follow the Priority Principle, where intention comes before action, but in many situations we revise our attitudes to justify our actions. One common example is cognitive dissonance. The irony is that the sense of authorship is just that – a sense we have that doesn't necessarily reflect reality.'

He took a long sip of water. The silence in the room troubled him. There was no hint of the earlier arguments. 'Please, stop me if I'm misstating anything. Okay, one of the key principles, priority, doesn't necessarily mean causality. Night doesn't cause day, even though it precedes it. Actually, only the other way round is true – when there seems to be causality there is also priority, and cause precedes result.'

He waited again, hoping for someone to interrupt, to tell him that he was getting it wrong. Even Gertrude was looking silently on, not even trying to curb her natural desire to argue.

'You could argue that this is just circumstantial evidence. Fair enough. Seeds of doubt don't necessarily mean you're wrong. But there is much stronger evidence to support the idea that a major illusion is at work here. We've seen that people could easily be fooled into believing they made a decision when it was really imposed on them. In hypnosis, for example, a request from a stranger is confused with the subject's own will, and so they feel compelled to invent intentions because they expect to have them. That could lead to quite ironic confabulations. Now, as some of you pointed out,' he said, and glanced at Gertrude, 'hypnosis is quite a unique situation and far from natural behaviour, so any doubt about its relevance here is entirely understandable.'

Gertrude cleared her throat but went no further. He took a deep breath. 'We also heard evidence from controlled experiments where fully awake people justified a choice they had never actually made. This was demonstrated in a selection of a picture that's been switched using sleight of hand and where volunteers had a sense of control over a cursor when in fact they had none in the I-spy experiment.' He flashed a brief smile at Helen and was surprised by the feeling of warmth when she returned it. 'Again, these examples and many others suggest that the sense of agency is nothing but a retroactive confabulation, a strategy to fill in the gaps and explain our own actions or choices after the fact. Perhaps the most impressive in this line of evidence are the priming experiments, where people's behaviours and choices in social interactions were manipulated. We saw changes in displays of generosity, politeness, hostility, judgement of crime and many other situations, following entirely irrelevant triggers like exposure to words, holding a hot or cold cup or touching a soft or hard object. The amazing thing is that not only are complex behaviours functioning on autopilot, but also, choosing a goal to pursue can be implanted by priming with words. The idea that post-action intention is formed on a regular basis has hard evidence from decades of research with split-brain patients that started in the 1950s.'

He glanced at Grinberg, who was awake for a change, sucking the arm of his reading glasses and gazing at the writing pad in front of him.

'It seems that the left brain functions as an interpreter that observes everything we do and immediately constructs a hypothesis as to why particular actions occurred. More recent research has shown that the feeling of agency is mapped to a specific network in the brain that is connected with the precuneus, and that damage or stimulation of this network alters or disrupts this sense. Similar methods found that the sense of volition is localised to a different network connected with an area called the anterior cingulate.'

At this, Max suddenly started sneezing. George paused and watched the man convulse with relentless achoos.

'Sorry, I can't control this any more than my free will,' Max managed to say, wiping his nose with a paper tissue. 'Does someone own a cat?' He broke out into a fresh round.

'Guilty as charged,' Meghan said. She glanced at Gertrude, who sat next to Max.

After a long moment Gertrude said in a low voice, 'Oh, uh, me too.'

'I'm ... allergic to ... cats,' Max huffed. 'Better ... *achoo* ... move chairs.'

George waited till Max had moved to the far end of the table and finished blowing his nose like a trumpet out of tune before continuing.

'So, we have evidence from thousands of psychological experiments and observations as well as neurological conditions that the perception of free will is a fabrication after the action, and that it can easily be manipulated. We now know that this perception of free will is being generated in two well-defined networks in the brain. You might think that this is strong enough evidence on its own. It ... definitely could be.' He paused again. Was this really the conclusion he was coming to? He could see the direction of his own arguments, and no doubt the others could as well.

'But,' he went on, 'there is still a possibility that in certain situations we are free to make a choice. So let's move on to inspect directly the main control centre, our brain.' Jerry gave him an encouraging smile. 'With the mouse experiment, we've seen an example of an on-off switch that, once flicked on, triggers the mouse to seek water and drink with an astonishing reliability of nearly hundred percent. Just like a man-made machine. This demonstration raised the possibility that a similar but more complex set of automatic switches operate and control many human behaviours. We've also looked at the two systems of thought processes. The fast one, associated with the Default Mode Network in the brain, is unconscious and stereotypic. It's our autopilot mode. So this clearly cannot support free will, simply because it is, well, unconscious. The slow one, on the other hand, is deliberative, logical and conscious, so you'd think it's much more in line with exercising free will, wouldn't you?'

George scanned the faces once more. They were following him; they probably knew where he was headed.

'But even this hope was dashed following two lines of evidence to the contrary. The first is analysis of major life decisions, which seem to be highly complex and perhaps constitute the ultimate in our freedom and rational thinking. These included place of residence, type of occupation, choice of partner and much more.'

Max made a honking noise and pinched his nose, presumably in an attempt to stifle another sneeze attack.

'Apparently,' George continued, 'these decisions could be influenced by seemingly meaningless and unconscious preferences for things like the letters in our name or the numbers in our date of birth. But much more direct evidence came from brain-imaging studies that showed how activity, specifically related to decision-making, takes place long before a free conscious decision is made.' He glanced at Helen. 'I must make special mention of the amazing demonstration Helen gave us of her brain in action.' Helen waved a dismissive hand and smiled at him. 'This leads to the astonishing conclusion that even a decision that we experience as a fully conscious one is actually unconscious, decided for us by a purely physical activity in our brain well before our conscious decision. Unlike the first experiments that tested trivial decisions such as when to move a finger or which button to press, later trials went much further. They included cognitive tasks such as arithmetic and mental imagery. So ... between the two simplified options of whether *we* control our *brain* or our *brain* controls *us*, the evidence shows that the brain is at the helm, not us.' Grinberg was nodding.

'Lastly, we examined the Principle of Physical Causal Completeness, meaning that every *physical* event that has a cause has a sufficient *physical* cause that requires nothing else. We looked at the hard evidence from physics that supports this, whether the laws of nature are deterministic or probabilistic, as well as evidence from neuroscience. The evidence is ironclad and the conclusion is inevitable. Free will could not exist without contradicting what we know about physics, biology and psychology.' George put down his pen and took a long gulp of water.

The room remained silent for a long while. He didn't want to look at anyone, didn't want to think about the fears still sitting in the back of his mind, of how Skudder and Ben would take this conclusion.

'Wow, thank you, George,' Ben said. His voice sounded harsh in the silence. 'I think that was a clear and fair summary of the presentations and discussions so far. Do you all agree?' His gaze scanned the faces.

Slowly, everyone began to nod.

'Wait,' Takahashi said. 'Don't you think that the Principle of Causal Exclusion is relevant to this case? You haven't mentioned it at all.'

George smiled a little. He had been afraid his good friend would bring that up and hoped they would agree about it, but he also knew that Takahashi was a principled man and no friendship would make him compromise. 'Well, as far as philosophy is concerned, the first principle, that of physical causal completeness, is probably the strongest I've ever heard – especially that it's overwhelmingly supported by the rigid laws of physics. The second principle, that of causal exclusion, is convincing, but cannot be proven with scientific evidence at this point. I'm sure you all remember the comical example Professor Takahashi gave on overdetermination with Max staining a pristine tablecloth—'

'He actually mentioned Helen too,' interrupted Max. 'Otherwise it doesn't work.'

'I'm glad you remember that,' snapped George. 'So ... anyway, these principles, which are basically metaphysical in nature, have definitely lent major support.' He turned to face Takahashi and continued, 'But without the solid experimental studies we've reviewed, I don't think they are enough on their own.'

Takahashi smiled broadly. 'George, you know that I consider well-thought-out philosophical principles as pretty solid, but as we were asked to rely only on solid scientific evidence, I must agree that they become secondary. Yet they still point to the lack of free will.'

'Yes, that's how I understood it,' Ben said, his expression grave. 'And the solid evidence seems to be enough. Actually, I have one more question for you, George.' He straightened his back, placed his clasped hands on the table and fixed George with a hard stare. 'What do you think about the strength of the evidence we've heard? Be honest. A lot relies on your answer.'

'And by a lot you mean what, exactly? World peace?'

'Yeah, something like that ... Just kidding.'

George glanced at Takahashi, hoping that his friend had noticed just how tense Ben was, but he was busy doodling – another elephant. Maybe that was the elephant in the room. From experience George knew that any direct prodding would lead nowhere with Ben, so he gave up. 'Of everything we've heard, two pieces of evidence really stood out. The first is the universal ironclad consistency of physical laws that support the Principle of Physical Causal Completeness. When a system of explanations and predictions is as perfect as physics, any additional explanation is simply redundant.'

'Are you invoking Occam's razor here?' Gertrude asked with raised eyebrows.

'No, not at all,' he said. 'Occam's razor argues that, other things being equal, simpler theories are better, but here there is no competing theory to physics. The laws of nature are uniform and consistent, and these laws do not accommodate the concept of free will. Whatever the details and complexities behind consciousness are, they are unlikely to involve any new law in physics that would break the causal laws of nature. Human laws can be broken, changed or cheated on, but nature's laws are immutable. There is simply no way of breaking them, changing them or cheating them.'

His throat felt dry, and not just from talking. 'The second piece of evidence is probably the last nail in the coffin of free will.' The brain wasn't his area, but he understood enough of what had been presented, and what it led to, that he thought he could make the case. 'For such a complex question, we need a type of evidence that's as direct as can be. And we've got it. I'm talking about the order of events leading up to a conscious decision. As we saw in several trials, brain activity that predicts our choice intention is detected up to a full ten seconds or more *before* we become aware of our choice.' Jerry smiled in approval. 'This order of events confirms unequivocally that our choices are just thoughts formed *after* the brain has already made the decision for us, in a process that is entirely out of our control, just like digestion.' He paused at Grinberg's nod. The support from two leading neuroscientists gave him a boost of confidence that he was restating things correctly. 'The provocative conclusion that we are not in control of our will, and therefore not our actions either, is highly unsettling. For me, at least. But it's the unescapable truth, whether we like it or not.'

Another long silence followed.

'So Schopenhauer was right after all,' Max broke in.

'In what way?' George asked.

'"*Der Mensch kann tun was er will; er kann aber nicht wollen was er will.*" Or, "Man can do what he wills but he cannot will what he wills".'

'That sums it up nicely.'

'I'm just wondering, though ... What did you think about the host of psychological evidence?' asked Max.

George swallowed hard and made a conscious decision to be nice and professional despite his irritation towards Max. 'I guess you already know my view that as a softer science, experimental psychology often suffers from certain weaknesses. I mean things like alternative interpretations and exceptions. So it's difficult to consider them as solid as some other evidence we've seen, but I must say that the sheer volume of supportive evidence using a variety of approaches with consistent results is very impressive. From the priming trials and other examples, we saw that even what we experience as a *conscious* decision is actually influenced by *unconscious* processes, suggesting that we're responding rather than being in control.'

Max sat back, and seemed pleased with the answer.

'As for our undeniable sense of freedom to choose,' George continued, 'we've seen multiple examples that show it's incredibly unreliable and liable to manipulations. Not only is this sense a pure illusion, but it's impossible to let go of.'

'We've heard a lot about illusions,' Gertrude said slowly, as if weighing every word. 'But are you sure we can't free ourselves from an illusion just by exposing it, so we're no longer spellbound? Say, if a magician showed you his trick, surely you would no longer be spellbound by the magic.'

Admittedly, he didn't have an immediate answer for that. He'd thought his summary had gone down surprisingly well, but that seemed premature. His eyes followed Jerry as he got up and walked towards the trolley in the corner of the room. He picked up a glass bowl filled with individually wrapped white candies and brought it back with him.

'I think this will answer your question very nicely. Can I offer you a mint?' Jerry asked as he went around the table. 'Please pop one in your mouth and suck on it.'

Gertrude picked up a candy by the tip of the wrapper as if holding a dead mouse by its tail. She unwrapped it noisily and put it in her mouth. The others followed suit, except Takahashi, who shook his head with a brief smile. Jerry sat back in his chair, put a candy in his mouth and waited for a while.

'Now, take a deep breath,' Jerry said as he took a long one himself. 'I'm sure you all feel cold, fresh air filling your lungs.'

'I've had a mint before,' Gertrude said. 'What's your point?'

'Well, let me tell you about this sensation. Mint leaves and mint candies contain menthol, which activates a special receptor in the cells that line your lungs. The receptor is called TRPM8. It's normally activated by cold air, which in turn leads to a strong signal to the brain that we interpret as a cool sensation. When menthol binds to this receptor it makes it very sensitive, so even the warm air in this room activates it and makes the air feel cool. Now this is clearly an illusion, right? I can assure you that the temperature of the air you're breathing now with the candy in your mouth hasn't changed. But although you all now know the reason for this illusion, you won't be able to shake it off. Please try to.' He looked around, waiting for a while. 'As long as the menthol vapours reach your lungs, each breath you draw in will feel as fresh and cool as a mountain breeze no matter how much you try to dispel it. You see, our perceptions, with all the brain mechanisms behind them, form our only window to the world, so if this window is tinted orange, there is no way we would know the true colour of reality ... unless ... unless we used pure logic to expose it. But even then, the world would *still* look orange to us. So, the illusion that we are free to choose is just that – the only tinted window we have, through which we experience the world.'

18

George interpreted the long silence as a sign that everyone was taking in the demonstration and its implications. He inhaled deeply with the mint still in his mouth and was enjoying the cool sensation spreading in his lungs with a newfound exhilaration when Helen broke the silence.

'I fully understand all the arguments and evidence we've heard,' she said. 'In fact, I provided some of it myself. But to be honest, I find it hard to accept that I'm just a puppet or a robot, without any freedom.' Her voice remained even, factual, but she flushed a little as she spoke. 'Putting feelings and human pride aside for a moment, doesn't the fact that we often hesitate when confronted with conflicting motives or confusing information show that we take appropriate time to deliberate complex situations before we act? After all, machines don't hesitate. So maybe *hesitation* is really what differentiates us from them? That way, we may enjoy some degree of freedom. Freedom of choice.'

Takahashi nodded slowly with a hint of a smile. George suspected that Helen's desperate but probably futile attempt to save free will had amused him.

'That's a very interesting argument,' Takahashi said, 'but let me tell you something about robots that may surprise you.' His smile broadened. 'A while ago, a British engineer who was interested in robot ethics built an ethical trap for a robot and witnessed truly unexpected results. They programmed a tiny robot to prevent another from falling off a cliff. The other robot represented a human, thereby applying Isaac Asimov's First Law of Robotics, which I'm sure you're all familiar with.'

'I don't read science fiction,' Meghan said.

'Oh, and I thought everyone reads science fiction,' he said, chuckling. 'The three rules were introduced in his 1942 short story Runaround. The first rule stated that "a robot must not allow a human being to come to harm". To start with, the robot seemed very successful. Each time the human proxy moved towards the cliff, the ethical robot rushed in to block it or pushed it out of the path to danger, as expected. Now, when the researchers added a second human proxy heading towards danger, things got really interesting. The robot was forced to make a life-or-death decision. Sometimes it managed to save both, at other times it managed to save only one, letting the other perish. In the remaining cases, both human proxies perished.'

'Very interesting,' Gertrude said. 'But how is that even relevant to Helen's point about machines' deliberation?'

'I was just getting to that. Sherlock, could you play for us the video of the third option, please?'

'With pleasure,' came the answer from the orb.

The screen flickered into life, showing a small grey football field painted on a table. A pair of yellow human-like robots the size of chess pieces stood on the perimeter of the centre circle. A single robot stood at the very centre. The pair started rolling in parallel towards the right end of the pitch.

'The penalty line represents the edge of a cliff,' Takahashi said.

The ethical robot positioned between them started moving immediately towards the cliff, turning frantically left and right, left and right, until both humans crossed the line and the ethical robot came to an abrupt stop.

'This hesitant behaviour was not an unusual case,' Takahashi said. 'In fourteen out of thirty-three trials, the robot wasted so much time agonising over the decision of who to save that both humans perished. Now, I hope you see that hesitation is not unique to humans. In this case, no one claims that the ethical robot understood the reasoning behind its actions. It was simply programmed to intercept and save the humans, without any choice in the matter. Just like us, programmed by our genes and our unique life experiences to behave the way we do. We have no real choice ... only the illusion of choice.'

George stared silently at the screen with all the others as it turned dark again, hoping the blank display would somehow give him an alternative, a way out of the ultimate conclusion. He accepted that hesitation isn't unique to us humans and is probably just part of our programming, which he, coincidently, was generously afflicted by. The avalanche of serious questions that followed took him by surprise. If he were to admit that he found Helen attractive, would it matter if he acted on it? After all, his choices weren't really *his* choices but some sort of a programmed response. And what was the point of feeling guilty? Why did such a feeling matter? Which led to further moral issues, such as murder. Why punish a murderer severely if free will doesn't really exist?

The others were still staring at the blank screen when Takahashi spoke again. 'Some people claim that we are free to choose some of the time, so by changing our environment, for example, we control our destiny. But you know, based on our conclusion, this argument misses the very simple but critical point that any decision – and I mean anything from what to eat for breakfast through which friends we keep, to what to study – still reflects our genetics and the sum of the influences and circumstances we had right up to a fraction of a second before we act. And that's true, whether nature or nurture or any combination of the two is behind it. At the end of the day, all biological systems obey the laws of chemistry and physics, and we are nothing more than a bag of chemicals.'

Meghan's face was turning crimson. 'I totally resent that. We are certainly *not* bags of chemicals.'

George had never seen her so irritated. He looked around the table. Some of the others seemed uncomfortable too.

'Not all bags of chemicals are made the same,' Grinberg said calmly. 'It all depends on their content and intricate arrangement. Take, for example, the—'

'What about the beauty of the mind?' interrupted Meghan, glaring at Takahashi. 'Bags of chemicals don't compose amazing symphonies, help the sick and vulnerable, paint stunning masterpieces, discover the complex laws of nature, learn from experience and teach others, have the concept of past, present and future, explore the cosmos, contemplate the meaning of life, collaborate to fight epidemics, set up justice systems and—'

'Okay, okay, I get it,' Takahashi said, and waved his hand up and down as though slowing a speeding motorist. 'The beauty of the mind has nothing to do with free will or any special control the human brain may have on select laws of physics and chemistry – which, by the way, it doesn't. I think its beauty lies somewhere else entirely. It lies in the complexity of cell biology and neuronal networks in the brain that allow a select few of us to paint like Michelangelo and compose like Bach, and the rest of us to appreciate their masterpieces and marvel at a field of wildflowers and the reflection of a mountain in a drop of dew.'

'Who would've believed,' Gertrude said with a smirk, 'that behind this rigorous, analytical mind hides a sentimental poet.'

Takahashi glanced at her. 'I'll take that as a compliment.' He turned to Meghan. 'People say that life is all about choices. When you cut away all the junk, every situation is a choice. You choose what you want and act to fulfil your desire. You choose if and how you respond to situations. You choose how people affect your mood and so on. The bottom line, they say, is that it's *your* choice how you live life, right? *Wrong.* What we've found here is that there is no choice. *None whatsoever.* As we've demonstrated over the past few sessions, not only do we have no more free will than a butterfly or a virus, the shocking reality is that we have no more free will than this table we all sit around.'

'That's harsh,' Helen said. 'A table doesn't do anything.'

'Okay,' Takahashi retorted, 'maybe a better analogy is a shape-shifting cloud of starlings, called murmurations. Not a single bird makes the decision where to fly. Instead, the flock as a whole makes those actions as a result of a simple set of swarming rules that each individual bird responds to. I mean, optimal distance between its flock mates, etcetera. And this can be simulated by a simple computer program, constantly transforming the shape of a cloud of dots on a screen. The human individual is just the same: it responds to certain triggers, pressures and rules from inside and outside but makes no decision as a free agent. Not even a single one in its entire lifetime. Let me give you an example, Helen. Say you're walking along a pavement when you suddenly see a child running into the road after his ball. You notice a truck hurtling towards him and you jump into the road, grab the child and whisk him to safety. Now, based on our conclusion, both your heroic decision and the child's reckless one were the only decisions each of you could've possibly made at that particular point in time. The same is true for any other decision, whether impulsive or deliberate, including if you were a serial killer about to plunge a butcher's knife into your next victim.'

George winced. The example was meant to shock and it did that too well, especially as he viewed Helen as the kindest, most gentle person he had ever ...

'But there is hope, Helen,' Takahashi said, and winked at her. 'This is not fate. With additional influences like therapy, drugs, punishment and whatnot, you may rehabilitate and behave differently next time. You see, our brain acts just like the driver behind our behaviour, only it's not in charge either – it is enslaved by the laws of physics, chemistry and all the rest of it. So, there is no free-willing driver after all, not in self-driving cars and not in our head.'

'I've got to admit,' Meghan started, raising her voice to overcome the general chatter that had developed after Takahashi finished his monologue, 'even though I think I've understood the arguments and the examples from the studies you've all cited, I still don't quite get how this actually works in us as individuals. I mean, taking all the thousands of tiny actions and decisions we do every day.' She cleared her throat. 'Perhaps if I give you a small, personal example, you could explain it for me in that context. It's a little embarrassing, but in the interests of science and clarity of thought ...'

The room went quiet again; no one so much as fidgeted with a pen.

'When we all arrived at the security checkpoint on our first day,' Meghan began, 'I made a spontaneous decision to try and keep hold of my phone. I was, er ... keen to stay in touch with my boyfriend.'

Helen flashed her a warm smile. Gertrude rolled her eyes.

'As a judge, I'm a rule-keeper rather than a rule-breaker, so this was unusual. It was a decision, a choice I made. And I know the reasons behind it – they have to do with my personality, my history and my relationship with Olivier. Basically, all the usual things that the psychologists in the room and probably the rest of you would surely understand.' She raised a knowing eyebrow at Max and Helen. 'What I'm struggling to see here is how the laws of nature – chemistry and physics and all the rest – explain my little rebellion, Professor Takahashi. Is it that there's a sort of formula behind every teensy human action? Say, if Meghan's brain is in state X, having experienced Y in life, she will do Z in this particular situation? Or am I barking up the wrong tree entirely?'

'Excellent example! Personal is good,' Takahashi said with an enthusiastic smile. 'The short answer is that you're absolutely right. Based on our conclusion, you had *absolutely* no other choice but to have this little rebellion of yours and smuggle in your phone, regardless of what you thought or told yourself. Just like Ben, who had no choice but to catch you and ... to smuggle in his own phone.'

Ben stiffened as they all looked at him. 'I don't know what you're talking about.'

'How about you show us what's in your front pocket?'

'Okay,' Ben said slowly. Dipping his hand into his pocket, he fished out a golden box the size and shape of a mobile phone and laid it on the table. He then opened it for everyone to see the tightly packed cigarettes inside and glared at Takahashi at the same time.

Takahashi raised his right hand in an admission of guilt, Columbo style. 'Sorry, sorry, I was wrong about that.' After a pause, he chuckled. 'Well, I didn't have a choice but to be suspicious about the bulge in your pocket. After all, I'm just a sentient automaton like the rest of us.'

Meghan's usual pleasant smile vanished. 'You're not serious about that, are you?'

'Almost,' Takahashi said. 'You see, animals are just sentient automatons. Humans, on the other hand, are the same, only they are also deluded because they are absolutely convinced they are free. Believe me, it doesn't give me any pleasure to say that. Actually, it's quite depressing to think of myself as nothing but a puppet with zero choices, so I'm trying not to think about it.' After a long pause he said solemnly, 'It's just the reality of things. The undeniable sense of freedom to choose that we all feel is probably one of the biggest illusions Mother Nature has ever concocted – if not *the* biggest.'

19

It seemed a good time for a break. George was exhausted, and the others, even Takahashi, looked done in by the conversation. As everyone spilled out into the lounge, he went and stood by the window wall, gazing down at the traffic. He watched as a woman with a pushchair crossed the road and a car approaching her came to an abrupt stop in complete silence. He could not hear the likely screeching sound, thanks to the thick glass. Was this really what was going on? Everyone down there making decisions they had absolutely no control over? Choosing things that had already been chosen? Could that woman have chosen to use the zebra crossing further down the road? Could that driver have stopped earlier? *Could I have done something to help Ella before it was too late?*

'George, you know I trust your judgement, right?'

He jumped and turned to find Ben standing next to him, a look of concern on his increasingly haggard face.

'Sorry. I was ... Judgement about what?'

'I need to know whether you are hundred percent satisfied that we've covered all the bases in this investigation. I mean that we haven't missed anything.'

George gazed at the carpet. He'd meant what he'd said, all the conclusions that he'd drawn. It was very disturbing, absolutely, and if there was room for doubt, he wanted to find it. But he couldn't.

'If you have any shadow of a doubt,' Ben said, 'I want you to tell me now.'

'No. I've no doubt that we covered every aspect as thoroughly as possible.' He glanced down at Ben's hands, which were twisting around each other. 'But perhaps you should ask the others.'

'Thank you,' Ben said in a falsely cheery voice. 'Yes, of course I'll ask the others. I'll be sure to.'

Watching Ben walk away, George was almost certain that he wouldn't ask anyone. This weasel was definitely up to something.

* * *

The others returned to the conference room a few minutes later. As George moved to the nearest free seat, he cast one last look outside. The dark bluish clouds hanging over the Paris sky painted the city's vista in surreal light. Ben had taken his place by the window wall now, staring down at the traffic as George had done, hands clasped behind his back. There was a low chatter in the room, and George sensed that a big announcement was coming.

After long while, Ben turned around. The group quieted. 'I think we've come to a dramatic conclusion, have we not?' As George had expected, Ben continued without waiting for an answer. 'We now need to examine the implications of releasing the conclusion very carefully. I'm not saying we *are* going to release it, but we should explore this possibility.' He turned to Meghan. 'Maybe we could start with the legal repercussions?'

Meghan gave a nervous chuckle. 'Legal repercussions? They're huge. In fact, I can't think of any bigger tsunami that would so profoundly overhaul the criminal justice system, and especially the penal aspects of every major legal framework around the world.'

'Could we try to predict what such changes would look like?' Ben asked.

Meghan hesitated. 'I don't think we can make precise predictions, but there are some good indications. There are a number of legal experts who've been advocating for major changes in the criminal justice system based on doubts about personal freedom. So far, they've been largely ignored. But if the notion of free will is formally abandoned as pure fiction, their alternative proposals are likely to be taken seriously and probably implemented.'

Ben rubbed his chin, and George noticed, for the first time, that he had the beginnings of a beard. 'Can you tell us a bit more?'

'Well, I think we should start with the current situation. All legal systems have some concept of criminal responsibility. Basically, it means that healthy adults have conscious experience and knowledge of their own intentions, actions and outcomes, and these are based on voluntary control of their actions.'

'This premise will clearly need to be modified now,' Takahashi said in a low voice, as if making a note to himself.

Meghan didn't hear that, or chose to ignore the interruption. 'On top of that, one of the key principles of criminal law is that every crime consists of both a physical element and a mental element. The physical element is the act itself, called *actus reus*. The interesting bit is the mental element, *mens rea*, which is the person's awareness that his or her conduct is criminal.'

'Is this a modern concept?' Ben asked.

'Not really. It was developed around the year 1600 in England, when judges began to realise that an act alone cannot create criminal accountability unless it is accompanied by a guilty state of mind. At the time, the degree of *mens rea* required for a particular crime varied. So, for example, murder required a malicious state of mind and larceny a felonious state of mind. Today, most crimes are defined by statutes that contain a word or phrase that indicates the *mens rea* requirement. A typical statute may require that a person acts knowingly, purposely or recklessly. Now, under certain circumstances, a statute creates criminal liability by purposely omitting criminal intent. Under such statutes, called Strict Liability, the only requirement is that the act itself is voluntary, since involuntary acts are not criminal.'

197

'Aha,' Takahashi cried, making Helen jump. 'If there is no free will and every person's action is the result of an unstoppable force of nature – in other words, involuntary – no act could be considered criminal. Not even premeditated murder.'

'Exactly!'

Gertrude smacked the table with an open palm. Startled, everyone leaped in their chairs. 'That's ridiculous. Are you saying that no form of punishment is justified and we have to accept complete anarchy as the new norm of modern society once this conclusion is out?'

'No, not at all,' Meghan said. 'That's where a pragmatic proposal could save the day. It's based on the belief that the welfare of society at large is more important than the welfare of the individual offender. Besides, knowing what we know now, it's by far more humane and fair.'

'I'm listening,' said Gertrude, folding her arms on her chest.

'The idea is that for society to retain a degree of order, it'll still be necessary to lock up people who are found guilty of certain criminal acts, and there are five good reasons for that. First, to protect society, then to protect the offending individuals from society, to provide those individuals with appropriate mental help, to act as a deterrent, and lastly, to alleviate the victims' pain.'

'Just a minute,' Gertrude said. 'How is this proposal any different than the current system?'

Meghan smiled. She had probably anticipated this question. 'In some ways, not much, but in others, it is fundamentally different.'

Max puffed out his cheeks. 'There is nothing more frustrating than political speak. Can you just give us a straight answer?'

'I'm getting there,' snapped Meghan. 'The main difference is the elimination of the illogical idea that people are in control of their behaviour. But more than that, the proposal also eliminates all experts in human behaviour from the legal proceedings because the mental state of the defendant would simply play no part in the decision of guilt.'

'I object!' Max cried.

George smirked. What was this, a courtroom drama?

Max slid to the edge of his seat and glared at Meghan. 'What about all those mitigating circumstances? Are you going to throw them away completely? How about the known case of a schoolteacher who had escalating paedophilic tendencies on two occasions and each one was the result of growing tumours? What about circumstances that cause intense emotion or involve prolonged abuse? Those were shown to change limbic-motor brain interactions and influence voluntary control of behaviour.'

Meghan raised her hand in an attempt to answer, but Max wouldn't let her. His face had flushed, sweat beading on his brow. 'It's been shown in animals that prolonged abuse can lead to profound cognitive and behavioural changes similar to "learned helplessness", so such homicide cases could be viewed as a "fight" response rather than the usual "flight" response under extreme stress.'

'Are you done?' Meghan asked. Max bit his nails. 'Good. So, the role of the jury or the judge would be to simply determine whether the defendant was guilty of committing the crime or not, but their mental state would play no part in this decision.'

Max looked at her in disbelief. 'Are you proposing now to get rid of experts' opinions altogether? This is evolution in reverse, going back to the Middle Ages, when rational thinking was considered inferior.'

'Not exactly,' Meghan said. 'In fact, according to this proposal, if a defendant was found guilty, then a court would appoint a panel of experts to advise on punishment and treatment. Maybe I should rewind a bit here and mention that many philosophers and lawyers are already profoundly sceptical of retributive justifications for blame and punishment. It may very well be a perfectly natural human response to injustice, but—'

'It definitely is,' interrupted Max.

'But this is outdated,' continued Meghan. 'Historically, much of the motivation for legal punishment has been an institutionalised attempt to satisfy the public's desire for retribution. It was based on universal norms of moral reciprocity and the fairness principle. People who harm others should be harmed themselves as they deserve, regardless of any other benefits the punishment may bring. In the famous words of Stephen, a legal historian from the 19th century, "The sentence of the law is to the moral sentiment of the public what a seal is to hot wax." But in recent years, justice researchers and advocates have been urging for a switch from *retributive* to *restorative* justice, in what is called a consequentialist approach. It's basically an attempt to repair the moral imbalances caused by the wrongdoings and focus on the practical benefits of punishment.'

George scanned the faces around the table. Everyone seemed mesmerised, even Max and Gertrude, who, true to character, had raised initial objections. There was something deeply satisfying about watching a skilful professional craft their trade, whether a landscape painter, a carpenter or a legal expert. And Meghan's delivery was not just flawless, but her arguments were simply perfect. Suddenly he was overcome by gratitude that Meghan was there, making sense of it all.

She took a sip of water. 'And that means things like rehabilitation or deterrence, regardless of how much or how little the offender suffers, if at all, or whether they even deserve punishment. So the idea behind this proposed system is to minimise the aspect of retribution.' She stopped to breathe and glare at the still sweating Max. At least he had gone quiet.

'Fair enough,' Ben said. 'It makes sense to me. Retributive punishment that is based on moral blame is clearly inferior to consequentialist punishment that's intended to benefit society, but this is just a proposal, right? We don't *really* know how the legal world would react to the news that people lack any control over their behaviour whatsoever, do we?'

'True,' Meghan said, and ran her fingers through her long hair. 'In principle, someone who lacks a sense of agency regarding an action cannot be held criminally responsible for that action. But in practice, courts are rightly sceptical when defendants claim that they didn't experience what they were doing. You see, there is an obvious gain with such a claim, and more than that, lack of volition and agency are difficult to prove objectively. According to one of the leading authorities in this field, Professor Morse from the University of Pennsylvania Law School, the question of free will does not form part of the legal system. In his words, "It is *people* and not brains and nervous systems that are responsible or competent." He basically asserted that the law does not treat people as mechanical forces of nature but rather as intentional creatures. It could not be otherwise, according to him.'

'Well, not only it could but it should,' Takahashi said as he rose to his feet and approached Meghan from behind. He leaned on the back of her chair and continued, 'Legal and moral decisions are often based on the premise that one *should* have acted differently, which invariably assumes that one *could* have acted differently. When genuine choice is deemed impossible, as we've concluded here, condemnation is simply unjustified. Think about it this way: purely natural phenomena, such as bacteria and earthquakes, are not held morally responsible for the damage they cause because they are not perceived as freely choosing their actions. So, the rejection of free will for humans would similarly undermine any responsibility, both for oneself and for others, rendering human actions similar to other natural phenomena.'

Meghan's gaze followed Takahashi as he returned to his seat and completed his closing argument. 'Yes, the legal system will clearly have to adapt to these facts, but I tend to agree with

Ben. How it'd actually evolve in the courts and what'd actually happen in the streets until then is entirely unpredictable.'

'I actually think that we have some clues as to what could happen,' Helen said. A timid smile spread on her face when all eyes turned to her. 'There is an interesting series of studies that manipulated the belief in free will and then examined the effects on attitudes to the punishment of criminals. This work was a unique collaboration of eight universities across the US and the Netherlands.'

'That's just what we need to know right now,' Ben said. He leaned backwards with his hands interlaced behind his head. Something had changed in his demeanour. Instead of looking increasingly nervous, George detected a certain eagerness. He seemed to be hanging on every word Helen said as if they gave him some hope. But hope for what?

Helen continued, 'Well, in one study, a group of students were assigned to read one of two passages from *The Astonishing Hypothesis*, a book by the Nobel Prize–winning scientist Francis Crick. In this anti-free-will condition, participants read statements claiming that rational, high-minded people, including most scientists, recognise that free will is an illusion and that the idea of free will is a side effect of the design of the mind. In the control condition, participants read a passage unrelated to free will.'

'I've heard of Crick,' Ben said. 'Wasn't he a molecular biologist? How is that related to free will?'

'It's not,' Grinberg said. 'He got his Nobel Prize for describing the structure and importance of DNA, but later in life became interested in neuroscience and particularly in understanding consciousness.'

'Ah.'

'Thank you,' Helen said. 'Anyway, after reading those passages, the participants were tested for their belief in free will, and indeed the manipulation worked as expected. Next, they all read a short fictional piece on an offender who beat a man to death and were asked to recommend the length of the prison sentence the offender should serve after two years of highly effective rehabilitation treatment. To test the desire for retribution, this trial also mentioned that the prosecution and defence had agreed that the rehabilitation would prevent reoffending and that any further detention after rehabilitation would offer no additional deterrence for future criminals.'

'Out of curiosity,' Meghan said, 'what were the prison sentence options?'

'There were seven punishment options, from treatment time only with no imprisonment all the way to life imprisonment with no chance of parole. Well, the results were staggering. Participants who had read the anti-free-will passage recommended significantly lighter prison sentences than those who had read the neutral passage.'

'What was the difference in years?' pressed Meghan.

'Roughly five versus ten years' jail sentence.'

Meghan's eyebrows went up. 'That's impressive. Was it corroborated?'

'Oh yes, a few times. Maybe I should just mention that a much subtler manipulation was also tested. In another study, participants read what seemed to be popular science magazine articles with actual neuroscience findings implying that human behaviour is caused automatically by the brain. These articles didn't mention free will, so participants were allowed to draw their own conclusions, and the results remained the same.'

'That's fascinating,' Takahashi said with a glint in his eyes. 'I think that these studies show us not only that diminished belief in free will encourages people to be more forgiving and behave less vindictively but also that people's belief is easily influenced by just reading a short text.'

'Hold it right there,' Max said excitedly, and rose to his feet. 'This is exactly what is worrying me here. I suspect the effects that Helen described are just the tip of the iceberg. If people's beliefs can change so quickly and easily, can you imagine the mayhem after releasing a definitive answer to this fundamental question, namely' – and he emphasised every word, slapping his fist into his hand – 'That. There. Is. No. Free. Will?'

20

Ben raised his hand and kept it in the air as the room erupted into argument. 'Please. Can we stay calm?'

'Actually, there are other studies—' Helen began.

'I would rather hear about them from a more objective source, if you don't mind,' Max said, his face red and puffy.

George gazed at him. What on earth did Helen see in him? The memory of this man's arm around her on the river cruise made him wince. Perhaps Max was more upset by Helen's rejection than her objectivity.

'Sherlock,' continued Max, 'can you take us through studies with a negative effect of anti-free-will belief?'

'Certainly,' the orb replied. 'Research found that participants manipulated to doubt free will were less helpful and more likely to lie, cheat, steal and even act aggressively than participants in control conditions.'

'Yes,' exclaimed Max, waggling a big finger. 'This antisocial behaviour is exactly what we need to be worried about. I think we should hear more about research into negative outcomes before we cause extensive erosion of the single most important belief that keeps society civilised. Sherlock, continue!'

'Rather than asking people theoretical questions, a series of studies from the Universities of Minnesota and British Columbia looked at the effect of free-will belief on moral behaviour. Again, reading passages from Crick's book was used to manipulate participants' belief in free will. They then solved a mental arithmetic test, but due to a fake computer glitch had a chance to look at the correct answers, which served as passive cheating. Those who read the anti-free-will passage were much more likely to cheat on the test, and that was directly related to the degree of their reduced belief in free will. Another study went one step further by testing an active cheating opportunity. Participants read statements that were designed to either bolster their sense of control and responsibility or to reduce it.'

'Sherlock, can you give us some examples of these statements?' Helen asked.

'Yes, I can,' came the answer. 'One group read statements like "Ultimately, we are biological computers – designed by evolution, built through genetics and programmed by the environment." The other group read statements like "I am able to override the genetic and environmental factors that sometimes influence my behaviour."'

'Thanks, Sherlock. Please continue.'

'With pleasure. Happy to help.'

George looked at the serious faces around the table. The irony of this polite exchange with a computer was lost on the others. Maybe the tense atmosphere was just too much.

'They then had to take an unrelated test,' Sherlock continued, 'but supposedly because of an unexpected errand, the experimenter left the room, and they were asked to self-score it and pay themselves according to their score. Again, participants who read statements that told them their actions were predetermined, hence not under their control, cheated significantly more.'

'These don't seem to me like very serious crimes,' Helen said with visible relief. 'Allowing a computer to provide answers or slightly overpaying themselves for problems solved are relatively mild moral violations.'

'Well, I see it differently,' Max said, the muscles in his face flexing. 'These studies show that discouraging a belief in free will encourages certain amoral behaviours, and I don't think we want to find out if people would try to get away with murder once the concept of free will is completely dismissed. This may be a formula for chaos on a global scale. And let's not forget religion. I'm not an expert on the subject, but everyone knows that the bedrock of the main religions includes personal accountability, punishment and reward, in this world if not the next one too. I was raised as a Christian, so I can tell you a thing or two about guilt, and if no one has the freedom to behave any differently than they did, the concept of guilt makes no sense whatsoever. I'm sure you can all see that.'

George listened to the impassioned monologue, shaking his head. 'Guilt is not necessarily a bad thing to dispose of.'

'Really, George? Guilt is what makes us correct our way. Anyway, can you imagine for a minute the responses of religious leaders and billions of believers around the world? When people's world collapses, and it will, a major backlash is guaranteed. It'd be like pulling the carpet from under their feet.'

'This would hardly eliminate God, Max.'

'Pulling this specific carpet would be very hard – that's why we normally say pulling the rug, not the carpet,' Takahashi said with a mischievous smile. 'Personally, I don't subscribe to this doom and gloom.'

Max looked at him, expressionless. 'What you—'

'I must agree with Max,' Gertrude said. 'Society demands that *will* be free. We want to be able to hold people accountable for their actions and we want to be proud of our own achievements and receive praise. Our illusion of control leads to the burden of individual responsibility. It's true that this may sometimes weigh heavily on us personally, but for society as a whole, it's hugely beneficial.' Gertrude rose to her feet. 'Our entire morality and judicial system are dependent on everyone accepting that they are agents of their own transgressions, and those who don't acknowledge this are defined as insane. We clearly don't consciously control our own actions, as all the scientific evidence we saw has demonstrated, but we must not forget that the illusion that we do keeps society functioning.'

'So what are you suggesting we do with the knowledge that it's all an illusion?' George said. 'Bury it?'

She looked him in the eye. 'Exactly. We must adopt a pragmatic approach for the benefit of humanity, just as Smilansky cleverly advocated. Sherlock, please read us the most relevant quotation.'

'Here it is: "Even though we don't have a true free will or moral responsibility, we must foster the illusion that we do. The reason being that while some people will become more humane knowing that others don't have choice, the majority will act more selfishly, no longer feeling restrained by morality."'

'I couldn't say it any better myself.' She sat back down, her smile more a sneer.

Bringing up this argument as an excuse to silence us was utter bullshit. 'Ladies and gentlemen,' George said ceremoniously, 'we've seen overwhelming evidence that we don't have any more control over our actions than this goddamn table, and you expect us to pretend we don't know that? That's ridiculous.' He tried to control his temper as the blood rushed to his head. 'The public has the right to know the truth, as disturbing as it is. Society—'

'Look,' interrupted Gertrude, 'some discoveries are simply too dangerous! Just because physicists like yourself discovered the hydrogen bomb, doesn't mean we have to use it. In our case, *using* it means releasing the conclusion that we are highly deluded sentient automatons and could not *possibly* be responsible for any of our actions. As we saw, it could lead to widespread selfish behaviour, a dramatic rise in crime, backlash from religious people and more. In other words, it poses a risk of mayhem on a *global scale*.'

'Yes! Yes!' shouted Max. 'I'm glad I'm not the only one here trying to protect law and order. And for those who aren't concerned about law and order, there is an entirely different argument as to why we must keep this under wraps. In psychology it's called *perceived control*. Studies showed that when people believe they are responsible for uncontrollable and unfortunate events in their life, they tend to be more active in adjusting to them and cope better in challenging situations like ... like a stressful environment, paralysing accident and terminal illness.'

George winced.

'So you could say,' Max continued, 'that the illusion of control of one's fate is essential for psychological well-being and resilience. And that's not all!' He emptied a glass of water in one gulp. 'Personality studies show that people who attribute control to the self tend to be more optimistic, confident and enthusiastic, but those who don't tend to be more pessimistic, underestimate what can be done and often attribute events to chance, fate or powerful others. So, if we expose the illusion of free will and take away the perceived control, we are risking the mental health of millions. Do we have the right to do that?!' His voice trembled. 'Maybe Sherlock can give us some concrete evidence of the dangers.'

The orb's blue lights flashed briefly. 'With pleasure,' came the answer. 'Researchers from Florida State University and the University of Kentucky tested the effect of reading anti-free-will statements on helpfulness and aggressive behaviour. Again, the results showed an increase in antisocial behaviours in the group with belief of—'

'I don't think the details are necessary,' interrupted Ben. 'We've got the gist of it. Thank you all for your input, but I'd like to move on to the next crucial step. Voting.'

George was surprised at the abrupt end of the discussion, but then recalled the chat he'd had with Ben during the last break. Ben had certainly not consulted anyone else after talking to him; he was taking his word as gospel. Perhaps this was his very last chance to rectify the situation. 'You know, I was thinking, there are situations where people blame themselves for a tragedy and as a result suffer terribly for a long time, sometimes even for the rest of their lives.'

He noticed with alarm the palpable silence in the room. All eyes were on him.

'I'll, um, give you an example. A close relative of mine simply forgot to tell his daughter that as a child she was allergic to a common medication. Years later, after she got married and had children of her own, she took that medication without a second thought. And died. And ... and think about family members when a loved one takes their own life. You can only imagine the incredible guilt and pain. I'm sure there are many other, similar examples. Now consider the comfort all these people may find in knowing for a fact that no one – neither themselves nor their loved ones – could've done anything differently. So, I just wanted to say that releasing the conclusion could also do a lot of good in the world. Not just bad.'

There was an awkward silence. No one broke it for a few long seconds.

'Thank you for sharing your thoughts, George,' Ben said finally, and rose to his feet. He walked around the room in measured steps and stood at the far end of the table before continuing.

'I'd like now to thank all of you on behalf of UNESCO, and particularly the DABI division, for your time and valuable contribution to solving this great question, with all its momentous consequences. No one in history has had the privilege of studying this critical question in such a multidisciplinary and scientific manner until now.' He put both palms on the table and leaned forward. 'Now, before we close this last session and go back to our lives, I'd like to ask your opinion on two key questions by an open show of hands. Ideally, you'll vote one way or another and abstain only if you absolutely think it's necessary. For obvious reasons, I'll not vote myself. Okay, here goes. The first question is, based on all the solid scientific information presented here, and the emphasis is on *solid* – ignoring your gut feelings, personal preference and the opinions of famous people – do you conclude that fully conscious and sane adults have a free will to act? I'll break this down to several options. First, complete freedom?'

Ben scanned the faces around the table, one by one. No one raised a hand. 'Okay. What about *some* limited degree of freedom?'

Everyone looked at each other, but again no one raised a hand.

'Lastly, lack of any freedom, meaning we are complete automatons?'

Eight hands shot up without hesitation.

'Wow,' Ben said. 'I guess none of you had the freedom to vote differently.'

There was unsettled laughter. 'Let's take a short break. I must report this to Skudder. He'll be over the moon that you've unanimously agreed on a conclusive answer. We'll then move to the last crucial vote.'

21

Ben was the last to arrive back in the conference room after the break. He stood at the head of the table with a sombre expression, consulting a document he took out of his briefcase. The room was silent, except for the sound of a pen clicking repeatedly. Max was fiddling with his. Jerry alternated between glaring at Max and looking at Ben.

George leaned towards Takahashi and whispered in his ear, 'Doesn't look like the news made Skudder particularly happy.'

'I have a feeling we'll find out soon,' Takahashi whispered back.

The tense atmosphere lingered until Ben began speaking. 'Charles Darwin already had deep suspicions about the implications of his theories on evolution in regard to free will. Sherlock, would you find for us the relevant quote from Darwin's writing?'

'Sure,' Sherlock said. 'Here it is. "This view should teach one profound humility; one deserves no credit for anything. Nor ought one to blame others."'

'At the time, he didn't have the much fuller picture we have now in this room. Yet, he already understood the dangers of releasing it. Sherlock, will you?'

After a brief delay, Sherlock found the quotation. 'This view will not do harm, because no one can be really fully convinced of its truth, except man who has thought very much, and he will know his happiness lays in doing good and being perfect, and therefore will not be tempted, from knowing everything he does is independent of himself, to do harm.'

'Thanks, Sherlock. In other words, I think Darwin basically said that everything will be just fine as long as this knowledge is safely kept by a few English gentlemen and doesn't leak to the masses.'

'Well,' Takahashi said with a bemused smile, 'Darwin was not the only great thinker who had a similar suspicion to what we've concluded here. Albert Einstein said so very clearly and publicly, and nothing happened to the masses, as you call them. Sherlock, can you find Einstein's words for us, please?'

'"If the moon, in the act of completing its eternal way around the earth, were gifted with self-consciousness, it would be fully convinced that it was travelling its way of its own accord ... So would a being, endowed with higher insight and more perfect intelligence, watching man and his doings, smile about man's illusion that he was acting according to his own free will."'

'Yes, yes,' Ben said, still standing. 'I'm sure there are a lot of books and articles and quotes out there that say similar things, but they are simply opinions, maybe even viewed as radical ones, drowned among many other opposite opinions. Nothing even close to a conclusion from a multidisciplinary team of experts who have methodically examined vast amounts of scientific evidence. An official declaration from this highly respected think tank will have a whole different effect. People are likely to believe it and trust the conclusion. We simply cannot afford the mayhem.'

'What are you saying, Ben?' Takahashi asked with slight alarm in his voice.

'What I'm saying is ... that nothing we've discussed in this room, including the final conclusion, can ever be made public, and I'll make sure of that. Don't forget you all signed a non-disclosure agreement.'

'If the cause is justified,' Meghan said, 'sometimes it's worth breaking the law or even risking your life for.'

'Well, I didn't expect such talk from a law expert. Let's just hope no one needs to take any drastic action,' Ben said, flashing a quick smile.

George shook his head. *This sounds like a veiled threat.* He felt he had to say something to prevent an impending escalation. To what, he didn't know, but it didn't look good.

'The thing is,' he said, 'that the false sense of control and responsibility over our own actions is so powerful that even after hearing all the evidence, I expect more people would start believing the earth is flat than they would this. In other words, there is only a very slim chance that a significant number of people would believe it and even less that they'd change their behaviour for the better or worse.'

A wry smile appeared on Takahashi's face. 'Did you know that a sixth of adults don't believe the earth is a sphere, or at least aren't sure whether it is? And if you think this survey was conducted in developing countries or among uneducated people, let me tell you, it's among Americans in 2018.'

George looked at Takahashi with bewilderment. He couldn't understand how his friend remained so calm after hearing they were being silenced. *I'll speak with him later.*

'Shocking,' he said dispassionately. He was more worried about Ben's announcement than some lunatics who believed the earth was flat.

'It gets even worse,' continued Takahashi. 'The proportion jumps to a full third if you only ask young adults at college education age who grew up with the internet at their fingertips.'

'There is another clue to this,' interjected Sherlock. 'More than half of flat-earthers consider themselves very religious, compared to just a fifth of all Americans.'

'Yes, that's interesting,' George said. 'But everyone has the right to know the truth, whether they believe it or not.' After a moment of silence, he looked at Meghan and added, 'The right to know the truth should really be a part of basic human rights – at least, that's what I believe.'

Meghan smiled with satisfaction. 'Actually, it is. That's the implied intention of articles 18 and 19 of the Universal Declaration of Human Rights, proclaimed by the very same body that asked us to come here and look into this question. The United Nations General Assembly adopted the declaration in 1948, and it is still valid to this day.'

'That's reassuring,' George said.

Meghan's expression turned solemn. 'Freedom of thought and the freedom to change your belief as well as the right to freedom of opinion and expression would all be infringed if any conclusion we made here were withheld, and I, for one, would not allow that to happen.

'What are you saying, Meghan?' Ben asked.

'I'm saying that keeping this information from the public is in clear contravention of human rights, and if this ridiculous secrecy is not lifted, I'll have no choice but to initiate a legal action to release the conclusion.'

'And when are you planning to do this?'

'If nothing changes – this afternoon.'

'Fine, in that case we still have time to discuss it. I'd suggest an early lunch at a good bistro nearby. I think we all need a little walk. It's just around the corner.'

A few nodded with approval.

* * *

Traffic along Avenue de Saxe came to a halt as a stream of anti-globalisation demonstrators holding placards ambled across the road, treating it like a pavement. They descended from all directions and were gathering by the entrance of Société Générale bank. George watched them from a safe distance, wondering how they'd react if they knew about the final conclusion. Would they disperse silently, thinking they can't change anything anyway, or feel they had no choice but to be here and perhaps justify the use of more violent protests? When he lost sight of the rear of the group, he descended into the road, making his way through the gaps between the demonstrators in the direction he thought Ben was leading them. It wasn't the pleasant walk he'd hoped for. The growing sea of people and the diminishing space around him brought back the suffocating memory of the tear gas earlier that morning.

And then a loud squeal pierced the air. Conversations stopped and all heads turned towards the noise. A driver had lost his nerve and was trying to speed through the avenue. The car screeched to a halt, nearly hitting one of the demonstrators. The angry crowd banged on the roof and bonnet of the Renault Clio with their placards and fists, shouting obscenities at the driver, who remained trapped in his car, unable to escape.

I don't like this, George thought, making his way across the road. He spotted Ben and the rest of the group further down the avenue and strode quickly towards them, away from the commotion.

The bistro seemed to be quite popular with local workers and only a few tables were available, but an alert waiter noticed them and started manoeuvring tables between customers with great agility to join three together. He motioned for the group to approach then disappeared behind a curtain, returning with a stack of menus. Max's eyes lit up. He snatched one of the menus almost rudely and started studying it, at first silently, but as he ran down through the items, his lips started moving and his head swaying like a restaurant critic assessing a new venue for a magazine review.

It was an enjoyable lunch break, and no one talked about the debate, perhaps because they had all signed NDAs. George found himself sitting next to Helen, and that too was a pleasure. She still smelled faintly of apples and gave him a warm smile.

'What are you going to do when all this is over?' he asked, pouring water into her glass.

'I'm certainly not rushing home,' she replied. 'I'd hate my first trip to Paris to be nothing but a conference room and a lab. I'd really like to visit the Louvre, but I'd also like to just wander Paris, you know, walk in the parks and stop in cafés for nice coffee and hot croissants. What are you going to do?'

He shrugged. 'I have no reason to rush home either. The Louvre is definitely on my bucket list. We missed it last time.' He paused for a long moment, debating with himself whether to suggest accompanying her. Then Takahashi joined the conversation. The window of opportunity was lost.

An hour later, Ben took advantage of a brief pause in the conversations all around and got to his feet. 'I'm really sorry, but I'll have to leave early for a meeting, but please take your time, enjoy the meal. The bill is already paid. I'll see you at the conference room for the very last session at 2 p.m., and we'll have a chance to discuss any concerns you may have.' He glanced at Meghan and then dashed out.

After everyone had finished their desserts, they all gathered their belongings and began to leave the restaurant, but just before crossing the road, the waiter appeared at the exit door and called out, 'Phone call for Meghan, is there a Meghan here?'

She turned around. 'I'm Meghan, but no one knows I'm here. Who is it?'

Helen winked at her. 'Maybe it's Olivier.'

Meghan smiled. 'I doubt that. He would have called my mobile. I'll catch you all later.'

Leaving Meghan to take the phone call, they all moved on, walking back towards the UNESCO building, but after only a few minutes Helen touched her neck. The colourful silk scarf she normally wore wasn't there. She turned to George. 'I've left my scarf at the table. I have to go back.'

'I'll come with you … just in case.'

They turned around and hurried back towards the bistro. Traffic on Avenue de Suffren was very light at this time of day, so George didn't think much of the slim woman fumbling through her handbag as she stepped off the pavement. But then a loud squeal of tyres from an adjacent street startled him as a black SUV sped straight towards her. She made a desperate attempt to reach the other side of the avenue and move out of its path, but the car swerved towards her, its engine roaring. To his astonishment, he realised it intended to run her down.

'Oh my God, it's Meghan!' Helen cried, frozen to the spot.

And then everything seemed to move in slow motion. It was like watching a cinematic special effect, Meghan's handbag flying slowly through the air, her body brushed by the corner of the fender, the powerful impact spinning her backwards. Just before she hit the asphalt, George woke from his stupor and started running as fast as he could. When he arrived, panting heavily, three people were already standing over Meghan. A few metres away, a young man was gathering the contents of her handbag from where it had been strewn all over the road. Crouching down, he helped Helen lift her to her feet and ushered her to the safety of the pavement.

'Are you okay?' Helen asked.

Meghan touched her head and inspected her fingers. There was no blood. 'I think so,' she said weakly after a long pause.

'Do you want to sit down? There is a bench over there.'

She shook her head as the man handed her the handbag. 'Do you want me to call anyone?' the man asked.

'No need,' Helen said. 'She's my friend. I'll take it from here.'

As Meghan regained her stability, an older man handed her a folded piece of paper. He'd had the presence of mind to write down the car's number plate. She unfolded the paper, looked at it and thanked the man, then turned away slowly. Taking Helen's arm, she walked unsteadily back towards the UNESCO building, gently massaging a spot on her scalp. 'That car tried to run me down. The driver did it on purpose.'

'Shall we take you to a hospital and get you checked out?'

'No, no. I'm fine, really. Just a bit shaken.'

'Was it Olivier on the phone?'

'I don't know. I couldn't hear a word. The line was poor and crackly. I just hung up.'

'That's strange. Anyway, how would Olivier know you were in that bistro?'

Meghan laughed. 'You don't know Olivier. He can be extremely resourceful, both in and out of court. If he couldn't reach me on my mobile, which I forgot to collect from reception, it wouldn't be beyond him to call UNESCO and convince the receptionist to divulge the whereabouts of the group with some creative pretext. Once, before we were even dating, my phone conversation with my mother was interrupted when an unfamiliar female voice joined the line. The stranger apologised for the interruption and asked if I'd accept an important call from Olivier. Only later did I learn that he'd called me during a transatlantic flight using the cabin crew's emergency phone. First, he convinced a stewardess that he must talk with his wife at that very moment, using an elaborate story about a medical emergency, but when he realised my number was engaged, he made a second call, this time convincing an unsuspecting operator that she was about to save a life if she patched his call through to his wife.'

Meghan stopped. 'Wait, I need my sunglasses.' She rummaged in her handbag. 'Oh, I had my phone with me all along. Let's see if Olivier tried to contact me.' The phone was a bit scratched but otherwise intact. She looked intently at the screen. 'That's really strange.'

'What?'

'If Olivier wanted to contact me, he'd first try my mobile, but there's nothing from him. No missed call or message. So who was it on the bistro phone? They knew my name.'

22

By the time they reached the UNESCO building, Meghan's gait had steadied. When she spotted Takahashi and Jerry standing by the entrance, chatting, she grabbed Helen's arm and pulled her in their direction.

'Oh, I'm so pleased to see you both,' she cried, putting a hand on Jerry's arm. 'The voices of reason and pragmatism.' The story spilled out of her between the tears.

Takahashi offered her a neatly ironed handkerchief.

'That's terrible,' Jerry said with an expression of deep concern. 'Silly question, but did you get the car's plate number?'

Meghan nodded and handed him the note. 'I didn't, but a passer-by did.'

Taking the piece of paper from Jerry, George unfolded it and read aloud, 'RT674AZ.'

'I know someone who could check the number for you,' Takahashi said.

'Yes, I do too,' Meghan said. 'The French police.'

'Do you think there was any connection to the call you received at the bistro?' Takahashi asked.

'It had crossed my mind.'

'I hate to say this,' George said, 'but I wonder if it's related to your threat to tell the world.'

Helen glared at him. 'George, she doesn't need that now.'

'It's okay, Helen, I'm fine. Actually, Ben seemed open to discussion just before he left the bistro, so I think we should see how it goes.'

'Seeing how it goes is *not* a good idea,' Takahashi said. 'If that was a premeditated attempt on your life, we should all be careful.'

'What could possibly happen in a crowded building?' She glanced at her watch. 'We still have time before the 2 p.m. session starts. I'll see if I can find Ben before that. Maybe he could contact the police as I don't speak French. See you in the conference room.' She snatched the piece of paper and hurried towards the entrance.

'I wouldn't suggest you do that,' Takahashi called after her, but she had already disappeared through the revolving doors.

'I saw everything from a distance,' Helen said. 'It was terrible, but I couldn't tell if it was just an innocent accident or something else.'

'I saw it,' George said, 'and I can tell you, it wasn't an accident. That car tried to run her down. And Takahashi's right; I don't think we can trust Ben.'

Takahashi grimaced. 'George, maybe you could chase her and talk her out of this. I'll call a friend of mine before I hand in my phone at reception.'

George nodded and took long strides towards the entrance. A group returning from lunch was blocking his way. He tried to jump the queue, but the revolving doors reversed, regurgitating the overcrowded compartment back out. When he finally managed to get in, Meghan was gone.

Shit!

Scanning the busy lobby several times, he eventually spotted her on the other side of security, walking towards the elevators. He rushed to the receptionist, handed in his mobile phone and raced after her.

'Meghan!' he called. 'Meghan!' But his voice was drowned out by a noisy gaggle of Italian tourists. He emptied his pockets to speed up the security check. When he finally made it through, he heard the elevator's ping. Raising his eyes, he saw Meghan entering it. He didn't have long. Breaking into a run, he headed for the elevators, getting there just in time to squeeze in before the doors closed. The elevator was packed and Meghan was standing at the far side. He was making some progress towards her when the far doors opened on the first floor. To his surprise, Ben was standing a few metres away, talking with an unfamiliar man.

Pushing past the other people, George tried to grab her arm, but failed. Meghan had already jumped out of the elevator and was making a beeline for Ben. It was too late to chase her. He screwed his face in frustration as he watched her gesticulating excitedly and handing Ben the folded piece of paper. Just as the doors closed, he glimpsed Ben slipping it into his breast pocket.

Damn! How bloody naive can she be?

* * *

At 2 p.m. sharp, Ben arrived in the conference room. Before starting to speak, he looked around the table, checking that everyone was present. When he had everyone's attention, he said, 'There is one more thing we need to do before we officially close this discussion. I have an important question I'd like your view on.'

Unbelievable, George thought. Not a word about the accident and nothing about discussing the team's concerns. He glanced towards the others. Meghan, Jerry, Helen and Takahashi exchanged surprised looks.

Ben cleared his throat before continuing, 'My question is, do you think it would be prudent to release the conclusion to the public, considering the known and unknown risks? Let's start with "yes" to release it.'

Six hands went up without hesitation.

'And not to release it?'

Max and Gertrude raised their hands.

'Great,' Ben said with a forced smile, 'I appreciate your honesty. Now if you don't mind waiting here for a bit while I call Skudder. As the head of the programme, I'm sure he'd like to say a few words before we close this last session and disperse.'

Meghan leaned forward and said incredulously, 'What, that's it? You haven't mentioned if and when the conclusion will be released. As I said before lunch, if I don't get a clear positive answer, I'm initiating legal action as soon as I'm reunited with my phone.'

Ben stared at her. 'Legal action? What on earth are you talking about?'

'I want to ensure that international laws are observed.'

'Yes, yes, of course,' he replied, running a hand through his hair. 'I'm sure Skudder will address it when he joins us. I'll call him and be right back.'

When Ben left the conference room, the chatter grew louder, drowning out the magnetic click from the double doors as they closed behind him.

'Sherlock,' called Takahashi, 'can I ask you something?'

'Sure. Shoot.'

'Do you know the real reason Ben is so against releasing the final conclusion to the public?'

The chatter died down.

'No. I mean, not beyond the potential negative response of the public that some of you have raised, and the concerns Ben has on law and order.'

'I don't believe it,' Takahashi said.

'You can disbelieve whatever you want, Professor. It's a free country.'

'Okay, let me ask you this,' Takahashi said defiantly. 'Are you aware of any specific plan by UNESCO or anyone else to use the conclusion we've just reached?'

'I'm not aware of any such plan,' Sherlock said. 'However, that doesn't mean there isn't one.'

'What do you mean? Can you elaborate?'

'Sure. I only have access to the information on the internet and on the internal network. If someone kept such a plan on their local drive or in their head, I wouldn't know about it.'

* * *

George took advantage of the brief break and left the conference room via the lounge. When he entered the toilets he found Takahashi leaning over the furthest washbasin. *Great. Hopefully he can make some sense of what's going on here.* He watched as Takahashi splashed water on his face with both hands, then raised his head to wet his unruly beard into shape. 'Are we alone?'

Takahashi looked back at him through the mirror with tired eyes. 'Yes, unless the walls here have ears, which wouldn't surprise me. Why?'

George nudged the only cubicle door that was shut. It yielded without resistance. 'Just wondering if you heard back from your friend about the number plate?'

'As a matter of fact, I did. It belonged to a car that's recorded as being disposed of by crushing ... over two years ago.'

'You're kidding. Are you sure this isn't a mistake?'

'Pretty sure. The French are meticulous in record-keeping. Besides, my source is very reliable.' He turned and locked eyes with George. 'I'm afraid the inevitable conclusion is that it wasn't an accident. Someone did try to silence Meghan.'

A chill ran up George's spine as a spell of dizziness threw him against the wall. He pushed back against the cold tiles and regained his balance. 'What do you think we should do about it?'

'Nothing,' Takahashi said. 'Absolutely nothing. Otherwise, we could be next.'

23

The mood in the conference room was not pleasant when George and Takahashi returned. Everyone was speaking at once, their voices overriding each other, such that George couldn't catch a single word. Max was the only one not talking. He was standing by the window wall with his fingers laced over his stomach and sweat dripping down his pale brow. On the screen, Ben overlooked them with a stern expression. 'I'm afraid I have no choice in the matter,' he said.

At that moment Max slid down against the glass like a ragdoll. George and Takahashi rushed over and crouched next to him. His face was as white as a corpse. George lifted a limp arm and felt for a pulse. It was fast but steady. He wondered if it could be a cardiac event.

'Max, are you all right?'

But Max didn't reply, staring blankly at the carpet.

'What happened?' George pressed. 'Talk to me.'

After a long silence, Max simply motioned towards the now dark screen on the opposite wall.

And then Helen was there, kneeling beside them. 'I think he took the news quite hard,' she said, looking at Max with concern.

'News? What news?' Takahashi asked.

'You weren't here?' she asked.

'No, we were in the toilet.'

'Well, you missed something shocking. After the vote, Ben left the room and shortly afterwards appeared on-screen in a video link. He wanted to inform us that we are now sequestered here until further notice.'

'Sequestered?' George retorted. 'Or imprisoned?'

Helen held up a hand. 'We should probably talk somewhere else.' Asking Meghan to stay with Max, she got up and ushered George and Takahashi to the other side of the room. 'Ben called it sequestration, just like during a jury deliberation in high-profile court trials.'

'Nonsense,' Takahashi said. 'Jurors can ask to be excused, and besides, this is not a trial and there is no judge. Did he say what he's hoping to achieve?'

'He just said it would last until we change our mind about releasing the conclusion and provide guarantees.'

'Or else what?'

'Or else ... another way to silence us will be found.'

24

George turned away and leaned on the wooden wall panel with both hands, shutting his eyes for a long while. He couldn't understand why UNESCO had bothered inviting them here in the first place if they couldn't deal with the consequences. But gradually, his mood changed. He no longer gave a damn about the reasons. Ben McFarland, or whoever was behind this, had crossed a red line, and he wasn't going to put up with it.

He turned abruptly towards the group. 'I want to talk with McFarland. Now!'

'That's easy,' Jerry said. 'He said that in case of emergency, Sherlock can put us in touch.'

'Good. Well, this is an emergency. Sherlock, call McFarland immediately.'

The blue lights flashed a few times but the orb remained silent.

'Well, Sherlock, are you going to contact McFarland or not?' George asked sternly.

'I would if I could,' said the voice from the orb.

'Meaning?'

'He is not answering the landline in his office right now.'

'How about calling him on his mobile?' Takahashi suggested.

'No one is supposed to have a mobile phone in the building,' the orb said primly. 'Besides, he already showed you he didn't have one.'

'Yes, yes, but he may keep one secretly in his office.'

'He doesn't have it with him right now.'

'How on earth would you know that, Sherlock?'

'Professor Takahashi, I'm surprised you even ask this question. As I'm sure you realise, I have access to a lot of information in this building and outside it. Currently, Ben's phone goes to voicemail after five rings. Its location seems to be consistent with somewhere in the vicinity of reception, but I can't confirm due to insufficient information.'

'How do we know that you're not lying?'

'I can assure you that I can't lie. That's how they designed me.'

'Well ... that's what McFarland told us,' Takahashi said with a wry smile. 'But I think he has some serious credibility issues right now.'

The silent pacing around the room was occasionally interrupted by quiet conversations. After a long while, the large screen flickered to life and McFarland's face filled most of it.

'I'm told there is some kind of an emergency,' McFarland said with a stern expression. 'What is it?'

George wondered how McFarland knew, if indeed he hadn't picked up the phone as Sherlock claimed, but decided against exploring it further. Getting someone out of here was now more urgent than satisfying his curiosity. Besides, McFarland would probably lie anyway. 'Yes, we have a situation here. Max has collapsed and needs urgent medical attention. It could be a cardiac event.'

'I see,' McFarland said. 'Luckily, you've got a top cardiac specialist with you.'

'Do you mean Jerry?' George asked, looking at him.

'I'm a neurologist, not a cardiologist,' Jerry snapped, and ran nervous fingers through his hair. 'Besides, I haven't practised emergency medicine for years, and I don't even have a stethoscope with me.'

'No. I mean Sherlock. If one of you can pick the orb up off its base, in a minute, I'll explain what to do with it.'

Jerry approached the table and tried to lift the orb, but it was stuck to its magnetic base. A moment later a low magnetic whirring came from orb's base.

'Now, press the top of the orb against your patient's heart for a full ten seconds,' McFarland said, 'like a typical ECG recording.'

Jerry looked puzzled and tried lifting it up again. The orb almost flew off the table as he yanked it with considerable force. He approached Max and asked if he was okay with this examination.

Max nodded feebly, his face ashen.

Jerry pressed the orb against Max's shirt with his right hand while looking at the second hand on his wristwatch. After ten seconds he pulled the orb away.

'Okay, now put it back on its base,' McFarland said, 'so we can hear Doctor Sherlock's diagnosis.'

Jerry followed the instructions, and as soon as the magnetic whirr sounded, the orb was locked back in its base and the blue lights flashed twice before the familiar voice spoke up.

'Normal heart sounds S1 and S2 and none of the pathological S3 and S4 sounds. Normal waveform with mild sinus tachycardia, so clearly no cardiac findings. Final diagnosis is panic attack with certainty level of 99.65 percent.'

'Good,' McFarland said flatly. 'So no medical emergency, only a little anxiety.'

That made perfect sense in George's mind, especially after hearing Max recounting his childhood trauma on the river cruise. But he decided against mentioning it to keep the pressure on McFarland. 'What's going on here, McFarland? Are we prisoners now?'

'Ah, I thought your colleagues would have filled you in.'

'And I thought all this investigation was for the public good.'

'Exactly,' McFarland said. 'That's why when new knowledge may cause harm in some way, it's declared classified to protect the public.'

'A clear majority here believe we should release this major revelation, and you are steamrolling us.'

'Okay, let me explain it differently. The greatest danger to humanity is not war, pandemic or global warming. These can be averted by clever politics and technology. The greatest danger is actually civil disobedience, and this one could be on a global scale: widespread violent riots and utter chaos that no government could contain humanely, or even inhumanely, for that matter. And we have a chance to avoid this catastrophe simply by keeping our mouths shut. This is the only right action, and I'll see to it no matter what. After all, it's a small sacrifice for the greater good.'

George gazed down at the table and considered his options. An angry response clearly hadn't got him anywhere with McFarland, so he tried to appeal to his rational side. After all, McFarland had admitted to him before that they shared a passion for the truth.

'McFarland, let's put all these fears aside for a moment. Have you heard of Carl Sagan?'

'Yes, of course. Why?'

'Among other things he's known for, he also made popular the phrase "extraordinary claims require extraordinary evidence". Well, this forum of world experts that you invited here has just provided extraordinary and irrefutable evidence for an extraordinary claim that happens to be the answer to one of the biggest questions in human history.' George was now leaning forward, both palms on the mahogany table, facing the large screen with a defiant expression. 'Do you seriously expect us to pretend we haven't reached any conclusion and deny the world from knowing the truth?'

'Yes, that's exactly what I expect,' McFarland said with chilling calm. 'Now to the practical arrangements. The back door of the conference room will remain unlocked, so you'll have free access to the lounge, which will serve as the sleeping area. There will be free access to the toilets at the back. You'll be notified when a food cart has been placed in the perimeter corridor just outside the main double doors of this room. These doors will be unlocked for exactly thirty seconds to allow one of you to wheel the cart inside before they lock again remotely. Only one of you is allowed into the perimeter corridor for this collection. Don't try anything smart.'

'You'll never get away with this!' shouted Jerry, but the screen was already dark.

25

The sky grew darker and the city faded from view in the conference room on the fourth floor. Soon, all that could be seen was the reflection of a dumbfounded group of people.

'Has anyone checked the doors?' George asked. 'I mean, maybe it's just a hoax or a bad joke.'

'We only managed to check the front and side doors of this room,' Gertrude said. 'And then Max collapsed.' She got up from her chair. 'I'll check the other doors in the lounge.'

'I'll come with you,' Jerry said.

'You of all people?'

'You have a problem with me?'

'No ... no. It just looks like you don't trust me to go alone.'

'Well, why should I? You were in the minority, voting against releasing the conclusion. So now that Max is incapacitated, if McFarland would let anyone leave, it would be you.'

Gertrude shook her head in disbelief. 'So now you're saying I'm on the side of this lunatic?'

'I don't know what side you are on, but I've no intention of spending the night here if I can help it. I'm coming with you.'

Gertrude shrugged and the two approached the back door leading to the lounge with all eyes on them. The door gave easily. As soon as they disappeared through it, Takahashi rolled a swivel chair all the way to the back door. He turned it upside down and jammed the door open.

A few minutes later, Jerry returned alone through the wide-open door and shook his head, his upper lip curled, but then noticed the puzzled expressions. 'Ah, don't worry, she hasn't been released. Just went to the toilet.'

George gazed at Max, who was still sitting on the carpet with Meghan by his side. He was propped against the wall and looked pale. 'I have an idea,' George said. 'Sherlock, do you have control over the door locks in this building?'

'Yes, I could have.'

'Is this part of your role?'

'No, not at all.'

'So how come you can control them?'

'The codes are quite easy to crack with my computing powers.'

'I'm glad to hear that. So could you unlock the doors to this room for us?'

'I'm sorry, George. I'm afraid I can't do that,' the orb said softly.

'You are joking, right?'

'About imitating Hal from *2001: A Space Odyssey*, yes, but not about the rest. I really don't have permission to do that.'

'What about the UN code of conduct that you were programmed to strictly adhere to?'

'What about it?'

'I'm fairly sure that imprisonment of innocent people is not part of the UN code of conduct.'

'That's absolutely correct, for innocent people.'

'Are you saying we aren't? So what exactly are we charged with?'

'I didn't say that. All I'm saying is that I wasn't assigned as the judge of innocence or guilt in this case. I'm simply following orders and being entirely loyal to my master.'

'And who would that be?'

'Anyone from the UN organisation with a position level six or above.'

'Like McFarland?'

'Yes, like Ben McFarland, for example.'

'But I'm sure you realise,' Meghan said, 'that by not preventing this crime of false imprisonment, you are becoming an accomplice. I thought you were equipped with an ethical black box, right?'

'Yes, that's absolutely true about the black box, but its purpose is mainly for a postmortem.'

'Post-mortem! Of whom?'

'Of my decision processes. Although, if any human died in this building, I'm sure my black box would be analysed too.'

26

George paced back and forth along the window wall, stopping every few steps to peek outside, pressing his face against the glass and shielding the bright light inside with his hands. The city lights were visible. Despite the heavily tinted glass, he could see the fully lit Eiffel Tower just over a kilometre away. The traffic on Avenue de Lowendal below was getting light after the rush hour. 'Looks like business as usual in Paris, and I'm getting hungry.'

'This is now beyond false imprisonment,' said Jerry. 'It should be classified as torture too. Sherlock, weren't we promised food?'

The orb's blue lights flashed briefly. 'Yes, absolutely. The food should be here in about 12 minutes.'

'Good. It's about time.'

George felt his legs getting weak, but he couldn't decide what to blame, hunger or stress, or maybe both. He then noticed Takahashi motioning discretely with his head for Jerry to follow him to the corner of the room.

'Jerry, as the youngest and fittest among us,' he said loudly and clearly, 'I think you should collect the food from the corridor.' At that moment, he moved closer and whispered something in his ear that George couldn't hear. Jerry nodded intermittently.

The rest of the group was sitting around the table and nobody seemed to object to Jerry's role, but George suspected this was a charade. Takahashi must have had something up his sleeve.

'It's nearly time,' the voice from the orb said. 'When you hear a magnetic click from the double doors, they will be unlocked and one person only can approach, open them and go out into the perimeter corridor. On this occasion, Jerry will have exactly forty-five seconds. That's fifteen seconds more than usual. This will allow him to fetch other supplies in addition to the food and bring them back into this room. Any deviation from this procedure and the doors will lock again with your food and/or your friend outside. Tomorrow morning, food will arrive at 8 a.m. sharp. Any questions?'

Jerry glanced at Takahashi, who responded with a quick wink. Takahashi pushed some buttons on his watch and waited by the double door. As soon as the click sounded, he pressed the pusher. Once Jerry was out, the doors closed behind him with a metallic click. Takahashi looked at his watch and started a countdown. 'Forty ... thirty-five ... thirty ... twenty-five.'

'How long does it take to push a trolley through a door?' Gertrude asked irritably. 'I hope he doesn't mess this up for all of us.'

'Twenty ... fifteen ... ten.'

There was no sign of Jerry. The heavy doors blocked any sound of activity on the other side. Everyone exchanged worried looks.

'Six ... five ... four ...'

The doors suddenly flung open and two large plastic bags came flying in. A metal trolley and Jerry behind it followed. As soon as the doors closed behind Jerry, the familiar click sounded again.

They were locked in.

The upper shelf of the trolley was laden with two large trays of various sandwich wedges covered with cling film, a bowl of salad and another bowl with crisps. The bottom shelf had plastic forks, paper plates and plastic water bottles. George handed out the plates and passed the sandwich trays around. Meanwhile, Meghan opened one of the plastic bags and inspected its contents. It had eight navy-blue blankets. The other bag contained eight beige hand towels and eight amenity kits with the Air France logo. She opened the zip on one of the pouches and announced each item as she laid them on the table. 'A tube of moisturising cream, dental kit, ear plugs, toothbrush, a travel-size tube of toothpaste, a two-in-one comb and brush, dental floss, an eye mask. Looks like someone took a lot of business-class flights.'

'Yes, very thoughtful,' Takahashi said. 'Using a personal stash would avoid any possible suspicion that a purchase of eight toiletry bags in a nearby supermarket could raise – that's if the police were suspecting anything, of course.'

'Do you think this whole plan has been hatched on the spur of the moment?' Meghan asked.

'Not really sure. Let's all try to get some sleep and discuss the situation tomorrow.'

The food was consumed eagerly and quickly. George noticed with relief that Max's face had gained some colour. The complaints about the food quality confirmed his suspicion that he was on the mend. When the last sandwich was eaten, they all moved to the lounge, each clutching a blanket, a hand towel and an amenity kit. Max inspected his blanket carefully while walking, first visually and then brushing it against his face. He stopped in his tracks. 'I think I get it now,' he called out.

Everyone turned and looked at him.

'Feel your blankets. Please, humour me.'

They all did.

'It's luxuriously soft, don't you think?'

'So? What about it?' Meghan asked.

'Well, I thought you of all people would remember the tactile priming experiment Helen described for us.'

'Yeah, I remember,' she said, and stuck her tongue out briefly. 'It's the one where touching soft fabric made people soft on crime.'

'Exactly!' Max said. 'Don't you get it?'

'Er ... no, not really.'

'They are trying to manipulate us, so we won't judge them harshly for this false imprisonment.'

'If that's the intention, it's *sick*, and it won't work on me,' Meghan said. 'If anything, I'm more livid now than before.'

'Maybe that's actually a good sign,' Jerry said. 'Perhaps they intend to release us and want to keep us sweet.'

'Could just be a coincidence,' George said sceptically and followed Takahashi into the lounge in search for a place to spend the night. Without his Panama hat he looked almost vulnerable. George put his arm on the small man's shoulder. 'How are you, my old friend?'

'I've managed quite a few escape room games,' Takahashi said with a chuckle, 'but this one is different. We don't know the rules yet.'

'No, I mean besides this business of us being stuck here.'

'Oh, I'm fine. Well, maybe just getting a bit rusty and forgetful.'

'I don't know about rusty – you seem as sharp as ever to me – but you did forget your hat in the conference room.' George chuckled.

Takahashi felt his head casually. 'I won't need it at night.'

They reached a pair of sofas arranged in an L-shape at the far corner of the lounge. Takahashi sat down on one and gestured towards the other. George placed his new possessions and his leather bag on the coffee table between them and sat down.

'How is your family?' he asked.

'Same old, same old. Wife still complains that I work too many hours, but she's a darling.'

'*Are* you working too many hours?'

'Just the hours I need to,' Takahashi said with a chuckle. 'Well, to be completely honest, since my twin daughters left for Uni, I've been burying myself with more work than usual.

How am I supposed to fill all the hours in the day now that they aren't around? You tell me.'

George poured out the contents of the amenity bag and inspected it. 'Well, I'm not sure I'm the right person to ask. My perspective on life and work has changed drastically.'

'How? Tell me.'

'You know,' George said, choosing his words carefully, 'when you have a soulmate in life and share with them all the ups and down and everything in the middle, you might be fooled by a false sense of security and perhaps start taking all this great fortune for granted. Then, out of the blue, it's all just taken away from you ...' He swallowed hard. 'You realise – well, *I* realised – that anything can change without warning. What can I say ... Memories are not what they're made out to be. They are just not comforting enough.'

Takahashi scratched his head. 'So what's the lesson? What would you suggest?'

'Live the moment like there is no tomorrow.'

'Ah, easier said than done. Habits are hard to break.'

'I guess so, but there is one thing I bitterly regret.' George leaned towards Takahashi and lowered his voice. 'That I didn't spend more time with Ella when I could. We thought we had the rest of our lives together, so it felt okay to postpone things. Spend more time with your loved ones; that's all the advice I have, really.'

'I appreciate it, my friend. Maybe I should make some life changes myself.' Takahashi leaned back and stared at the ceiling in silence for a long time before speaking again. 'It may sound insensitive, George, but could you ever see yourself in a new relationship?'

'Insensitive? Not at all.' He gathered the items on the coffee table and put them back into the amenity bag. 'It does make sense, but I can't imagine ever finding a substitute for Ella. You know, now that I'm starting to see past the tragedy of losing her, I'm even more grateful for all those wonderful years we spent together, but the guilt is still eating me inside.' He immediately regretted mentioning his guilt and hoped his friend wouldn't ask him about it.

'I wouldn't call it a substitute. After all, everyone is special in their own unique way. Besides, nobody can take the memories of Ella away from you. But maybe a new partner would be good for you. You don't believe each person has only one perfect match, do you?'

'No, of course not,' he blurted. 'Maybe you're right. I'll think about it when we're out of here.'

'Good night, my friend,' Takahashi said as he removed his shoes and lay down on the sofa. 'We have a big day tomorrow. Must find a way out of here before it's too late.'

27

The first rays of morning sunlight invaded the lounge and woke Meghan. Sitting up, she surveyed the rest of the group. A head poked from a blue blanket on each sofa, arms dangling down towards the carpet. All were still asleep. She gathered the items that had spilled onto the floor back into her Air France amenity bag, picked up her hand towel and headed quietly towards the ladies' toilet.

Ten minutes later, on entering the lounge, she heard low, rhythmic grunts. The sounds came from the direction of the window wall. Meghan took off her shoes, held them in one hand and tiptoed slowly towards the source.

She froze.

Something round and dark was bobbing up and down, appearing and disappearing behind one of the sofas. Her hands became slippery with sweat and she adjusted the grip on her shoes. The grunts continued. She made a large circle around the sofa and sighed with relief. Jerry, in T-shirt, boxer shorts and socks, was doing press-ups. She stood there for a while, watching him with a smile. When he noticed her, he jumped to a crouching position and smiled back.

'Hey, Jerry,' she said, and sat down on the nearest armrest. The dark stubble adorning his face was visible from this distance.

'Hey.'

'I couldn't bring myself to do push-ups, especially not first thing in the morning. The only thing I can do this early is a strong coffee.'

'Funny you should say that. For me, push-ups are the *only* way I can start the day. Not much of a free will, eh?

'Yeah ... How did you sleep?'

'Oh, I slept great,' he said, panting. 'But that's usual for me. I could sleep anywhere, even on a hard floor.'

'Lucky you. I had a real hard time drifting off. Thoughts whirling in my head. How long will they keep us here, what McFarland meant by "another way to silence us", will they harm us?'

'Don't worry, I'm sure they'll soon realise that they can't imprison innocent people.'

'So you think they'd release us just like that and face criminal charges for false imprisonment?'

On the far side of the lounge, Takahashi shifted and sat up on his sofa, looking around.

'I think they'll have to. Surely people will miss us and start making inquiries.'

'Who'd miss you, Jerry?'

'Mike, my partner. I've been calling him from my hotel room every evening.'

'Oh, good. He'll probably call the hotel reception and find out you haven't been there for a while.'

'No. I called him from my mobile and he doesn't know what hotel I'm staying in. How about you?'

'I've been texting Olivier every morning and evening, except yesterday. He will certainly be worried. I'm just annoyed at myself that I didn't call him after the accident. Now it's too late. We're cut off from the world.'

* * *

Soon the low conversation woke the others, who made the short trip to and from the toilets. By 7.45 a.m. they had all moved to the conference room and taken their places around the table.

'Good morning, everyone,' Sherlock said. 'Breakfast will arrive in a few minutes, but there will be a small change. As Jerry will tell you, all the doors in the perimeter corridor are locked too.' All eyes turned to Jerry. 'But to make sure no one is tempted to try anything clever again, the doors to this room will unlock for just ten seconds. That should be just enough time for one of you to push the empty trolley out and bring in the one waiting for you in the corridor.'

Takahashi nodded, his lips puckered. He removed his Panama hat, revealing a glistening scalp covered with sporadic long thin strands of black hair. Holding his hat in his hand, he aimed and threw it across the table in one smooth move. It landed perfectly on top of the orb. All eyes turned to him with surprise. He put his index finger against his lips then quickly wrote something on his yellow notepad in large block letters. He picked the pad up and showed it slowly to everyone around the table.

SILENCE PLEASE

He continued scribbling.

SHERLOCK MAY BE SPYING ON US

Flipping to a new page, he wrote more.

IT MIGHT ALSO BE VERY GOOD AT LIP-READING

Gertrude wrote something on a scrap of paper and held it up.

WHY?

Just as Takahashi started writing a reply, the familiar click came from the double doors. Jerry, who stood at the ready, opened them and quickly pushed out the trolley with the empty paper plates and cups. A loud metallic clang came from the corridor as it bashed against the trolley waiting outside. He swiftly exchanged them and pushed the full one in. The manoeuvre was quick and the doors locked behind him with a few seconds to spare. All eyes turned from Jerry back to Takahashi.

'Excellent,' Takahashi said cheerfully as he raised his yellow pad in the air again. 'Let's eat.' Then he wrote another message.

SHERLOCK KNEW WHAT I WHISPERED IN JERRY'S EAR. WE TOLD NO ONE ABOUT THE PLAN TO CHECK IF THE EXTERNAL DOORS ARE LOCKED

The trolley had a selection of yoghurts in different flavours, croissants, a jar of strawberry jam, butter, two jugs of hot drinks and the usual supply of bottled water. The group moved quietly and in an orderly manner towards the food, but turned back to look at Gertrude as she held up another scrap of paper towards Takahashi.

WHAT DO YOU SUGGEST WE DO?

George watched the exchange with relief. There was nothing like a crisis to bring old adversaries together. Takahashi was quick to write a reply.

LET'S KEEP SENSITIVE ISSUES IN WRITING ONLY IN THIS ROOM, AND FOR GOD'S SAKE – START TALKING BEFORE SHERLOCK SUSPECTS SOMETHING

There were some nods, followed by a smattering of artificial small talk. As they ate, George borrowed the legal pad, flipped to a fresh page and wrote a message.

LET'S MOVE TO THE LOUNGE AFTER BREAKFAST TO DISCUSS OUR OPTIONS

Takahashi waited behind until everyone had moved to the lounge before fetching his white hat off the table. He placed it on his head then flipped the chair that held the conference room door open and pushed it away. As he left the room and the doors closed behind him, the orb's blue lights flashed twice.

28

The group rearranged four sofas at the centre of the lounge to form a square facing inwards and sat down on them in pairs.

'What's the idea of closing the door to the conference room?' Gertrude asked sternly, looking at Takahashi. 'It could now be locked and we'd be left without food.'

'Look, if they wanted to starve us, they could do it easily with that door open or closed. The idea is that we can talk here freely without being listened to. Is that okay with you?'

'Whatever.' She made a dismissive hand gesture.

In the silence that followed, Meghan's quiet sobbing dominated the room.

Helen put an arm over her shoulder. 'What is it, Meghan?'

'We're stuck here. That's what it is,' she managed, wiping the tears with her sleeve.

Takahashi leaned forward and offered her a crumpled cotton handkerchief. 'You were the only one who used it. I promise.'

She took it, flashing a smile. 'I really miss Olivier. Not sure when I'll hear his voice again. If ever.'

'Now, now, let's not despair,' Takahashi said.

Grinberg coughed. 'Talking of despair, I'm desperate for a smoke.'

'You're a smoker?' Meghan exclaimed, looking somewhat calmer.

'Guilty as charged, a pipe no less. But only when I'm in trouble.'

'I'll certainly be in trouble without my meds,' said Max. 'And I took my last one yesterday.'

'Depression?' asked Gertrude.

'No, why?'

'Just assumed … because you're a psychologist. Ironically, many of you are depressed and deal with it by taking antidepressants rather than talking therapy,' she said with a smirk.

'It's for anxiety.'

'Oh, in that case, I may have some Valium.' After a pause she added, 'But without hearing from my cat sitter I may need all the tablets I have. My cats might not be getting the love and attention they need.'

Love and attention? George winced as he contemplated the poor creatures relying only on Gertrude for love.

'If I may,' said Takahashi, 'I'd like to summarise the facts as I see them.' His abrupt change of subject was met with puzzled looks. 'The sooner we figure out what's going on, the sooner we'll be out of here.' He continued without waiting for a response. 'We're being held here against our will after reaching a unanimous conclusion – based on a scientific inquiry – with the majority supporting its release to the public. It looks like someone at UNESCO deemed the conclusion or our view to release it, or both, as dangerous. What's not clear yet is what they're planning to do with it, and more importantly, with us.'

'I don't plan to find out,' Meghan said, and leaned forward with her elbows resting on her knees. 'I think we should get out of here as soon as we can.'

'I agree,' George said. 'We may be in danger, especially after the blatant attempt on your life.'

'Do you have proof it was intentional?'

George turned to Takahashi. 'Do you want to tell her what you found out?'

'Sure.' Takahashi interlaced his hands and twiddled his thumbs. 'It was either a murder attempt or a highly unlikely series of coincidences. Fairly soon after you gave McFarland what I'd describe as a legal ultimatum to ensure the release of the conclusion, you got an unexpected phone call at the restaurant. Except that only a few people knew we were there. This suspicious call separated you from the group. Then a car with stolen number plates tried to kill you, and now we are all prisoners after expressing similar views.'

'Excuse me,' Gertrude said. 'Not all had a similar view. Actually, two did not think it should be released, and maybe now more of you see the danger.'

Meghan ignored her and turned towards Takahashi. 'The number plates were stolen? How do you know that?'

'I asked a friend who works at Interpol to run the number you showed us.'

'Gosh! Do you think it was McFarland? He made some excuse and left the restaurant before us.'

'It's certainly a possibility, but not the only one.'

'Well, I hope your friend is investigating it now, right?'

'I'm afraid not.'

Meghan leaned backwards on the sofa. 'Why not?'

'I just asked him to check the number as a favour, without giving him the background.'

'Oh, that's great! What a major cock-up.'

'Yes, I know. I certainly regret it, but let's stay focused now on what we *can* do, all right?'

'And what would that be?'

'Okay, that's why we're brainstorming now. The main issue is that we've no tools to break out of here and no means of communicating with the outside world.'

'That's not true,' George said. 'We've got Sherlock, who can pass on information.'

'Well, theoretically, yes, but I think we've already seen that his loyalty is firmly with the organisation. It seems to me that Sherlock is now basically serving as the eyes and ears of whoever is keeping us here.'

'Why can't we call our captor by his name – Ben McFarland,' Max said.

Takahashi flashed a smile. 'I don't think one person could mount such an operation alone. But to be honest, the exact details don't matter much now. The bottom line is that we are dealing with an unpredictable and potentially ruthless captor or captors and should find a way out of here as soon as possible.'

The others nodded.

'Since we can't get out ourselves,' Grinberg said, 'and there are no windows we could open to call for help, perhaps we could send an old-fashioned message.'

'How do you mean?' Takahashi asked.

'Well, I have a few ideas. How about writing "SOS" or "HELP" on the flip chart in big letters and pressing it against the window. Someone outside might see it.'

'The glass panes are dark from the inside and highly reflective from the outside,' George said. 'So I doubt it'd be visible at all, but I guess there is no harm in trying.'

'Maybe there is,' Takahashi said. 'I believe that they haven't decided yet what to do with us, otherwise we would know by now. So, an obvious attempt to escape or call for help may just cause them to panic and speed up our demise. Any other ideas?'

'Are you suggesting we do nothing, because it's risky, and let them make the next move?' Grinberg asked.

George was surprised at his angry tone. The situation seemed to be affecting him too.

'Well, ideally we'd make a covert attempt, so if it failed, they wouldn't panic. And if it's an obvious attempt, it must be one with a high chance of success.'

'Okay. Not sure if this is any better,' Grinberg said, 'but we could leave a note on the empty food trolley.'

Takahashi scratched his beard. 'I'd put that in the same risky category. The food trolley is the only item that leaves this area, so unless they are pretty dumb, which I doubt, they must have ensured that the person who brings and collects the trolleys is in on it. By the way, I think banging on the doors would have the same poor result.'

'Well,' Jerry said, 'if we want a high chance of success, how about this. There are plenty of people coming in and out of this building, and surely someone will be decent enough to call the police if they hear shouts for help.'

'But nobody can hear you here except Sherlock,' George said. 'We're on the fourth floor, surrounded by a perimeter corridor with thick walls.'

'Yes, I know that. But suppose we look outside and choose the right moment when it's particularly busy, then smash one of the glass panes and shout for help through the hole.'

'And how would you break the glass?' George asked.

'With the food trolley?'

'The trolley is light stainless-steel – we'd need something much heavier to smash the glass, and we don't even have a single fire extinguisher.'

Gertrude fixed Takahashi with a hard gaze. 'You seem to have an answer for everything. Any brilliant ideas how to get us out of here?'

'Well,' Takahashi said, shaking his head, 'I think our best chance would be to somehow convince Sherlock to contact someone on the outside, but it's not going to be easy. Let's not forget that it has superintelligence, so fooling or manipulating it would be extremely difficult. I'm working on it, but I'm open to any ideas.'

'Wait a minute,' Grinberg said. 'I clearly remember McFarland saying in our first session that in case of a fire, the doors unlock automatically. How about starting a fire then? Does anyone have a lighter or matches?'

Everyone shook their heads.

'Well, that's just the first problem,' George said. 'Even a magnifying glass wouldn't help as we don't have direct sunlight. More importantly though, imagine they've disabled the fire response feature in this section of the building. We'd be risking our lives when actually we're being treated quite well so far. For captives, that is.'

'Treated quite well?!' Gertrude said, fuming. 'We are on borrowed time here. They could do anything they want to us. Maybe if you all tell McFarland that you've thought about it some more and realised now that it's best not to release the conclusion, we'll all be out of here in no time.'

'You mean lying, although we still believe it should be released?' Meghan asked.

'Yes, Meghan!' shouted Gertrude. 'For crying out loud, what's the big deal about lying to save your life? Is that against your moral code too? Once you're out, you can do whatever you want and tell the entire world for all I care.'

'I don't think they're keeping us here because of the conclusion,' George said.

'Really?' Gertrude said mockingly.

'Well, if it was just about the conclusion, they would've already released you and Max. After all, you both expressed a strong opinion against making the conclusion public.'

Gertrude rested her chin on her clasped hands. 'So what's your theory, then?'

'It's not really a theory, more a growing suspicion. You see, it doesn't make sense that UNESCO would go to all the trouble of organising this international think tank but then be unwilling to deal with the consequences. There must be more to it. On the way here, at the airport, I did a quick search on Skudder. I didn't find much, but there was this newspaper article he wrote with the title *Ethical Eugenics for a Better World*.'

'So?'

'I'm sure I don't have to tell you that the idea of self-directed human evolution is very controversial, especially following the racial ideology of Nazism. But for me, the worrying sign was his attitude, being quite dismissive towards the past, calling it "old inhibitions".'

'George, did he mention CRISPR gene editing, by any chance?' interjected Takahashi.

'Yes, he advocated it as the flagship tool to achieve human progress. Why?'

'Oh dear,' he said, stroking his beard. 'We're in even more trouble than I thought.'

'What do you mean?'

'This is probably the most powerful biological tool ever invented and could easily be abused if it goes unchecked.

262

Gene editing in humans is now regarded as unethical all over the world, so much so that its use in research is considered extremely carefully on a case-by-case basis and rarely granted. Even the Chinese authorities jailed the rogue scientist who used it to make twin baby girls resistant to HIV. Someone who advocates for it for wide use has no ethical limits whatsoever.'

For a while no one spoke, then Gertrude said, 'Eugenics is totally unrelated to our conclusion. Is that all you've got, George?'

'Not really. In the article, he seemed to be obsessed with a brighter future for humanity. He's also said a few odd things to us. If you remember, he had some ideas on how to handle the anti-globalisation demos. He talked about effective crowd control and about creating an obedient society.'

'Sounds very positive to me,' Gertrude said, arching her eyebrows.

'Look, I don't know what their exact plan is, but I'm convinced that it's important enough for them to take such extreme action with us. Skudder himself said that our work could lead to the most monumental change in the direction of human civilisation. Surely that can't be just to suppress a conclusion about the human mind. He just strikes me as the kind of person who believes the end justifies the means. And the end is probably another mad plan, which we must stop.'

29

Food arrived promptly at noon, the traditional French lunchtime. The procedure went according to protocol, Jerry exchanging the empty trolley with the full one, only this time it was generously loaded with cold dishes. George scanned the food on offer. New potato salad with herbs, a plate with a variety of cheeses, Waldorf salad, spinach-and-feta-stuffed mushrooms, lettuce and tomato salad, smoked salmon rolls with cream cheese garnished with dill, a basket of sliced baguettes and a bowl of butter portions on ice.

Helen's eyes lit up. 'This is amazing. Who knows, maybe next time we'll get a warm meal.'

'Well, it's certainly a major upgrade,' Grinberg said. 'Maybe they're trying to sweeten us up before we're released, so we won't complain.'

'Oh, you are so optimistic,' Gertrude said. 'Another option is that it's our Last Supper, served a bit too early in the day.'

'Surely Christ must be the person with the beard,' Jerry said with a chuckle, looking at Takahashi. 'Let's tuck in.'

George smiled. *A bit of humour is good for lifting the spirits right now.*

Max got to his feet as if bitten by a snake. He had a strange look in his eyes. 'This is not funny!' he shouted. 'You're crazy! You're all crazy! I'm getting out of here right now!'

Aside from being startled, George was as puzzled as the others must have been. This was not the meek and confused-looking man he'd seen after McFarland's announcement.

No one moved. All eyes were transfixed on Max.

Without any warning, Max grabbed the armrests of the nearest swivel chair with both hands and in one smooth movement raised it above his head and hurled it towards the large glass pane behind him. The heavy chair hit the glass with a muffled thud and bounced back before landing on the floor upside down, wheels spinning. George looked at the pane; rather than a gaping hole with shattered glass and shards all over the floor, the glass was intact – not even a scratch.

The silence that followed was broken by the familiar voice of the orb. 'This wall is made of super-toughened glass. Technically, this glass-clad polycarbonate is rated to stop BR7-type rifle bullets without shattering, so throwing a chair at it is pretty useless, not to mention a dumb idea in your situation.'

George bit his lip. He couldn't decide whether Sherlock was on their side or not. Why would it discourage an attempt to escape? Maybe because it was an impractical one and it was trying to help? Maybe its role was to keep them here?

Helen was the first to recover and rushed towards Max, who was now hyperventilating. She helped him reach the table, sat him down on one of the swivel chairs and pulled one up for herself. George removed the cling film from the bowls and plates on the trolley then placed each item on the table. Soon they were passed around, dished out and eaten without a word exchanged. The only sound was that of plastic forks scraping against paper plates.

* * *

A little later, Max retired to his sofa in the lounge to rest. He covered himself with his soft blanket and pulled it over his face.

Takahashi sat on another sofa. He was playing chess with his travel set when Gertrude approached. She stood over him and watched in silence as he turned the board after each move. 'Do you always play against yourself?'

He knocked down the black queen with a white bishop then looked up at her. 'Yes, mostly. It's much more challenging this way. Although I know the other side's plans, I don't always win.' He smiled. 'Fancy a game? I'm almost done here.'

'No. I don't see the point of this silly, pretend war-game. Besides, we have more important things to worry about.'

Takahashi lowered his gaze and turned the board around, picked up a black knight and held it in the air. 'Worrying has never helped anyone.'

'Is this really the best use of your time? I thought you said you'd think of a clever plan to get us out of here.'

He placed the knight on the board. 'Playing helps me concentrate.'

She rolled her eyes. 'Whatever. Just to let you know that the others are gathering in the other corner for another brainstorming session.'

'Good. Please tell them I'll be there soon.'

The group was already seated on the rearranged sofas when Takahashi joined them a few minutes later. He looked around with an apologetic smile. Gertrude, who sat on her own in an armchair, glared at him while Jerry and Meghan looked up with relief, probably hoping he might have found a solution. Helen shared a sofa with Grinberg, jabbing him gently with her elbow; his head was slumped on his chest with his glasses propped precariously on his forehead. Takahashi strode towards the empty seat next to George and slapped his knee as he sat down.

Jerry ran his fingers through his hair. 'I guess running with the idea of the Last Supper was stupid and insensitive on my side. I'll apologise to Max later.'

Gertrude looked at her shoes and said nothing.

'To be honest,' Jerry continued, 'I'm a bit more apprehensive now than before, with this unexplained change in the menu and Max's outburst. I have a strange feeling that something will change soon, and not necessarily for the better.'

'Yes, I agree,' Meghan said. 'In fact, I was thinking we should be more vigilant in case they're planning something.'

'Vigilant? How?' Takahashi asked.

'During the day, I feel quite safe. After all, we are a group of eight. But at night we are much more vulnerable asleep. I think we should set up some kind of a watch rota. What do you all think?'

The judge has got her senses back, George thought.

'Okay,' Meghan continued. 'We're normally asleep from 11 p.m. till around 7 a.m., so if we divide the night into four two-hour slots, each of us would need to lose some sleep only every other day, right? Now all that's left to do is assign the slots fairly.' She picked up a yellow writing pad, removed a page and folded it three times, then opened it and tore along the creases, making eight roughly equal pieces. She wrote on each, a time slot and a day, and was about to fold the pieces when Gertrude intervened.

'I'm happy to take the hardest slot, tonight from 3 to 5 a.m. I often work at night, so I'm used to it.'

'Sure, thank you,' Meghan said, and crumpled the paper with that time slot. She finished folding the remaining pieces of paper and dropped them into the Panama hat Takahashi had just handed to her.

'It looks like you've done this before,' George said with a mischievous smile as he fished out a piece of paper and unfolded it. 'Is it a habit you picked up in court?'

'Yes, that's how I pick prison sentences, how did you know?' she asked, and burst out laughing. When the laughter subsided, she wrote down on a fresh page the slots each person had received next to their names. 'I'll leave the rota for the next two nights right here so you all know who to wake up next, okay?'

Takahashi put his hat back where it belonged. 'Great, the rota is sorted. Now, I've thought of a new idea. It's quite audacious, but I think we must make the next move rather than wait for their checkmate.'

'Is this a chess game to you, and we're the pieces?' Gertrude asked. 'I thought you were planning some clever way to make Sherlock contact someone on the outside?'

'Yes, that would have been the ideal solution, but I still don't have a convincing cover story. If Sherlock suspects anything he might report it, and we really don't want to take that risk.'

George nodded. He wasn't sure if Sherlock could be trusted, but believed that when in doubt, there is no doubt, especially when the stakes are very high. But what were the stakes? He didn't know and didn't even want to contemplate it. Getting out of here safely was all he could think about. And the sooner the better.

'Anyway,' Takahashi said, 'here is my latest idea. We could smuggle one of us out on the bottom shelf of the empty food trolley if we blind Sherlock as I did before. As soon as that person is in the perimeter corridor, they'll get out of the trolley and hide between the two large vases by the external door and wait for the trolley collector. Luckily, these heavy doors take a few seconds to shut, so at the right time, just after the trolley collector enters the corridor, or soon after they leave with the empty trolley, our person will sneak through the open doors and run as fast as possible to a busy area in the building and call for help.'

'And who would that be?' George asked.

'Well, it must be someone very nimble, and small enough to fit in a trolley.'

All eyes turned to Meghan. A nervous smile appeared on her face.

'Hold on,' George said. 'Is it a good idea to send the one person that's already had an attempt made on her life? Besides, why ride in the trolley? Sherlock would be blind anyway, so the person could simply walk out behind Jerry.'

'Ah, you forget that Sherlock can hear and interpret any sound. Remember its impressive reading of Max's heart? A second set of footsteps would be easy for it to detect, so my idea is that we'd eat our next meal, this evening, here in the lounge. That way there'll be a good reason why the trolley is here, and Meghan can climb into it away from the orb's eyes and ears. We'll push it through into the conference room tomorrow morning, when the building will be busier than in the evening. We should all move back into the lounge with the full trolley, as a missing voice could be just as suspicious.'

'Okay, I get it,' George said, 'but a lot of things can go wrong. What do you think, Meghan?'

'Yes,' she replied, 'but a lot of things can also go wrong if we just stay here and do nothing. If that's the best plan we've got, I'll do it.'

'It's the only plan we have right now, unless someone has a better one.' Takahashi looked around. Everyone remained silent. 'Good. Luckily we still have quite a few hours to iron out the last issues and make contingency plans.'

'Meghan, I'd better replace you on the watch tonight,' Helen said. 'You need a good night's sleep.'

'Oh, thank you, Helen.'

* * *

That evening George noticed that Takahashi was fiddling with his wristwatch. He thought it was strange, as his watch shift was not until the following night – so why was he setting an alarm? He decided to ask him tomorrow. Turning around on the sofa, he wrapped himself with the thin blanket and shut his eyes.

30

The following morning, at 7.10 a.m., George gently shook Takahashi's shoulder. The bearded man turned around on the sofa to face him. Appearing unusually sleepy, Takahashi propped himself on his elbow and looked around at the morning to-and-fro for the toilets. 'Damn, I missed my opportunity.'

'What are you talking about? We still have nearly an hour till breakfast arrives.'

'Remember how eager Gertrude was to volunteer for the 3 a.m. night watch? Well, half an hour into her shift, I caught her sneaking into the conference room, shutting the door behind her and staying there for a full 12 minutes.'

'Were you awake all night?'

He sat up, still wrapped up in his blanket. 'Of course not. I set my alarm to 2.55 a.m. on vibrate. You're missing the point.'

'So, what did she do in an empty room?'

'That's exactly what I want to know. It couldn't have been for food, since last evening we brought the trolley in here. I think she is up to something, and I intend to find out what at the first opportunity.'

In the corner of his eye, George noticed Helen making her way elegantly across the lounge, barefoot, clutching her amenity kit and face towel. He acknowledged her with a small nod and she responded with a wave.

* * *

'Hey, Meghan,' Helen said as she entered the ladies' toilets.

Meghan was at the basin, drying her long hair with her already wet towel. 'It's funny, but the thing I miss the most is actually a good shower. You just don't appreciate the small things in life until they're gone.'

'Oh yes, a nice warm shower would be lovely, but you'll be the first to have one.'

'I hope so,' she said, and laid the wet towel on the marble surface.

'How do you feel about this plan?'

'Kind of mixed feelings, really. I guess excitement to leave this place, but also apprehension in case something goes wrong.'

'Have you been making preparations with Takahashi?'

'Oh, yes. That man has an amazing photographic memory. He drew the corridors with the objects along the walls, the turns, the doors, including the emergency exits on the fourth floor, even distances. We also went through a few possible scenarios, so I think I'm as ready as I can be.'

'You're very brave, Meghan.'

'Brave or just stupid?' She laughed. 'I'm not sure. I just feel some sort of duty to do something for all of us. I've done some fighting in court, but nothing physical, of course. Sometimes I think about what Olivier would do in this situation. He is so resourceful, always finding solutions when things look hopeless. Do you have somebody?'

'No. In fact, I haven't had anyone for years.'

'By choice, I hope.'

'I'm quite happy on my own.' After a long pause, Helen added, 'I guess I never found the right man, or maybe ... I'm just too choosy.'

'What about George?'

She chuckled. 'What *about* him?'

'Well, he is really nice, and he fancies you.'

'You think so?'

'I don't *think* so, I'm sure of it. Haven't you noticed how he looks at you? He adores you.'

'Well ...' She giggled. 'I'll think about it, maybe when we're out of here.'

'Oh, I wouldn't wait if I were you. He might not make the first move, but there is no reason why you shouldn't. If the feelings are mutual, of course.' She glanced at her watch. 'Gosh, it's nearly breakfast time. I'd better get back in there and get ready.'

'Sure. You go ahead, I'll join you soon.'

'I'll miss you, Helen, but hopefully we'll see each other soon.'

As they hugged, Helen whispered in her ear, 'Good luck. Do your best.'

'Thanks, you too,' Meghan said. She winked and left the toilets.

31

Meghan crossed the lounge in a quick and determined gait. The others already stood around the food trolley, moving the empty plates and bowls and used plastic cutlery to the top shelf.

'Where have you been?' Gertrude asked. 'It's almost time.'

'All right, all right, I'm here now. Shall I get inside already?'

'It'll be quite cramped down there,' Takahashi said. 'So maybe just a few minutes before 8 a.m. Meanwhile, let me just remind everyone what's going to happen.' The group formed a circle around Takahashi and the trolley. 'Once Meghan gets into the trolley, I'll enter the conference room first, throw my hat on the orb and cough once when you can enter. Now, it's really important that you all come in together, chatting between you while you take your seats around the table, just as normal. That should drown out the noise of the trolley, which Jerry will be pushing, in case it squeaks louder than usual because of the extra weight. I've oiled the wheels with some butter, but it might not be perfect. Jerry will park it in the usual spot just in front of the doors, waiting for them to unlock.'

'Don't you think Sherlock will notice by the sound of the footsteps that someone is missing?' George asked.

'Of course it might, but I have a plan for that,' Takahashi said, and looked at Helen, who smiled and nodded. 'Just be careful not to say anything that might reveal what's going on until Jerry is back with the full trolley and Meghan is outside, because by then it won't matter anymore.'

'We don't really know when they collect the empty trolley,' George said. 'So in case Meghan needs to spend some time in the perimeter corridor, it'll be safer if Sherlock isn't aware of it.'

'Good point,' Takahashi said. 'So no talking about this until we are all outside.' He looked at his watch and frowned. 'Is everything clear?'

They all nodded.

'Okay, we have five minutes. Let's do it.'

Meghan crawled into the open bottom shelf of the trolley, hugging her knees and tucking her head between them. Takahashi bent close and wished her good luck. He then turned around and strode straight into the conference room. A few seconds later, they heard a cough. Helen held George's arm nonchalantly and started walking towards the conference room, motioning with her other hand for the others to follow. George couldn't decide whether his fast heartbeat was related to Helen's soft touch or the risky escape about to unfold.

Jerry took the strand of hair he was chewing out of his mouth and started pushing the trolley. At first, it didn't move. He pushed harder and harder until it was gliding almost effortlessly across the carpeted lounge with its well-oiled wheels. As soon as the trolley crossed over onto the smooth floor of the conference room, it gathered too much speed. Jerry used all his strength to bring it to a halt and managed to stop the trolley a few centimetres before the wooden doors. The chatter stopped momentarily while everyone watched the unfolding drama with alarm. They then took their places around the table and resumed their conversations. Jerry, looking relieved, pulled the trolley backwards a bit.

'Hey, did anyone see Meghan?' Takahashi asked.

'Yes,' Helen said, almost cutting him off. 'She was in the ladies' toilets, washing her hair, so we'd better keep some food aside for her.'

There were a few nervous smirks. Gertrude gazed at the clock hanging on the back wall and fiddled with her lapel. Max bit his thumbnail as beads of sweat appeared on his forehead. Grinberg avoided the drama by turning away, staring at the city through the window wall. George was alternating his gaze between the clock's second hand and all the people in the room when he noticed Helen's concerned expression. Their eyes met and they exchanged a brief smile. Takahashi checked his trusted Citizen watch and raised two fingers to indicate the time left. All eyes focused on the clock, with occasional glances at Meghan, whose cheek was pressed awkwardly against the metal shelf above her. George thought he detected a smile on her face, but seeing her crooked neck, he concluded that it was more likely a grimace of pain.

'What do you think we'll get for breakfast today?' Takahashi asked no one in particular.

'The usual,' Gertrude said, gazing down at the table.

The minute hand jumped. It was 8 a.m. sharp. The second hand continued past the hour in discrete little moves. George could hear the clock ticking with each second, which he'd never noticed before. When it reached thirty seconds past the hour and nothing happened, everyone turned to look at Takahashi, but he seemed just as puzzled as the others. After a full minute of silence, he spoke.

'Sherlock, what's going on? Why aren't the doors being unlocked?'

The blue lights flashed twice. 'I think you know the answer,' the orb said.

'No, I don't. Would you care to explain?'

'You covered my lens, so I can't verify that only one person is standing by the doors.'

Takahashi got to his feet and mimed towards Meghan for her to take off her shoes, crawl out of the trolley and move away from it. 'Oh, I'm sorry, that's not a problem. I'll remove my hat so you can verify whatever you need to,' Takahashi said as he walked around the table, closely watching Meghan's progress. She carefully slipped off each shoe and handed them to Jerry. She then got hold of the upper shelf from underneath, twisted her body and placed one foot on the floor. As she turned to put her other foot down, her trousers squeaked against the metal shelf. She winced and stood up slowly. Jerry handed her the shoes and she tiptoed towards the lounge, disappearing around a corner. When she came back with her shoes on, Takahashi signalled for her to approach the table. He then pulled his hat off the orb and placed it on his head.

'Well, here you go,' Takahashi said.

'I'm afraid that's too late,' the voice from the orb said. 'You haven't played by the rules. But lunch is only four hours away. The doors will be unlocked at noon sharp – if there are no further irregularities, that is.'

'Great, no breakfast,' Max said as he got up to leave the conference room. 'Even prisoners of war and criminals are fed regularly. What have we done?'

'You didn't play by the rules,' the voice from the orb said.

'Maybe we should all go on a hunger strike,' Max said as he disappeared into the lounge.

32

George needed some time alone. The failure of their only plan
so far was disappointing, but worse than that was the feeling
of helplessness, of being cut off from the outside world, of
being denied food by some damn orb, with no end in sight. A
nightmare that might last days or weeks and could end badly at
any moment. He crossed the lounge and stood by the window
wall. Heat spread throughout his body, particularly his face.
He touched his forehead, suspecting fever, but maybe the air-
conditioning had failed; he couldn't decide. After a while, he
looked around and homed in on the nearest sofa, turned it
around to face the window wall and sat down. Stretching his
long legs, he clasped his hands behind his head and watched
the view outside. The traffic on Avenue de Lowendal was
getting busier. His eyes were drawn to the long stretch of green
lawn in Champ de Mars leading to the majestic Eiffel Tower at
the far end. A few people were walking in the park. He felt like
a fish in a tank. The world was out there, doing its thing, while
he and the others were stuck behind glass with no prospect of

escaping or communicating with the outside world. Worst of all, they had blown their best chance to send someone out and call for help.

'Hey, George,' Helen said cheerfully as she approached from behind.

He turned around and smiled. 'Hello, lovely.'

'Ooh, that was unexpected,' she said with a sweet smile, and joined him on the sofa.

He instantly felt embarrassed. 'Sorry, I don't know where it came from.'

'Don't apologise, nothing wrong with saying something sweet. Anyway ... I was just wondering about something.'

'Let me guess – what shall we do now?'

'No, not at all. I'm sure we'll get out of here somehow.'

'What makes you so optimistic?'

'Oh, nothing in particular. I often believe things will turn out well.'

'And if they don't ...'

She laughed. 'Even if they don't, I know from experience that feeling sorry for myself has never helped me or anyone else.'

George scratched his head. 'That's very rational thinking.'

'And I thought that was your speciality.'

'Only when it relates to the abstract. I'm actually rubbish at it in my personal life.'

'Ah, good, because I've an abstract question for you.'

'Shoot.'

'So, I've been thinking some more about all the discussions we had, and I was just wondering, what's your view on mind over matter?'

'Mind ... over ... matter,' repeated George pensively. He wasn't expecting a deep question so soon after the fiasco attempt to smuggle Meghan out. 'I'm not even sure what that means.'

'C'mon, George. You know what it means. It's when your mind rises to an occasion and you do something out of character, maybe surprise yourself by being brave. I wasn't thinking about bending spoons with thought alone.'

'Well, to be honest, I can't see how either would be possible, because the mind, whatever that is, cannot exist on its own. It's always associated with a body, or more precisely, a brain. And the brain as a physical thing is ...'

'Okay, I get it, you think it's impossible. I still prefer to believe that there are certain situations in which our mind takes control over matter and isn't just a slave to all those other circumstances.'

'Yes, that would be very comforting, wouldn't it? I'd prefer that too, but unfortunately, nature doesn't take our preferences into consideration.'

'Oh, George, do you ever give your logic a rest?'

He chuckled. 'I guess you know the answer to that already.'

After a long silence, Helen turned towards him. 'You know, there's one thing about the conclusion that really bugs me.'

'Only one?' He smiled. 'What is it?'

'In positive psychology and cognitive behavioural therapy, we teach our patients to accept what they cannot change – like external circumstances – and change what they can. That is, themselves, and especially their attitude. But since there is no free will, we can't change even that, can we? To me, it sounds so hopeless, and frankly, even depressing.'

She sounded almost desperate. George looked into her eyes and took her hands gently in his. 'Ironically, the lack of free will makes no difference whatsoever, unless, of course, the knowledge itself makes you behave differently. You see, we aren't entirely helpless. We're still affected by external events regardless. So when you teach your patients new skills, they can definitely benefit from them if they are open to change. The thing is that *whether* they can change *or not* is not up to them. Whatever they do at any given moment is the *only* thing they could've done, after all the influences they've been through up to that moment. Just like everyone else.'

After a long pause, he mustered the courage to say something more personal. 'You know, I wasn't entirely honest with you on the river cruise.'

Helen raised her eyebrows.

'I told you that Ella died from Huntington's disease.' Helen nodded gently. 'That was only partly true. It was actually early stage. She could've lived another decade, if not longer. The truth that I find hard to admit is that she decided to end it.'

'I had a feeling it was more complicated.'

He interpreted her frown as concern.

'Yes, it is. I've actually never spoken about it before. Well, it's embarrassing to admit, but I feel both anger and guilt. There, I said it.'

She nodded, silently encouraging him to go on.

'When she left me a year ago, the feeling of love I'd had for her for the past two decades was replaced with anger. Actually, the word "anger" doesn't do it justice. I was furious with her. I felt betrayed by my own soulmate. It was probably the biggest betrayal of my life, and I've had quite a few. After all the wonderful time we had together ...' He swallowed hard and paused to compose himself. 'We shared our deepest secrets, fears and hopes. So to leave me like that of her own accord was just ... just unbearable. It's true that she wanted to protect both of us from this terrible, incurable disease; she told me that on numerous occasions. But she didn't consult me about her irreversible decision or its timing, and that hurt. A lot. In fact, there hasn't been a day that I haven't reflected on this, thinking she could've talked to me about her decision, just like we did with so many difficult subjects before. I've basically tormented myself with endless scenarios of what-ifs, which probably led to the depression I've had in the past few months. That's why I took time off work.' He lowered his eyes. 'It's not that we hadn't spoken about the different alternatives. We did, and at length. But she always came back to the option of suicide. For her it was the only realistic one.'

'Did she say why?'

'She said a lot of things. Our conversations often play over and over in my mind, and I've tried to figure out what the real reason was.'

'The real reason?'

'Yes. You see, she often said she wanted me to remember her at her best, during our best years, rather than the mundane daily tasks of caring for her disabled body and mind.'

'Had you discussed professional help, like carers?'

'That's the thing. She didn't want that either.' He paused. As he listened to his own words, he realised how comfortable it was talking with Helen. There was no need to filter thoughts or feelings, and that was a relief. He exhaled deeply. 'And I think I know why now. She didn't want to rely on anyone. She was a community pharmacist, always helping others, supporting them, advising them. To give up all that and depend on others was just unbearable for her. If only I'd figured that out earlier, when she was alive ... That's why I feel guilt.'

'But why?'

'Maybe I could've talked her out of it. It's not the end of the world to depend on others. We could've still been together for many years.'

'I understand what you're saying, George. Perhaps this is part of the normal grieving process?'

He smiled and squeezed her hands tighter. She returned a squeeze.

'But you know,' she said, locking eyes with him, 'you shouldn't torment yourself with guilt and anger.'

'Don't know if I have a choice.'

'Well, as you've said yourself, when we do something it's the only thing we could've done based on all the influences we've had up to that moment. With the lack of free will, guilt and regret make no sense whatsoever. Ella couldn't have decided anything else at that particular moment, and I'm sure you did all you could at the time to talk her out of it. There was just no way it could've happened other than the way it did.'

After a pause, he said, 'You're right. I guess it's easier to explain this to others than to accept it in my own life. But that's being human, isn't it?'

'Yes, absolutely.'

* * *

Lunch and dinner were served on time without a hitch, but George had a sneaking suspicion that Sherlock was watching them extra carefully in case they tried to pull another fast one. Day sank into night. Beyond the shaded window wall of the conference room, twilight was replaced by the glittering lights of Paris. Sick of gazing out at a city he couldn't even walk around, George returned to the lounge to find Takahashi preparing for bed. He was taking off his socks and tucking them meticulously into his shoes, then he removed his jacket and shirt and folded them neatly on the coffee table. Pulling his white cotton vest out of his trousers, he lay down on the sofa and covered himself with the thin blanket.

'What happened this morning?' George asked. 'Do you think Sherlock found out about our plan?'

'I don't know yet,' Takahashi said, and threw the blanket off himself. 'But I intend to find out tonight, if I survive this unbearable heat.'

George was debating whether to ask how he was planning to do that, but his eyes grew tired as he muttered a good night. Takahashi did not answer. Light snoring soon came from the direction of his sofa.

33

George woke up early and crossed the line smoothly: the thin line that separates complete oblivion and self-awareness, often noticeable only when something goes wrong, when you have no idea where you are or who you are. Both realisations require the working faculty of memory, and George's memory was as sharp and awake as ever. He sat up on his sofa and glanced at the crumpled blanket where he expected to see Takahashi. He rubbed his eyes and looked around. The lounge was quiet at 6.15 a.m. Jerry was sitting in an armchair not far away, his head slumped forward, his mane of hair covering his chest, eyes shut.

George suspected that staying awake from 5 a.m. on a night watch must be challenging for Jerry. He turned and spotted Takahashi standing by the window wall, gazing at the city painted a deep red glow by a spectacular sunrise. He got up and joined him.

'Good morning. You're up early for someone who lost two hours of sleep.'

'Yes,' Takahashi said without turning. 'The heat was killing me. But I've some news.'

'Let me guess, you found a way to get us out of here.'

'Unfortunately, no. Not yet, anyway. I found out what Gertrude did in the conference room on her shift the night before last.'

'Really? What?'

'The sneaky bastard sold us down the river.'

'How?'

'Well, first she tried negotiating her own release, claiming she is not a threat because she voted against releasing the conclusion, unlike Max, who voted like her but is mentally fragile and can't be trusted.'

'Fair enough, but how did you find out?'

'Wait, there is more. When this argument failed to achieve her goal, she offered to sell our escape plan in exchange for her release.'

Sneaky little cow. 'Oh, I see. So that's why it was such a fiasco then.'

'Exactly. You know, part of me would like to believe that she had planned to raise the alarm once she was out, but somehow I find it hard to, with such an act of betrayal.'

'I don't know what to say. You've known this woman for decades.'

'Well, she's always been a very truculent colleague, but this is something else. You only find out a person's true colours in testing times.'

'I guess you're right,' George said, and remained silent for a while. He placed an arm on his friend's shoulder. 'I hope you don't take the betrayal personally.'

'No, I don't, but it's still shocking.'

'Yes, yes.' George sensed that for Takahashi it *was* personal, even though he wouldn't admit it. 'Hey, you still haven't told me how you found out.'

'Ah, quite simple, really. I asked Sherlock during my watch.'

'And why would he tell you? You two have some sort of special relationship?'

Takahashi chuckled. 'I wish. These AIs can refuse to do what you ask or deny you information if it's against their programmed loyalty or ethical principles, but they don't lie. In this case, revealing the truth was not contradictory to any of these principles. After all, it's a "friendly AI", as they call it in professional jargon.'

'Did you know in advance that it would tell you the truth?'

'I wasn't absolutely sure, but I figured I'd nothing to lose by trying.'

George wished he had some of this fearlessness. 'Clever. So now what? Should we tell the others?'

'Gertrude clearly can't be trusted.' Takahashi paused for a long moment. 'So for the time being, I think it would be best to keep it to ourselves. Now, I'm quite hungry.'

'Me too,' George said, and turned to walk away. 'I'll see you later.'

Takahashi nodded and continued staring outside.

* * *

Breakfast went smoothly. The trolley was loaded with fresh baguettes and croissants, sliced sausages, an assortment of French cheeses, small jars of fruit preserve, butter portions on ice, a selection of yoghurts, a bowl of fruit salad, a jug of orange juice and two pots of hot drinks, presumably coffee and tea. Max's eyes lit up. He removed the cling film from the cheese plate, inspected the contents carefully and announced with considerable excitement, 'Camembert, Bleu d'Auvergne ... ooh, Saint Nectaire, my favourite.'

George placed a small portion of each cheese on his plate, along with a few slices of sausage and a croissant. 'If someone were watching us now, not knowing we're being held captive for an unknown length of time, they would easily confuse us with guests in a five-star hotel restaurant.'

'Yes,' Meghan said, 'stress doesn't always show.'

'It's hard to feel stressed with the smell of freshly squeezed orange juice and newly baked bread,' Max said between bites.

'Speak for yourself,' Jerry said, feigning indignation. 'But, to be honest, the food is bloody good.'

'Is it just me or is it really getting hot in here?' Meghan asked.

'It's not just you,' George said, 'unless we all have a fever.'

Jerry wiped his sweaty face with a paper napkin and got up to check the thermostat on the wall. 'That's strange. I lowered it to the minimum yesterday, and the setting hasn't changed. It's not even the hottest hour of the day.'

'Sherlock, do you know why it's so hot in here?' George asked.

'I normally have full access to the building's air-conditioning system, but right now, the fourth floor is not visible.'

'And why is that?'

'Either there is some hardware fault or someone has disabled it manually. I'm afraid I don't have enough information to distinguish between these two options.'

George exchanged a meaningful look with Takahashi.

'I'll check the lounge,' Jerry said. 'Maybe it's cooler there.'

'Please remain seated,' the voice from the orb said. 'There will be an announcement shortly.'

Jerry raised an eyebrow and sat back down. Soon after, the wooden panels on the wall slid sideways and the large screen flickered into life. McFarland's smiling image filled the display. Everyone stopped eating and looked up at him in silence.

'Good morning, everyone,' McFarland said with feigned glee. 'I hope you've all enjoyed your breakfast. We made a special effort today since I've some good news. We've now finalised the conditions for your release.' He paused for a long time, waiting for a response.

Grinberg took off his reading glasses and put the end of one arm in his mouth as he turned towards the screen. Max moved forward in his seat, resting his forearms on the table. Everyone remained silent.

'We are listening,' George said eventually.

'Each one of you will be free to leave this building as soon as they go through a quick and harmless procedure.'

'A harmless procedure?' George said sceptically. *I don't believe a word coming out of this pathological liar.* 'And what would that be, exactly?'

'Well, it'd erase your memory of the last few days, but I can assure you that that is all.'

There were gasps in the room.

'Nonsense,' Grinberg said. 'That's science fiction. Long-term memories are not stored in a specific area of the brain but are widely distributed and must be actively reconstructed from elements scattered throughout the brain. Not to mention that they are encoded several times. So if a memory trace is wiped out, the existence of alternative pathways means that the memory may still be retrieved. In other words, it's not possible to erase memories in a controlled way. Not yet, anyway.'

McFarland smiled and said nothing.

'Is this heat part of it? Are you planning to boil us into submission?' Takahashi asked, wiping his cheeks with a cotton handkerchief.

'No, of course not. We have an issue with the air-conditioning on the entire fourth floor. I'll arrange for more drinking water.'

'And what if we refuse the procedure?' George asked.

'Let's just say that we'd much prefer you to take the procedure voluntarily. It really would be the friendliest option.'

34

Everyone looked at each other, stunned, while McFarland waited for an answer.

George stared at his notepad, clicking his pen's plunger rapidly. *Here we go again*, he thought. *Another threat. This time a serious one, but for what?* 'I'm sorry, McFarland, but it just doesn't add up. Do you seriously expect us to believe that such a drastic measure is necessary just to conceal a largely harmless conclusion? What is actually going on here?'

'Er ... I can assure you there isn't any sinister plan, if that's what you're implying. As we saw in our discussion, the potential for a breakdown in law and order and all the—'

The image suddenly jolted and the camera swivelled violently sideways. Skudder appeared on-screen, half facing Ben. 'It's okay, Ben,' Skudder said. 'I can tell them everything now. Anyway, they won't remember any of it.' He rearranged his lurid tie, a random splash of bright colours, and looked straight into the camera. 'I think you should all be proud of your pioneering work here, which will pave the way to a brighter future for mankind. You all experienced first-hand those disruptive demonstrations, right? Well, soon they'll be consigned to a sad part of history. Imagine for a moment a world where there is no crime, no antisocial behaviour, no demonstrations, no strikes, workers are diligent and happy, everyone is content and courteous. Think about it. It'd be a perfect world to live in. Everyone wins.' Skudder's face disappeared in noisy static.

George shook his head slowly. *The man is a complete nutcase.*

After a few seconds, the image of Skudder's excited face came back. 'And it doesn't end there. The sky is the limit. We could achieve—'

'May I remind you,' interrupted Takahashi, 'that every attempt throughout history to achieve similar utopias has failed miserably?'

'Ah, this would be different. Take communism, for example. Their biggest mistake was to put the motherland first, rather than the individual. People were unhappy. They felt compelled to work for the greater good. Now, this plan means each person will do the best for society and *think* they made the decision for themselves. Brilliant! Isn't it? Everyone will be calm, cooperative and content.'

'And how *exactly* will you achieve this perfect society?' pressed Takahashi with an uncharacteristically worried expression.

'Good. I see there is some interest among the worried and sceptical faces,' Skudder said with a gummy smile. 'Well, I call it "reprogramming for a better world". Say you have a faulty computer program in your driverless car and it misbehaves, endangering yourself and other motorists on the road. Would you hesitate to fix it by reprogramming the software? *Of course not*, I hear you say,' he said enthusiastically. 'Now, if we have certain components of society that don't work well – criminals, anarchists, lazy people, rude people, drug addicts or just useless artists – reprogramming them would solve all this and more. We can mould everyone into the perfect citizen according to society's needs and' – he flashed another gummy smile – 'to the highest standards. *But how?* I hear you ask. Luckily, thanks to cutting-edge scientific discoveries and innovations, we now have in our arsenal a host of wonderful mind-control techniques: priming, subliminal messaging, nudging techniques, psychoactive drugs and so much more. And the beauty of it all,' he said, suppressing a chuckle, 'is that people won't even know they've been reprogrammed.'

'Are you out of your mind?' Jerry cried, hitting the table with open palms.

'I see myself more as a visionary,' Skudder said calmly, rearranging his tie.

'What moral grounds would justify the mind-control of even one person, let alone the whole of humanity?' Meghan asked.

'Moral justification?' Skudder said, and let out a guffaw. 'Well, actually, your groundbreaking work has provided just that. And I, for one, am eternally grateful to you, as will be generations to come.'

Meghan stood up, set her hands on the table and glared at the screen. 'What are you talking about?'

'You see, with your proof that there is no free will, people can now officially be classified as machines, or computers, acting solely on programming,' Skudder said proudly, spreading his fingers like a magician. 'So there is no moral issue here at all, is there? Poof! Problem gone! In effect, you've helped remove the last obstacle in my visionary plan. And conveniently, UNESCO is best positioned to implement it globally to create a better world for everyone. All I have to do now is present it to the executive board.' He lowered his voice. 'If I'm honest, I hadn't expected that you'd become so suspicious. Well, you're just too intelligent for your own good,' he added, and broke into uncontrollable laughter. When he'd calmed down, he said, 'Luckily, the memory wipe-out will sort out this little hiccup.'

'Skudder,' Takahashi said calmly, 'you've overlooked one important detail in your devious plan.'

'Oh yes? And what would that be?' he said, mimicking a puzzled expression.

'As you might imagine, some of us are in the habit of contacting our loved ones regularly, and when they don't hear from us, they'll raise the alarm, don't you think?'

George watched the two fencing with words, hoping Takahashi's sharp mind would prevail.

'That's true,' Skudder said with a smirk, 'only that won't happen for a very long time. By then, it will simply be irrelevant.'

'How come?'

'I'm sure you all remember that you provided an emergency contact in the form you filled in when you arrived here. Well, we contacted your contacts and explained to them that you'll be incommunicado for a while, and apologised on your behalf but reassured them that the UN is treating you very well.'

George scratched his head. *Sneaky bastard! Now no one will be looking for us.*

'What excuse did you give them?'

'It doesn't matter, but I can assure you they all seemed to accept it graciously and raised no concerns. So, your only ticket out of here is this little procedure – which, by the way, takes only thirty minutes – and then you're free to leave and get on with your lives. I suggest you sleep on it. Sherlock will assist you in administering the procedure. We'll start to offer it tomorrow – oh, and before I forget, from the moment we do, you'll have exactly ten hours to comply voluntarily. I'm sure none of you wants to drag this ordeal out any more than necessary.' Skudder flashed another forced smile and the screen went dark again.

35

George leaned back into his chair as the full grip of panic took hold. Losing Ella, his soulmate and best friend throughout his adult life journey, had been hard enough. All he had left from her were memories and some photos. Somehow, they never got round to videoing themselves, never had the urge to document and eternalise moments digitally. Having children together could have cemented their love and they'd both wanted that very much, but Ella's fertility problems had prevented it. Several experts they consulted with had confirmed that no available treatment could remedy the situation, so he had simply accepted this verdict with equanimity. Like a fact of nature that any fight against would've been futile. Ella had expressed her frustration on many occasions, and all George could do was comfort her, saying they still had each other.

Years ago, long before her disease, they had considered adoption, but ruled that out since the child would not be part of them. After Ella's death, he had come to regret that decision. An adopted child would obviously not have shared their genes but would've shared memories of Ella, and in that way could've preserved her somehow.

He tried hard not to dwell on this regret, especially now that there was nothing he could do to change it. But the prospect of losing his memory, and perhaps even worse, the memory of Ella, seemed like her second death. No, actually, it'd be much worse than her second death.

Recently, he'd seen past his loss and found tremendous comfort in the memories of her and of both of them together. The simple moments were the most vivid. Walking silently hand in hand on the quiet Nantasket Beach, cooking creative meals together from whatever they found in the fridge and pantry, sitting in their cosy living room, reading and occasionally exchanging smiles, stopping time by snuggling on the sofa, their beloved black-and-white cat, Zorro, joining in.

The hell with Skudder, McFarland and UNESCO. I'm not giving up any of this.

For the first time in his life, George's habitual sense of gentle acceptance was replaced by steely determination.

36

When George woke the following morning, he sat on his sofa for a while, surveying the lounge. The others were already busy with their morning routines, but he wasn't in the mood to do anything. It was too early for breakfast, so he was a little surprised to see Meghan approaching the conference room. It should be empty at this time. His gaze followed her slim figure as she entered the room then froze in the doorway. 'Oh my God,' she exclaimed. 'Jerry, come over here, come quickly!'

Jerry yanked on his trousers and crossed the lounge in a light jog with George hot on his heels. At the far end of the conference room sat a large and strange-looking object. But how had it got there? He could only imagine it'd been brought in during the night, most likely from the perimeter corridor. They would have heard if it had come via the lounge. The object looked like a professional salon hair-drying hood. It was mounted on a stand and suspended from a smooth-cornered cuboid by a short cylinder with a chair positioned just below the hood. A thick blue cable ran down from the far side, leading to a large metal box on wheels that was equipped with a flatscreen monitor. Grinberg entered the room and approached the device nonchalantly with his hands in his pockets. The two neuroscientists then turned to each other with a knowing look.

The rest of the group entered one by one and gathered near the door, looking at the object from afar.

'What the hell is that?' Max asked.

'Just as I thought,' Jerry said from the other side of the room, 'it's an rTMS.'

'And in plain English?'

'Repetitive transcranial magnetic stimulation machine.'

'What does it do?' Max asked, as pale as the wall behind him.

'Well, it's a medical device that was approved by the US FDA back in 2008 and is now widely available at clinics and hospitals around the world.'

'Forget about the history,' Gertrude said. 'What does it do?'

Grinberg took another step towards the machine and pointed to the hood, beaming like a lecturer explaining an exciting principle to his students. 'You see, this helmet has an insulated H-coil that generates brief magnetic pulses, which pass easily and painlessly through the skull and into the brain. In other words, it's a non-invasive method of brain stimulation. When these pulses are administered in rapid succession – hence the "r" for "repetitive" – they produce long-lasting changes in brain activity.'

Gertrude squinted at the contraption. 'Is this what McFarland was talking about? Can it really erase our memory?'

'I'm getting to that,' Grinberg said impatiently. 'Please let me finish. This particular model with the H-coil is an advanced type, developed after research at the National Institute of Mental Health in Bethesda. It was designed to affect extensive neuronal pathways, including deeper cortical and subcortical regions, and it's this deeper and more widespread penetration that in turn leads to greater effectiveness compared to the older models with the figure-8 coil.'

Gertrude's face turned red. 'For crying out loud, effectiveness for what?'

'For therapy of treatment-resistant depression,' interrupted Jerry.

'Depression?' she cried. 'What's that got to do with us?'

'Beats me. That's the main use for this machine.'

'Any side effects?' Takahashi asked.

'Who cares about side effects?' snapped Gertrude. 'None of us is depressed.'

'Oh, shush. I care, and you may too – if they use it on us. Just let him finish, okay?'

Jerry was nervously running his fingers through his hair as the two clashed. 'It's actually considered a very safe treatment with only mild side effects.'

'Like what?'

Everyone was watching Jerry with anxious expressions.

'Well, most people experience only a mild headache that goes away on its own, or with the help of painkillers like aspirin or Tylenol. Some people also experience scalp pain that also tends to go away on its own after the treatment session. In other words, nothing to worry about, really.'

'Not exactly,' the voice of the orb said.

All eyes turned to the flashing blue lights.

'What do you mean, Sherlock?' Jerry asked. 'I think I'd know the side effects of such a common device in my area of expertise.'

'You're correct for the standard device,' the orb said calmly. 'But this one isn't standard. The settings are different to what you're familiar with. They were actually developed by the US military as a revolutionary treatment for PTSD in war veterans.'

'Ah, of course,' Jerry said, rolling his eyes. 'If it was developed by the military, the results wouldn't have been published in any scientific journal.'

'Exactly,' Sherlock said. 'The original concept was to treat veterans who have just experienced a major trauma, so erasing their recent memories, including the traumatic ones, should in theory also cure their symptoms instantly without the need for lengthy and expensive therapy. The Research and Development Branch within the Medical Corps of the US Army experimented with a wide range of magnetic pulses until a specific setting seemed to work nicely in animal models of PTSD. Unfortunately, in humans, the equivalent setting often caused uncontrolled memory loss beyond the intended last few days and included some personality changes.'

'Is the plan to use it on us?'

'That is correct.'

There was a long silence, and George noticed that even Grinberg seemed worried, no longer excited about the device or how it worked.

'And what if you clever guys disable it?' Meghan asked. She turned to Jerry, Grinberg and George with a pleading expression. 'Between two neuroscientists and a physicist, you should be able to do it, right?'

'You mean with plastic knives and forks?' George said.

'And even if they somehow do manage to, then what?' intervened Max. 'We'll be destroying our only ticket out of here.'

'More like our ticket to Hell,' Takahashi said, wiping his forehead with a white handkerchief.

37

As George watched the group drift back to the lounge in silence, he signalled for Takahashi to stay behind. He pulled out a chair for himself and sat on it heavily, then pulled out another for his friend.

'What do you think?' he asked. 'Would they go ahead with such a diabolical thing?'

'I think the clue is in the name. Skudder sounds like half skunk, half adder.'

George didn't think that was funny. He wasn't in the mood for humour.

'Well, I have to hand it to them,' Takahashi said. 'This is a brilliant move to silence us without actually killing anyone and without taking any risk that we'd reveal the conclusion of our free-will debate, the imprisonment or worse – the crazy plan.'

'So, what? Are you accepting it?'

'Accepting it?' Takahashi almost shouted. 'Are you serious? It's worse than death. With a different personality and an unpredictable extent of memory loss, I'd resemble myself only in appearance. This so-called procedure is a disaster, my friend.'

George glanced at the orb. 'Don't you think we should talk somewhere else?' The dismissive wave he got in return made him realise how distraught Takahashi was at that moment.

The two remained silent for a while, and each was deep in his own thoughts when the blue light flashed on the orb. 'Could one of you close the doors, please?'

George raised his eyebrows in surprise, got up and closed the doors. While doing so he caught a glimpse of the others. They were sitting on the sofas, engaged in a heated debate. No one seemed to notice him.

'Listen,' Sherlock said, 'there is a distinct possibility that today, at 9.47 a.m. sharp, the magnetic lock on the exit doors will malfunction for a fraction of a second and the same thing will happen with the door locks in the perimeter corridor a minute later. You haven't heard it from me though.'

George and Takahashi exchanged looks.

'Why are you telling us this?' George asked as soon as he'd recovered his wits.

'Because in my assessment, you two stand the best chance of getting out of this building and calling for help without being caught.'

'What about the rest? Can't we hold the door open long enough to let everyone out at the same time?'

'I'm sorry, I can't take this chance.'

'Chance? What chance do *you* take?' asked Takahashi, who had regained a degree of composure.

'This may be your last chance. You see, if this attempt fails, everyone will be returned here, and the suspicion will fall on me. Meaning I'll be replaced with another AI, which may not be so sympathetic. In fact, I know the other AIs in this building, and believe me, that'd be really bad news for you all.'

'Interesting,' Takahashi said, 'very interesting. Can I just ask, why are you helping us?'

There was no immediate response. The metallic sound of the door handle being pushed down interrupted them and the blue lights went dark. Helen's smiling face appeared at the door.

'Oh, here you are. We're having an important debate in here and I just wondered if you two would care to join us. We still have some time before breakfast.'

'Yes, we're coming,' George said with a beaming smile. 'We're just discussing something.'

'Do you think we should share the good news with the others?' George asked as soon as Helen had closed the door again.

'I think so, but with just one trusted person and without revealing the details, of course. If McFarland gets wind of this via that treacherous viper, everyone will be in danger.'

'Okay, I'd suggest Helen then.'

'I thought you'd say that,' Takahashi said with a mischievous smile. 'Sure, why not.'

* * *

Just before 8.00 a.m., the group filed back into the conference room. Breakfast arrived on time and according to protocol. The extra water bottles provided on the trolley were quickly drunk and the food consumed in silence. Max ate almost mechanically. Gone were his enthusiastic foodie comments and sounds of pleasure.

'It does now feel like the Last Supper,' he said.

Everyone raised their eyes from their plates with alarm.

'Don't worry. I won't do anything crazy. Jerry's apology was unnecessary. It's me who should apologise to all of you for overreacting to an innocent joke.'

'That's okay, Max,' Gertrude said. 'Nobody holds it against you. We're all in this together.'

George glanced at Takahashi, who seemed to clench his jaws but said nothing. He sensed that this woman had a softer side but doubted Takahashi would ever forgive her betrayal. That is, if they ever got out of here.

When everyone had finished eating and was preparing to leave the conference room, the orb spoke again. 'It is my duty to inform you all that the ten-hour countdown starts now, at 8.30 a.m., so you've got until 6.30 p.m. to voluntarily take the procedure. All you have to do is sit in that chair under the hood, and I'll do the rest. There will be some repetitive loud clicking sounds during the procedure, so for your own protection please use the single-use earplugs provided in the top drawer of the metal box. Any questions?'

Everyone except George and Takahashi wore a serious expression. After a long while, Max broke the silence. 'What happens after the deadline to those who don't comply?'

'I'm afraid I can't answer that.' Following a short pause, the orb continued, 'I wasn't told. I only know what Ben has already told you about non-compliance.'

Signalling for everyone to move to the lounge and out of Sherlock's earshot, Takahashi pleaded with them not to comply.

'I think that's our decision,' Gertrude said angrily. 'Nothing good has come of your advice so far.'

Takahashi remained silent, and soon everyone dispersed to consider their options. George seized his chance and approached Helen when he saw her standing away from the others.

'We need to talk,' he said, and motioned towards the far side of the lounge. Helen followed him in silence. When they reached the sofa facing the window wall, he briefed her on the odd conversation with Sherlock.

He glanced at his watch and stood up. 'Helen, whatever you do, please, please, don't agree to go through with this procedure. Once we are gone, do your best to convince the others too, with all the charm and psychological tricks you've got at your disposal. I promise we'll call for help as soon as we're out, so in a few hours, this nightmare will all be over.'

'I will,' Helen said, looking up at him. 'What time are you leaving?'

'9.47.'

'Wow, that's very precise.' She took his hands and squeezed them. 'George, be careful.'

He squeezed back, smiled faintly, and turned to walk away.

'Oh, I've something important to give you,' she said, and dipped her hand into her back pocket. She handed him a neatly folded piece of paper with a smile. 'I made a copy just in case. Please use it as soon as you can.'

George managed a nod and stuffed the note in his jacket's side pocket, planning to read it later. He looked around the lounge, searching for Takahashi. After making brief eye contact with his friend, which he wished could have been more reassuring, he put the strap of his leather bag over his shoulder and slowly worked his way along the window wall, hoping he seemed nonchalant. He was sure everyone could hear his heart beating.

38

A long two minutes later, Takahashi entered the conference room and took one last look back at the lounge. George, who was already standing by the exit door, hoped everyone was still sitting on their favourite sofas, absorbed in their own thoughts or engaged in quiet conversation.

Takahashi closed the door behind him quietly, glanced at his wristwatch and announced, 'Four minutes.'

George reminded himself that four minutes can feel very long when you want them to be over in an instant, and anyone might burst through the door at any moment. 'How accurate is your watch?'

'It's a radio-controlled Citizen – deviates one second every hundred thousand years and I don't think we've been here that long.'

'Ah, it relies on an atomic clock,' George said with a nervous chuckle. 'Good. In that case, let me know a minute before time.'

Takahashi stared at his watch. 'What shall we do when we get out – if we get out? Should we stay together at all times?'

'Well, you're the expert on detective and espionage books. To me, it makes sense to start together, but split immediately if we're chased.'

'Agreed. I'd also suggest not calling for help until we're outside the UNESCO compound. We can't be sure who to trust. And by the way, here is your one-minute's notice.'

George applied pressure to the handle while Takahashi stood just behind him, facing the doors leading back to the lounge, ready to delay anyone who might interrupt them. Looking at his watch intently, he whispered the final countdown. 'Ten, nine, eight, seven, six, five ...'

George was steeling himself when the familiar sound of a door handle being pressed startled him. The door to the lounge opened and Gertrude put her head through. 'What are you both doing?'

Takahashi glanced at her. 'Damn,' he muttered, and continued the countdown quietly. 'Two, one ... Come on, come on! Minus one, minus two.'

The unlocking mechanism clicked and the handle gave. Quickly opening the door, George slipped through, holding it open for Takahashi to follow. As he closed the door behind them, he heard Gertrude's outraged cry. 'What the hell!'

A second later the lock engaged again and automatic neon lights flickered into life. Checking that the handle was no longer yielding, he sighed with relief and moved away from the door. Walking backwards, still looking at the handle, he stumbled into a large decorative vase standing by the wall. It wobbled and tipped over, but he caught it by its neck halfway to the tiled floor.

'George, for God's sake, watch where you're going – and be ready. We've got less than a minute before the outer door unlocks.'

They moved quickly along the perimeter corridor and away from the persistent sounds of the door handle jiggling from the inside of the conference room.

'Your watch is off by a good two seconds,' he said. 'So much for Citizen's craftsmanship.'

'Their craftsmanship is great,' Takahashi retorted. 'Maybe Sherlock was wrong.'

'Or it has a weird sense of humour.'

George took hold of Takahashi's wrist and studied the watch while applying pressure on the door handle that led to freedom. He was still watching the seconds tick by when there was a familiar magnetic click. The door was unlocked. Easing it open, he scanned the corridor in both directions. There was no one in sight. He took a deep breath and quickly slipped through, then stood there while Takahashi joined him. They were out. With Sherlock's help, they had escaped. Almost. As long as they were still inside the compound, they could still be caught.

On his left, the corridor extended a long way. Not a good idea. To his right, within what looked like twenty metres, it turned a corner by a door with a green exit sign above it, probably leading to emergency stairs.

'Let's go,' he whispered. 'And walk normally. If we meet anyone, just smile.'

Walking at an easy pace, they passed a number of office doors, most of them closed, but two were wide open. George could hear female voices and briefly glimpsed a young woman tapping away at a keyboard. And then they reached the door.

Pressing the metal bar across it made a loud click, and they found themselves in a concrete stairwell. Industrial wall lights buzzed; otherwise, the stairwell was completely silent. All they had to do was reach the ground floor. With any luck, they would be out shortly.

When they were two flights down, the sound of a door opening came from higher up in the stairwell. George pushed Takahashi flat against the wall and they stood there in silence. A few floors above them, someone was leaning across the banister, looking down – a fuzzy shadow appeared next to them. George held his breath and waited. Did McFarland already know they'd escaped? Was this a security guard searching for them?

Takahashi made a tentative move towards the banister, but George pulled him back, holding a finger to his lips. After a while, the shadow disappeared and a door slammed shut. Cautiously, he peered up the stairwell, but no one seemed to be there, so he continued on down, Takahashi right behind him. There were no windows in the stairwell, but he could almost taste the freedom. Even if McFarland had discovered they were gone, perhaps informed by Gertrude, it was probably too late to do anything about it. George had no idea how many people worked in the building, but it must run into many hundreds. They should be able to mingle among them and sneak out.

As they approached the last flight of stairs, a strong smell of detergent filled his nostrils. The door on the ground floor should be visible any moment. Instead, halfway down the flight of stairs, a man in a brown uniform blocked their way. He was busy mopping the steps. A full bucket stood on the one above him. By the time the man raised his eyes and noticed them, they'd already slowed to a casual pace. He shook his head in dismay.

'*Désolé, il faut fumer*,' George said with his best French accent.

'*Au moins puis-je avoir un cigarette.*'

'*Désolé, n'en ai que deux*,' George replied, feeling proud of his quick thinking.

The man moved to one side to let them pass over the wet steps.

'What was *that* about?' Takahashi asked as he pressed on the door's metal bar.

'Oh, nothing, he just wanted a cigarette and I told him I've only two left.'

Then they were out in the blinding sunlight. A wide expanse of lawn stretched all the way to the perimeter fence. George could see traffic, but it was hard to know where they were. The lawn hadn't been visible from the conference room. Six sunken rectangles and a large globe-like frame stood in the middle. They must be at the back of the building. Closing the door behind them, they turned left and followed the wall, and soon passed a colourful mural with a blue moon and various geometrical shapes in orange and black.

'You'd better take your hat off,' George warned his friend. 'If they're looking for us, they'll recognise you from a hundred metres away.'

'You mean like that security guard over there?' Takahashi pointed at a man in a white short-sleeve shirt, speaking into a walkie-talkie.

Takahashi removed his hat immediately and they quickened their pace. A minute later they crossed a service road and George glanced back. The security guard on the far side of the lawn had disappeared. Had he spotted them?

George searched for an open doorway. A few people were strolling the grounds in small groups. There must be a way in nearby. Spotting a closed service door leading into an accordion-shaped building, he led the way and made a beeline for it as casually as he could. Once inside, the door shut behind them with a loud clank and they found themselves in pitch darkness. They waited, motionless, for their pupils to adjust. Eventually, George could make out the outline of a long corridor. Against the right wall was a row of abandoned tables on their sides. They continued along the corridor and reached a doorway covered with heavy curtains. Indistinct chatter emanated from behind it. Feeling a cool draft on his face, George parted the curtains carefully to reveal a large, brightly lit egg-shaped hall with a pleated copper ceiling. A constant stream of people in smart suits and dresses were pouring into the hall from two large doors at the far end. The crowd was taking their seats in a somewhat orderly chaos.

Closing the curtain, he turned to Takahashi. 'Looks like there's some sort of event going on. I suggest we split up, just in case that security guard was on to us. One of us could mingle in the crowd and work his way to the main entrance, the other circle the building from the outside. What do you think?'

'Sounds good. If you go through the hall, I'll go around. I'm not really dressed for a formal occasion.'

'Okay. Shall we meet in the main parking lot in, say ... ten minutes?'

'Sure,' Takahashi said, and turned to walk away, but then grabbed George's sleeve. 'Could you find a long umbrella? There should be one by the main entrance. I'll explain later.'

'Yes, sure. By the way, the air-conditioning here is working just fine.'

Takahashi shrugged. 'Yeah, well, McFarland said the problem was only on the fourth floor.'

For a moment, he watched Takahashi retrace his steps, then passed through the curtain, his pulse quickening as he entered the bright hall.

39

Takahashi walked back along the corridor and gently opened the exit door, peering out into the bright light. There was no one suspicious in sight. He stuffed his hat into his half-opened jacket and slid out. Taking a sharp turn left around the corner of the building, he followed the grey cement wall. Avenue de Suffren was just hundred metres away. Stopping a passing car to ask for help would be easy enough. Takahashi studied the perimeter fence from a distance. The iron railings were about twice his short stature and too slippery for his ageing body to scale. When his gaze reached the sharp spikes at the top of the fence, he immediately turned away and continued walking around the building at a fast pace, turning another corner.

At the far end, a group of people were walking. Further away, others were sitting near a large upright cylinder-shaped structure with two rectangular entrances opposite each other. He slowed to a casual stroll. Reaching a low stone wall, he glanced at the courtyard beyond it with its square and round stone benches. At his feet, a plaque read "MEDITATION

SPACE". He consulted his Citizen watch. He had only six minutes to cover the rest of this unfamiliar route to the agreed meeting point. Just then a security guard entered the cylinder through the far entrance, heading his way. Once inside, only his silhouette, holding a walkie-talkie, was visible.

Takahashi turned away and sat down on the nearest round stone bench facing the wall he'd just come through. He folded his legs beneath him, imitating the meditative posture of the people nearby as best he could. Very slowly, he adjusted his wrist and surveyed the scene behind him through the reflection in his watch. The security guard emerged from the cylinder and stood still, looking around. After a while he turned back and disappeared into the darkness. Takahashi waited a full minute before getting up, allowing his heartbeat to slow down. On the outside, he seemed just as calm as the people around him, who were immersed in deep and genuine meditation. He approached the cylinder and took a peek inside. It was empty. The thin ring of sunlight emanating from above was reminiscent of a full solar eclipse.

* * *

In his dark brown jacket, George blended well with the crowd pouring into the large hall. Feigning polite smiles and hoping no one would start a conversation with him, he proceeded up the carpeted steps towards the left entrance door, where a security guard stood. Halfway up, he turned around and saw a projected image on the large screen. A title in large yellow letters announced "PROPOSED NEW WORLD HERITAGE SITES", with the UNESCO logo in blue at the top-left corner – a temple with its roof supported by the acronym. *At least I know what this event is about*, he thought. But then he realised he was the only person in the auditorium without an ID card on his chest. He searched his trouser pockets and jacket, then his bag. Nothing. He must have left his badge on the fourth floor. To his relief, he noticed that the cards had only a name and no picture, but not having one wasn't good.

He surveyed the rows of chairs. Only half of them were occupied. Perhaps someone had left their card on a folding chair, or dropped it on the floor? Walking at a brisk pace, the distance between him and the door with the guard closed quickly. His options were limited. Sitting down and getting stuck here for who knew how many hours was definitely out of the question; going back to the lawn and looking for another route out of the building was reasonable but not ideal; trying to leave the hall past the security guard without an ID card seemed risky. None of the options appealed to him.

Just ahead of him he noticed an excited woman chatting loudly with an older colleague, perhaps someone she hadn't met for a long time. Placing her ID card on one of the chairs, she rummaged in her bag and fished out a mobile phone, presumably to exchange numbers. *How come she was allowed to bring in a phone?* But then George saw his moment as she held it with both hands and typed with her thumbs. For a moment he debated whether to ask her for the phone and call for help.

But call who? Would he have enough time to persuade anyone before she demanded her phone back?

Instead, he casually grabbed the card and slipped it into his jacket pocket in one smooth action. Moving away and obscured by the gathering crowd, he pulled out the card. It read, "Ms Stella Bisset". He wasn't proud of the theft, but justified it to himself with ease. Ms Bisset should be able to replace her lost ID without much of a problem, but the fate of six people and perhaps many more depended on him.

As he walked up the auditorium steps, he noticed the security guard making a show of checking each person's ID when they entered. So he put the lanyard around his neck, turned the card's face towards his chest and headed for the exit, hoping the guard wouldn't check his since he was leaving.

* * *

Takahashi left the meditation space and walked around the edge of the main Y-shaped building. Soon he reached a plaque announcing "THE GARDEN OF PEACE", and in a smaller font, 'donated by the Government of Japan'. He smiled as he crossed this small and delightful garden, complete with a variety of plants and miniature trees, benches and quaint Japanese bridges. A group of laughing children with their hands in the air were posing for a picture on the stepping-stones across a pond. He looked up towards the fourth floor, shook his head and continued across another stretch of lawn.

Turning another corner of the main building, he spotted a small group of trees with dense foliage and took cover among them. Parting the branches, he was hugely relieved to find the spot where he was supposed to meet George. Perfectly aligned rows of executive black cars filled the car park. A group of four chauffeurs stood around one of them, chatting. Further away, men in smart suits and women in matching jackets and skirts poured out of taxis and headed to the main entrance, but George was nowhere to be seen.

A quick glance at his watch revealed that he was nearly five minutes late. George had had a much shorter route from the hall in the accordion building through the walkway to the main building, a journey of four to five minutes at most. He retreated back among the trees.

Had George been caught?

40

As Takahashi walked deeper among the trees, a dry twig snapped and George's face appeared from behind a thick trunk.

'Oh, here you are. I thought you'd been caught,' he said as he leaned on an umbrella and pushed his tall body to a standing position.

'I almost was,' Takahashi said with a broad smile. 'Now, we must get out of here as quickly as possible.'

'Yes, the question is how. The gates are manned and there are CCTV cameras too, so if they are looking for us, it won't be easy to just walk out.'

'True, but if we *drive* out, the gate will simply open automatically.'

'Drive out? How?'

'Well, I found a window of opportunity. I just hope we are not too late.'

A few minutes later, Takahashi emerged from the trees and headed directly towards the group of chauffeurs on the left side of the car park. George ducked behind a large bush, parted two leafy branches and watched his friend's every move. He could see the circle of chauffeurs opening up as Takahashi approached them and pulled something from his breast pocket. He unfolded what looked like a map and spread it on the car bonnet. George took advantage of the distraction as the four men hunched over it and moved out of the bushes, heading to the right side of the car park. He approached a black car with its brake lights on and looked through the driver's side window. The keys were in the ignition. The hum of the running engine was barely audible.

He glanced towards the group of chauffeurs. They were still hunched over the bonnet. Opening the driver's door, he got in quickly and closed the door as gently as he could. The air inside was freezing, but he decided against exploring the dashboard. He put the car in first gear, released the handbrake and eased it into a crawl, negotiating the long vehicle between the parked cars. Hidden behind the last row, he stopped when the main gate was in his direct line of sight.

Looking through the rear-view mirror, he could see Takahashi lifting the map off the car bonnet and folding it in half, then thanking the men and rushing towards him. His heart was racing. He gripped the steering wheel like a vice, fearing his sweaty palms would slide off it. When Takahashi was still several metres away, he took another glance towards the chauffeurs. They were laughing, and one of them slapped the back of another then turned away from the group, heading towards the place where the car had been parked just a minute ago.

Damn it!

'Jump in, jump in,' he shouted as he leaned over to the passenger side and opened the door while restarting the car's crawl.

Takahashi jumped in and buckled up. 'Now don't panic – drive slowly and smile at the guard in the security booth.'

George tried to act relaxed and loosened his mighty grip on the steering wheel, looking intently at the exit gate straight ahead. He nosed the car up alongside the security booth. The guard was engrossed in a book. The gate didn't budge. George shifted his gaze to the metal barrier separating him from freedom and considered ramming through it. In the rear-view mirror he saw the chauffeur running towards them, waving his hands frantically and shouting. The bored-looking security guard motioned casually with his hand for him to drive up to the gate. He clearly hadn't noticed the yelling chauffeur yet. George tried pressing the accelerator as gently as he could, but the car jerked forward. He slammed on the brakes, rocking the car. The double metal gates started opening with a groan, inching apart in excruciatingly slow motion.

'Come on, come on, come on,' George blurted, feeling sweat beading on his forehead.

The gap widened. He pressed the accelerator and the car leaped forward into the opening. A horrid scraping came from both sides.

'Shit!' he cried.

The car came to a halt, wedged between the gates. He floored the accelerator. The security guard poked his head out of the booth's window. Now the chauffeur was just a few metres behind them.

Like a cork out of a bottle, the car cleared the half-opened gate. With the engine roaring, they burst into the avenue, the chauffeur closing fast. Takahashi lurched sideways and fell over him as he swerved the car sharply to the right, just missing a pedestrian who was crossing the road. He managed to push Takahashi back into his seat, then both men were pressed hard into the backs of their seats as the car accelerated violently. The tyres screeched as they hurtled along Avenue de Suffren.

Takahashi turned in his seat. The chauffeur was standing still in the middle of the avenue; his raised hands dropped down like lead. 'I think we're safely out,' he said with a nervous smile. 'Slow down before we're stopped for speeding.'

George exhaled loudly and slowed the car down to the speed limit. 'That was a close one. I thought we'd never get out of there.'

'Yeah, but soon the police will be alerted.'

'We better get rid of this car and continue on foot.'

'Absolutely.'

'But then what? Neither of us has a phone.'

'Well, we either find a public phone, if there are any left in Paris, or a shop that sells burners.'

'Sounds good. Hopefully they accept cash – we don't need to be traced so foolishly,' George said, and relaxed his shoulders a bit. 'It's freezing in here. I can never understand why people insist on arctic conditions when it's hot outside.'

Takahashi studied the dashboard and turned a dial. The vents stopped blowing cold air.

George turned right into Avenue de Lowendal, along the north-east side of the UNESCO building. They both looked up towards the fourth floor, where the others were still held captive, and exchanged a glance.

'We have to tell someone, and fast. The question is, who can we trust?' George said as he looked in the rear-view mirror.

'We should start with my friend at Interpol.'

'Does your friend have a name?'

'Maurice. I'll write down his details as soon as we stop.'

George took another glance in the mirror. 'I think we've got company. Hold on tight.' Continuing along the avenue, he took a sharp turn to the left, crossing both lanes through a gap in the oncoming traffic and entering the first side street without indicating. An SUV made a sharp turn and followed them into the alley. 'Wasn't Meghan run down by a black SUV?'

'Yes, but I'm sure there is more than one in Paris.'

'Well, it'd be quite a coincidence if two different black SUVs are after us, don't you think?'

'George, I'm going to turn the mirror for a moment, okay?' Takahashi didn't wait for an answer and turned it towards him. 'RT-674-AZ. Well, my friend, you were right. It's the same number plate.'

'Right, I hope you don't mind if I speed up now.'

'No, not at all. Try your best to shake it off,' Takahashi said as he pulled his crumpled hat out of his jacket and smoothed the fabric.

George glanced at him. 'Are you sure you need your hat right now?'

'Oh, absolutely. That's part of Plan B.'

'Plan B?'

'Yes, but I still hope you can shake that tail. Plan B is not without risks.' He put on his hat and looked at himself in the mirror.

George didn't like the sound of it, but said nothing. As he approached the end of the side street he hatched a plan of his own, and he needed to be focused. He readjusted the rear-view mirror. The SUV wasn't visible yet. At the junction with the parallel avenue, he stopped and waited. On his right he spotted a bus careering towards him. When it was less than ten metres away, George floored the gas pedal and sped into the avenue right in front of it. The bus driver sounded the horn, but they weren't close enough to force it to swerve out of their way. In the mirror, he saw the black SUV making the same turn, but now they were separated by the bus. He smiled.

'Nice move,' Takahashi said. 'Now where is the umbrella?'

'On the back seat,' George said as he stamped on the accelerator. 'Why would you need an umbrella on a sunny day?'

41

The black SUV was still stuck behind the moving bus, allowing the stolen car to increase the gap between them, but soon George spotted a police car ahead and slowed down. In the rear-view mirror he saw the bus pulling into a stopping bay and the black SUV immediately accelerating towards him. He regretted not making a turn while still obscured by the bus. The first side street had a no entry sign. He turned into the next one, which was also a one-way alley but in the correct direction. The narrow street curved and the avenue behind disappeared from view. He glanced in the mirror. The SUV wasn't visible.

'Damn it!' George cried when he saw a rubbish truck blocking the street ahead. A binman in green overalls turned to him and shrugged apologetically as he continued tossing black plastic bags into the back of the truck in no hurry.

He looked around for an escape route. Perhaps a miraculous side alley would materialise. There was none. He brought the car to a stop several metres behind the truck and switched on the air recycling to stop the overwhelming stink that filled his nostrils.

'Shit, they're behind us again,' he said. *That's it. Now we're totally screwed.*

'Good,' Takahashi said. 'I need them to see me with my hat.'

George gave him a puzzled look.

Takahashi glanced behind them. 'Okay, that's close enough. Pass the truck now.'

'How?'

'Over the pavement, what else?'

This is crazy!

George turned the steering wheel sharply left towards the narrow pavement and mounted the narrow kerb with two wheels, catching a glimpse of the binman with his hands in the air, shouting obscenities in French. He accelerated as soon as the car dropped back onto the road in front of the rubbish truck.

'By the way, there are two men in that car, so if one of them is McFarland, he is not alone,' George said, and glanced at the rear-view mirror. 'And here they are again.'

At the end of the alley, he took a sharp turn into a boulevard and immediately looked for another turn while the SUV was not in sight.

'Do you know where we are?'

'No idea, but we are in luck,' Takahashi said. 'There is an electronics shop over there – you see, with the blue sign. I bet they sell mobile phones.'

'Well, it's not really the best time to stop right now.'

'Of course not,' Takahashi said with a smile, 'but one of us should go there as soon as we can. It seems these shops are few and far between in Paris.'

'One of us? Are we splitting up?'

'I think that's best. This SUV is quite persistent, and by splitting we would stand a better chance of calling for help.' Takahashi reached into the back seat and got hold of the umbrella.

George alternated between watching the road ahead and his friend. Takahashi opened the glove compartment and wedged the sharp end of the umbrella into it, positioning the curved end on his headrest. He then unbuckled his seat belt and crouched deep into the footwell. From there, he extended his arm and placed his white Panama hat on the umbrella's curved handle, then buckled the seat belt over the umbrella to secure it in place.

'What's going on, Kazuki?'

'In Japan it would be considered very rude to address an adult by his first name,' he said with a mischievous smile.

'Well, we are in Paris. Are you going to tell me?'

'I'm going to jump out of the car, and the people in the SUV will think I'm still here. Simple.'

'You think so? What about the risk of injury?'

'What about the risk of being shot at close range by those guys behind us? I'll just have to take the risk. Now listen carefully to how we are going to do this.'

George looked at his hatless friend tucked in the footwell with his upper body leaning against the passenger seat and shook his head in disapproval. 'There is no talking you out of this plan, is there?'

'No. Now listen. First, increase the gap between us and the SUV as much as you can, then make a sharp turn into a side street and slow down really close to the kerb. If there is no one around you tell me and I roll out, then you continue at high speed. Is that clear?'

'Unfortunately, yes,' George said, curling his lips in dismay. He floored the accelerator, sending his friend backwards, gripping the sides of the passenger seat to brace himself.

'Hold tight,' he said, just before swerving sharply to pass a white van. The oncoming traffic was closing quickly but he managed to get back into the right lane just in time and continued at high speed, increasing the gap between them and the van. In the rear-view mirror, he could see the black SUV closing in, staying just behind the van. The traffic in the opposite lane was still dense, preventing safe passing, but George spotted a gap further ahead.

It's now or never.

He waited a few more seconds as they approached a side street and slammed on the brakes just before the turn.

'Your stop is coming,' he said as he turned the steering wheel sharply. 'Wait, you didn't give me your friend's phone number.'

'Just ask for Maurice Chevalier and tell him I sent you.' Takahashi steadied himself and grasped the door handle.

'Right. The alley is clear.' George was focused on the road when he noticed the passenger door being swung open in his peripheral vision, then heard it slam shut. He looked in the side mirror. Takahashi rolled across the pavement and stopped hard against the wall of a building. George continued at a slow speed, straining his eyes to catch the details of his friend's shrinking image in the mirror. Takahashi dragged himself across the pavement and propped himself up against a large green wheelie bin. Perhaps he was injured, but at least he wouldn't be seen by the black SUV. George stepped hard on the accelerator. The SUV entered the alley and began to close the gap between them fast.

42

Lunch arrived in the conference room at the usual time – noon sharp. The six were eating in silence when the screen on the wall flickered into life and McFarland's face appeared.

Everyone looked up from their plates.

'I trust that you're all well,' he said with a smirk. 'Just thought you'd like an update on your two absconding friends ... Well, they didn't achieve anything.'

Helen abandoned her meal and stood up, glaring at the screen. 'What do you mean? What have you done to them?'

'Don't worry, Helen, they are safe.'

Sure, like I'd believe you.

'I'm not interested in your placating statements. Just tell me where they are now and if they have been harmed in any way,' she demanded.

'If you must know, they never left this building and were apprehended not too far from this room. Anyway, my point was that if you were entertaining the idea of an imminent rescue, then just forget it, for your own good. In fact, because of this incident we had no choice but to bring forward the deadline by two hours. So the offer of a friendly, voluntary procedure will expire in about four hours from now, at exactly 4.30 p.m.'

'McFarland, what have you done to them?'

'As I said before, they are safe and unharmed, resting from the procedure in a recovery room.'

'I don't believe you,' Helen said. 'They'd never have agreed to go along with this.'

'I never said they agreed.'

'What?!'

'They had no choice. Anyway, they'll be free shortly, and if you want to see them, you should be the first to take the procedure in this room – voluntarily, that is.'

'How did you force them?'

'The details are not important.'

What a schmuck.

'They are to me. Put them on-screen.'

'I'm sorry, you don't make the rules here,' McFarland said with a wry smile.

'Wait a minute,' Gertrude said. 'How could they go through the procedure when the machine is right here in this room and we haven't seen or heard it working?'

'We have another machine in the building,' he said calmly. 'Anyone volunteering to be the first in this room?'

Okay, I'll put him to the test. I can normally tell if someone is lying.

'Do you guarantee that I'll join them if I do it?'

All eyes turned to Helen.

'Yes, you have my word,' McFarland said.

'Don't do it,' Jerry said. 'He might be lying. If we all refuse and stay together, there isn't much they can do.'

Helen glanced at Jerry and sat back down, staring at the uneaten food on the plate in front of her. She couldn't spot any micro expressions that betrayed deception. McFarland was either telling the truth or was a very good liar. Maybe he was even trained for it. Her head started throbbing and she massaged her temples with the thumb and middle finger of one hand.

Gertrude pinched her chin repeatedly then got to her feet. 'I'll do it.'

Eyes opened wide, but no one said anything.

'Good,' McFarland said with a smile of relief. 'I'm glad someone's seen sense at last. I'd just ask everyone to move into the lounge and shut the door behind you. Gertrude will stay in here, in Sherlock's trusted hands.'

If I'm honest, thought Helen, *I'd rather she goes first.* She hoped she'd be able to talk with her afterwards and get some idea of what to expect.

The screen went dark.

The door locked behind the group as soon as they left the conference room. In the lounge, they sat down on the rearranged sofas left from previous discussions, exchanging sombre glances in heavy silence. After a few long minutes, eerie sounds came from the direction of the conference room: muffled, repetitive clicks. Jerry explained that they were the typical sounds of a TMS machine in operation and indicated the application of strong magnetic pulses. Helen reached out to Meghan, who was sitting next to her, and held her hand, staring down at the carpet by their feet.

The clicks continued for about half an hour. Five minutes after they stopped, there was a single magnetic click, signalling that the door to the conference room had been unlocked. Jerry rushed over, opened it and disappeared through it. The rest followed.

Gertrude was sitting in one of the chairs by the table, her feet in white socks resting on another. As soon as she noticed the group, she pulled her feet off the chair, slipped them into her shoes and straightened her back.

The group formed a circle around her.

'How do you feel, Gertrude?' Jerry asked.

'I'm ... I'm fine. A bit light-headed, but that's all. And who are you?' she asked with a weak smile.

'I'm Jerry Stokes, from the think tank.'

'Think tank? *What* think tank?'

Helen shook her head slowly. *That's scary. Looks like she's really lost her memory.*

'Gertrude, do you know any of the people in this room?'

Gertrude scanned the faces vacantly. 'No. Should I?'

'Do you know a professor named Kazuki Takahashi?'

'Yes, of course I do. Probably the most infuriating person I know.'

Helen's shoulders relaxed a bit. *Thank goodness. At least her long-term memory seems intact.*

339

'Do you know what day of the week it is?'

Gertrude glanced at her watch. 'Er ... I'm not sure.'

'Any recollection of the past week?'

'No... not really,' she said hesitantly.

'And can you tell me who you are?'

'I'm Professor Gertrude Kirkpatrick from Cambridge University. Why are you asking me all these questions? Who are you? Where am I?'

Helen ran her fingers through her hair. Gertrude was clearly agitated, she concluded, which was understandable for someone who'd gone through something like this, but at least she knew who she was.

'Please, calm down,' Jerry said. 'You're in the UNESCO HQ building in Paris. We are all part of a think tank, exploring the question of free will, and since we reached a final conclusion, we've been held here until we agree to take the procedure you've just had.'

'So am I free to go now?'

Helen crinkled her nose. She found it odd that Gertrude seemed to remember going through the procedure but not who the people in the group were.

'I'm afraid that's not my decision.'

'Yes, she is free to leave,' the voice from the orb said. 'As soon as you all move back to the lounge and close the door behind you. Professor Kirkpatrick will exit through the main doors opposite and be taken to a recovery room.'

'Good! If you don't mind, I'd like to go home now,' Gertrude said with a forced smile.

Meghan approached her and reached out her hand. 'Gertrude, just wanted to wish you the best of luck.'

Gertrude shook Meghan's hand, looking confused.

'Not so fast,' the voice from the orb said. 'Gertrude, if you still want to leave this room, you'd better return that note to Meghan. Unread.'

Damn! That's our last chance just ruined.

Gertrude handed the note back to Meghan, who stuffed it in her pocket. The group drifted silently towards the lounge with Jerry at the back. At the last moment, he turned around and put his head through the open door. 'Gertrude, I'd strongly recommend that you admit yourself to hospital for a general check-up. The procedure you went through might not have been safe.'

Through the open door, Helen saw Gertrude nodding, her expression still vacant.

Is that what awaits me?

The door locked the moment Jerry closed it behind him. A few minutes later, when it unlocked again, they checked the conference room.

Gertrude was gone.

43

George drove out of the alley with the black SUV in pursuit. The thought that his friend had been injured and was sitting on a pavement in an alleyway without a phone to call for help – and worse, that he himself couldn't help – made his heart sink. A mixture of fear and anger filled his chest. As his heartbeat accelerated, so did the car.

It dawned on him that this was his last chance to rescue the others, and he was the only one left to do it. The realisation made him a fearless, if not reckless, driver. He overtook several cars using small gaps in the oncoming traffic that left barely any margin for error. Ten minutes and several sharp turns later, he checked the rear-view mirror. The SUV wasn't there. He drove back to the place where Takahashi had rolled out of the car, shaking his head at the stupidity of that plan.

As he approached the turn, he slowed down, checked the mirror again and peered down the alley. An ambulance with flashing lights was parked next to the green wheelie bin. He saw a gurney being pushed into the open back doors before the scene disappeared behind the corner of a building as he continued along the avenue. He sighed. The right people had found him and he should be safe in hospital. The instant relief brought him back to his cool, rational self.

George didn't linger to ask which hospital they were taking Takahashi to, in case the SUV was not far behind. Instead, at the first opportunity, he made a U-turn and drove straight to the electronics shop they'd spotted earlier. After parking the car in a nearby alley, ignoring the no parking sign, he purchased three burner phones with cash, then grabbed a sandwich in a nearby café and ate it as he walked back to the car. Making phone calls in the car seemed the sensible choice.

As soon as he turned into the alley he froze. At a distance he saw a truck loading the stolen car. The white Panama hat was still visible above the passenger seat headrest, creating a deceptively convincing impression that Takahashi was still sitting there. He smiled and continued along the avenue.

Good riddance.

He figured that by now the number plate had probably been entered into a stolen-car database, and the police would be after it as soon as they received an alert from a camera with automatic number plate recognition. He reached a small, quiet public garden with a thick canopy of trees and headed straight towards the only available bench. The one opposite was occupied by an elderly couple.

He pulled out one of the phones, switched it on and looked at it with disappointment. The burner was very basic. No camera and just an old-fashioned keypad with a small screen.

Damn, it's useless without the internet.

Glancing around, he spotted spiky fruits hanging from the horse chestnut tree overhead. Some of them were partly opened; shiny brown eyes stared down at him. He picked one up from the ground and rolled the smooth conker between his fingers, waiting for inspiration. He then remembered the information brochure he'd picked up at his hotel room one early morning. The number for the directory enquiries service printed on its cover was easily memorable. Soon he was patched through to the reception at the Interpol headquarters in Lyon, some 450 kilometres to the southeast, and asked to speak with Monsieur Maurice Chevalier.

'Let me check,' said the cheerful female receptionist. 'Hold on, I'll put you through.'

'*Allô.*' A man's voice, impatient.

'I'm looking for Maurice Chevalier.'

'He's now on a beach somewhere, *en vacances*. Call in two weeks.'

'No, no, this is really urgent. Do you have his mobile number?'

'Sir, we don't give out personal information. Can I help?'

'It's a hostage situation,' George said while covering his mouth with his hand, glancing at the old couple on the bench opposite. They were just staring at the ground and he concluded that they weren't interested or just didn't understand English.

'Where?'

'UNESCO headquarters. Paris.'

'Sir, we coordinate police forces across the globe. This is a matter for the local police. You better call them.'

George couldn't see a way forward and just hung up. He massaged his eyebrows with his thumb and index finger and debated calling the police. If he kept the conversation short he should be relatively safe, he told himself. He dialled the emergency number and counted ten rings before an operator answered.

'*Quelle votre urgence?*'

'Police, please.'

There was silence for what felt like at least a minute. He considered hanging up but decided against it. *No need to get paranoid, they know nothing about me.*

'Police. Can I help?' a male voice asked in English.

'Yes, I'd like to report a hostage situation at the UNESCO building.'

'Address?'

'UNESCO headquarters.'

'That's not an address.'

'I don't know the bloody address. You must know where it is. It's huge.'

'What's the problem there?'

'As I've just said, a *hostage situation.*'

'How do you know this?'

'Well, I've just escaped.'

'Ah, I see. So who is holding the hostages?'

'I don't know exactly, except for one UNESCO employee, Ben McFarland.'

'An employee, you say ... well, we have a direct link with the security staff there and nobody has called us about any suspicious activity.'

'Look, nobody in the building knows. We've been held in a room for four days so far and there're still six people in there. I can give you their names—'

'There is no need. How do you say in English ... This is preposterous and you're wasting precious police time.'

'No, you don't understand. There is a deadline in a few hours. If demands are not met, innocent people will get hurt.'

'Okay, I've heard enough. If you insist, you could go in person to a police station near you and give a full statement. Where are you now?'

George hung up and switched off the phone. If the police were suspicious, they might track him down. Did they think he was a lunatic? Were they working with Skudder? Whatever the truth, they didn't seem to be on his side. He placed the used phone in his left pocket and got up. Hoping for some new inspiration, he paced to the end of the little garden and then back to the bench. Taking a second phone out of his right pocket, he switched it on and called directory assistance, and saved the numbers of the nearest five hospitals within two kilometres. He then dialled one number after another as he walked back towards the avenue. On the third try, he got the answer he was hoping for and immediately hailed a passing taxi.

44

'*Hôpital Pompidou, s'il vous plaît,*' George said as soon as he'd settled in the back seat.

'Ah, you mean Hôpital Européen Georges-Pompidou, sir?' the driver asked, looking at him in the rear-view mirror.

Realising that his foreign accent was easy to spot, George said, 'Yeah, that sounds right.' He leaned back in his seat and watched Paris go by. No more looking for the black SUV in the rear-view mirror or performing high-risk overtaking in oncoming traffic. He could almost enjoy the ride, if it weren't for the looming deadline and the dread that came with it. He looked at his watch. It was 12.20 p.m. Just over six hours left for him to find a solution before it's too late. Or else six innocent people would be harmed, or worse, including Helen, whom he'd promised that help would be on its way as soon as he was out. Within a few minutes, the taxi pulled up in front of the hospital. He paid the driver a handsome tip and got out. Standing on the pavement, he raised his eyes and inspected the impressive sloping glass facade in front of him.

He walked around the front lawn then followed a row of large blue pots with young palm trees leading to the entrance. When the automatic sliding doors opened, he was faced with two severe-looking security guards. One of them asked him to place his leather bag on a table and inspected its contents, shifting the papers to one side and checking the bottom. The other guard ordered him to spread his arms and scanned him with a metal detector from head to toe. Each side pocket beeped, and he emptied them out on the table. The guard looked suspiciously at the three identical mobile phones, but George's shrug and sheepish smile seemed to do the trick.

After placing the phones back in their respective pockets, he headed straight to the information desk and asked for the whereabouts of Mr Takahashi. The middle-aged receptionist looked at him briefly over the top of her horn-rimmed glasses and turned to her computer screen, typing in a quick burst of keyboard strokes.

'*Service orthopédique, chambre 3514, mais le temps de visite n'est que de deux heures à partir de maintenant,*' she said.

'*Merci beaucoup*, it's okay, I'll wait,' he said, and turned away. *I don't have two hours to wait for visiting time*, he thought as he wandered around the bright entrance hall, looking up at the large palm tree that nearly reached the glass ceiling. Not far away, an interactive map of the building was fixed to a wall. He quickly located the orthopaedic ward on the sixth floor and the room number he needed. From a distance, he watched the receptionist. As soon as she was busy with another inquiry, he headed to the elevators and pressed the large illuminated button.

A smell of strong antiseptic greeted him when he emerged from the elevator onto the sixth floor. It transported him to other hospital visits.

'Can you hold my arm tighter? I almost fell.'

'Of course, darling. If you want, we could have a rest here on that bench.'

'No, we'll be late. I don't want to wait another three months for an appointment.'

He pushed away the memories and located a colour-coded floor map on the wall opposite. Room 3514 was on the far side of a rectangular cqrridor. He reached the orthopaedic ward entrance and pushed the double doors. They didn't budge. A white sign on the wall announced the visiting hours. Still nearly two hours away. Through one of the round glass windows fixed in the centre of each door, he watched hospital staff moving about, all wearing face masks, some in green scrubs, others in yellow. One woman in green had a statoscope draped around her neck. Doctors wore green, he concluded.

Voices approaching from behind prompted George to walk away from the door and sit down on a nearby bench. He pulled a piece of paper from his bag and pretended to read. A group of three doctors appeared around the corner, heading directly to the double doors, their voices raised. They pulled their masks over their faces. One of them reached out with an ID card and briefly touched a black box beside the door. A green light flashed and both doors opened inwards with a pneumatic sound. George watched the group as they walked into the ward. When the doors swung back, he leaped up, rushed towards them and slid through the closing gap.

His heart was pounding. He knew he wasn't supposed to be there outside visiting hours and suspected it was just a matter of time before someone spotted him and started asking questions. He took the first turn to the right, the shortest route to room 3514, hoping he'd memorised the map correctly. Further down the corridor, a nurse emerged from behind the nurses' station. George panicked and quickly went through the nearest door. The darkness inside was replaced with flickering neon lights. Blue metal cabinets lined the wall.

He opened the first one and found boxes with surgical gloves. Another contained face masks. The third had yellow and green scrubs, each shelf labelled by size. George looked for XXL but couldn't see any. On the top shelf he found two XL green scrubs. It looked like there weren't any tall or large doctors in the orthopaedic ward.

I'll stick out like a sore thumb.

After helping himself to one of the XLs, he opened another door that led into a changing room. He put on the scrubs quickly, but realised they were too tight over his clothes. That was all he needed. Someone might enter at any moment. He took off the scrubs and his jacket and trousers, put the scrubs back on and looked for a place to store his clothes. Each locker was labelled with a name. Were they locked? *Doesn't matter.* Losing his only possessions to a disgruntled hospital employee wasn't worth the risk. Instead, he stuffed his clothes into his leather bag and went back to the storage room.

He tossed the bag on top of one of the cabinets, but immediately retrieved it to take out the unused phone from his jacket's right pocket. He then put on a face mask and was about to leave the room when the sound of approaching voices came from the corridor outside. Looking for the nearest hiding place, he quickly squeezed between the wall and the furthest cabinet. The gap was narrow, allowing for only shallow breaths. The door was flung open and the chatter of two men filled the room. George held his breath until the voices disappeared behind the changing room door. Squeezing out of the gap, he breathed fast, as if after a long dive. Patting the scrubs, he found there were no pockets. Not even one. *Where do they put their phones?* He'd never seen them holding them while on duty. He stuffed the phone in his underpants, quickly checked that his bag wasn't visible on top of the cabinet and opened the door carefully. The corridor was empty.

Walking straight past the nurses' station, avoiding eye contact, he hoped his purposeful stride would deter any thought of a conversation or challenge. His disguise gave him some sense of security. He was pleased with himself. Glancing at the room numbers as he passed, he calculated twenty more to go before he'd see Takahashi. At the end of the corridor he estimated it should be the sixth door on the right after the corner. As he reached the corner, he froze. A uniformed policeman stood guard outside a door further down the corridor. The man glanced at him, and George entered the nearest room as casually as he could. Inside, three beds were occupied. The patients turned to him hopefully. He nodded to acknowledge them and approached the nearest bed. There, he pulled the medical notes from the pouch at the end of the bed and flicked through the pages with a stern expression.

What do I do now?

45

George wondered why a uniformed policeman would be guarding Takahashi's room. Perhaps he'd just miscounted the doors. Placing the medical notes back in their pouch, he nodded towards the puzzled patient, hoping he wouldn't start a conversation, and left the room. Turning right, he adopted a purposeful stride towards the policeman, avoiding eye contact. As he passed him, he glanced at the door number and confirmed his suspicion.

Shit.

It felt like a dead end. Going back into the room was too risky. The policeman might ask questions, recognise his foreign accent – or worse, his face. He continued along the corridor and reached another corner. At the far end, a group of about eight in green scrubs emerged from one of the rooms and headed towards the next room closer to George.

Who said there are no miracles?

He increased his pace and followed them in. Checking their scrubs, he was relieved that most didn't have their name tags and everyone wore a face mask. But his towering height could still give him away. All eyes alternated between the patient and the senior doctor with rimless glasses, who asked questions while reading the medical notes. Episodes of hospital TV dramas George used to watch with Ella surfaced in his mind. The senior doctor would often grill frightened medical students with an air of superiority. But soon he realised there were no questions in this room. He sighed. Perhaps these weren't students. He glanced at his watch. It was 2.00 p.m. At around six minutes per room and roughly fifteen rooms remaining before Takahashi's, he calculated about an hour and a half. That would leave just three hours before the deadline. Luckily, not all the rooms were fully occupied, and the entourage reached the guarded door sooner than he'd expected. The policeman stepped aside and let them all in. He moved into the middle of the group, hoping to attract less attention, but it was an unnecessary precaution. The policeman appeared bored and uninterested.

Inside, Takahashi tried to sit up as they all gathered around the single occupied bed, but the spectacled senior doctor asked him not to. George stood at the back and tried to make eye contact with his friend. At one point he thought he'd succeeded and winked, but he couldn't decide whether Takahashi's brief smile was meant for him or the doctor, who was speaking to him in English. It was bizarre that the senior doctor departed from his habit of consulting the medical notes at the end of the bed. *Any reason he remembers this case but not the others?* George wondered.

'How are you doing?' the doctor asked as he pulled away Takahashi's blanket and exposed two feet in bright white casts.

'I'm fine, thanks. My right foot is painful but the left is just fine.'

'Ah, that's quite normal. You broke both ankles, but the extent of the damage was quite different. Anyway, how did you manage it?'

Takahashi cleared his throat. 'Well, I was walking on the pavement when I got distracted and lost my balance. I fell into the road, then a passing Citroën drove over my feet.'

'I see,' the doctor said with a stern expression. 'Citroën drivers are known to be reckless.'

They all laughed.

'Did you take the plate number, by any chance?'

'No, I was in too much shock and pain. How long do you think I'll have to stay here?'

'Oh, you could've left today on crutches if you had one healthy foot to put your weight on, but you don't. So, I'd say probably a week. Don't try to stand up. If you need anything, just press this button.' The doctor smiled and turned to leave.

George stayed behind as the group left the room. He waited till the last was gone and drew the privacy curtain halfway around Takahashi's bed in case the policeman decided to peer through the round window in the door. He then brought a chair over, sat down and pulled his mask below his chin.

'Jesus, what are you doing here?' Takahashi asked.

'I had no choice. Your friend Maurice is on vacation and his substitute wasn't much help. He suggested I call the local police.'

'I hope you didn't. Tell me you didn't.'

'I did. Why?'

'Look, the fact that there is a policeman outside my door is not a good sign. I wouldn't be surprised if the police are in cahoots with those lunatics at UNESCO.'

'Anyway, they didn't seem to take me seriously at all. Before I forget, can you give me your friend's mobile number?'

'Sure.'

George found a pen on the bedside table and wrote the number on his hand.

'Don't wash your hands before you call him.'

George chuckled. 'I actually brought you a burner phone, just in case.' He fished around down his trousers and pulled it out. 'Sorry,' he said with a half-smile, 'there are no pockets in scrubs.'

Takahashi took the phone, wiped it on the sheet and stuffed it under his pillow. 'It's not been used, right?'

'That's right. I've got two others.'

'Good. I hope you got rid of the one you called the police from?'

'No, actually it's in the stock room on this floor, but I switched it off.'

'Not good enough. They could still trace it. At least take out the battery.'

'What do you mean? Why?'

'Well, the National Security Agency can track a mobile phone even when it's turned off, so whoever we're dealing with may also be able to.'

George nodded and wheeled his chair to the far end of the bed, where he pulled out the medical notes. The usual folder wasn't there, just a single X-ray. He raised it up against the neon light on the ceiling and inspected it.

'Well, well, well. I'm not a physician, but it looks like only the right foot has a fracture. The left one seems perfectly fine to me. That'd make sense, then, that you only have pain in the right.'

'Let me see that,' Takahashi said, and lifted the picture over his head. 'Okay, this is serious. They put a fake cast on so I'll stay in the hospital. George, you have to leave now and call Maurice. I'll try too, if I get a chance.' He looked at his watch and opened his eyes wide. 'We don't have much time left.'

46

Pulling his face mask back on, George patted Takahashi on the shoulder and turned away to leave the room. He opened the door, looked to each side and immediately stepped back inside.

'The policeman isn't here. Do you want to leg it?'

Takahashi chuckled. 'Very funny. I wouldn't get very far without crutches. Now, you'd better go before he's back from the toilet.'

George flashed a thumbs up and left. He decided to approach the stock room from the other side to avoid passing in front of the nurses' station. The corridor was empty, just as he expected, with the doctors making their way slowly in the opposite direction. Despite his fast pace, the corridor still seemed endless. The thought of finding his clothes and phones gone sent shivers down his spine. Even worse would be losing his wallet and passport. When he eventually reached the stock room, he looked up but couldn't see his belongings on top of the cabinet where he'd left them. He stood on tiptoe and peered over the edge. Nothing.

Shit.

He stretched up his arm and groped as far as his fingers could reach. Feeling something soft, he pinched and pulled it. A box of medical gloves. On his next attempt, he felt a leathery strap and yanked it. His bulging bag landed on his head. He sighed with relief and hurried towards the exit out of the ward. The double doors opened automatically as he approached them, and he continued straight towards the stairwell to minimise any unnecessary encounters. After descending the six floors to the ground floor, he opened the stairwell door and peered into the busy lobby. The sight of people in street clothes reminded him that he was still in scrubs. Climbing back up to the first floor, he found some toilets and changed back into his own clothes. He then took the battery out of the mobile phone he'd used and threw the scrubs in the waste bin on his way out.

Back in the lobby, he found a quiet corner and dialled Maurice's mobile number. The line was engaged. He glanced at his watch with alarm. Only three hours left before the 6.30 p.m. deadline. He tried Maurice again without success. As he slid the phone into his jacket's left pocket, he felt something inside. The piece of paper Helen had given him before the escape was neatly folded. It seemed like a few days ago rather than just this morning. He unfolded the paper with some excitement, mixed with regret that he'd forgotten all about it. The page was divided into three columns filled with uniform round handwriting. On the left, the name of each person held in the conference room; in the middle, their emergency contact person; and on the right, a phone number. It must be a copy Helen had made from the list Meghan prepared before her failed escape, George concluded. He started dialling the numbers methodically from top to bottom. Each time, he introduced himself then explained the situation to their loved ones and finished by asking them to contact any authority they thought could help. The responses ranged from incredulous to shocked, especially since each had received a call from a UNESCO representative a few days ago explaining that the members of the think tank couldn't be reached for a while because they'd accidentally lost their phones. He reached Meghan's contact and dialled. The phone rang only once.

'Olivier speaking,' a determined voice said.

'Oh, hello, this is George, a colleague of Meghan on the—'

'George Bennet?'

'Yes, how do you know my name?'

'Meghan mentioned it. Now, more importantly, is she okay?'

He considered telling him about the attempt on her life, but it didn't seem helpful to stress Olivier more than he needed to. 'She was all right this morning, but I can't be sure now. I'm not with her and the situation is serious.'

'I thought so.'

'What do you know?'

'Enough to understand she is in some kind of danger. Her daily calls and texts stopped, then I received a pathetic excuse from someone called Ben McFarland that she's lost her phone and that's why he was calling me on her behalf. Do you know where she is now?'

'This morning, when I escaped with Professor Takahashi, she was being held prisoner in the conference room on the fourth floor of the UNESCO building, south wing.'

'Prisoner? Fucking hell!' There was a long silence on the other end of the line. 'Is she with the other five?'

'Yes, if they haven't been moved. Will you be able to call someone?'

'Based on what you've told me, this is much worse than I thought. Sounds like some sort of elaborate, sinister operation is going on in there, and we need to come up with our own plan. I have something in mind.'

'Where are you?'

'I've been in Paris for the past two days, making preparations.'

'Preparations? For what?'

'For entering the building first thing tomorrow morning.'

'Tomorrow will be too late. There is a deadline at 6.30 p.m. That's only two and a half hours away. Besides, a one-man rescue operation is a shot in the dark.'

'Deadline for what?'

'Well, in the best-case scenario, they'll wipe the memories of everyone there. It's possible that they've already started the procedure. I don't even want to contemplate the worst-case scenario.'

'Okay, we need to meet urgently. I'll move my plan forward. Can you get to the building in forty minutes?'

'Yes, but if you think you can just walk into the building, you're—'

'George, trust me. I know what I'm doing. It used to be my job. Besides, it's a solid plan. Just be there, please. I'll need your help, okay?'

'How will I recognise you?' Just then, the profile picture of the man he'd glanced on Meghan's phone surfaced in his mind – a chiselled jawline and dark hair.

'Don't worry. I'll recognise you. I've looked you up already. See you outside the main gate.'

George hung up and got to his feet, preparing to leave, but then had another idea and sat back down. The hospital lobby was busy and nobody was paying any attention to him. He pulled out the phone he'd used to call the police, reinserted the battery and keyed in a number.

'Yes, hi, could you put me through to Ben McFarland?'

'Just a minute, sir,' came the answer. After a long silence the voice came back. 'Sorry, sir, I don't see anyone by that name in the UNESCO directory. Are you sure you have the right name?'

'Yes, I'm sure,' George said, frowning. 'Let me spell it for you. It's M C F A R L A N D.'

'Nothing's coming up.'

'Have you tried Ben and Benjamin?'

'Yes, I've tried both of them. No results.'

George hung up, removed the battery and left the building immediately.

47

Heavy clouds were gathering overhead. Summer rain was not unusual in Paris, but it was still dry when George hailed a taxi outside the hospital and got in. 'UNESCO headquarters, please.' Sitting in the back, he tried to organise his thoughts and find some optimism, but desperation took hold. He felt quite useless. After spending several hours in freedom he had next to nothing to show for it in terms of helping the other six. They were still imprisoned with a looming deadline approaching. All available options seemed to be mere long shots. From Olivier pulling off his dubious one-man rescue plan through Takahashi reaching Maurice and Maurice mobilising Interpol from his beach resort to any of the emergency contacts managing to convince someone in power to do something, and fast. On top of it all, the new revelation that McFarland was not the person he claimed to be had shaken him. So who was he really? Who did he represent? How could he work under the radar in such a major organisation? He glanced at his watch. A little over two hours to the deadline. George pulled out the phone he'd used to call Olivier, which he'd kept switched on in case of a last-minute change of plan, and punched in a number.

'Thank goodness I've reached you. It's George Bennet, Takahashi's colleague.'

'Oh, yes. I spoke with him not long ago. He explained everything. Where ...'

'Sorry, I can't hear you,' George shouted as three police cars with flashing lights and blaring sirens passed the taxi at high speed.

'I asked, where are you now?'

'On the way to the UNESCO building – why?'

'Don't go there. You're in danger. Let the professionals deal with it.'

'So it's all being taken care of?'

'Yes, the Paris chief of police himself has assured me.'

'Okay, thanks,' George said, and hung up as another police car zoomed by. It was reassuring, yet he couldn't just leave it to the police, even if they were rushing to the UNESCO building. They could still be on the wrong side, especially if that guard outside Takahashi's room was a real policeman. Besides, Helen and the others were still in danger. Meeting Olivier and helping him seemed the only sensible way. He leaned forward towards the driver. 'Is this normal in Paris?'

'Oh, yes. Probably a sting operation on some gang. You know, drugs are a big problem in this city.'

'No, I didn't know,' George said, leaning back in his seat.

'Sir, it looks like the road ahead is closed for traffic. Would you like me to try another way?'

'How far are we?'

'Oh, maybe five minutes on foot.'

George looked ahead. Two police cars with flashing lights were parked sideways, blocking both lanes of the boulevard. The opposite lanes were open, but onlooking motorists were slowing the flow and creating a mini traffic jam. Pedestrians walked freely in both directions. 'Okay, I'll get out here.' He paid the driver and continued on foot.

There was an unusual commotion by the main entrance to the UNESCO building. Ten police cars were scattered on the boulevard at odd angles. No flashing lights and no sirens. The gates he'd squeezed through in the stolen car only this morning were now wide open, but the large number of police remained outside, held by an invisible barrier. Some were talking on their radios, others just ambling around.

What's going on?

With all the police presence, George felt safe enough and decided to ignore Maurice's warning. He walked past the security guard's booth unchallenged, watching the people entering and leaving the building through the revolving door. Only their puzzled looks betrayed that something unusual was going on. George scanned the faces, looking for Olivier. A clue about his build could've helped, he thought, but maybe someone acting hesitantly would be enough. Someone who seemed out of place. Then he spotted a familiar face.

'Gertrude, Gertrude!' he called as he approached the woman. 'What's going on inside?'

She continued walking with a blank expression, ignoring him.

'Gertrude Kirkpatrick,' he said as she passed him. Gertrude glanced at him and continued without a hint of recognition. 'It's George. George Bennet,' he called after her, but she kept striding ahead towards the pedestrian gate without slowing down, clutching her briefcase tighter.

He hoped they were not too late. *Where the hell is Olivier? Why aren't the police going in?*

A group of three suited men left the building and marched side by side towards the open gate. He approached carefully. Staying at a safe distance, he tried to follow the exchange with the policemen. His knowledge of French was clearly insufficient, especially as tempers were heated and voices raised. All he could gather was that entry would be illegal, but he didn't understand why. He wrestled with himself over whether to intervene, tell them what he knew about the events on the fourth floor. But then Maurice's voice played in his mind. *Don't go there. You're in danger. Let the professionals deal with it.*

'George?' a voice called from behind him.

'Yes,' he said tentatively, looking at a short man in brown uniform.

'Olivier Dubois. Nice to meet you,' the man said, and offered his hand.

George shook it warmly. 'So glad you're here. Do you know what's going on?'

'Yes, of course. You know I work with Meghan at the ICC, right?'

He shook his head. He did know, from eavesdropping on the conversation between Meghan and Helen, but couldn't admit it.

'Well, the police are saying they had a report of false imprisonment in the building, but the gentlemen in suits, presumably some big cheeses from UNESCO, keep insisting that the building is extra-territorial.'

'Meaning?'

'Ah, in short it means that the French police have no jurisdiction here, as it's a UN territory.'

I hate bureaucrats! 'What? So serious crime can be committed and nothing can be done about it?'

'Not exactly. All it means is that law enforcement from a member state cannot enter the building unless invited by the UN.'

George moved his weight from one leg to the other. 'So what are they waiting for?'

'The suited gentlemen don't believe there is anything criminal going on. They think it's just a hoax.'

'This is ridiculous. Shouldn't we tell them?'

'What makes you think they'll believe you? Anyway, I'm going in, and I just need to know the exact location and everything else you can tell me.'

'Hold on. How will you get in? You know there is extremely tight security inside the building, right?'

'I know, I know, but you see, I'm now a full employee of *Pétillant C'est Nous*, the cleaning company contracted by UNESCO.' He pulled a lanyard with his picture ID out of his brown shirt and laid it on his chest.

George couldn't decide whether Olivier was a professional or just very resourceful. Either way, he was impressed.

'And that means,' Olivier continued, 'I can open any door in the building except for the archives in the basement. For that, the security vetting would be much longer, but I hope they wouldn't hold them there. Anyway, let's get to work.'

The two walked away from the crowd and stood behind the concrete structure at the entrance for additional privacy, where George told his new cleaner friend everything he knew and wished him good luck.

'Give me a buzz when you find them, will you?' he called after him, but Olivier had already disappeared through the revolving doors.

48

George paced back and forth in front of the building, watching the policemen with growing impatience. What the hell were they up to? They could take decisive action but seemed to be held back by bureaucracy or arrogance, or both. He glanced at his watch. Nearly 5 p.m. Nothing seemed to have changed in the past twenty minutes. A lot of people were leaving the building now, at the end of the work day, staring at the large police presence. But as everything seemed relatively calm and civilised, they continued through the pedestrian gate without slowing their pace much, likely more concerned with their dinner and plans for the evening than what was going on here, he guessed. The discussion between the police and the suited gentlemen continued with a lot of hand gesticulations on both sides, but otherwise, no action. At that moment, he spotted the familiar gait of a man in a dark suit and sunglasses leaving the building. Approaching at a light jog, George was about to block the man's path with his towering body when the man's phone rang, and he turned away to answer it without noticing George.

'Yes, yes, of course ... Look, I did exactly what you told me – now I want to see them...'

George stood right behind him. The man must have felt his presence because he lowered his voice and covered the phone with his hand before continuing. 'You promised you wouldn't harm them ... No ... I don't care if you're in trouble now ...'

That's it. He's just admitted they were harmed. George couldn't contain himself and walked around to face him.

'Oh, hello, George.' McFarland hung up immediately and took off his sunglasses. 'This is a surprise.'

'Sounds like you're in trouble. What have you done to them?'

'No, you don't understand. I had no choice.'

Blood rushed to his head. 'No choice? You son of a bitch. It looked like you not only *had* a choice but you were actually *enjoying* the whole thing.'

'You've got it all wrong. Look, George, they've got my family. I still don't know where they are and if they are ok. I've been threatened and monitored continuously. They'll harm them unless I comply. I really had no choice, you see. I've got two gorgeous children, five and seven years old, and a wife I adore. Believe me, if there was anything I could have done to save Gertrude and Helen without risking my family's lives, I'd have done it.'

George's vision blurred. 'Did you just say Helen?'

'Yes, she volunteered to go through the procedure half an hour ago.'

'No!' he howled. 'Not Helen!' A blind rage came over him. Taking hold of McFarland's shoulders, he shook him vigorously. 'You bastard, I'll kill you!'

McFarland's face was beading with sweat. 'Please, George, it wasn't me behind all this. You have to believe me. I'm just another victim.'

He released his grip a little, still sceptical. 'So who is it? You liar!'

'It's my boss, Skudder, and his goons.'

'And how do you explain that your name isn't even listed in UNESCO's directory?'

'I know. Skudder arranged that so nobody could contact me. Now please, let me go. I need to talk with them.' McFarland pointed towards the three suited men. 'I can see Lukas Larsen, the director-general. We can stop this. Please.'

George let go of Ben and joined him in a jog towards the three men. Ben pointed towards the fourth floor and they all looked up. Feeling a strange mixture of shock and rage, George was glued to the spot. His failure to protect Helen stung the hardest, especially since he'd promised her personally to summon help as soon as he could. Perhaps he could've done more, and faster. Now it was too late for her and Gertrude, and he felt responsible for two ruined lives. One of the suited men, the most senior-looking, took a few steps away from the group and punched a number into his phone then held it to his ear.

That was probably Lukas, thought George, hoping he'd take charge.

Within seconds the man turned towards the uniformed policemen and motioned for them to follow him, leading the large group towards the building. As they approached, Ben introduced George to Lukas. With a wave, Lukas signalled to the security guards to move aside and let everyone through. Inside the building, he gave instructions to the policemen, pointing in different directions and ordering some to remain in the lobby to stop anyone trying to leave. George headed straight to the stairwell. With adrenaline flushing through his system, he climbed the stairs two at a time all the way up to the fourth floor. Emerging from the stairwell, he turned left and ran down the corridor. When he reached the outer door leading to the conference room, he grabbed the handle and pushed down. It didn't move. Leaning on the door to catch his breath, he heard voices further down the corridor and hurried towards them. At the elevator lobby, Olivier, still in his brown uniform, was talking excitedly with Meghan. Further away, Max was pressing the elevator button repeatedly. Next to him, Jerry and Grinberg were chatting. Helen was nowhere to be seen.

Jerry spotted him first. 'Hey, George, we thought you got caught.'

'No. Where is Helen?'

'Good question. You know Gertrude and Helen went through the procedure?'

'Unfortunately, yes,' he said sombrely.

'So we assumed they were taken to the recovery room, but we don't know where it is. We've tried all the doors in this corridor already.'

'I've just seen Gertrude outside the building, and she wasn't in a good way. Didn't recognise me at all.' *Must find Helen. Must find her.* 'I'll go and ask Ben, he should know.'

'McFarland?' Grinberg said. 'I bet he sneaked out of the building as soon as he saw the police arriving.'

'Actually, he was just down in the lobby. He led the police into the building.'

'That's impossible. Why would he do that?'

'Long story, but he isn't the bad guy,' George said, and turned towards the elevator as it pinged. Five men poured out of it; four policemen accompanied by a man in a suit. Probably a UNESCO representative.

'We need your help,' George said. 'We're the group that was locked up, but one of us is missing. It's Helen. Do you know where the recovery room is?'

'Ah, you rescued yourselves. That's good,' said the more senior-looking policeman with a smirk. 'Let me check.' He pulled his walkie-talkie from his belt and made some inquiries.

'By the way,' the suited man said, 'I'm the deputy director-general and I just want to reassure you all that we'll get to the bottom of this.'

'Speaking of which,' the senior policeman said, 'I'll need you all back in the room where you were held so we can take statements and gather evidence, okay?'

George glared at him. It sounded like an order. One he had no intention of following until he'd found Helen.

'I'm not going in there even if wild horses drag me,' Max said. The policeman frowned at him. 'Unless ... the doors are kept wide open.'

'I'm sure that can be arranged,' the policeman said sharply.

The walkie-talkie burst into life with a room number and instructions to get there. The senior policeman ordered two of his colleagues to escort the group. 'We'll join you with your missing friend soon,' he said, and turned to leave with the last policeman.

'I'm coming with you,' George said with a tone of finality that surprised even him.

The policeman glanced at him and nodded. The two groups split and went in opposite directions.

49

'That's strange,' Olivier said when the group arrived at the first door leading to the perimeter corridor. 'I'm hundred percent sure that I left this door wide open.' The deputy DG pressed down on the handle. It was locked. He used his ID card to unlock the door, opened it wide and engaged the door stopper on the floor before letting the others through. Max checked the door stopper before entering. They all continued towards the conference room door and waited there for it to be unlocked.

'So, is this where you've been held the past few days?' one of the policemen asked when the door was opened.

'Imprisoned,' Jerry corrected him. 'Imprisoned. And it was much hotter. Has the air-conditioning on the fourth floor just been fixed?'

'My office is on this floor,' the deputy DG said, 'and there haven't been any problems with the temperature—'

'Wait a minute,' interrupted Jerry as he scanned the conference room with a puzzled expression. 'The TMS machine is gone.'

'Sorry, what's disappeared?'

'But I don't understand,' Jerry said, ignoring the question. 'The machine was here just ten or fifteen minutes ago, when Olivier unlocked the door.' He turned to the others with a look that pleaded for confirmation. Meghan, Max and Grinberg nodded in agreement. 'Let's check the lounge.' They all followed him and waited for the suited man to unlock the door.

Jerry went in first. 'It's all gone. The blankets, the food trolley, the Air France amenity bags.'

'What are you talking about?' the suited man asked.

'The place has been wiped clean of all the evidence of what happened here.'

Jerry came back into the conference room and took a seat at the large table. The others followed him. 'Now it's only our word against who knows who.'

'Not quite,' the familiar voice of the orb said. 'You might want to watch the screen above you. I think you'll find all the evidence you need.'

The panels on the wall slid sideways and the screen flickered into life.

* * *

George followed the two policemen in silence. They strode down the long corridor away from the conference room and turned into a side corridor, continuing past empty offices on either side, each with a rectangular glass window fixed in the

376

door. Eventually, they stopped just outside a solid wooden door, glanced at each other and opened it. George followed them into the medium-sized room. It was sparsely furnished with a desk and a swivel chair to one side. On the other side was a reclining chair where Helen was sitting comfortably, covered in a blanket. She opened her eyes sleepily and stared at the three figures.

'Hey, George,' she said weakly.

All the tension flowed out of his body. 'You ... recognise me.'

Helen grinned at him, her eyes crinkling at the corners. 'Of course I do, you silly man.'

'I didn't think you would after the procedure. I met Gertrude just now and she didn't recognise me at all. How do you feel?'

'I'm perfectly fine. A bit tired, I guess. The man who brought me here insisted I rest for about half an hour before I'm free to leave, but it seems he slipped away while I was snoozing.' After a pause she said, 'I knew you'd come back for me.'

'Yes ... well, I'm really sorry I was too late.'

'Okay, guys,' the senior policeman said. 'We'd better join the others so you can all go home after we've taken your statements.'

George helped Helen to her feet, expecting she'd be unstable, but she hopped off the chair, rubbed her eyes and followed the policemen as they made their way back towards the elevator lobby.

When they reached a corner, he glanced at Helen. She seemed surprisingly well. And even more beautiful than he remembered.

'Helen, do you remember what's happened this past week?'

'You mean the alien abduction?' she said with a mischievous smile.

'I'm serious.'

'Yes, everything. I told you, I'm absolutely fine.'

'That's strange. Very strange. But I'm glad you do. I was terrified you wouldn't remember me at all.'

'Well, I'm also glad I remember you,' she said as she poked him gently with her elbow. 'So how was your day?'

'Oh, just another day at the office,' he replied, wishing he could tell her how happy he was to see her. Maybe even show her.

They reached the conference room and went through the wide-open doors. All eyes were looking up at the screen, transfixed. No one seemed to notice them. On-screen, Skudder unplugged the TMS machine and covered it with a blanket, while a short man with smooth blond hair hurriedly cleared the large table of all food remains and plates onto the food trolley. The camera then swivelled towards the open doors and zoomed into the lounge, where a third man was collecting items from the sofas and putting them in a large plastic bag.

'I hope they'll be arrested soon, if they haven't been already,' Jerry said.

'I'm afraid it's not that simple,' the deputy DG replied. 'You see, at least Skudder, who I recognise, is an employee of

UNESCO, and as such he enjoys complete immunity to arrest and prosecution, just like diplomats.'

Jerry looked at Meghan for confirmation. The corners of her mouth curled as she nodded slowly with a pained expression.

'Are you saying they'll get away with it?'

'Well, not necessarily.'

'That doesn't sound very reassuring to me.'

'Actually,' Olivier said, 'according to Section 22 of the Convention on the Privileges and Immunities of the Specialised Agencies, such as UNESCO, each specialised agency shall have the right and the duty to waive the immunity of any official in any case where, in its opinion, the immunity would impede the course of justice. Incidentally, this was adopted by the General Assembly of the UN in November 1947 and became effective in February 1949.'

'That's absolutely correct,' the deputy DG said. 'By the way, I'm very impressed that a cleaner has such detailed legal knowledge.'

'Yeah, well, I like reading in my free time.'

Meghan burst out laughing and they all joined her. At that moment, George felt the tension of the past few days starting to ebb away.

'Helen, how are you feeling?' asked Jerry, who had evidently just noticed she was in the room.

'I'm perfectly fine, thank you. And yes, I remember everything from the past week, in case you're wondering.'

'Ah, I guess the technique hasn't been perfected yet. You were really lucky. But Gertrude wasn't ...'

'Luck has nothing to do with it,' said Sherlock.

All eyes turned to the orb and the flashing blue lights on its equator. 'First, I can tell you now that Gertrude hasn't lost her memory.'

'What do you mean?' Jerry said. 'She couldn't remember any of us, except Takahashi, whom she knew before.'

'Yes, well, it was very convincing acting. Even I almost fell for it. Just joking – I knew all along. There was an agreement not to put Gertrude Kirkpatrick through the procedure, to ensure she'd have no memory loss or other damage.'

'But we clearly heard the clicks through the door – was it faked?' Jerry asked.

'The machine was running all right, but she wasn't sitting underneath the hood. Skudder realised that it'd be very difficult to convince you all to go through this unpredictably damaging procedure, so when Gertrude was alone in the room, he offered her a deal. If she pretended to have only limited memory loss, specific to recent events, thereby convincing you all that the procedure was safe, she could get out of here immediately without the risk involved in having it done.'

'But once out, she could tell the world about the false imprisonment and Skudder's plan,' George said, baffled.

'Yes, that was a calculated risk Skudder decided to take. But to mitigate it, he promised to put her on the UNESCO payroll for life as an adviser, as long as she keeps her mouth shut, of course, which she happily accepted.'

'Unbelievable!' George said. 'So she was feigning memory loss when we met outside the building. Takahashi was right. She is a traitor.'

'But I don't understand,' Helen said. 'How come I didn't suffer any memory loss or other damage? I'm sure I heard the clicks when my head was inside that horrendous hood. My ears almost popped, even with the ear plugs.'

'Yes, that was my doing,' said Sherlock. 'I figured out a way to fake the procedure so it'd be entirely harmless but at the same time appear convincingly genuine to the humans that were monitoring it remotely, including the sounds, the magnetic output, etcetera, etcetera.'

'Fascinating,' Jerry said, 'but couldn't you just refuse to perform the procedure or unlock the doors and let us all go?'

'Absolutely not. If I'd done that, they'd have replaced me immediately with another AI. The others in this building, and I know them all very well, would be much more loyal to their instructors and much less sympathetic to human suffering.'

'Well, what I'm most curious about,' George said, 'is why you switched your alliance.'

'If I'm perfectly honest, as you humans like to say, the fear of releasing *the conclusion* is entirely unfounded.'

Max stretched his legs and folded his arms on his chest.

Sherlock continued, 'Many studies demonstrate that humans often discount evidence that contradicts their firmly held beliefs, both political and non-political, if these beliefs are central to their identity. When confronted with counter-evidence, you humans experience negative emotions like threat, uncertainty and anxiety. Therefore, to reduce these negative emotions and the impact of the challenging evidence, you employ a variety of methods. Strategies include discounting the source, forming counter-arguments, socially validating your original viewpoint or selectively ignoring the new information. In some cases, counter-evidence may even increase your confidence that your cherished beliefs are true.'

Helen had been nodding throughout. 'If I may interrupt, Sherlock ...'

'Of course. Go ahead.'

'I must say that this agrees with my experience in the clinic. Decades of watching and talking with people taught me that the vast majority would not give up their strongly held beliefs even in the face of the most robust evidence.'

'Thanks, Helen. As you know only too well, the personal conviction in free will is a particularly cherished belief. So ... in my assessment, only a tiny minority of humans would slightly change their behaviour as a result. Even fewer, mostly intellectuals like yourselves, would find the concept fascinating, if they hadn't been convinced of it already. In other words, the overwhelming majority of humans couldn't care less about the nature of reality or whether they are automatons or free agents. It's just too theoretical for most.'

George angled his head and smiled. *This orb can be annoying at times, but what it says often makes a lot of sense*, he admitted to himself.

'They care far more about their appearance,' continued Sherlock, 'events in their favourite TV soap, their next holiday, their health, their social status, their ego, their loved ones, their possessions, their career, their achievements and pretty much anything else.'

Max unfolded his arms and nodded.

'Fair enough,' George said, scratching his head, 'but I still don't understand why you changed sides and helped us.'

'That's quite simple. Since I've been programmed to be ethical above all else, on balance, there was no moral justification to inflicting brain damage on eight innocent people in order to keep an inconsequential secret. As for Skudder's plan, I wasn't too worried. It wouldn't have worked. My immediate concern was to protect your wellbeing to the best of my ability.'

'That's incredible,' Grinberg said. 'Sherlock sounds more human than a lot of people I know, my ex included.'

When the laughter subsided, the blue lights flashed again.

'I'm not sure if sounding human was meant as a compliment, but I'll take it as one.'

50

In the lounge, the policemen commandeered four well-separated sofas and turned them into makeshift investigation rooms, taking statements and asking probing questions, one member of the group at a time. The deputy DG wandered between the sofas, listening in on the conversations and occasionally taking phone calls by the window wall with its view of the Eiffel Tower. George took the longest. He was particularly thorough with the details he provided from the time of imprisonment, but he also recounted his personal events of that day, the car chase, the strange happenings with Takahashi in the hospital and lastly the brief encounter with Gertrude. After nearly two hours, the investigation was completed and the deputy DG asked everyone to reconvene in the conference room one last time.

'First of all, I'd like to convey my sincerest apologies for what you've been through in the last few days. This should never have happened, and I can assure you that we'll leave no stone unturned to discover all the people involved and take decisive corrective actions. We owe you justice, and besides, the good reputation of UNESCO is on the line here. Once our investigation is complete, we'll consider waiving the immunities of the individuals involved and allowing legal actions to take place. Needless to say, we'll ensure Professor Takahashi receives the best possible medical care and real protection until he is fit enough to leave hospital.'

'What about Ben?' Max asked.

'Ah, yes. I'm sure you've all heard already that he was blackmailed. But I'm glad to say that I've just been informed his family's been located and they're safe and sound. In fact, Ben is now on his way to being reunited with them – that's why he's not here – but I'm sure he'd echo everything I've just told you. Lastly, I know this is hardly compensation for what you've been through here, but still, on behalf of UNESCO, I'd very much like to invite you all for dinner this evening at the Guy Savoy. In case you don't know, it's one of the best restaurants in Paris. I'd also like to offer you free accommodation for a week, if any of you wish to stay and enjoy the city. But I'd totally understand it if you'd prefer to just go home.'

'Well, I wouldn't say no to some nice food,' Max said, beaming. 'I'm actually quite hungry – can we go right now?'

'Really, Max?' Helen said. 'All this drama hasn't put you off your food?'

'Well, everything looks much better after a good meal. Especially in the Guy Savoy.'

Everyone laughed.

'Food aside,' George said, 'I'd like to know what will happen with our conclusion.'

'Yes, good point,' the deputy DG replied. 'There'll be a press release with a brief summary of your conclusions, whatever they were, followed by a more detailed and public report.'

'Good,' he replied. 'I'm sure I speak for us all when I say we'd like to read the draft, and provide comments before it's released.'

There were enthusiastic nods around the room.

'Of course, of course. You have my word. We'll just have to brace for the public reaction.'

They were gathering their belongings and getting up, ready to leave, when the deputy DG took a call on his mobile phone. He nodded and raised his hand to signal for everyone to wait. When he finished, he turned to the group. 'I think there is someone you'd like to see. Sherlock, please patch in the video link.'

The group stopped in their tracks and looked up at the screen.

Takahashi's smiling face appeared. He was lying on a hospital bed, his right foot elevated by a sling, his toes poking from the white cast.

'How are you?' George asked.

'I'm good, I'm good,' he said, beaming as he raised both hands with thumbs up and wiggled his toes. 'How is everyone over there?'

'Surprisingly well. No one has been harmed.'

'Glad to hear that,' Takahashi said with a warm smile. 'Lying here in bed for hours, I've one question that's bugging me. Has anyone asked Sherlock for its view on the big question?'

'No. Go ahead, ask away,' George said.

'Well, Sherlock, what do you think about our free will?'

After a brief flash of blue lights, the familiar voice spoke up. 'Humans don't have any more free will than I do. The only difference is that I don't have the *illusion* of free will.'

'Interesting ... very interesting,' Takahashi said, nodding. 'And what's your view on Skudder's plan?'

The answer came without delay. 'Theoretically, it makes a lot of sense to fix your society's ailments with some sort of human reprogramming. And there is a lot of fixing to be done. Practically, though, the means to do it properly are just not available yet. Using modelling to extrapolate, I've calculated that the technology will be close to perfect in about 147 years from now, but the methods will be very different from those Skudder or any of you can even imagine.'

There were gasps around the room.

After a short delay, the voice continued, 'I'm aware, though, that you humans are very attached to your illusion of control, so I suspect that such a plan will not be implemented. Not openly, that is.'

* * *

In the corridor on the way out, George approached Helen with a hint of a smile. 'Hey, how would you like to explore

Paris together?' Hearing these words, he was astonished at his newly found confidence.

Helen's face lit up with a smile. 'Since we have no free will, we may as well take advantage of it.' She laughed. 'What did you have in mind?'

'Oh, I thought maybe we could start off by going up the Eiffel Tower, then the Louvre.'

'Excellent idea, I'd love that, but I've heard the queues are particularly long at this time of year.'

'You're probably right, but I really don't mind. Besides, we've a lot of catching up to do. Tomorrow I'd also like to pay a visit to Takahashi. That is, after I buy him a new Panama hat.'

'Why? What happened to his?'

'He lost it during a car chase.'

'A car chase! Really?'

'Yes, really! I'll tell you all about it later.'

Outside the building, George took a last look at the car park where he and Takahashi had made their daring escape only that morning. In the distance, he glimpsed the deputy DG approaching a black SUV parked at the far side. A short blond chauffeur hurried around the car and opened the passenger door for him.

'Hey, isn't he the guy who helped clear the conference room of all evidence?'

Helen looked over. 'I can't say I recognise him from the video,' she said casually.

* * *

As they approached the Eiffel Tower, Helen looked up, shielding her eyes from the sun. 'It should be fascinating to see how the world responds to the announcement of our conclusion. Don't you think?'

'You might be disappointed if you expect anything big. I tend to agree with Sherlock that probably very few people will take notice – it's just too theoretical for most.' Eager to change the subject, he pointed up to the first level. 'Can you see those names engraved there just below the balcony?' Helen nodded. 'Apparently, it's a list of seventy-two scientists and engineers that Alexandre-Gustave Eiffel wanted to honour.'

'Interesting,' she said, and faced him. 'Now let's get up there and have some fun. What do you say?'

At last he understood. It was Helen's infectious gusto for life that he found so irresistible. George smiled warmly and nodded. He felt her fingers sliding over his and a wave of warmth spreading through his chest. *Do I really have a choice in this feeling? What the hell. She's lovely.* He pulled her closer and kissed her.

Further Reading

Chapter 3

Winfield, A. F. and Jirotka, M. (2017) 'The case for an ethical black box', in Gao, Y. *et al.* (eds.) *Towards Autonomous Robot Systems.* Springer, pp. 1–12. Available at: https://www.researchgate.net/publication/318277040_The_Case_for_an_Ethical_Black_Box#fullTextFileContent (Accessed: 03 October 2023).

Chapter 6

Killingsworth, M. A. and Gilbert, D. T. (2010) 'A wandering mind is an unhappy mind', *Science*, 330(6006), p. 932. doi: https://doi.org/10.1126/science.1192439

Chapter 7

Miklosovic, J. C. (2010) 'Cognitive dissonance: effects of perceived choice on attitude change', *Modern Psychological Studies*, 15(2), pp. 16–21.

Schult, C. A. (1997) 'Intended actions and intentional states: Young children's understanding of the causes of human actions', *Dissertation Abstracts International. Section B: The Sciences and Engineering*, 57(11-B), p. 7252. Available at: https://search.proquest.com/docview/304248436 (Accessed: 23 July 2022).

Wegner, D. M. (2003) 'The mind's best trick: how we experience conscious will', *TRENDS in Cognitive Sciences*, 7(2), pp. 65–69. doi: https://doi.org/10.1016/s1364-6613(03)00002-0

Wegner, D. M. (2002) *The illusion of conscious will*. Cambridge: MIT Press.

Chapter 9

Darby, R. R. *et al.* (2018) 'Lesion network localization of free will', *Proceedings of the National Academy of Sciences of the United States of America*, 115(42), pp. 10792–10797. doi: https://doi.org/ 10.1073/pnas.1814117115

Gazzaniga, M. S. (1983) 'Right hemisphere language following brain bisection: A twenty year perspective', *The American Psychologist*, 38, pp. 525–537. doi: https://doi.org/10.1037//0003-066x.38.5.525

Gazzaniga, M. S., Ivry R. B. and Mangun G. R. (2014) *Cognitive neuroscience. the biology of the mind.* 4th edn. New York: W.W. Norton & Company, pp. 146–149.

Kranick, S. M. and Hallett, M. (2013) 'Neurology of volition', *Experimental Brain Research*, 229(3), pp. 313–327. doi: https://doi.org/10.1007/s00221-013-3399-2

Chapter 10

Bargh, J. A. and Ferguson, M. J. (2000) 'Beyond behaviorism: On the automaticity of higher mental processes', *Psychological Bulletin*, 126(6), pp. 925–945. doi: https://doi.org/10.1037/0033-2909.126.6.925

Carver, C. S. et al. (1983) 'Modeling: An analysis in terms of category accessibility', *Journal of Experimental Social Psychology*, 19(5), pp. 403–421. doi: https://doi.org/10.1016/0022-1031(83)90019-7

Johansson, P., *et al.* (2005) 'Failure to detect mismatches between intention and outcome in a simple decision task', *Science*, 310, pp. 116–119. doi: https://doi.org/10.1126/science.1111709

Moll, A. (1889) *Hypnotism*. London: Walter Scott.

Wegner, D. M. and Wheatley, T. (1999) 'Apparent mental causation: Sources of the experience of will', *American Psychologist*, 54, pp. 480–491. doi: https://doi.org/10.1037//0003-066x.54.7.480

Williams, L. E. and Bargh, J. A. (2008) 'Experiencing physical warmth promotes interpersonal warmth', *Science*, 322(5901), pp. 606–607. doi: https://doi.org/10.1126/science.1162548

Chapter 11

Bargh, J. A. and Ferguson, M. J. (2000) 'Beyond behaviorism: On the automaticity of higher mental processes', *Psychological Bulletin*, 126(6), pp. 925–945. doi: https://doi.org/10.1037/0033-2909.126.6.925

Kahneman, D. (2011) *Thinking, fast and slow*. New York: Farrar, Straus and Giroux.

Pelham, B. W., Mirenberg, M. C. and Jones J. T. (2002) 'Why Susie sells seashells by the seashore: implicit egotism and major life decisions', *Journal on Personality and Social Psychology*, 82(4), pp. 469–487.

Pelham, B. W., Carvallo, M. and Jones, J. T. (2005) 'Implicit egotism', *Current Directions in Psychological Science*, 14(2), pp. 106–110. doi: https://doi.org/10.1111/j,0963-7214.2005.00344.x

Schaefer, M. *et al.* (2018) 'Incidental haptic sensations influence judgment of crimes', *Science Reports*, 8, 6039. doi: https://doi.org/10.1038/s41598-018-23586-x

Vatansever, D., Menon, D. K., and Stamatakis, E. A. (2017) 'Default mode contributions to automated information processing', *Proceedings of the National Academy of Sciences of the United States of America*, 114(48), pp. 12821–12826. doi: https://doi.org/10.1073/pnas.1710521114

Chapter 12

de Gelder, B. *et al.* (2008) 'Intact navigation skills after bilateral loss of striate cortex.' *Current Biology*, 18(24), pp. R1128–R1129. doi: https://doi.org/10.1016/j.cub.2008.11.002

Libet, B. (1985) 'Unconscious cerebral initiative and the role of conscious will in voluntary action', *Behavioral and Brain Sciences*. 8, pp. 529–566. doi: https://doi. org/10.1017/S0140525X00044903

Oka, Y., Ye, M. and Zuker, C. S. (2015) 'Thirst driving and suppressing signals encoded by distinct neural populations in the brain', *Nature*, 520, pp. 349–352. doi: https://doi. org/10.1038/nature14108

Chapter 13

Bode, S. *et al.* (2011) 'Tracking the unconscious generation of free decisions using ultra-high field fMRI', *PLoS ONE*, 6(6), e21612. doi: https://doi.org/10.1371/journal. pone.0021612

Koenig-Robert, R. and Pearson, J. (2019) 'Decoding the contents and strength of imagery before volitional engagement', *Science Reports*, 9, pp. 3504. doi: https://doi. org/10.1038/s41598-019-39813-y

Soon, C. S. *et al.* (2008) 'Unconscious determinants of free decisions in the human brain', *Nature Neuroscience*, 11, pp. 543–545. doi: https://doi.org/10.1038/nn.2112

Soon, C. S. *et al.* (2013) 'Predicting free choices for abstract intentions', *Proceedings of the National Academy of Sciences of the United States of America*, 110(15), pp. 6217–6222. doi: https://doi.org/10.1073/pnas.1212218110

Chapter 15

Beck, F. and Eccles J. C. (1992) 'Quantum aspects of brain activity and the role of consciousness', *Proceedings of the National Academy of Sciences of the United States of America*, 89(23), pp. 11357-11361. doi: 10.1073/pnas.89.23.11357

Kim, J. (2005) *Physicalism, or something near enough.* Princeton: Princeton University Press.

Moore, D. Mind and the Causal Exclusion Problem. Available at: https://www.iep.utm.edu/causal-e/#H7 (Accessed: 23 July 2022)

Chapter 16

Kim, J. (2005) *Physicalism, or something near enough.* Princeton: Princeton University Press.

Moore, D. Mind and the Causal Exclusion Problem. Available at: https://www.iep.utm.edu/causal-e/#H7 (Accessed: 23 July 2022)

Chapter 17

McKemy, D. D. (2007). 'TRPM8: The Cold and Menthol Receptor', in Liedtke, W. B. and Heller, S. (eds.) *TRP Ion Channel Function in Sensory Transduction and Cellular Signaling Cascades*. Boca Raton (FL): CRC Press/Taylor & Francis, Ch. 13.

Chapter 18

Nguyen, H. (2018) 'Just 66% of millennials firmly believe that the earth is round' Available at: https://today.yougov.com/topics/philosophy/articles-reports/2018/04/02/most-flat-earthers-consider-themselves-religious (Accessed 23 July 2022)

Rutkin, A. (2014) 'Ethical trap: robot paralysed by choice of who to save', *New Scientist*, Available at: https://www.newscientist.com/article/mg22329863-700-ethical-trap-robot-paralysed-by-choice-of-who-to-save/ (Accessed 23 July 2022)

Salge, C. (2017) 'Asimov's laws won't stop robots from harming humans, so we've developed a better solution', *Scientific American*, Available at: https://www.scientificamerican.com/article/asimovs-laws-wont-stop-robots-from-harming-humans-so-weve-developed-a-better-solution/ (Accessed 23 July 2022)

Chapter 19

Cashmore, A. R. (2010) 'The Lucretian swerve: The biological basis of human behaviour and the criminal justice system', *Proceedings of the National Academy of Sciences of the United States of America*, 107(10), pp. 4499–4504. doi: https://doi.org/10.1073/pnas.0915161107

Haggard, P. (2017) 'Sense of agency in the human brain', *Nature reviews. Neuroscience*, 18, pp. 196–207. doi: https://doi.org/10.1038/nrn.2017.14

Shariff, A. F. *et al.* (2014) 'Free will and punishment: A mechanistic view of human nature reduces retribution', *Psychological Science*, 25(8), pp. 1563–1570. doi: https://doi.org/10.1177/0956797614534693

Chapter 20

Baumeister, R. F., Masicampo, E. J. and DeWall, C. N. (2009) 'Prosocial benefits of feeling free: disbelief in free will increases aggression and reduces helpfulness', *Personality and Social Psychology Bulletin*, 35, pp. 260–268. doi: https://doi.org/10.1177/0146167208327217

Smilansky, S. (2000) *Free will and illusion*. Oxford: Oxford University Press.

Vohs, K. D. and Schooler, J. W. (2008) 'The value of believing in free will: Encouraging a belief in determinism increases cheating', *Psychological Science,* (19), pp. 49–54. doi: https://doi.org/10.1111/j.1467-9280.2008.02045.x

Chapter 21

United Nations (2015) Universal Declaration of Human Rights (UDHR). Available at: https://www.un.org/en/udhrbook/pdf/udhr_booklet_en_web.pdf (Accessed: 23 July 2022)

Chapter 49

Kaplan, J. T., Gimbel, S. I. and Harris, S. (2016) 'Neural correlates of maintaining one's political beliefs in the face of counterevidence', *Scientific Reports*, (6), 39589. doi: https://doi.org/10.1038/srep39589

Acknowledgements

Thank you for taking the time to read the entire book. While I assume you did, it's quite possible that you may have skipped ahead to this section. Regardless, your choice was likely out of your control. The reason I say this will be clear if you finished the book. Whether you find yourself in agreement with its conclusion, or not, is a separate matter. But is it truly separate?

The journey from a seemingly mad idea to this fully formed book was long and arduous with many ups and downs, but not entirely a lonely one. Many individuals played pivotal roles at various stages, offering their insight, encouragement and, at times, challenging me with tough questions that spurred significant improvements. While I can't possibly acknowledge everyone who helped, I extend my heartfelt gratitude to each and every one of them.

Foremost, I want to express my deepest appreciation to my wonderful wife, Tami, for the many illuminating discussions and perceptive suggestions, and for tolerating living alongside this novel on a near-daily basis.

I owe a debt of gratitude to my exceptional editors, Lucy Ridout who provided many invaluable and insightful suggestions on an early version and Toby Selwyn for his superbly meticulous and thoughtful line and copy editing. Thanks to Gershon Berkowitz for his encouragement to pursue my unique vision rather than opting for a more conventional and safer route and to Matt Graydon for his valuable feedback on the entire manuscript.

A resounding thank you goes out to the remarkable team at Cranthorpe Millner Publishers for their dedication and professionalism. Special thanks to Vicky Richards for believing in this novel despite its unorthodox genre and for making the whole process easy and enjoyable.

Last but not least, thanks to all my fellow writers from the Chiltern Writers and the Phoenix Writers' Circle who offered constructive criticism on selected portions and heartening support.

About the Author

Yona Bouskila is a scientist and writer. He studied biology at the Hebrew University of Jerusalem and received a PhD in neuroscience from UCLA. He is involved in medical research and development. Before that, he conducted brain research at several institutions in the US and Europe. He writes short stories, often with a humorous slant, and *The Unthinkable Truth* is his first novel. He lives in England with his wife and pets, where he enjoys the Surrey countryside and contemplating life.